CURSED PRINCESS CLUB

LambCat

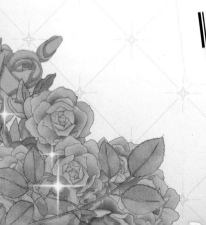

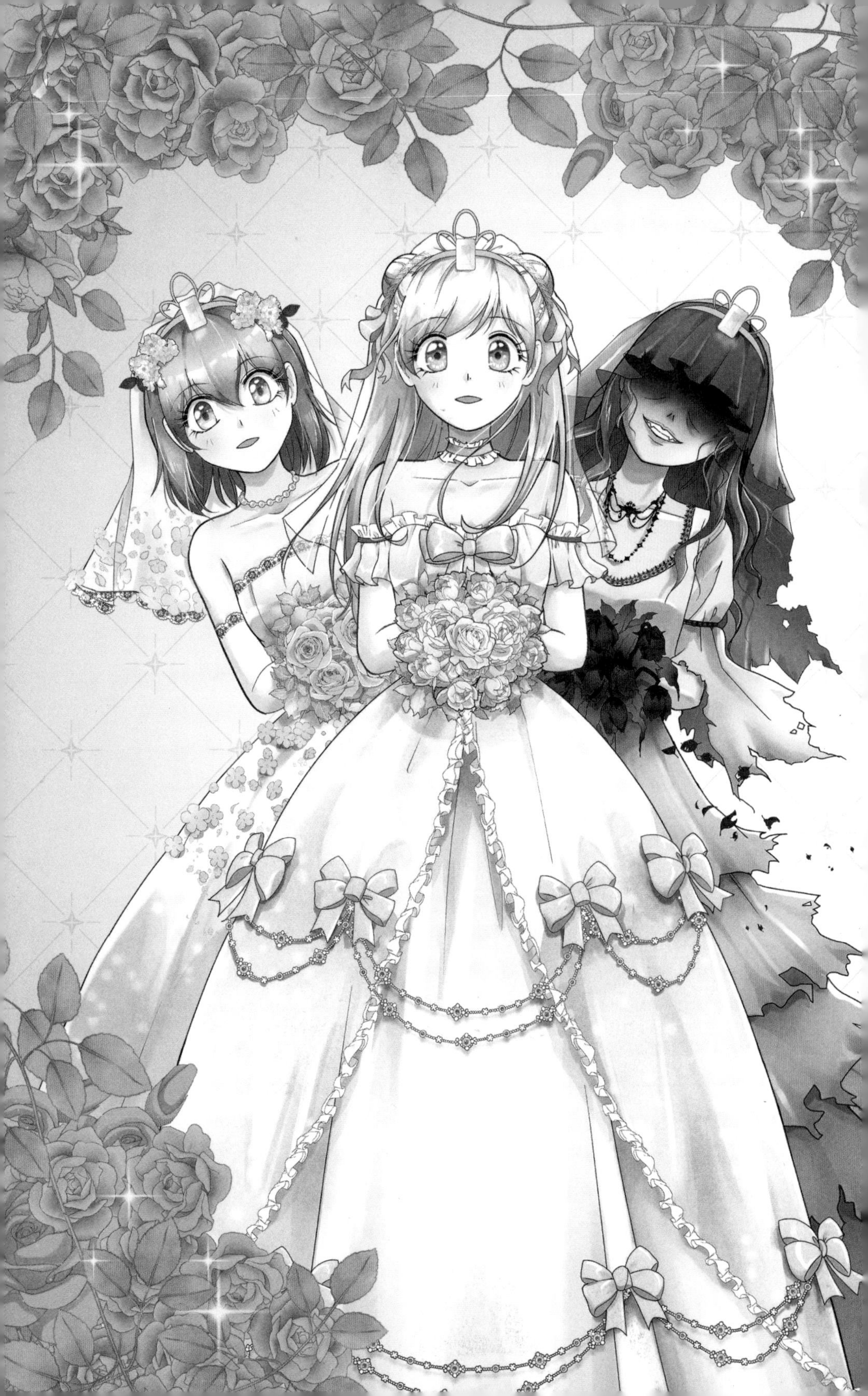

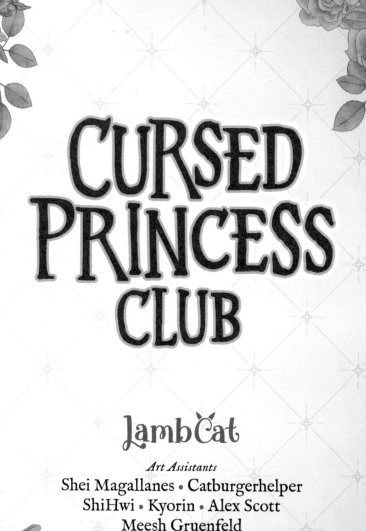

CURSED PRINCESS CLUB

LambCat

Art Assistants
Shei Magallanes • Catburgerhelper
ShiHwi • Kyorin • Alex Scott
Meesh Gruenfeld

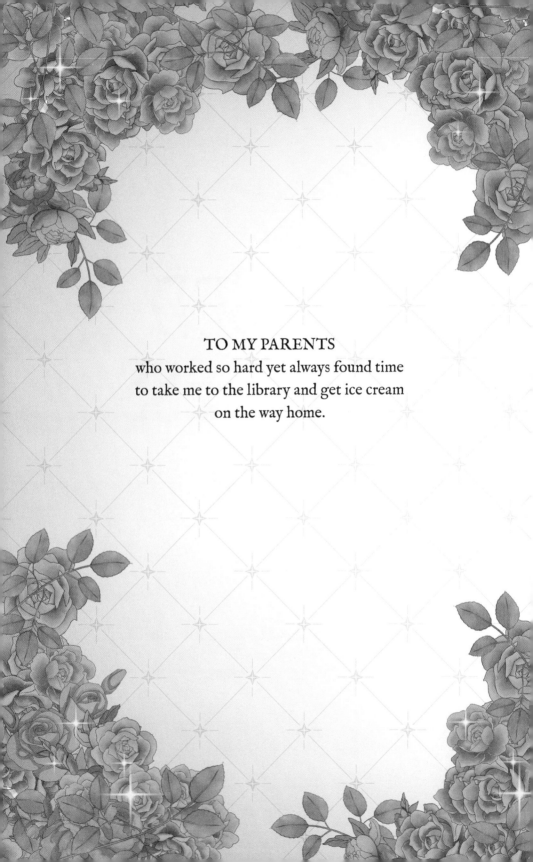

TO MY PARENTS
who worked so hard yet always found time
to take me to the library and get ice cream
on the way home.

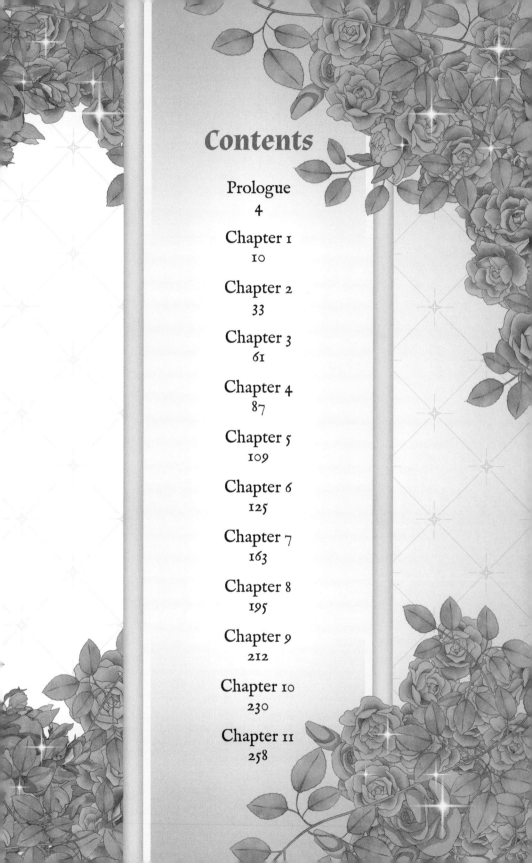

Contents

Prologue
4

Chapter 1
10

Chapter 2
33

Chapter 3
61

Chapter 4
87

Chapter 5
109

Chapter 6
125

Chapter 7
163

Chapter 8
195

Chapter 9
212

Chapter 10
230

Chapter 11
258

BOBBIE CHASE *Executive Editor*
JOSH BEATMAN *Publication Design*
NIKO DALCIN *Sequential Story Design*
PATRICK McCORMICK *Production Manager*
EUNICE BAIK *Original WEBTOON Editor*

ARON LEVITZ *President*
ASHLEIGH GARDNER *SVP, Head of Global Publishing*
DEANNA McFADDEN *Executive Publishing Director, Wattpad WEBTOON Book Group*
DAVID MADDEN *Global Head of Entertainment*
TAYLOR GRANT *VP, Head of Global Animation*
LINDSEY RAMEY *VP, Head of Global Film*
SERA TABB *VP, Head of Global Television*
TINA McINTYRE *VP, Marketing*
CAITLIN O'HANLON *Head of Content & Creators*
DEXTER ONG *Managing Director, International*
RYAN PHILP *SVP, Operations*
MAXIMILIAN JO *General Counsel*
AUSTIN WONG *Head of Legal and Business Affairs*
COREY HOCK *Director, Legal & Business Affairs*
KEN KIM *WEBTOON CEO*

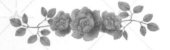

Prologue

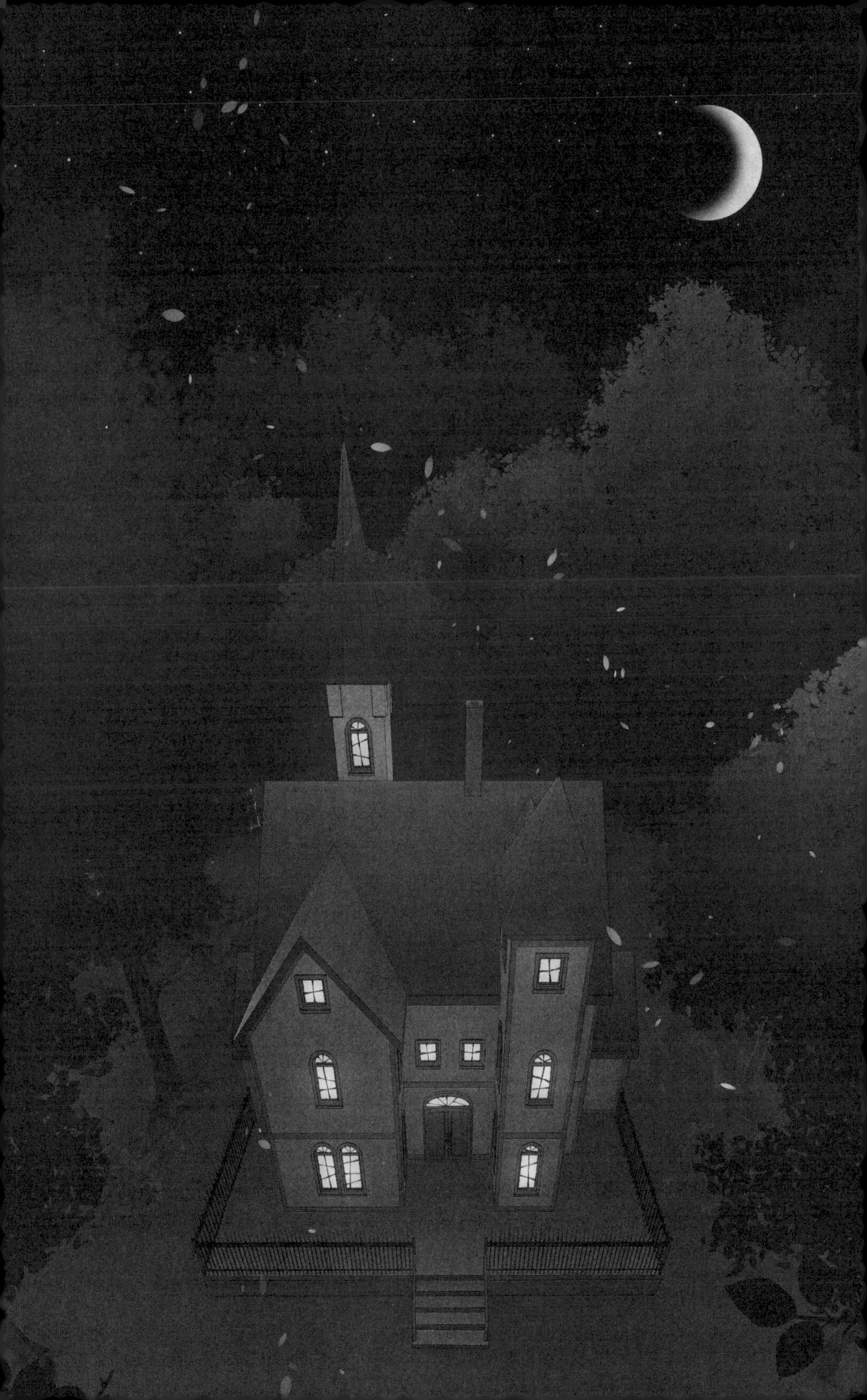

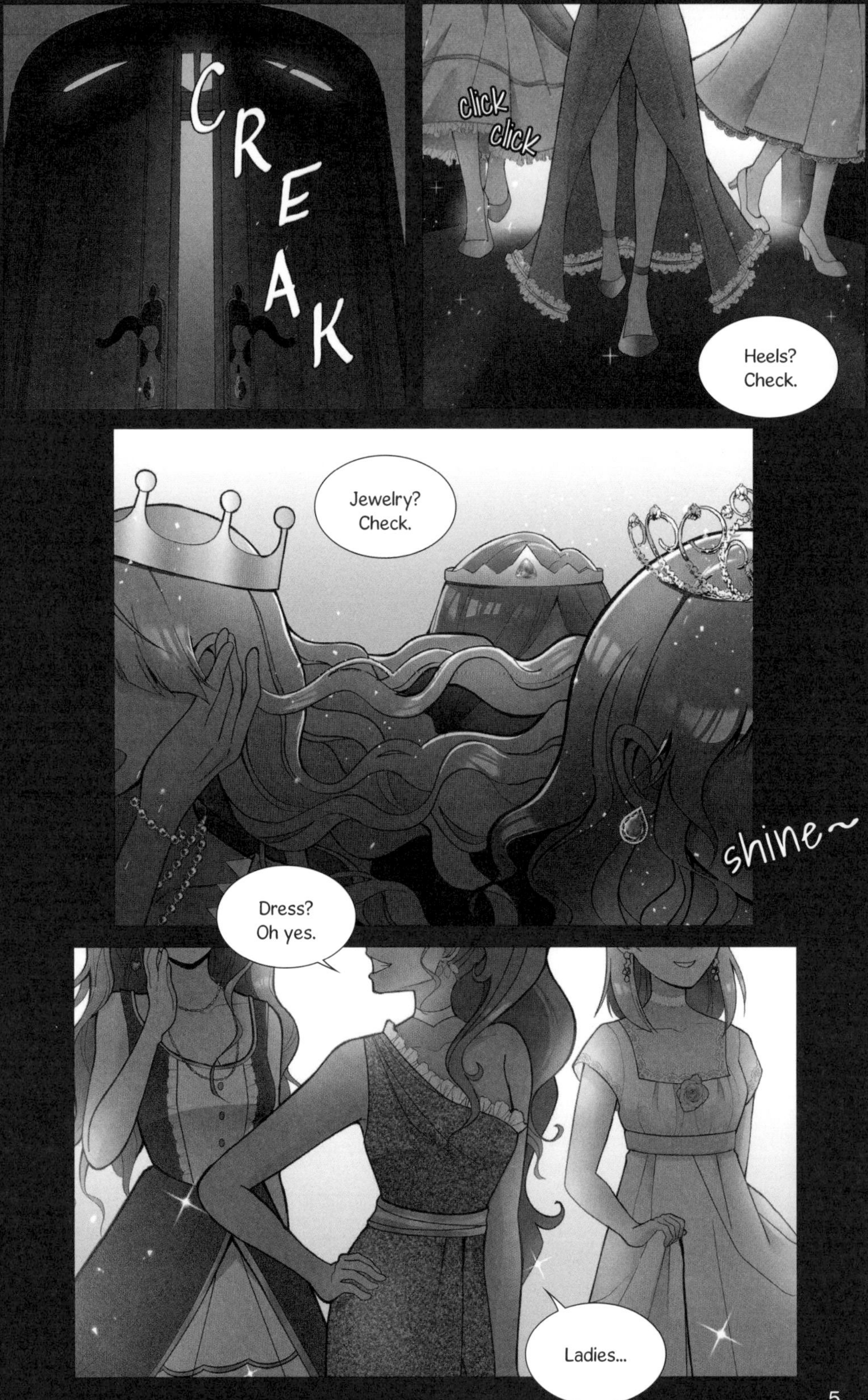
CREAK
click click
Heels? Check.
Jewelry? Check.
shine~
Dress? Oh yes.
Ladies...

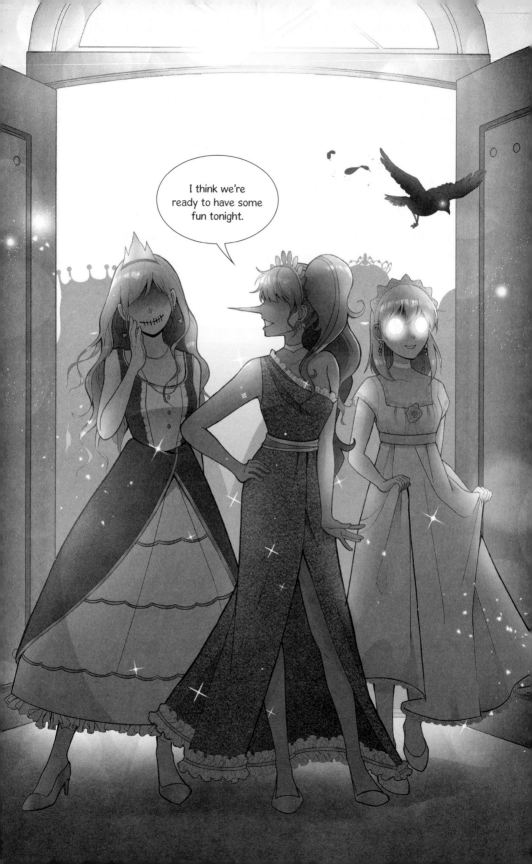

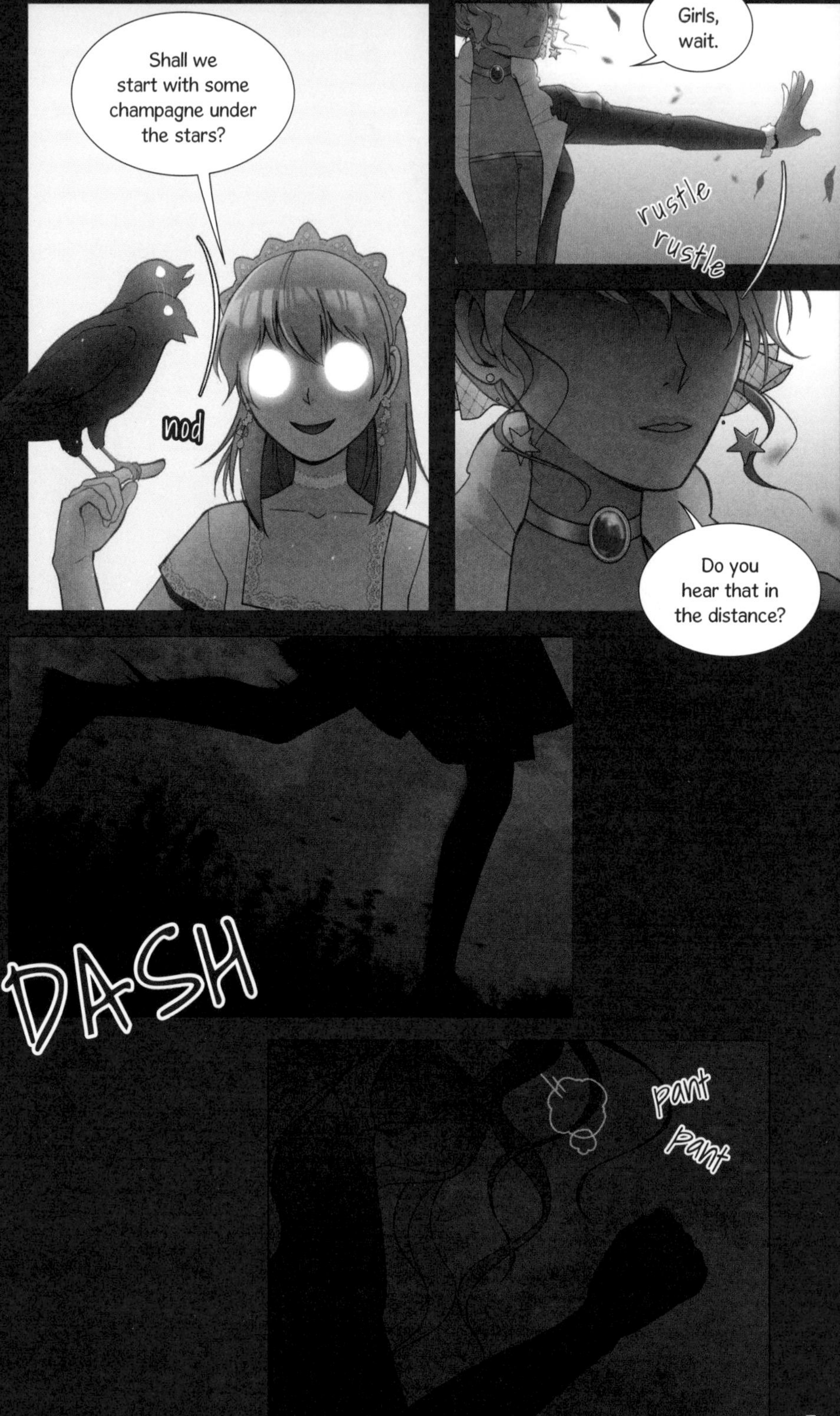

7

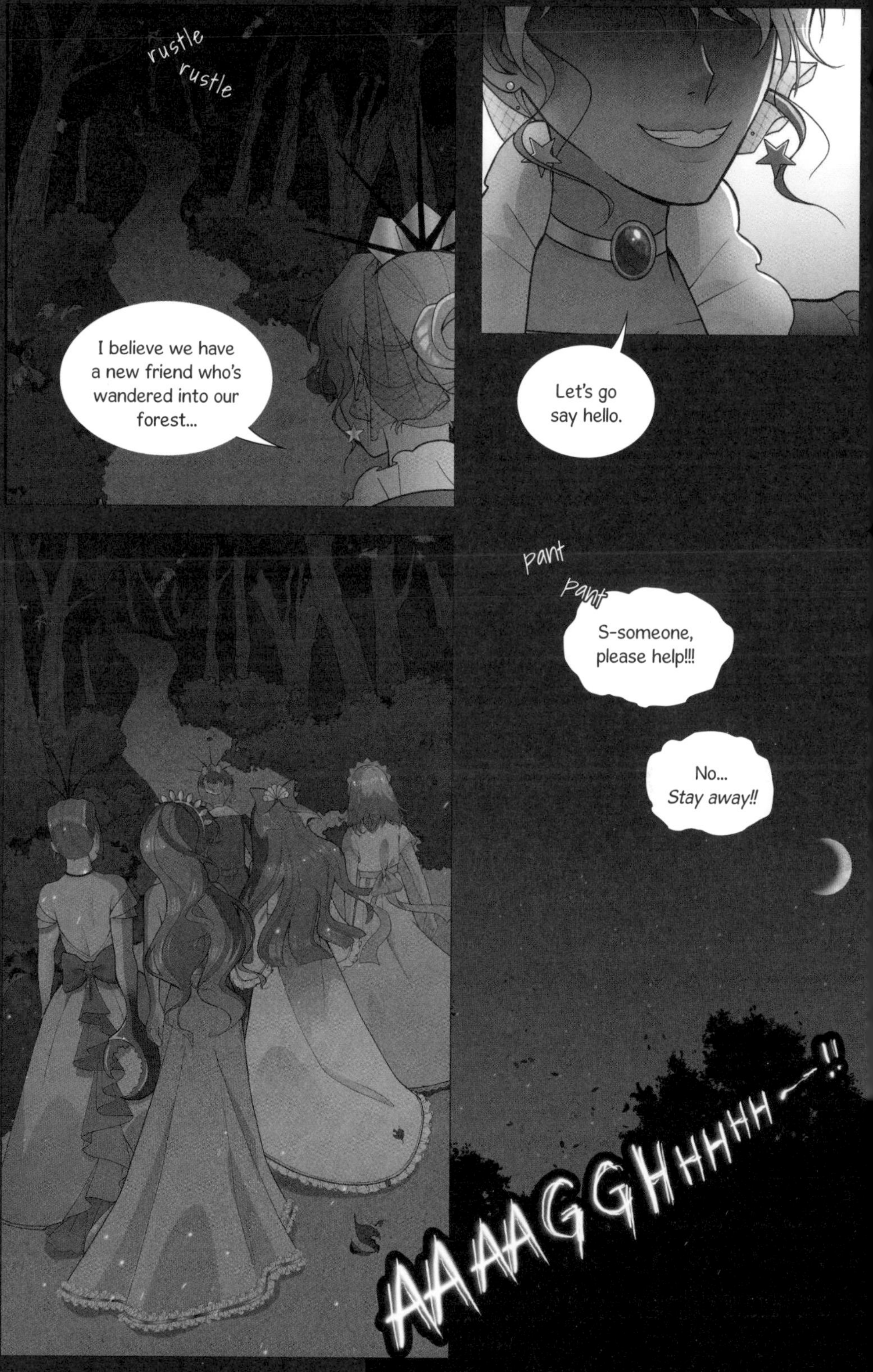
rustle rustle
I believe we have a new friend who's wandered into our forest...
Let's go say hello.
pant pant
S-someone, please help!!!
No... *Stay away!!*
AAAAGGHHHHH—!!

Chapter
1

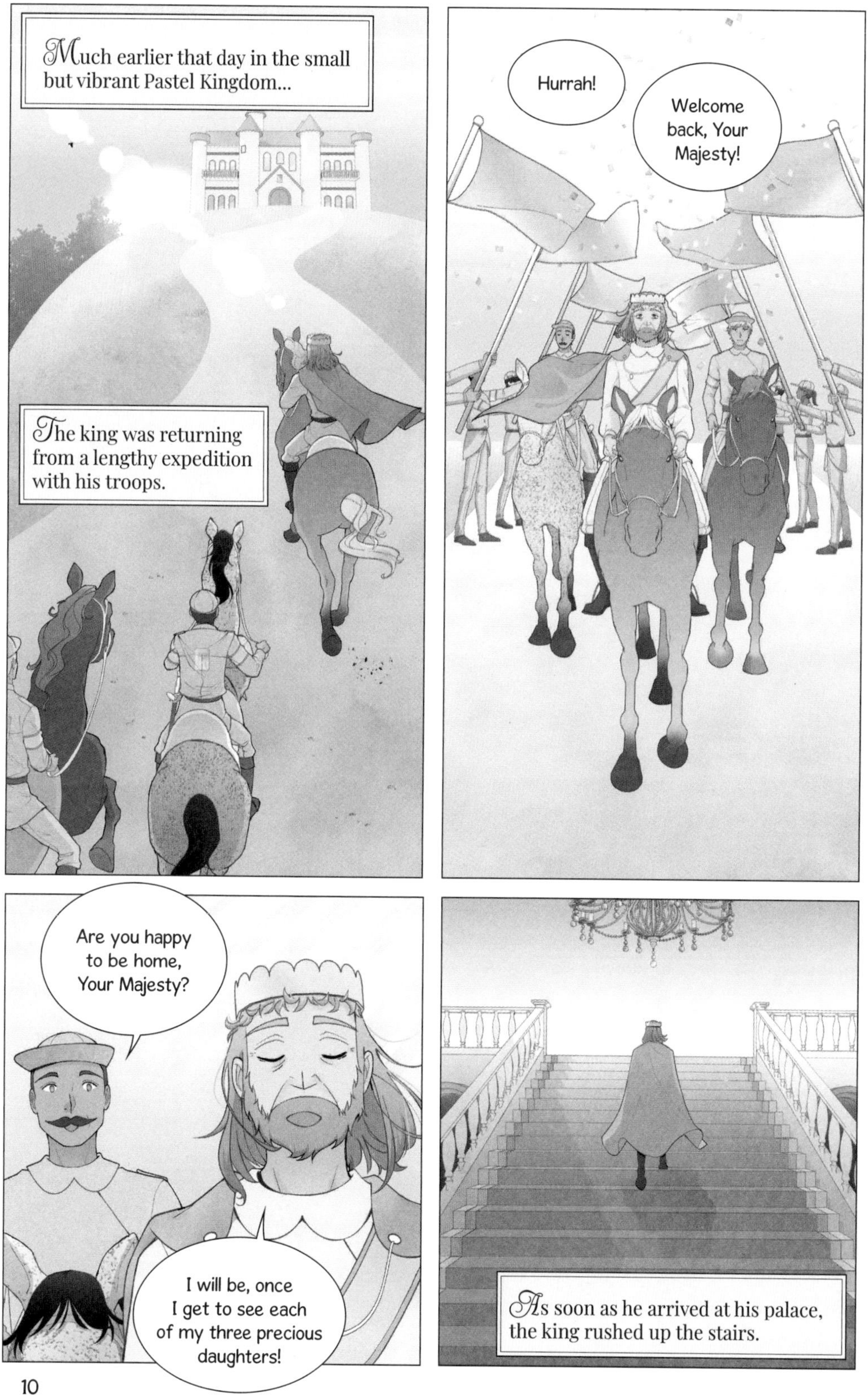
Much earlier that day in the small but vibrant Pastel Kingdom...
The king was returning from a lengthy expedition with his troops.
Hurrah!
Welcome back, Your Majesty!
Are you happy to be home, Your Majesty?
I will be, once I get to see each of my three precious daughters!
As soon as he arrived at his palace, the king rushed up the stairs.

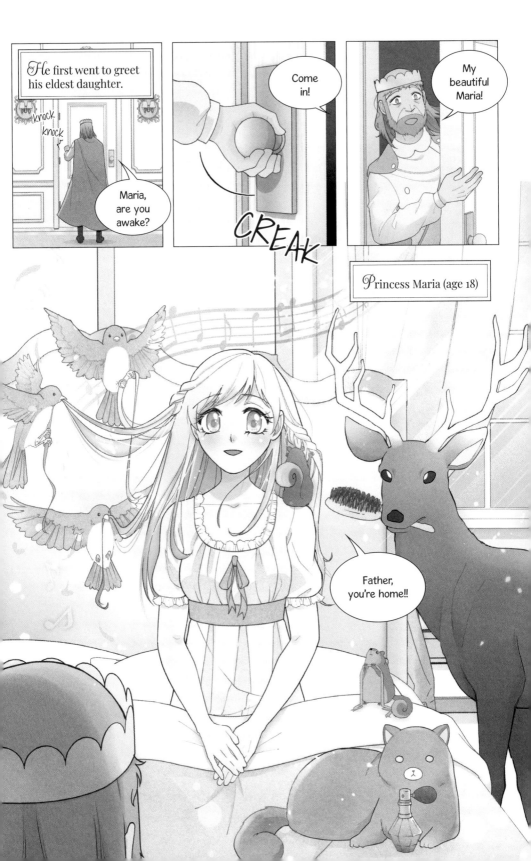

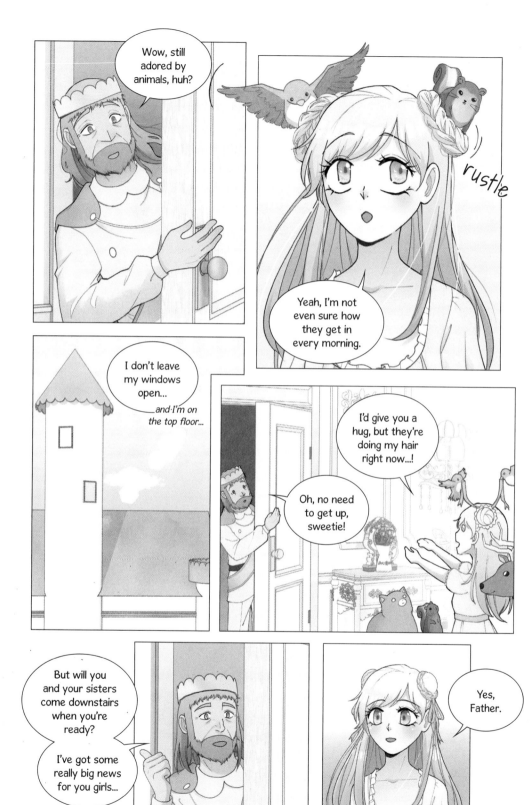

12

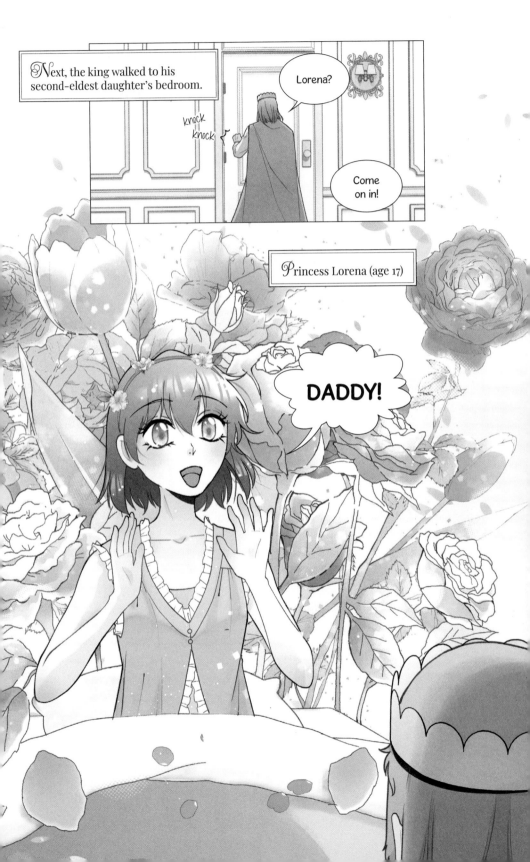

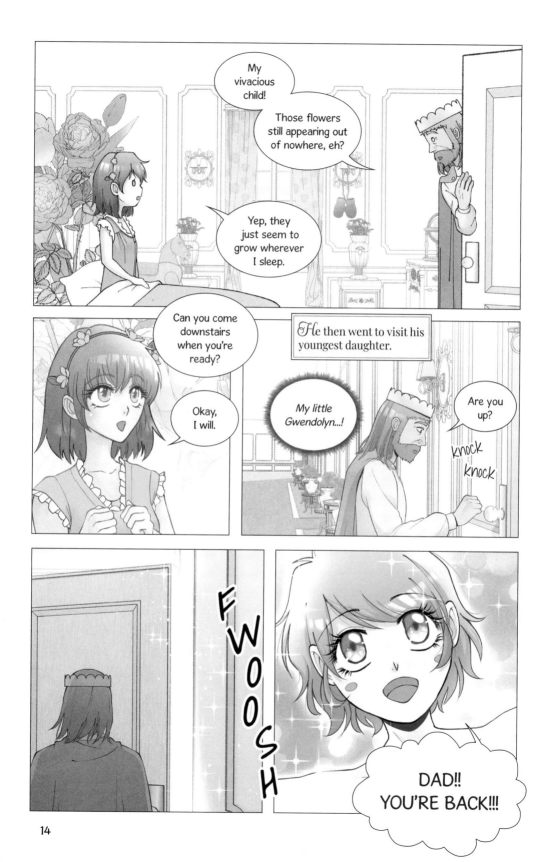

14

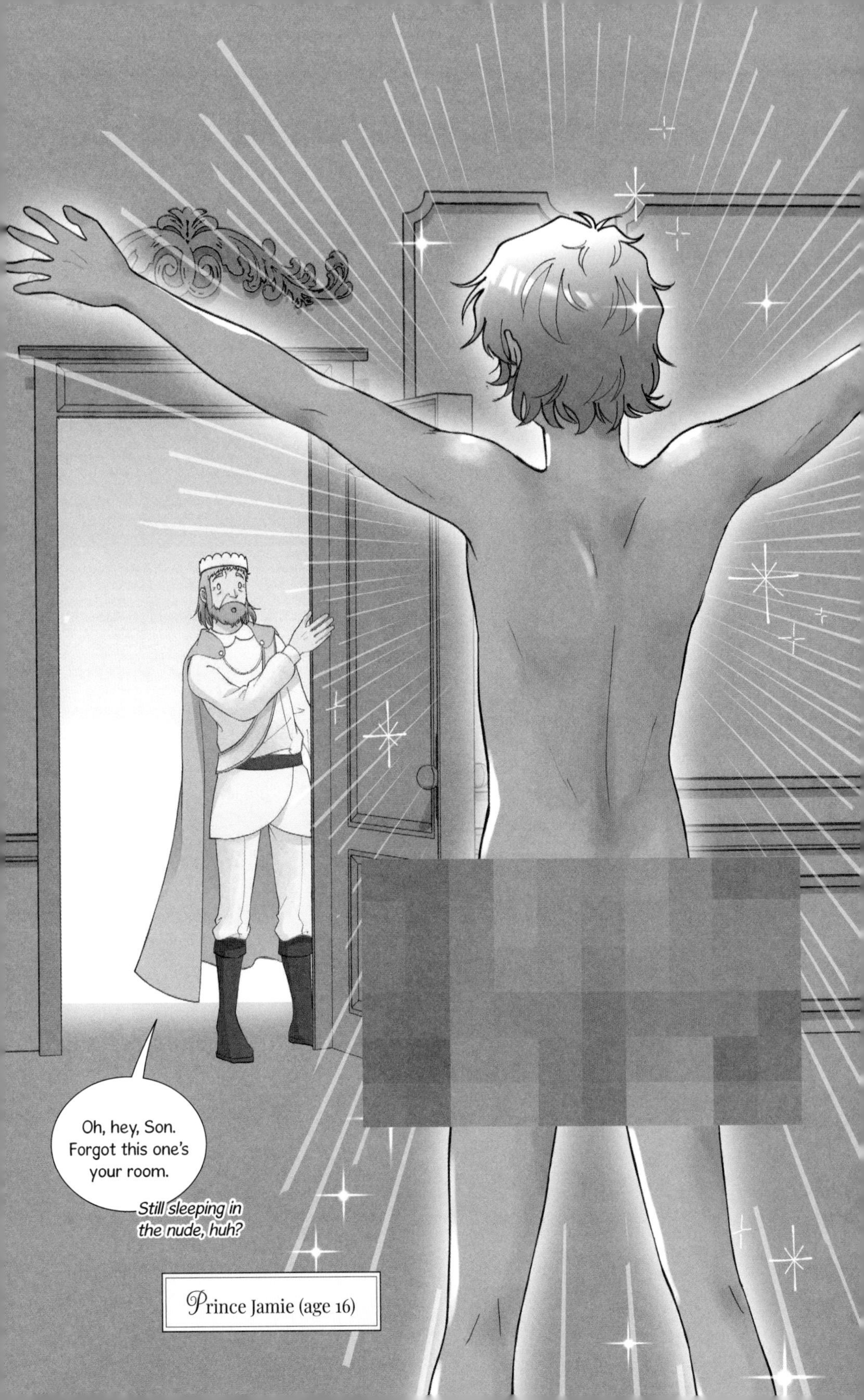
Oh, hey, Son. Forgot this one's your room.
Still sleeping in the nude, huh?
Prince Jamie (age 16)

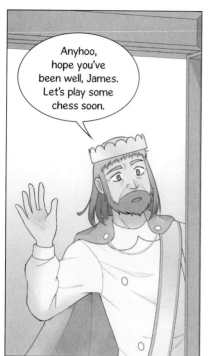

Anyhoo, hope you've been well, James. Let's play some chess soon.

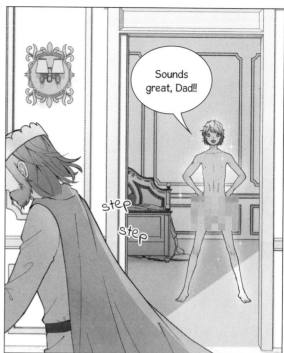

Sounds great, Dad!!

step
step

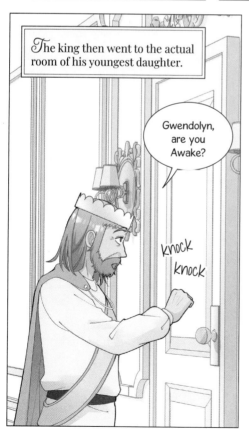

The king then went to the actual room of his youngest daughter.

Gwendolyn, are you Awake?

knock
knock

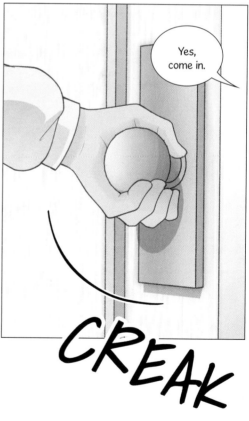

Yes, come in.

CREAK

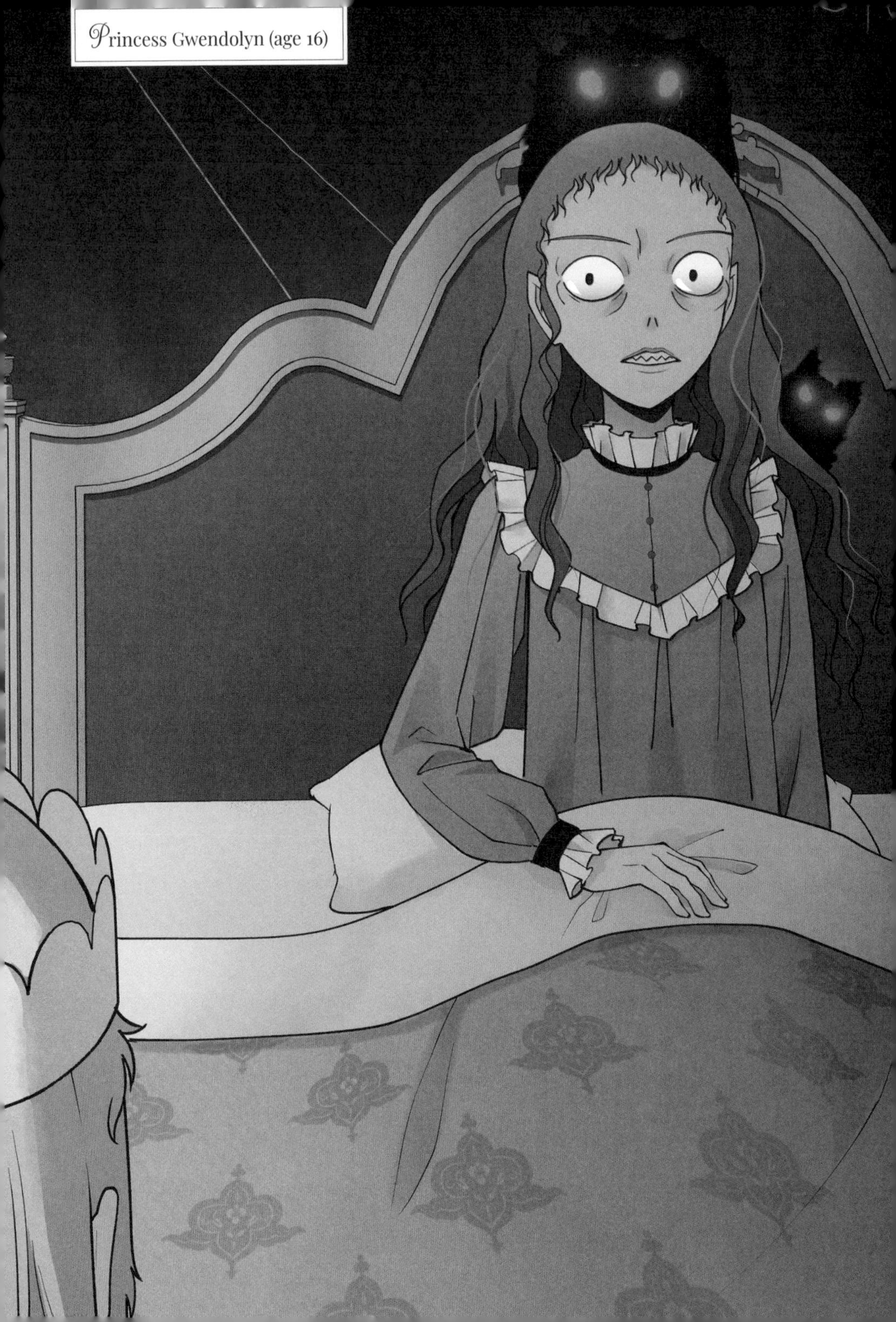
Princess Gwendolyn (age 16)

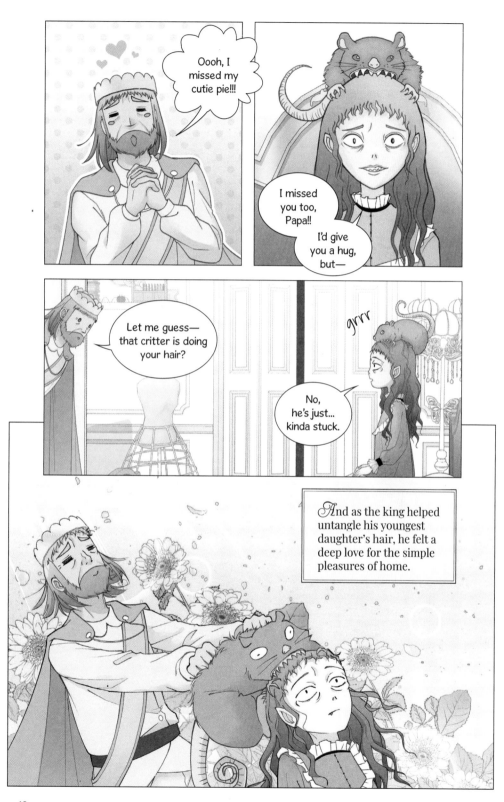

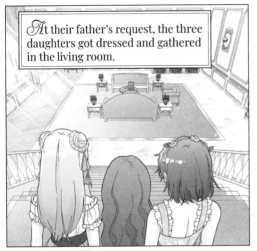

At their father's request, the three daughters got dressed and gathered in the living room.

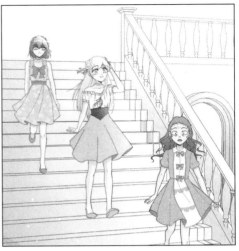

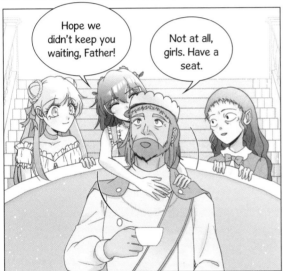

Hope we didn't keep you waiting, Father!

Not at all, girls. Have a seat.

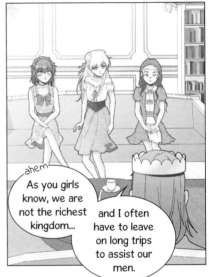

ahem

As you girls know, we are not the richest kingdom...

and I often have to leave on long trips to assist our men.

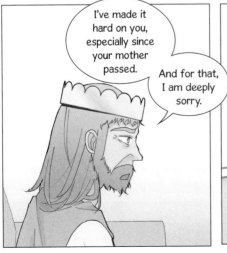

I've made it hard on you, especially since your mother passed.

And for that, I am deeply sorry.

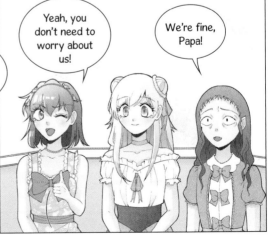

Yeah, you don't need to worry about us!

We're fine, Papa!

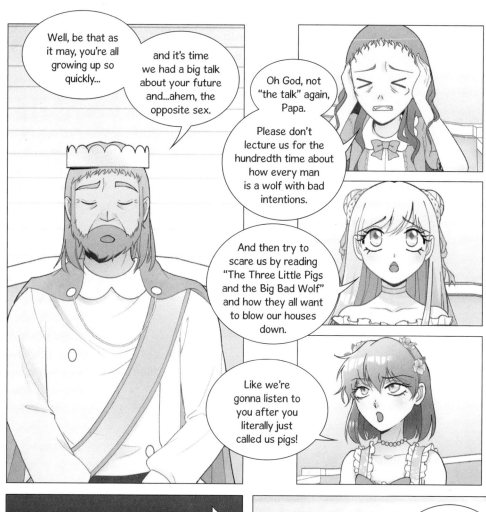

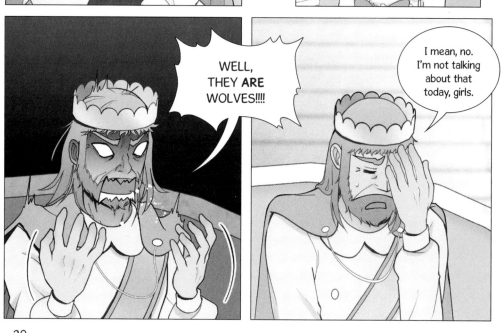

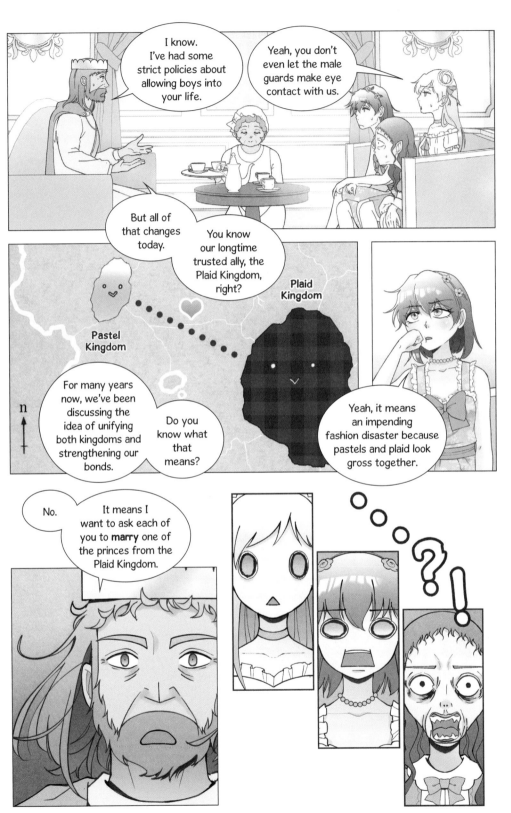

21

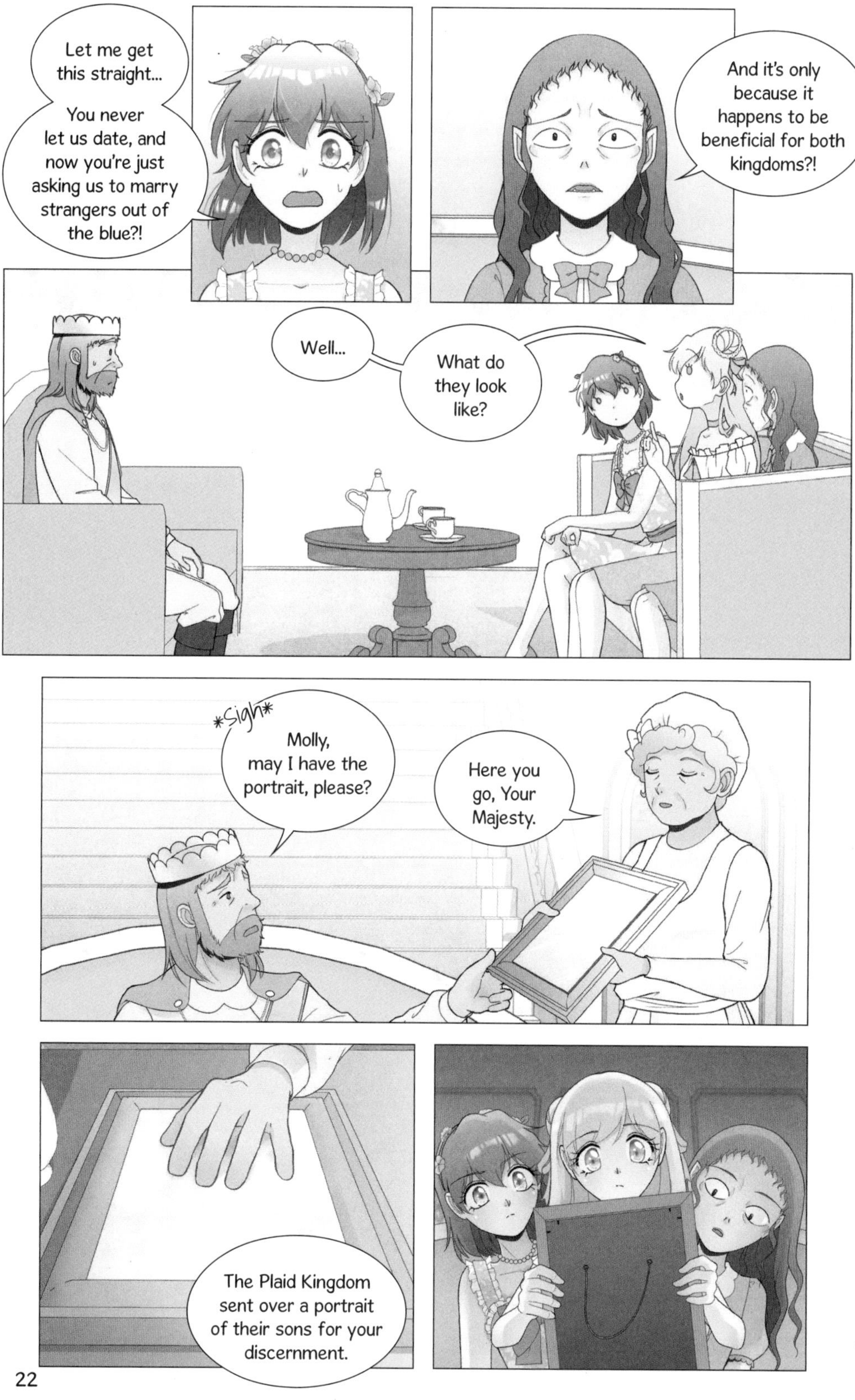
Let me get this straight...
You never let us date, and now you're just asking us to marry strangers out of the blue?!
And it's only because it happens to be beneficial for both kingdoms?!
Well...
What do they look like?
Sigh
Molly, may I have the portrait, please?
Here you go, Your Majesty.
The Plaid Kingdom sent over a portrait of their sons for your discernment.

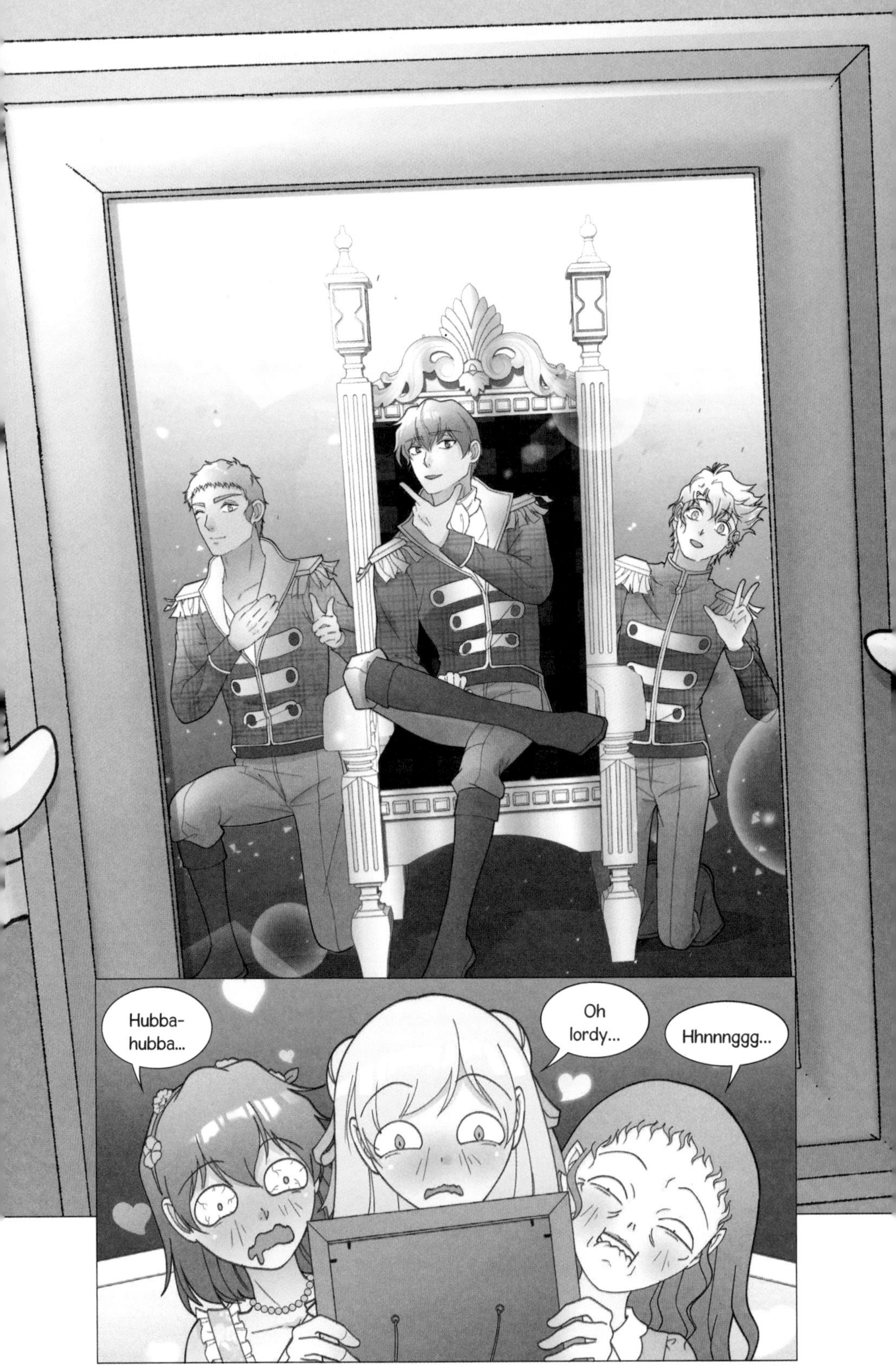

Hubba-
hubba...
Oh
lordy...
Hhnnnggg...

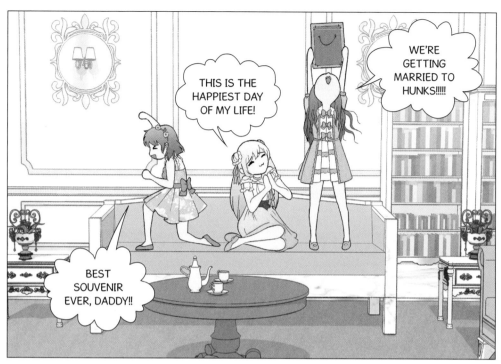

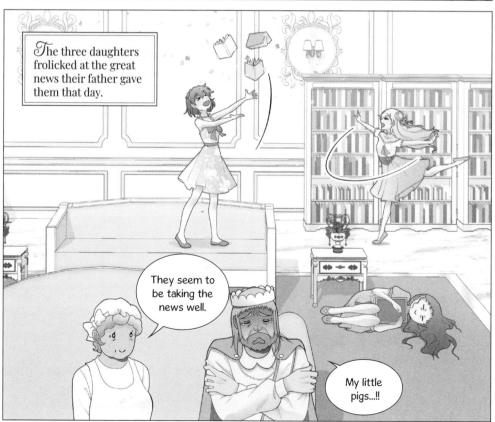

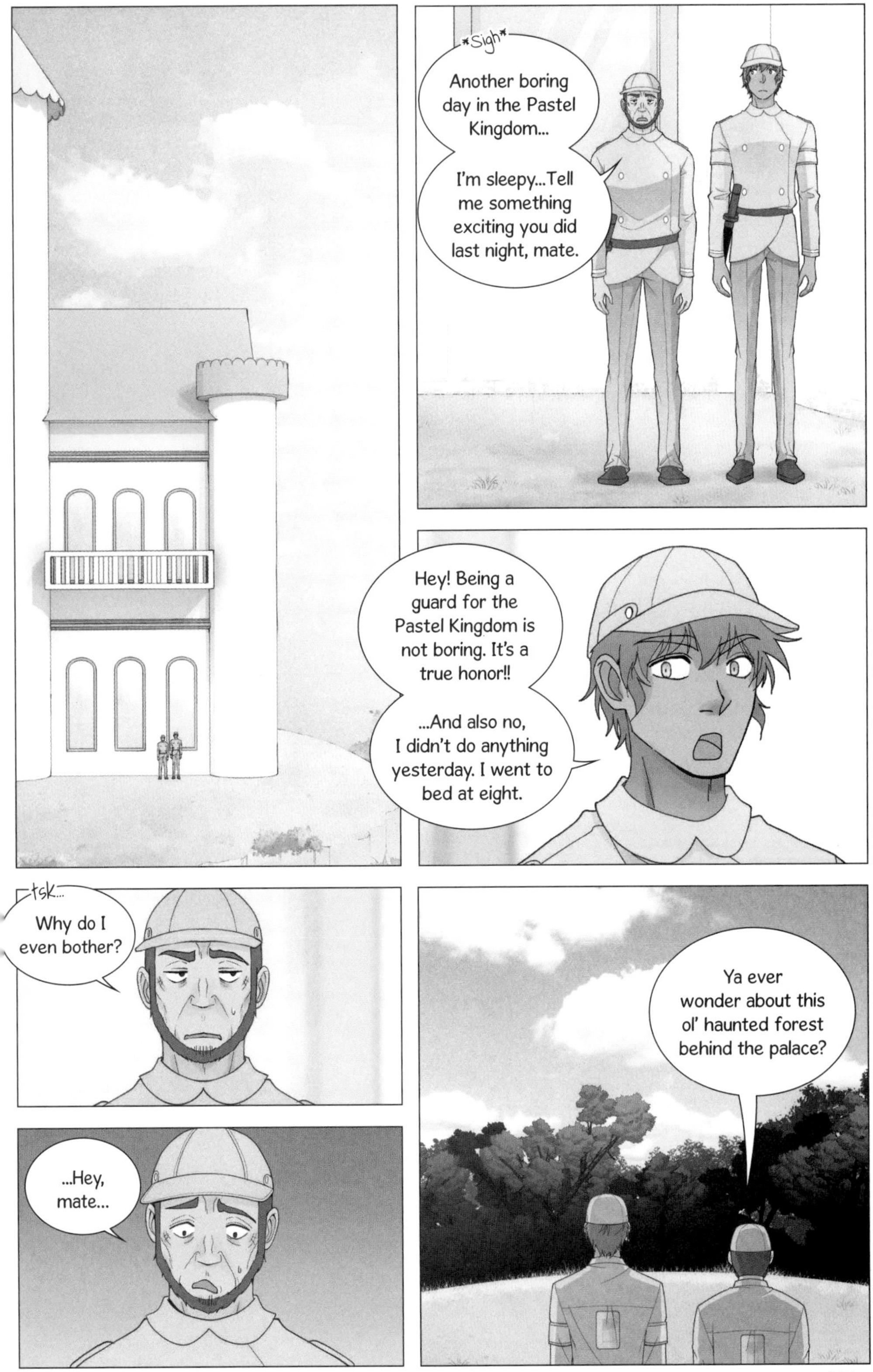
Sigh
Another boring day in the Pastel Kingdom...
I'm sleepy...Tell me something exciting you did last night, mate.
Hey! Being a guard for the Pastel Kingdom is not boring. It's a true honor!!
...And also no, I didn't do anything yesterday. I went to bed at eight.
tsk...
Why do I even bother?
Ya ever wonder about this ol' haunted forest behind the palace?
...Hey, mate...

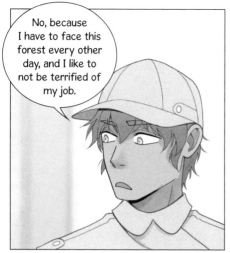

No, because I have to face this forest every other day, and I like to not be terrified of my job.

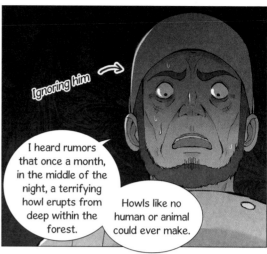

Ignoring him →

I heard rumors that once a month, in the middle of the night, a terrifying howl erupts from deep within the forest.

Howls like no human or animal could ever make.

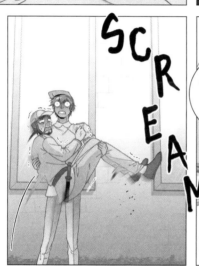

SCREAM!

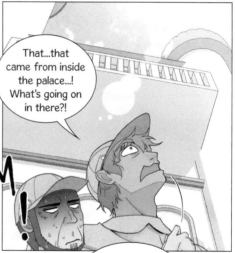

That...that came from inside the palace...! What's going on in there?!

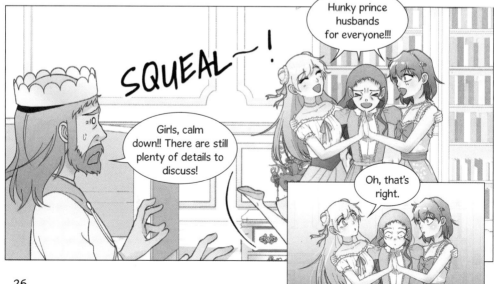

SQUEAL~!

Hunky prince husbands for everyone!!!

Girls, calm down!! There are still plenty of details to discuss!

Oh, that's right.

26

What are their names?

Their ages?

Are they a big spoon or little spoon?

Let's see... that's Lance on the left (age nineteen)...

...Blaine in the middle (age twenty), and Frederick on the right (age seventeen).

Since we're so close to the Plaid Kingdom, how come we've never heard of the princes?

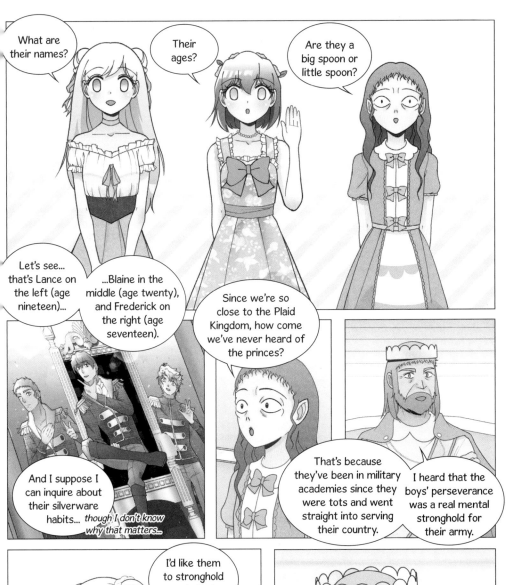

And I suppose I can inquire about their silverware habits... *though I don't know why that matters...*

That's because they've been in military academies since they were tots and went straight into serving their country.

I heard that the boys' perseverance was a real mental stronghold for their army.

I'd like them to stronghold me in their armies...

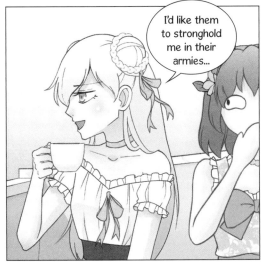

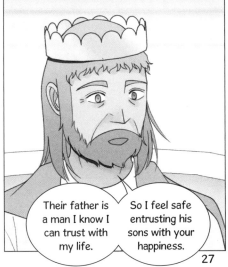

Their father is a man I know I can trust with my life.

So I feel safe entrusting his sons with your happiness.

27

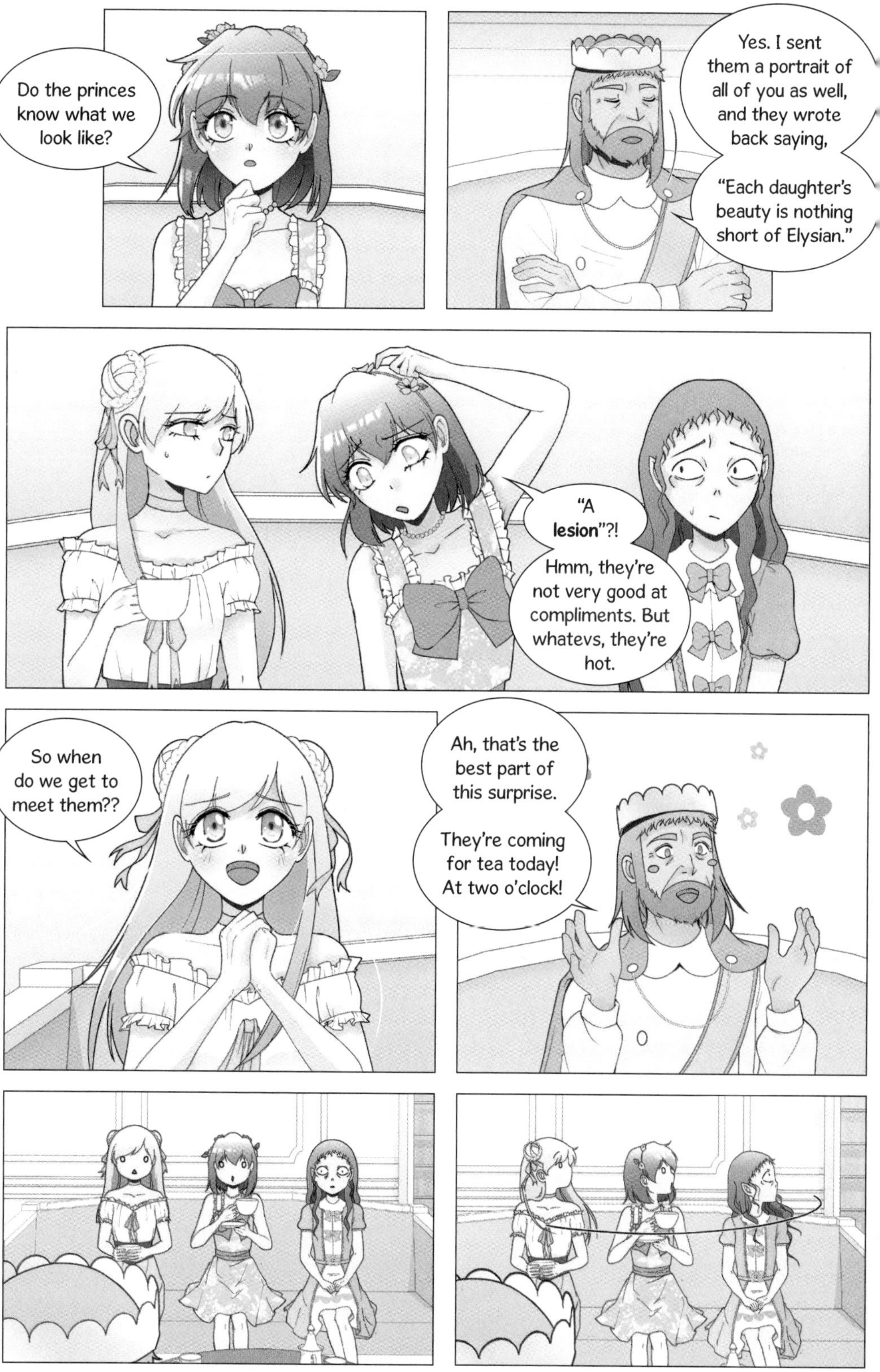
Do the princes know what we look like?
Yes. I sent them a portrait of all of you as well, and they wrote back saying,
"Each daughter's beauty is nothing short of Elysian."
"A **lesion**"?!
Hmm, they're not very good at compliments. But whatevs, they're hot.
So when do we get to meet them??
Ah, that's the best part of this surprise.
They're coming for tea today! At two o'clock!

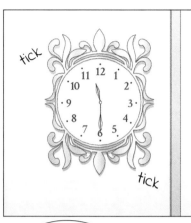
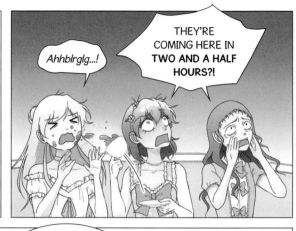
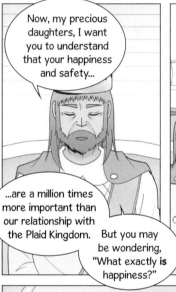
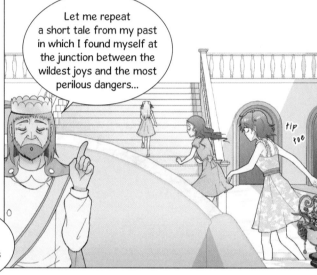
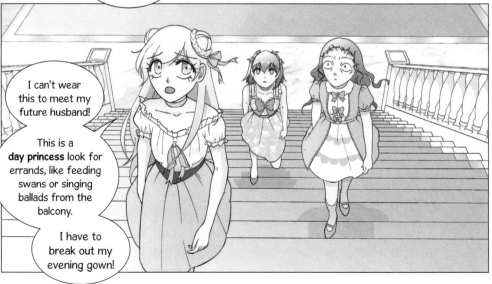

29

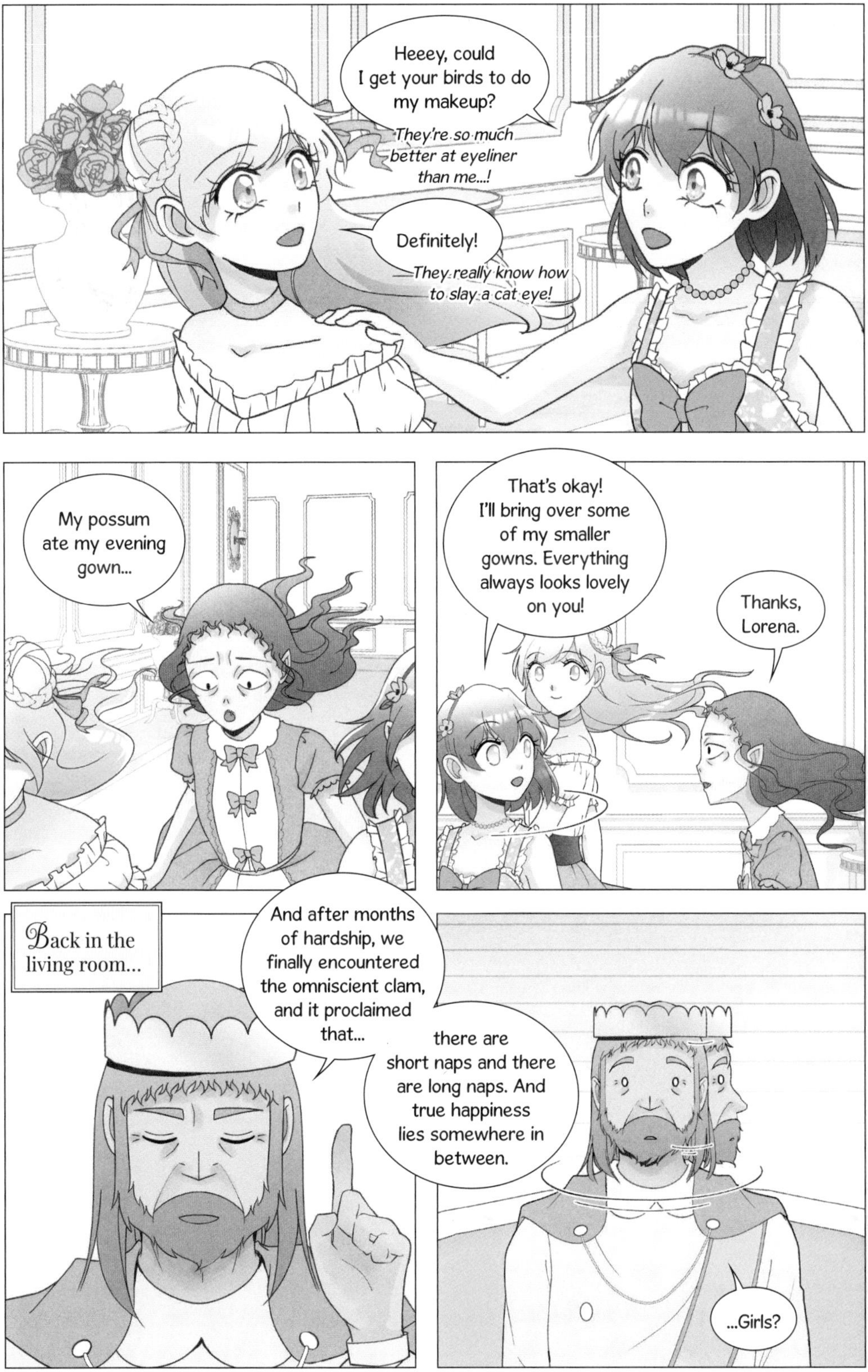
Heeey, could I get your birds to do my makeup?
They're so much better at eyeliner than me...!
Definitely!
They really know how to slay a cat eye!
My possum ate my evening gown...
That's okay! I'll bring over some of my smaller gowns. Everything always looks lovely on you!
Thanks, Lorena.
Back in the living room...
And after months of hardship, we finally encountered the omniscient clam, and it proclaimed that...
there are short naps and there are long naps. And true happiness lies somewhere in between.
...Girls?

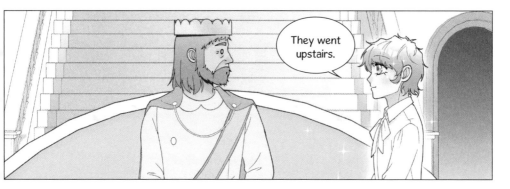

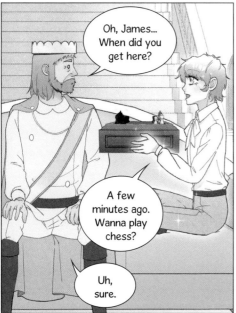

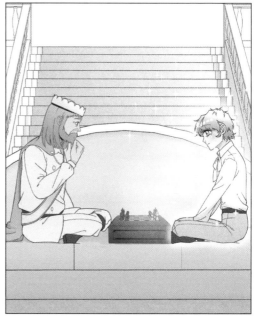

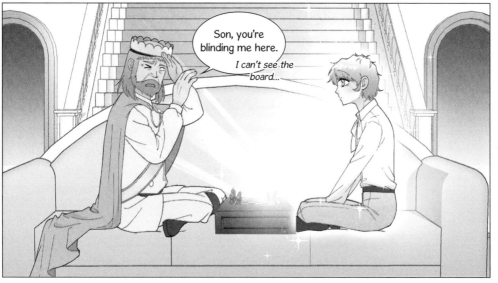

Chapter

2

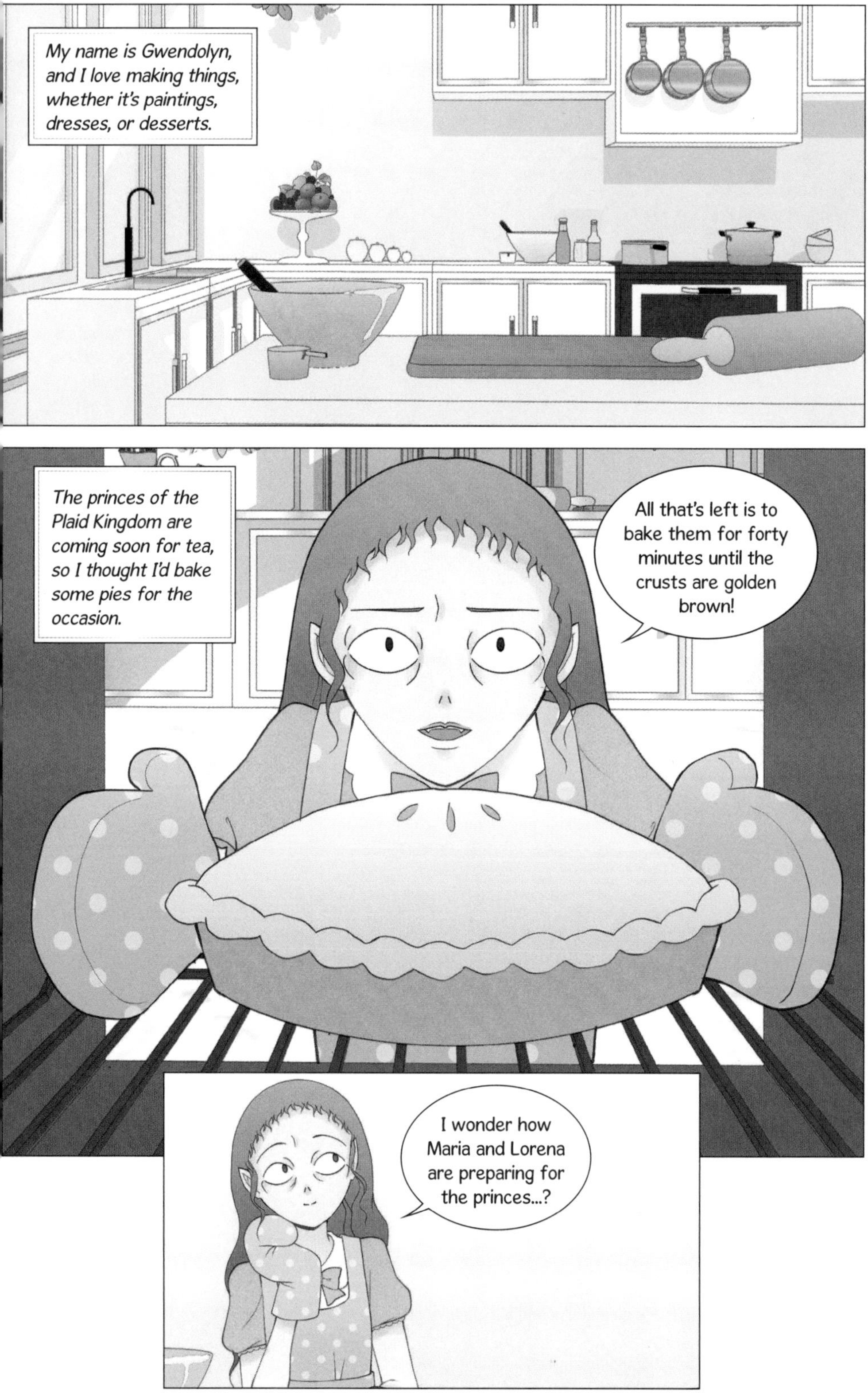
My name is Gwendolyn, and I love making things, whether it's paintings, dresses, or desserts.
The princes of the Plaid Kingdom are coming soon for tea, so I thought I'd bake some pies for the occasion.
All that's left is to bake them for forty minutes until the crusts are golden brown!
I wonder how Maria and Lorena are preparing for the princes...?

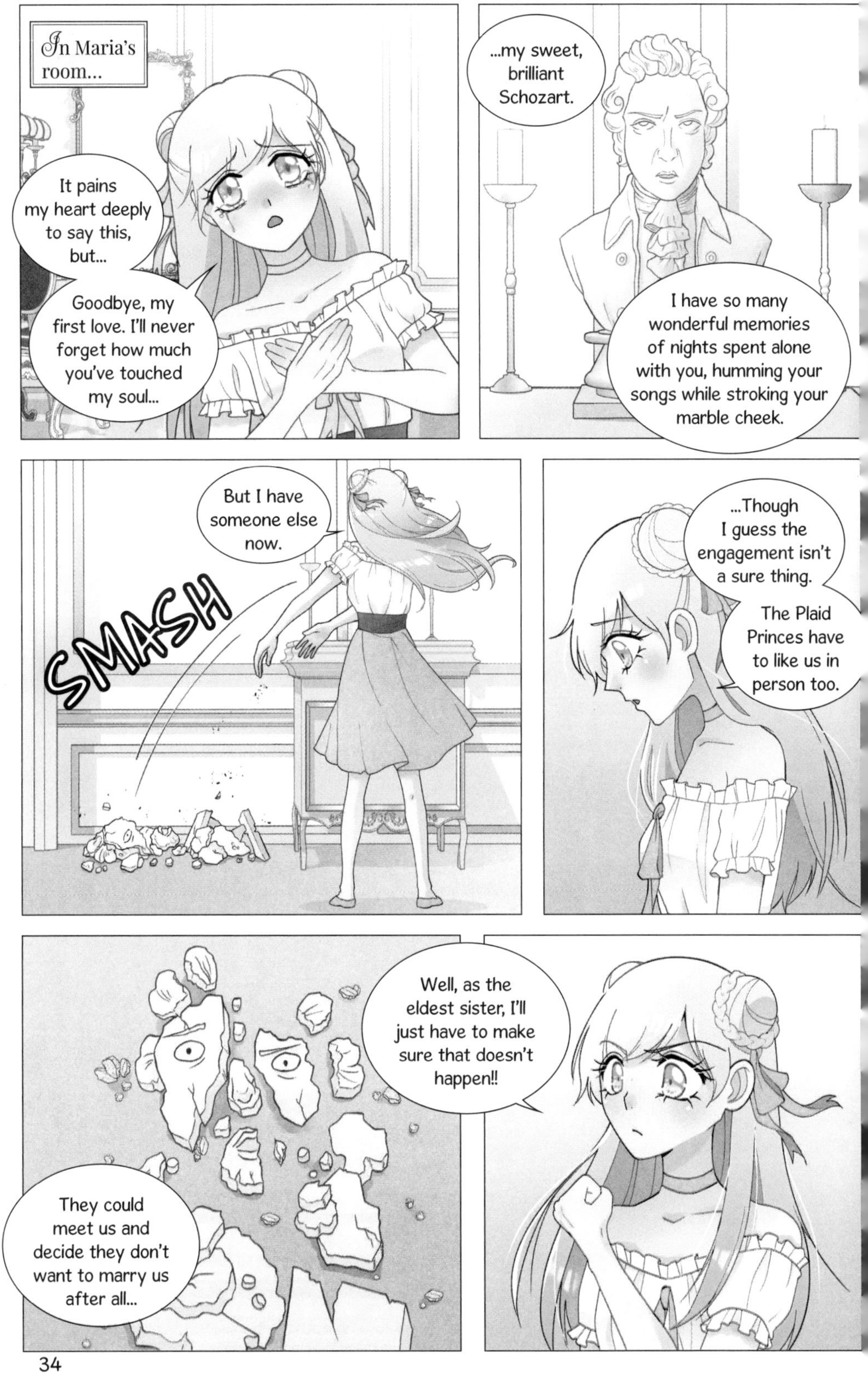
In Maria's room...
It pains my heart deeply to say this, but...
Goodbye, my first love. I'll never forget how much you've touched my soul...
...my sweet, brilliant Schozart.
I have so many wonderful memories of nights spent alone with you, humming your songs while stroking your marble cheek.
But I have someone else now.
SMASH
...Though I guess the engagement isn't a sure thing.
The Plaid Princes have to like us in person too.
They could meet us and decide they don't want to marry us after all...
Well, as the eldest sister, I'll just have to make sure that doesn't happen!!

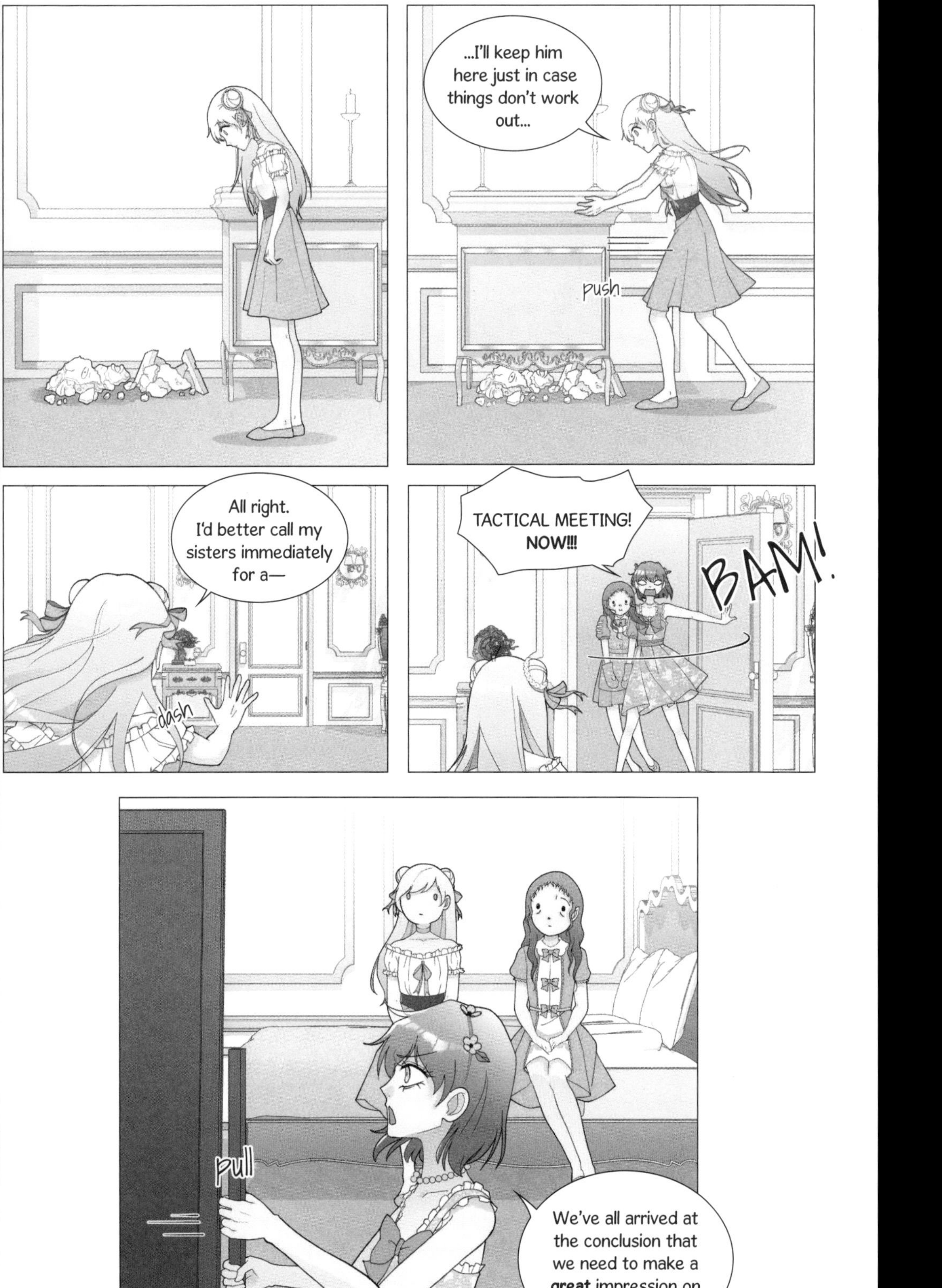
...I'll keep him here just in case things don't work out...
push
All right. I'd better call my sisters immediately for a—
dash
TACTICAL MEETING! NOW!!!
BAM!
pull
We've all arrived at the conclusion that we need to make a great impression on the princes.

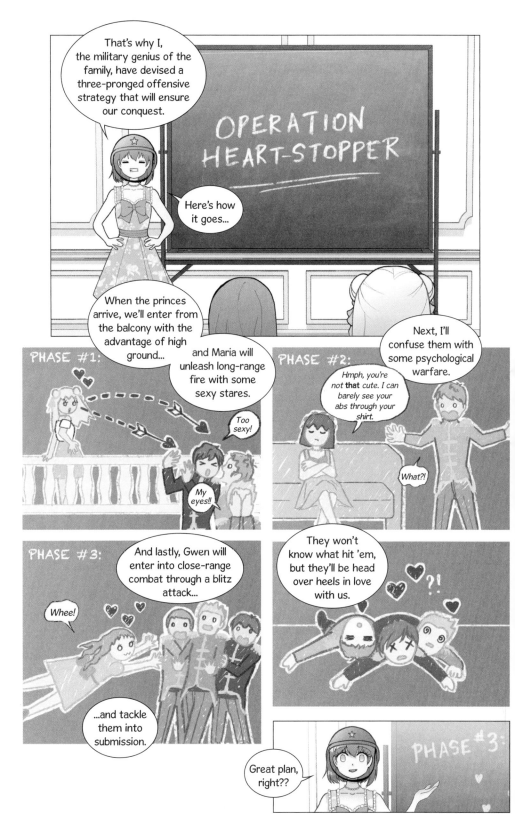

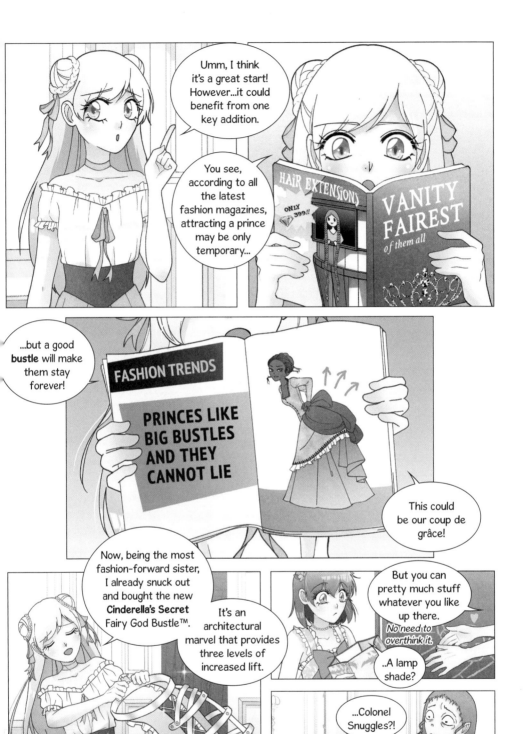

37

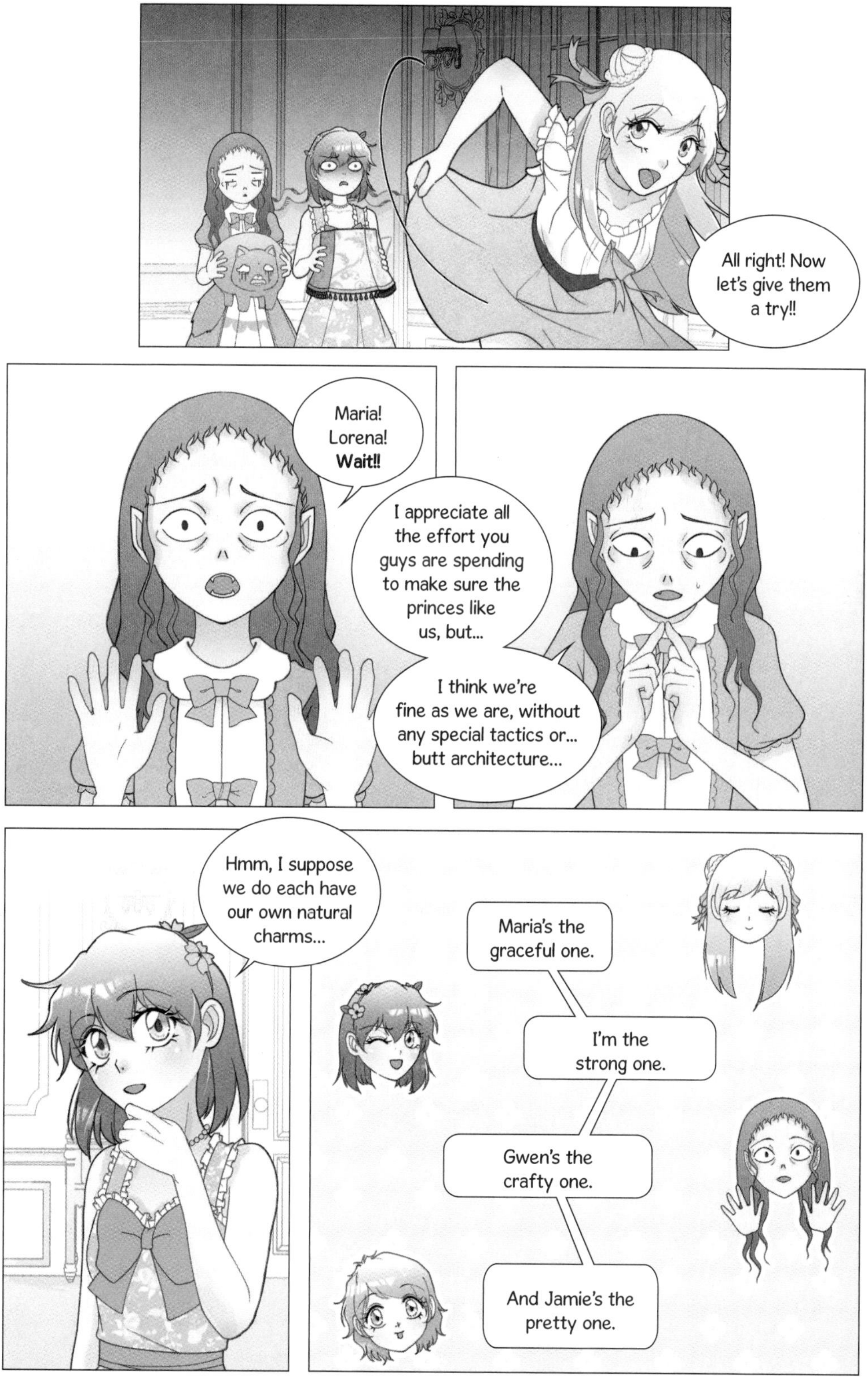
All right! Now let's give them a try!!
Maria! Lorena! **Wait!!**
I appreciate all the effort you guys are spending to make sure the princes like us, but...
I think we're fine as we are, without any special tactics or... butt architecture...
Hmm, I suppose we do each have our own natural charms...
Maria's the graceful one.
I'm the strong one.
Gwen's the crafty one.
And Jamie's the pretty one.

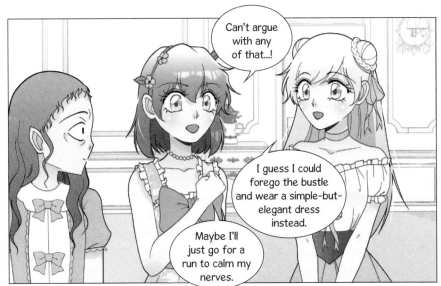

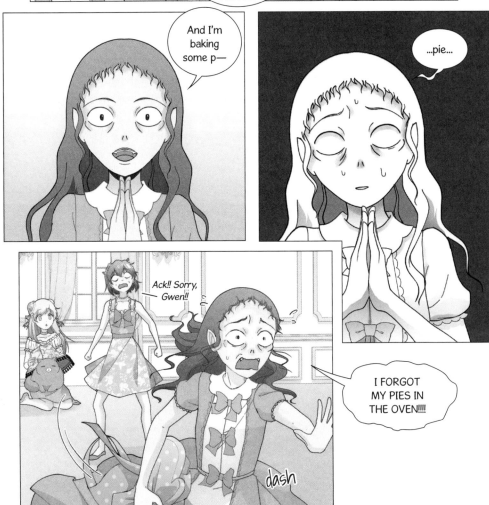

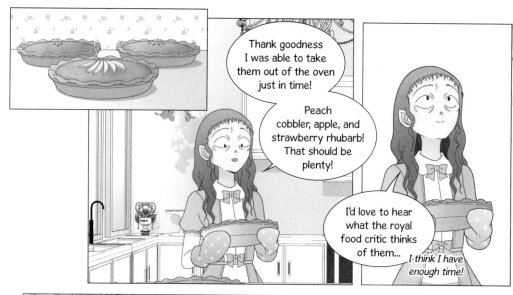

Thank goodness I was able to take them out of the oven just in time!

Peach cobbler, apple, and strawberry rhubarb! That should be plenty!

I'd love to hear what the royal food critic thinks of them...

I think I have enough time!

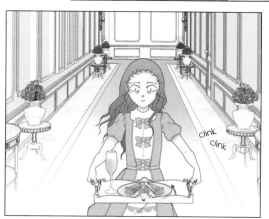

clink clink

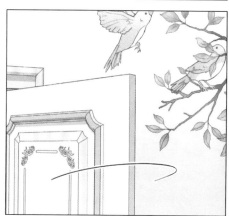

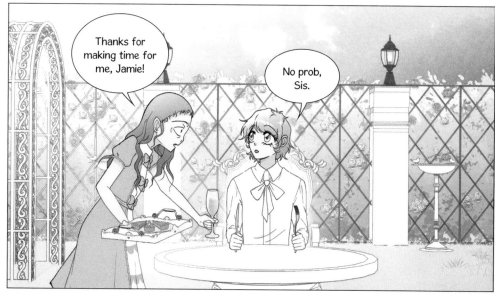

Thanks for making time for me, Jamie!

No prob, Sis.

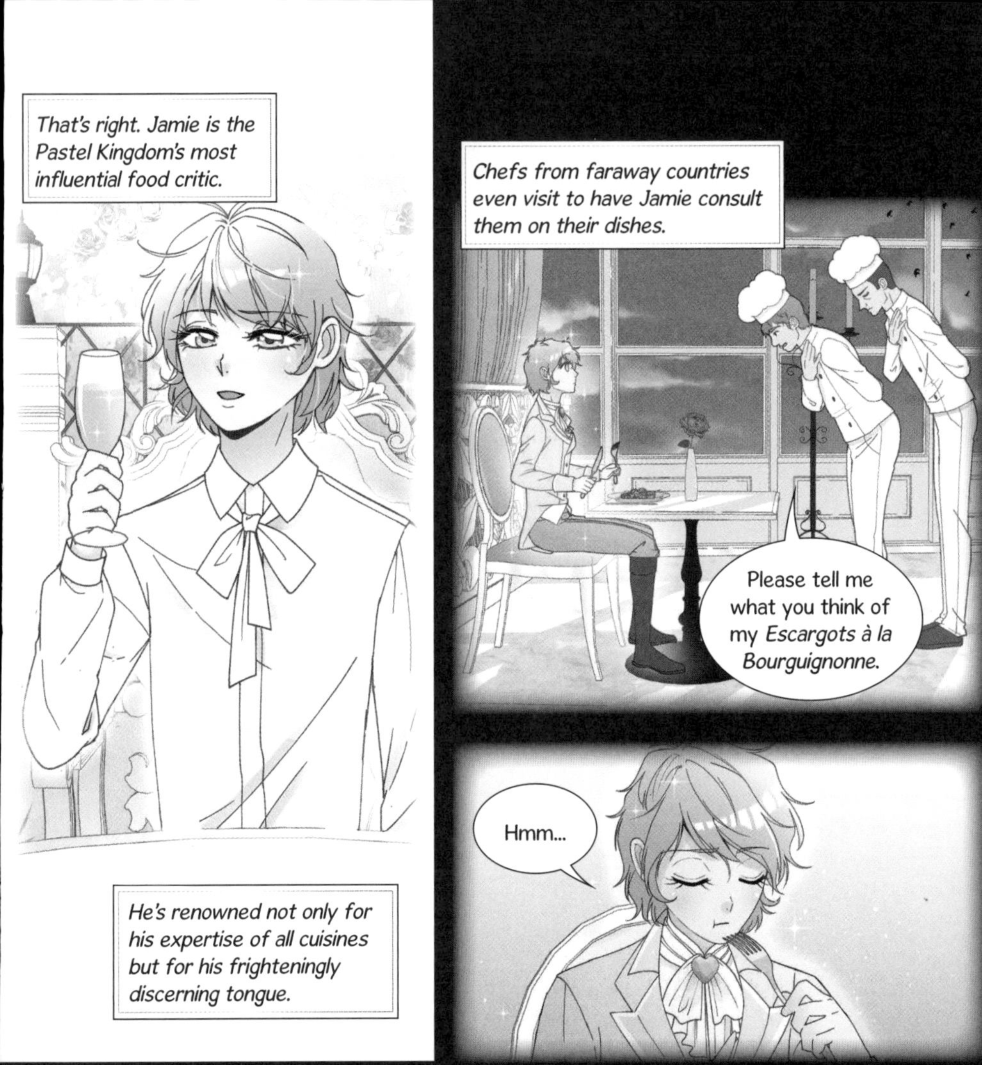
That's right. Jamie is the Pastel Kingdom's most influential food critic.
He's renowned not only for his expertise of all cuisines but for his frighteningly discerning tongue.
Chefs from faraway countries even visit to have Jamie consult them on their dishes.
Please tell me what you think of my *Escargots à la Bourguignonne.*
Hmm...

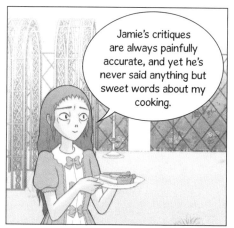

Jamie's critiques are always painfully accurate, and yet he's never said anything but sweet words about my cooking.

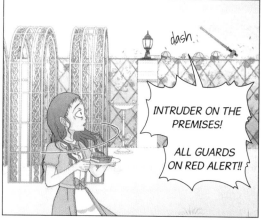

dash

INTRUDER ON THE PREMISES!

ALL GUARDS ON RED ALERT!!

Oh no!! Papa has been saying there's been an increase in crime and petty sorcery lately.

Jamie, we better get ins—

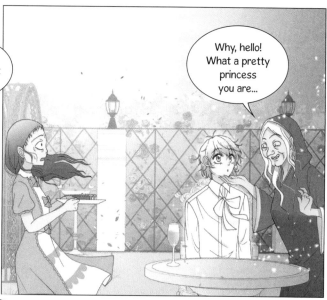

Why, hello! What a pretty princess you are...

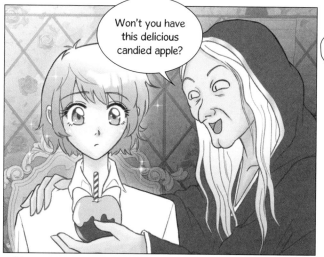

Won't you have this delicious candied apple?

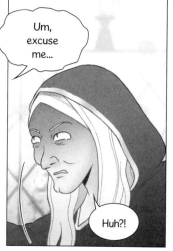

Um, excuse me...

Huh?!

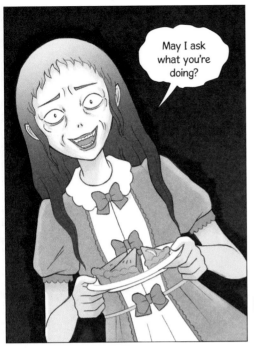

May I ask what you're doing?

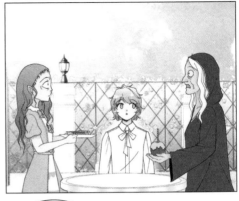

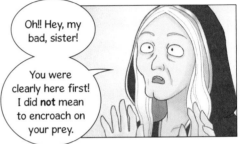

Oh!! Hey, my bad, sister!

You were clearly here first! I did **not** mean to encroach on your prey.

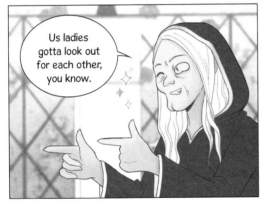

Us ladies gotta look out for each other, you know.

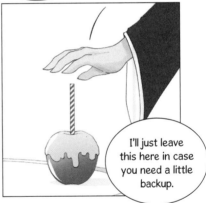

I'll just leave this here in case you need a little backup.

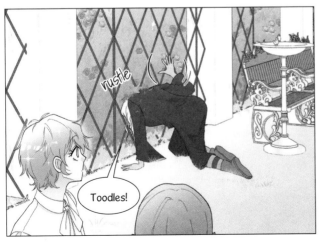

rustle

Toodles!

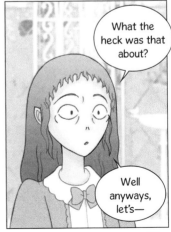

What the heck was that about?

Well anyways, let's—

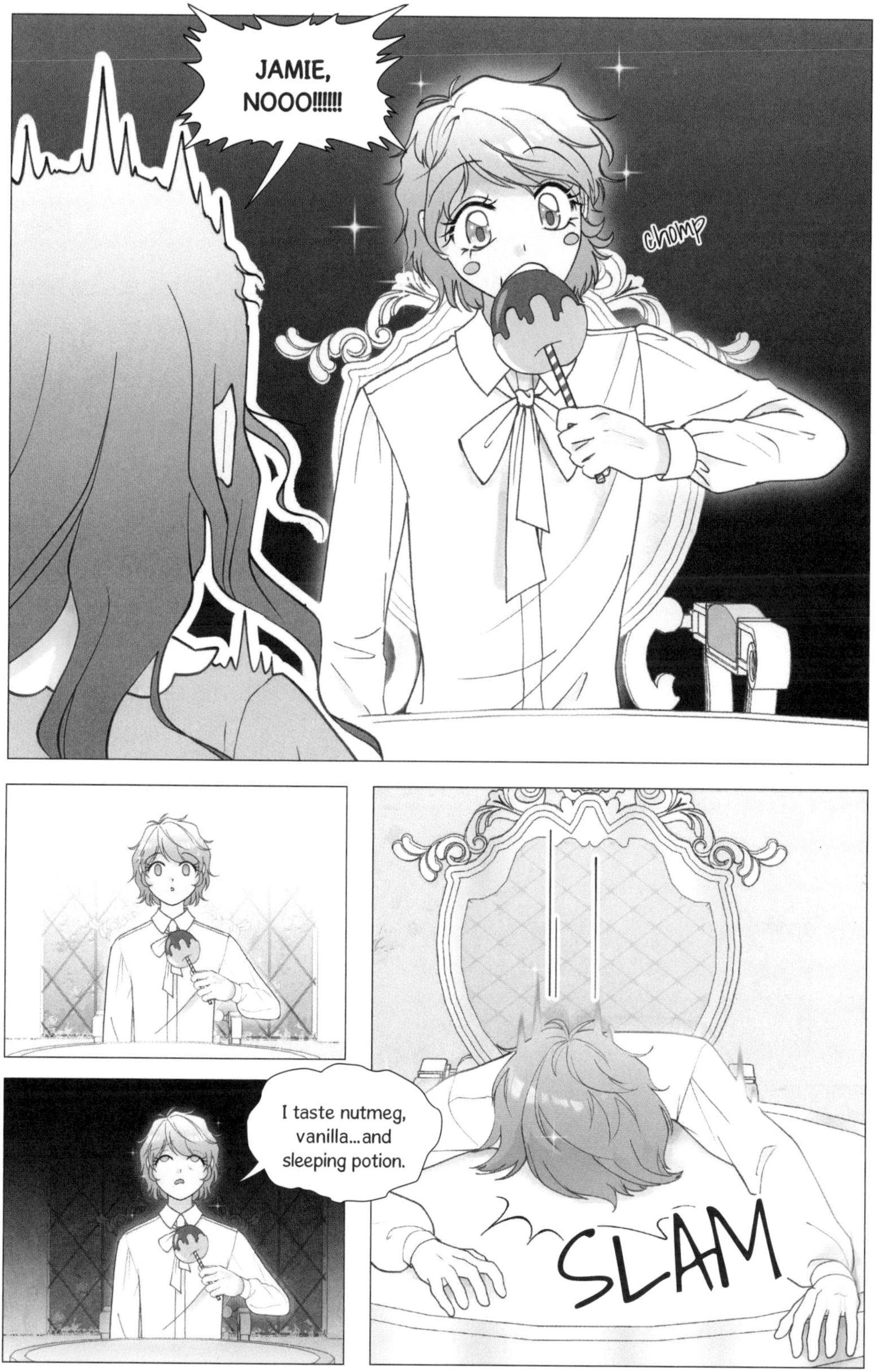
JAMIE, NOOO!!!!!!
chomp
I taste nutmeg, vanilla...and sleeping potion.
SLAM

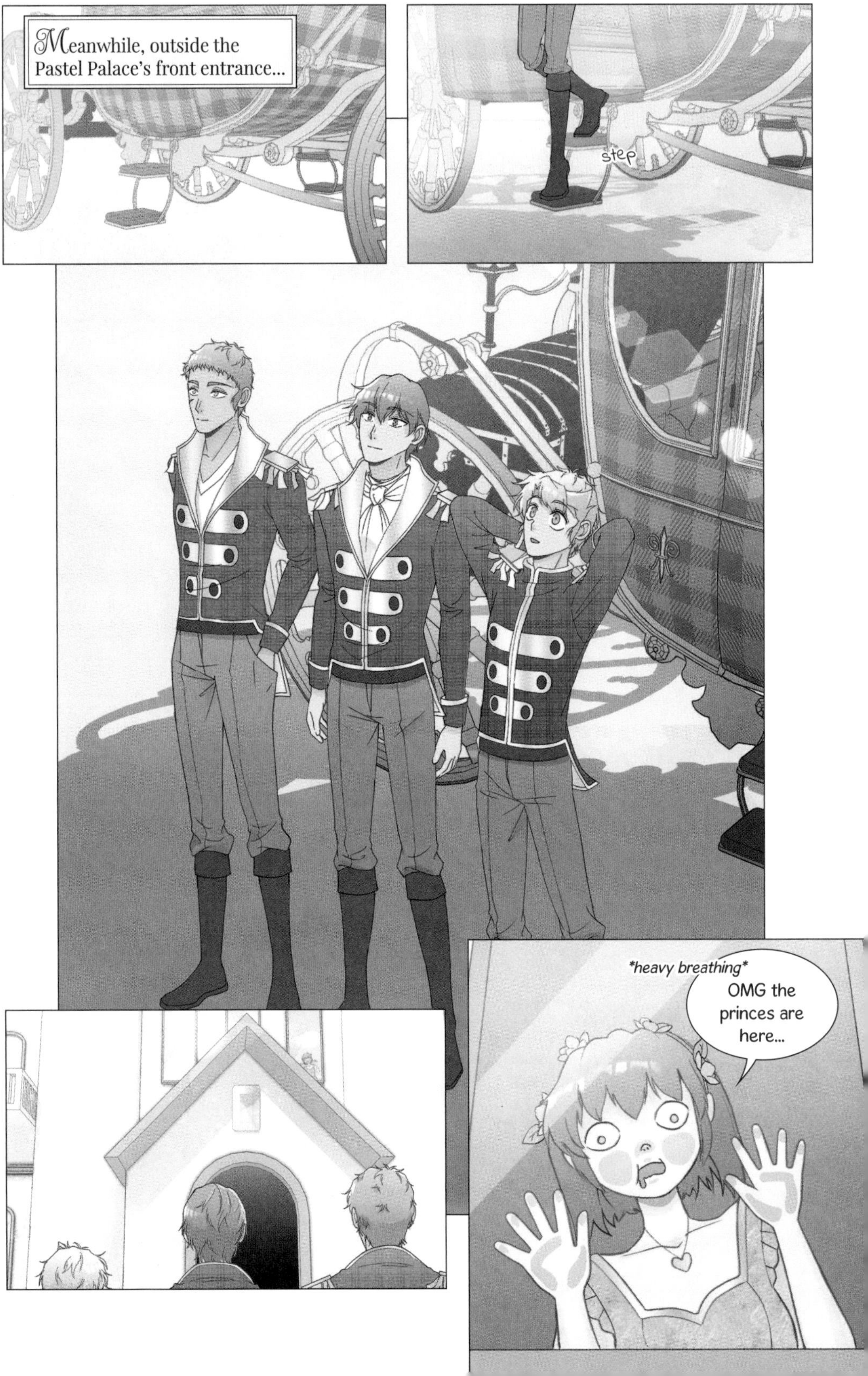
Meanwhile, outside the Pastel Palace's front entrance...
step
heavy breathing
OMG the princes are here...

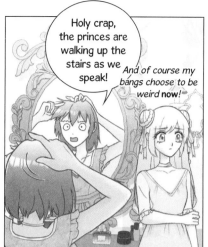

Holy crap, the princes are walking up the stairs as we speak!

*And of course my bangs choose to be weird **now**!*

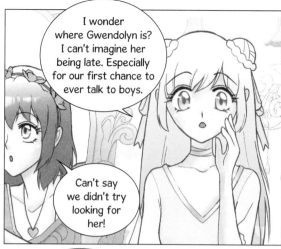

I wonder where Gwendolyn is? I can't imagine her being late. Especially for our first chance to ever talk to boys.

Can't say we didn't try looking for her!

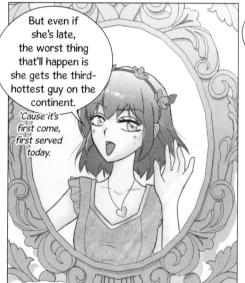

But even if she's late, the worst thing that'll happen is she gets the third-hottest guy on the continent.

'Cause it's first come, first served today.

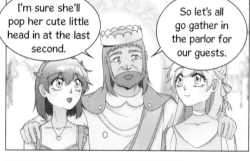

I'm sure she'll pop her cute little head in at the last second.

So let's all go gather in the parlor for our guests.

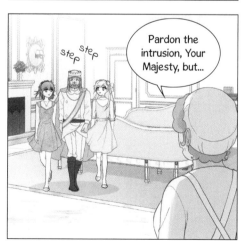

step step step

Pardon the intrusion, Your Majesty, but...

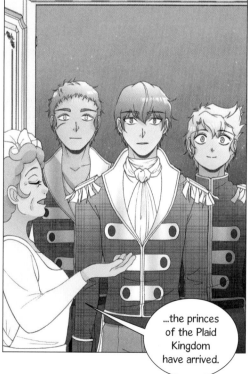

...the princes of the Plaid Kingdom have arrived.

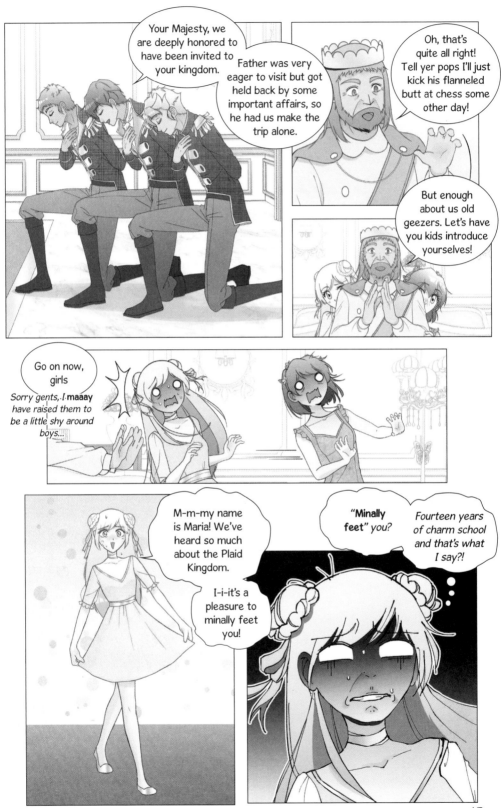

47

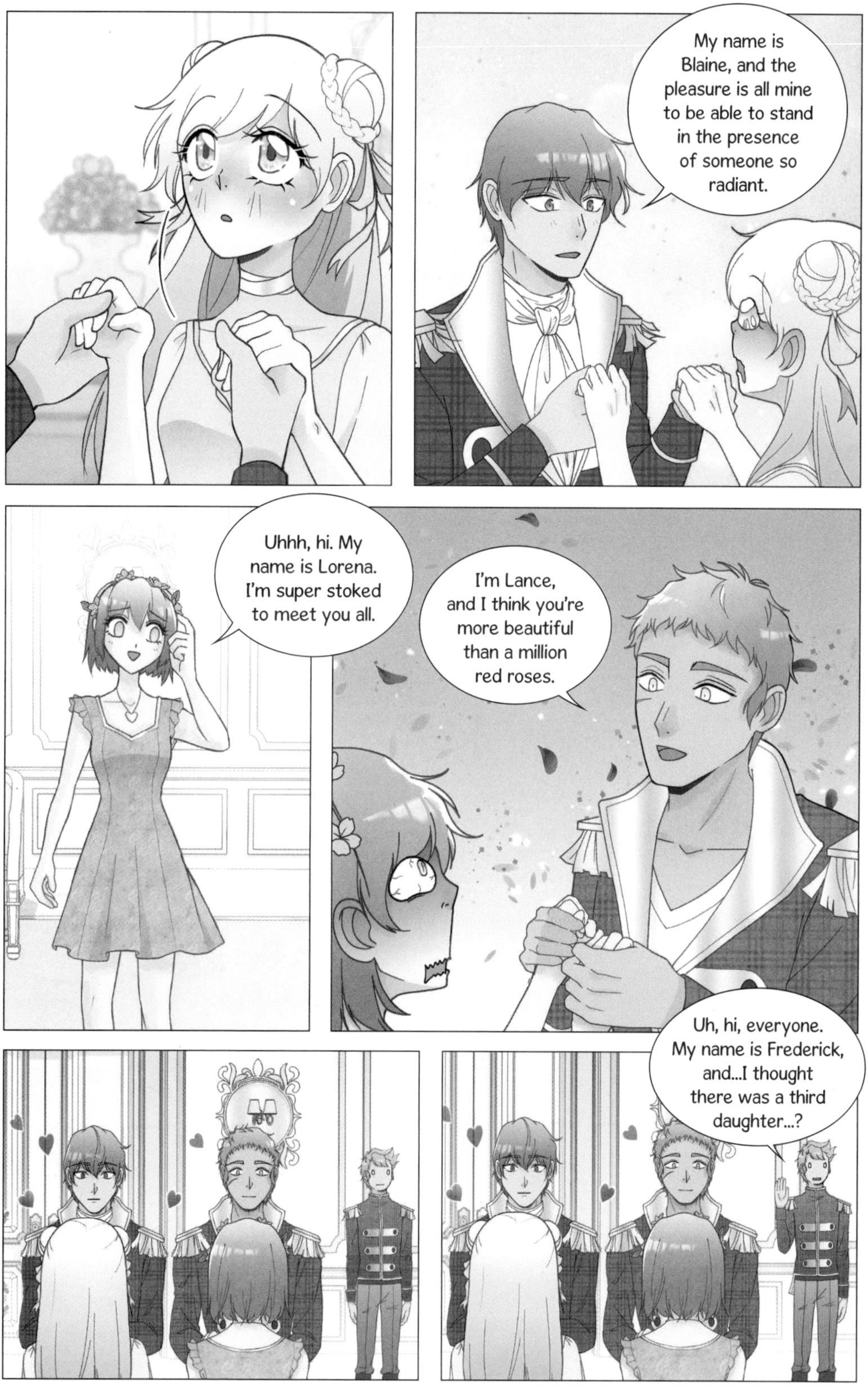
My name is Blaine, and the pleasure is all mine to be able to stand in the presence of someone so radiant.
Uhhh, hi. My name is Lorena. I'm super stoked to meet you all.
I'm Lance, and I think you're more beautiful than a million red roses.
Uh, hi, everyone. My name is Frederick, and...I thought there was a third daughter...?

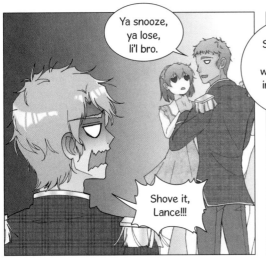

Ya snooze, ya lose, li'l bro.

Shove it, Lance!!!

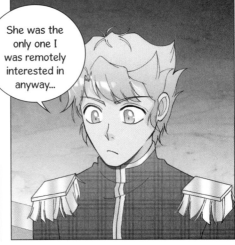

She was the only one I was remotely interested in anyway...

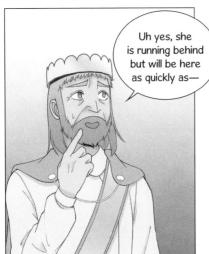

Uh yes, she is running behind but will be here as quickly as—

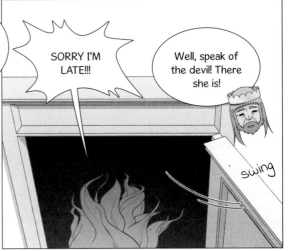

SORRY I'M LATE!!!

Well, speak of the devil! There she is!

swing

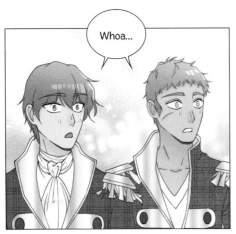

Whoa...

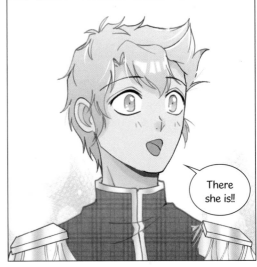

There she is!!

49

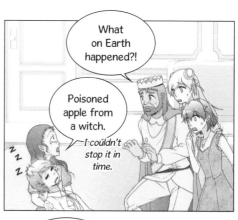

What on Earth happened?!

Poisoned apple from a witch.

I couldn't stop it in time.

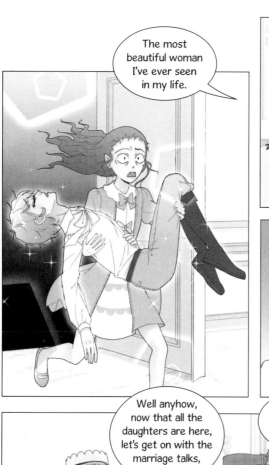

The most beautiful woman I've ever seen in my life.

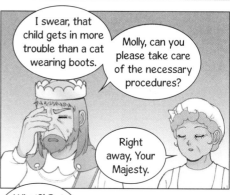

I swear, that child gets in more trouble than a cat wearing boots.

Molly, can you please take care of the necessary procedures?

Right away, Your Majesty.

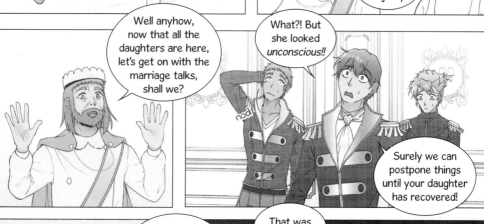

Well anyhow, now that all the daughters are here, let's get on with the marriage talks, shall we?

What?! But she looked *unconscious!!*

nod

Surely we can postpone things until your daughter has recovered!

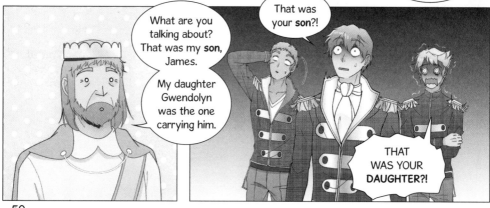

What are you talking about? That was my **son**, James.

My daughter Gwendolyn was the one carrying him.

That was your **son**?!

THAT WAS YOUR **DAUGHTER**?!

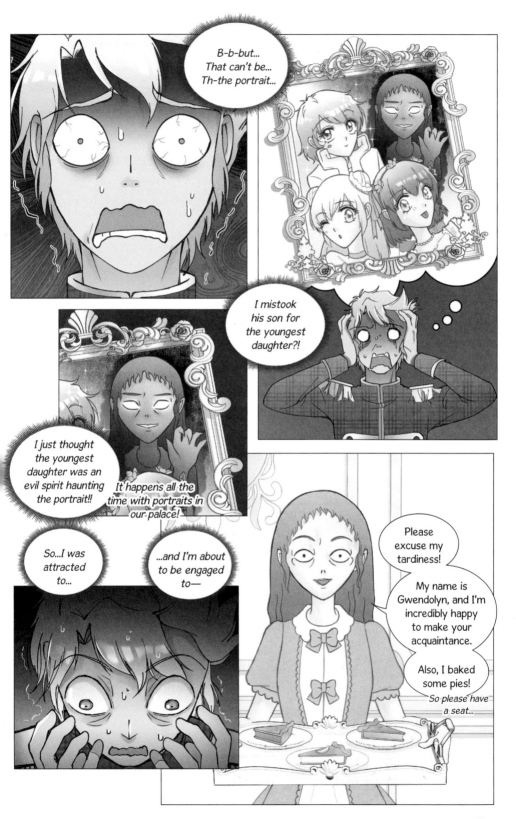

51

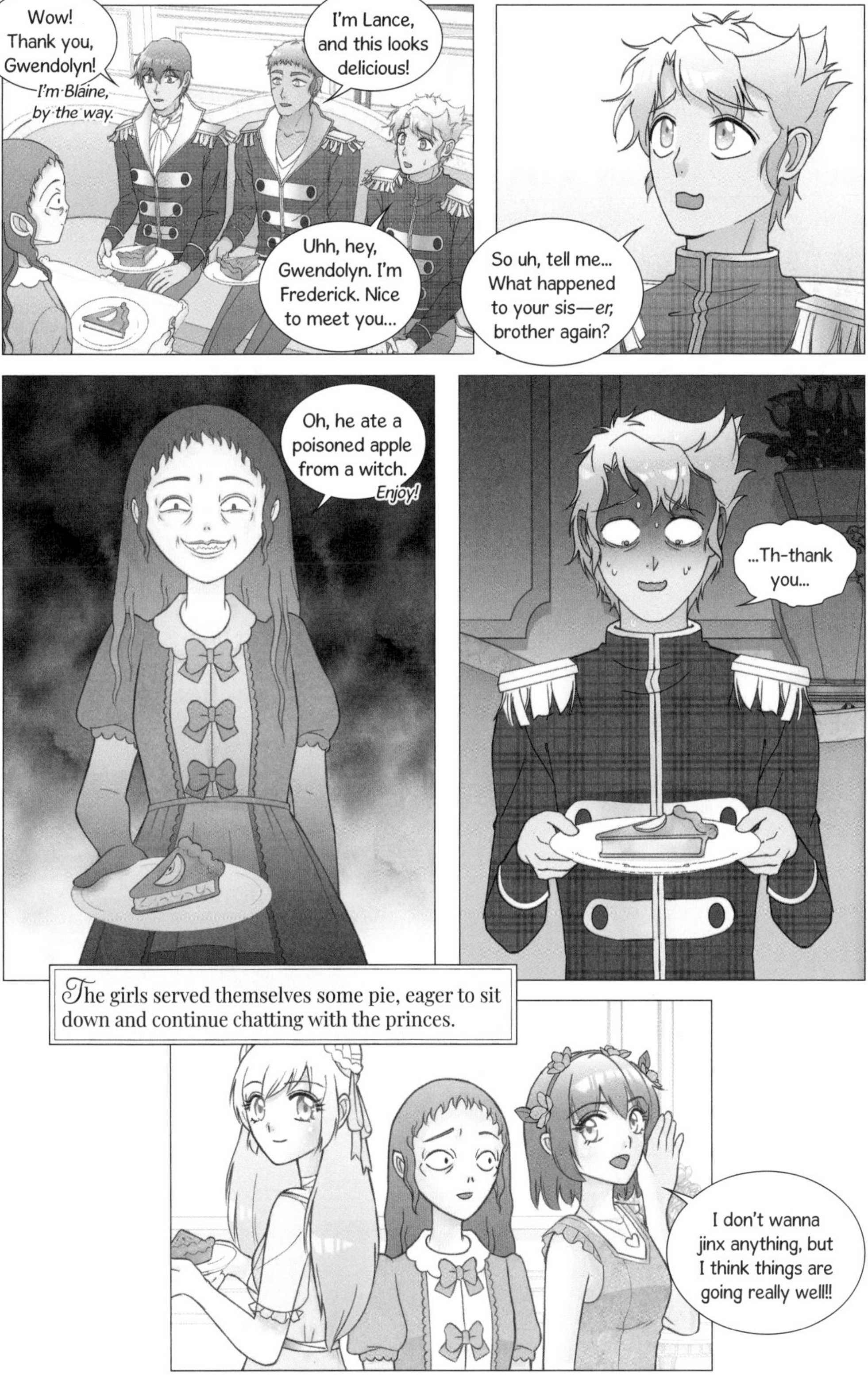
Wow! Thank you, Gwendolyn!
I'm Blaine, by the way.
I'm Lance, and this looks delicious!
Uhh, hey, Gwendolyn. I'm Frederick. Nice to meet you...
So uh, tell me... What happened to your sis—*er,* brother again?
Oh, he ate a poisoned apple from a witch.
Enjoy!
...Th-thank you...
The girls served themselves some pie, eager to sit down and continue chatting with the princes.
I don't wanna jinx anything, but I think things are going really well!!

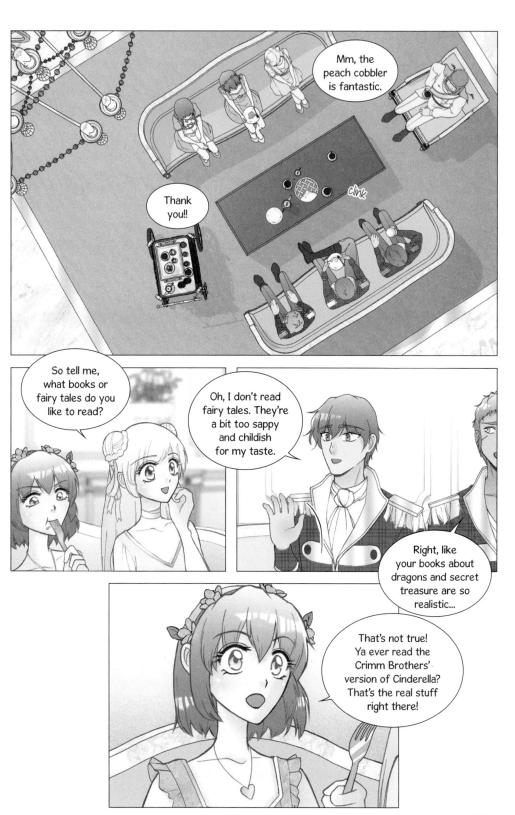

53

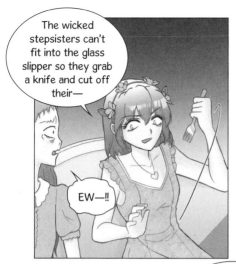

The wicked stepsisters can't fit into the glass slipper so they grab a knife and cut off their—

EW—!!

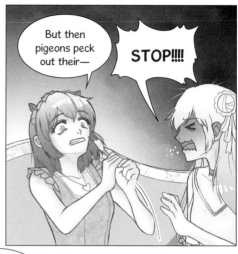

But then pigeons peck out their—

STOP!!!!

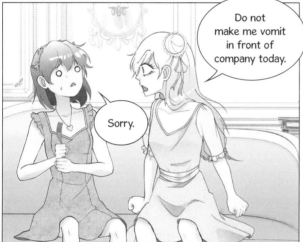

Do not make me vomit in front of company today.

Sorry.

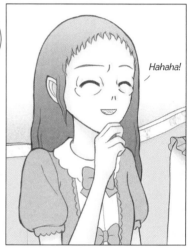

Hahaha!

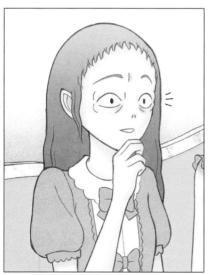

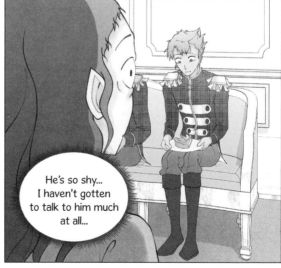

He's so shy... I haven't gotten to talk to him much at all...

54

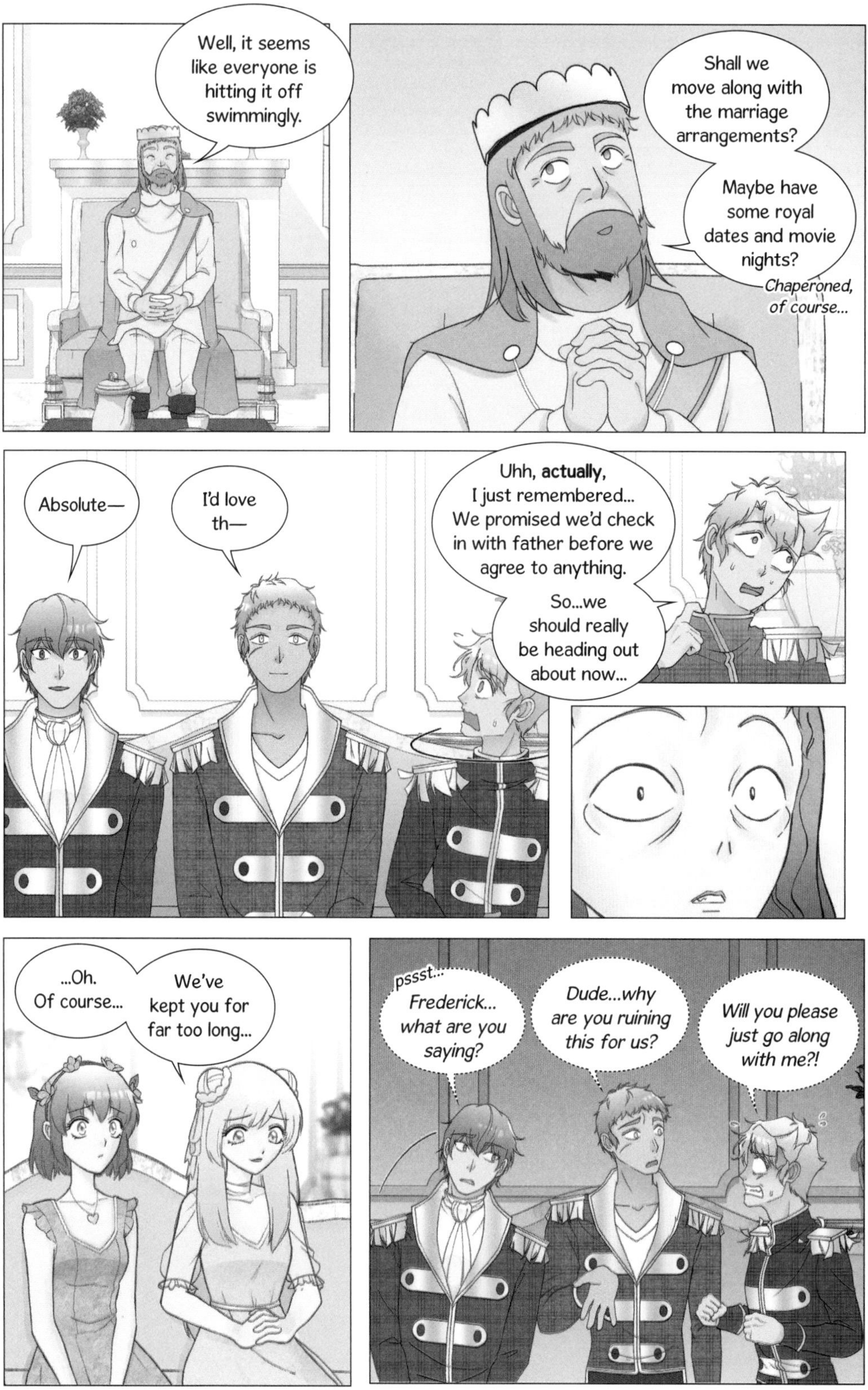
Well, it seems like everyone is hitting it off swimmingly.
Shall we move along with the marriage arrangements?
Maybe have some royal dates and movie nights?
Chaperoned, of course...
Absolute—
I'd love th—
Uhh, **actually**, I just remembered... We promised we'd check in with father before we agree to anything.
So...we should really be heading out about now...
...Oh. Of course...
We've kept you for far too long...
pssst...
Frederick... what are you saying?
Dude...why are you ruining this for us?
Will you please just go along with me?!

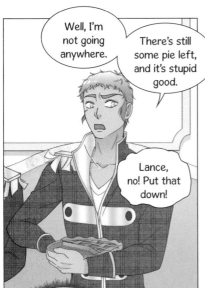

Well, I'm not going anywhere.

There's still some pie left, and it's stupid good.

Lance, no! Put that down!

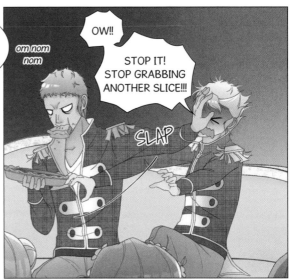

OW!!

STOP IT! STOP GRABBING ANOTHER SLICE!!!

om nom nom

SLAP

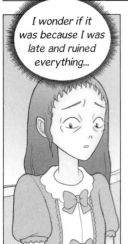

I wonder if it was because I was late and ruined everything...

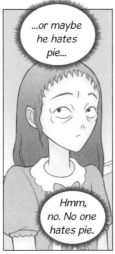

...or maybe he hates pie...

Hmm, no. No one hates pie.

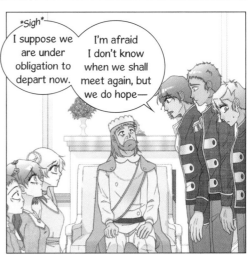

Sigh
I suppose we are under obligation to depart now.

I'm afraid I don't know when we shall meet again, but we do hope—

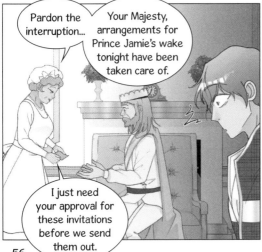

Pardon the interruption...

Your Majesty, arrangements for Prince Jamie's wake tonight have been taken care of.

I just need your approval for these invitations before we send them out.

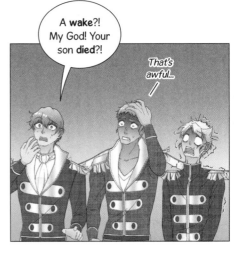

A **wake**?! My God! Your son **died**?!

That's awful...

56

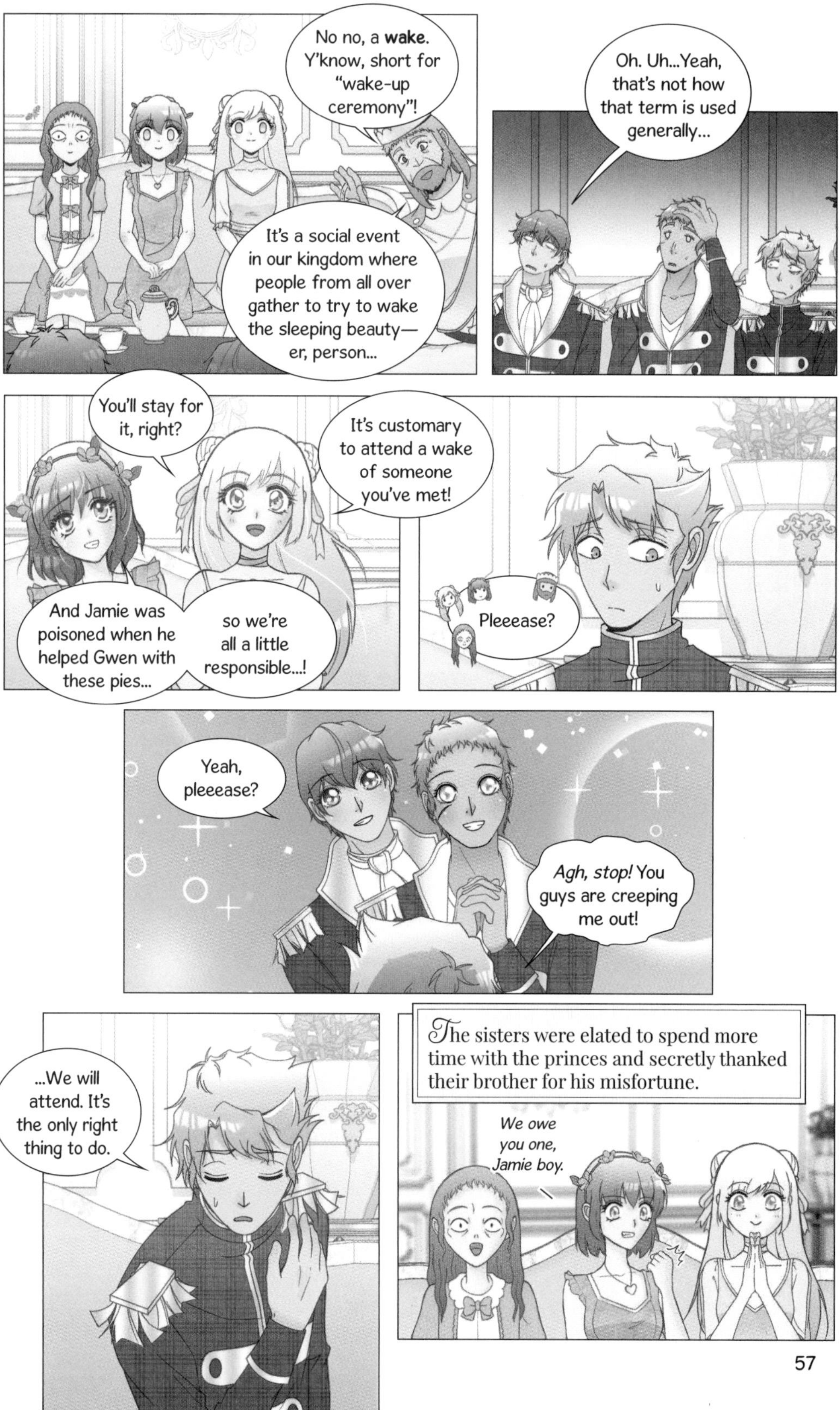
No no, a **wake**. Y'know, short for "wake-up ceremony"!
It's a social event in our kingdom where people from all over gather to try to wake the sleeping beauty— er, person...
Oh. Uh...Yeah, that's not how that term is used generally...
You'll stay for it, right?
It's customary to attend a wake of someone you've met!
And Jamie was poisoned when he helped Gwen with these pies...
so we're all a little responsible...!
Pleeease?
Yeah, pleeease?
Agh, stop! You guys are creeping me out!
...We will attend. It's the only right thing to do.
The sisters were elated to spend more time with the princes and secretly thanked their brother for his misfortune.
We owe you one, Jamie boy.

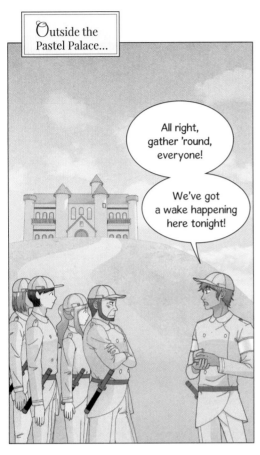

Outside the Pastel Palace...

All right, gather 'round, everyone!

We've got a wake happening here tonight!

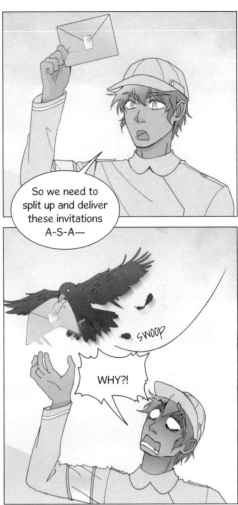

So we need to split up and deliver these invitations A-S-A—

SWOOP

WHY?!

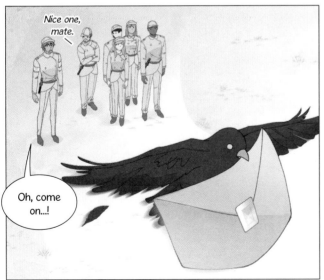

Nice one, mate.

Oh, come on...!

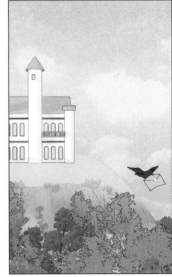

58

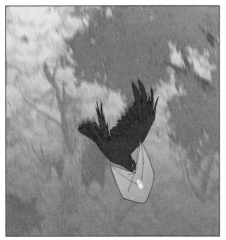

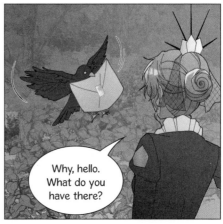

Why, hello. What do you have there?

Oh? It seems like there's a wake being held at the Pastel Palace tonight.

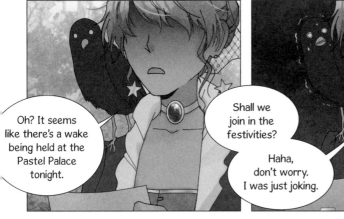

Shall we join in the festivities?

Haha, don't worry. I was just joking.

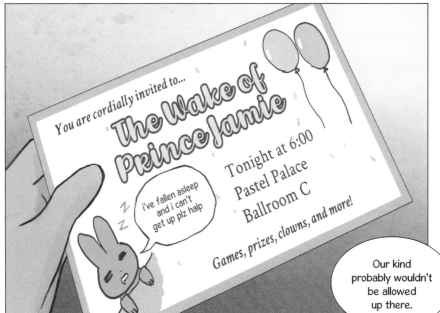

You are cordially invited to...

The Wake of Prince Jamie

i've fallen asleep and i can't get up plz halp

Z Z

Tonight at 6:00
Pastel Palace
Ballroom C

Games, prizes, clowns, and more!

Our kind probably wouldn't be allowed up there.

Chapter

3

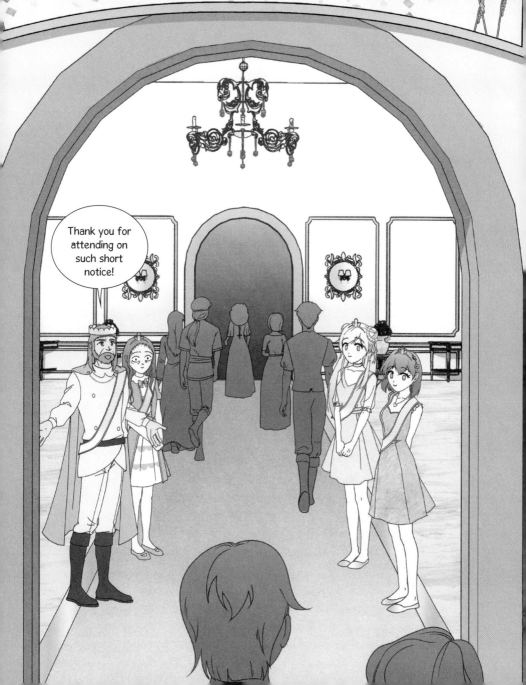

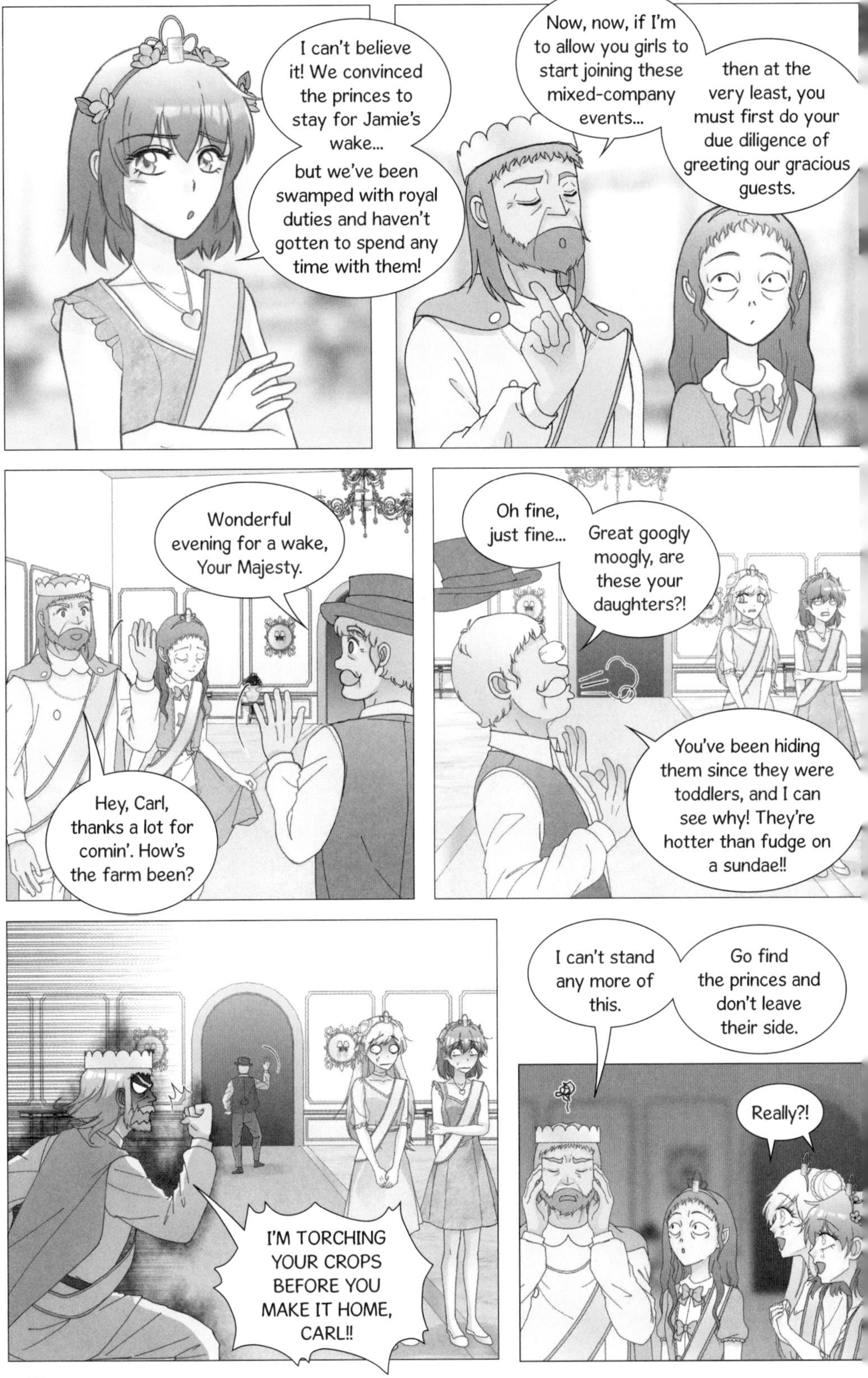
I can't believe it! We convinced the princes to stay for Jamie's wake...
but we've been swamped with royal duties and haven't gotten to spend any time with them!
Now, now, if I'm to allow you girls to start joining these mixed-company events...
then at the very least, you must first do your due diligence of greeting our gracious guests.
Wonderful evening for a wake, Your Majesty.
Hey, Carl, thanks a lot for comin'. How's the farm been?
Oh fine, just fine...
Great googly moogly, are these your daughters?!
You've been hiding them since they were toddlers, and I can see why! They're hotter than fudge on a sundae!!
I'M TORCHING YOUR CROPS BEFORE YOU MAKE IT HOME, CARL!!
I can't stand any more of this.
Go find the princes and don't leave their side.
Really?!

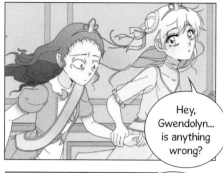

And tell them they have my permission to slay anyone who so much as looks at you!!

I can't wait to ditch these dorky tiaras!

dash

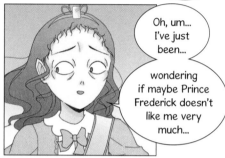

Hey, Gwendolyn... is anything wrong?

Oh, um... I've just been...

wondering if maybe Prince Frederick doesn't like me very much...

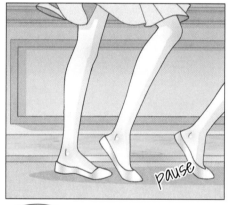

pause

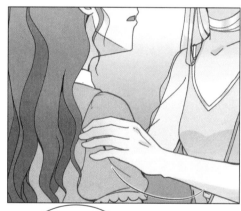

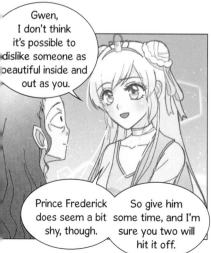

Gwen, I don't think it's possible to dislike someone as beautiful inside and out as you.

Prince Frederick does seem a bit shy, though.

So give him some time, and I'm sure you two will hit it off.

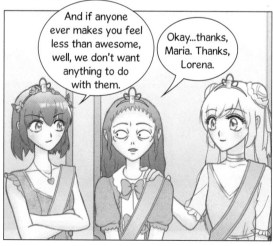

And if anyone ever makes you feel less than awesome, well, we don't want anything to do with them.

Okay...thanks, Maria. Thanks, Lorena.

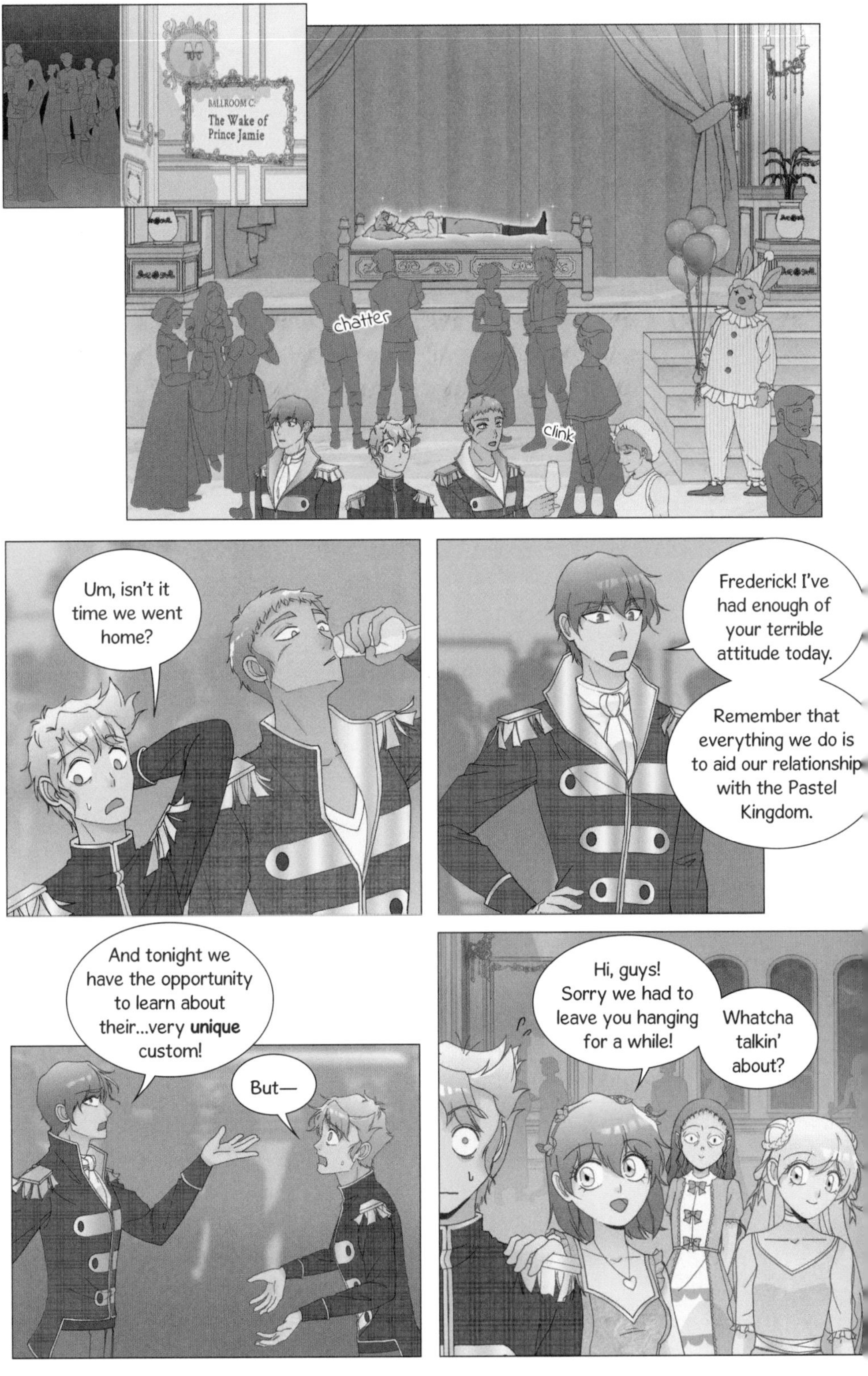
BALLROOM C:
The Wake of Prince Jamie
chatter
clink
Um, isn't it time we went home?
Frederick! I've had enough of your terrible attitude today.
Remember that everything we do is to aid our relationship with the Pastel Kingdom.
And tonight we have the opportunity to learn about their...very **unique** custom!
But—
Hi, guys! Sorry we had to leave you hanging for a while!
Whatcha talkin' about?

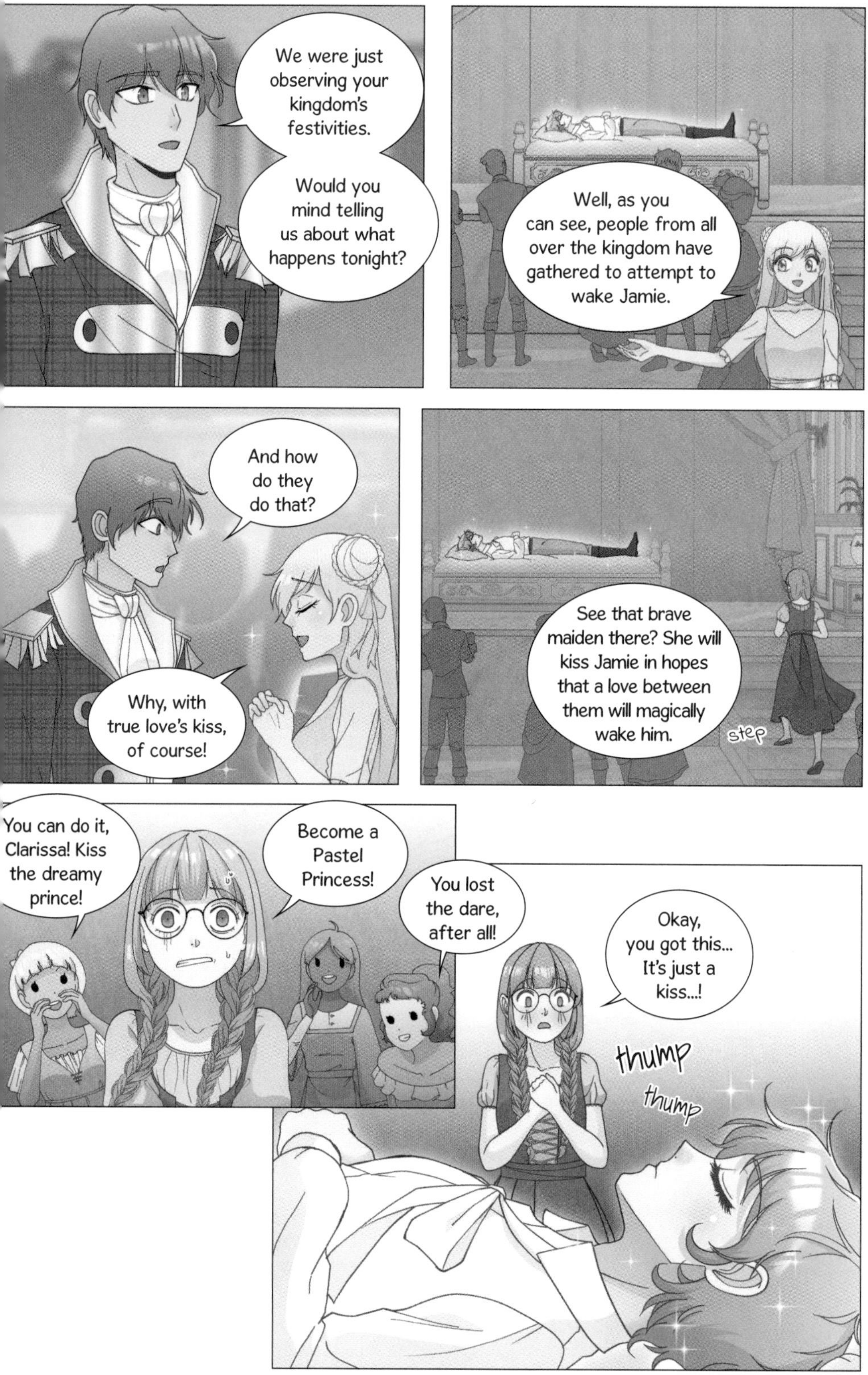
We were just observing your kingdom's festivities.
Would you mind telling us about what happens tonight?
Well, as you can see, people from all over the kingdom have gathered to attempt to wake Jamie.
And how do they do that?
Why, with true love's kiss, of course!
See that brave maiden there? She will kiss Jamie in hopes that a love between them will magically wake him.
step
You can do it, Clarissa! Kiss the dreamy prince!
Become a Pastel Princess!
You lost the dare, after all!
Okay, you got this... It's just a kiss...!
thump
thump

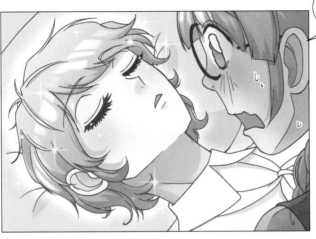

Wow, he's... he's...

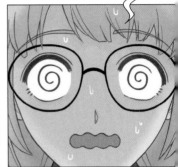

TOO PRETTY!!!!!!

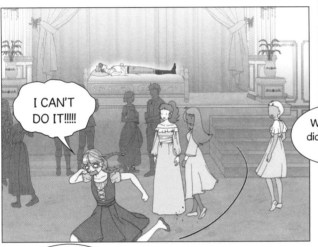

I CAN'T DO IT!!!!!

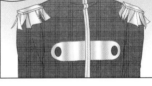

Well, that didn't work out...

Well, if none of these silly maidens can get the job done, I guess I'll just have to give it a try myself...

Me too!

Me next!

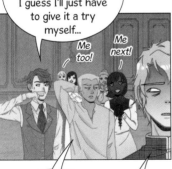

T-to save the kingdom...!

I don't think I like this tradition...

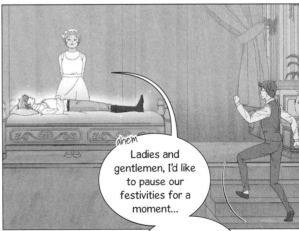

ahem

Ladies and gentlemen, I'd like to pause our festivities for a moment...

to thank you all for participating in the wake of Prince James.

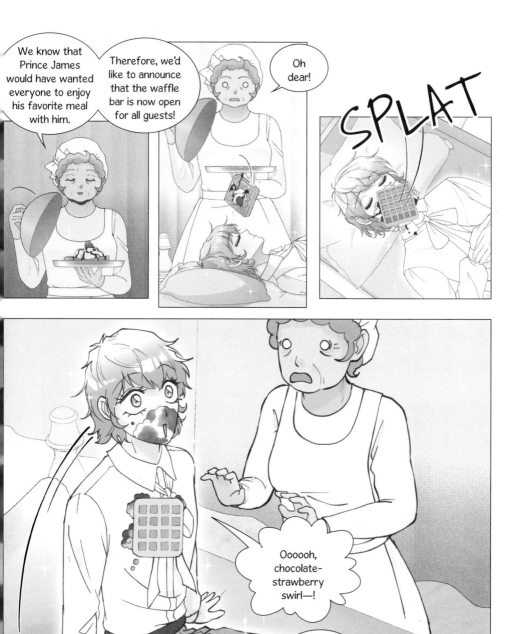

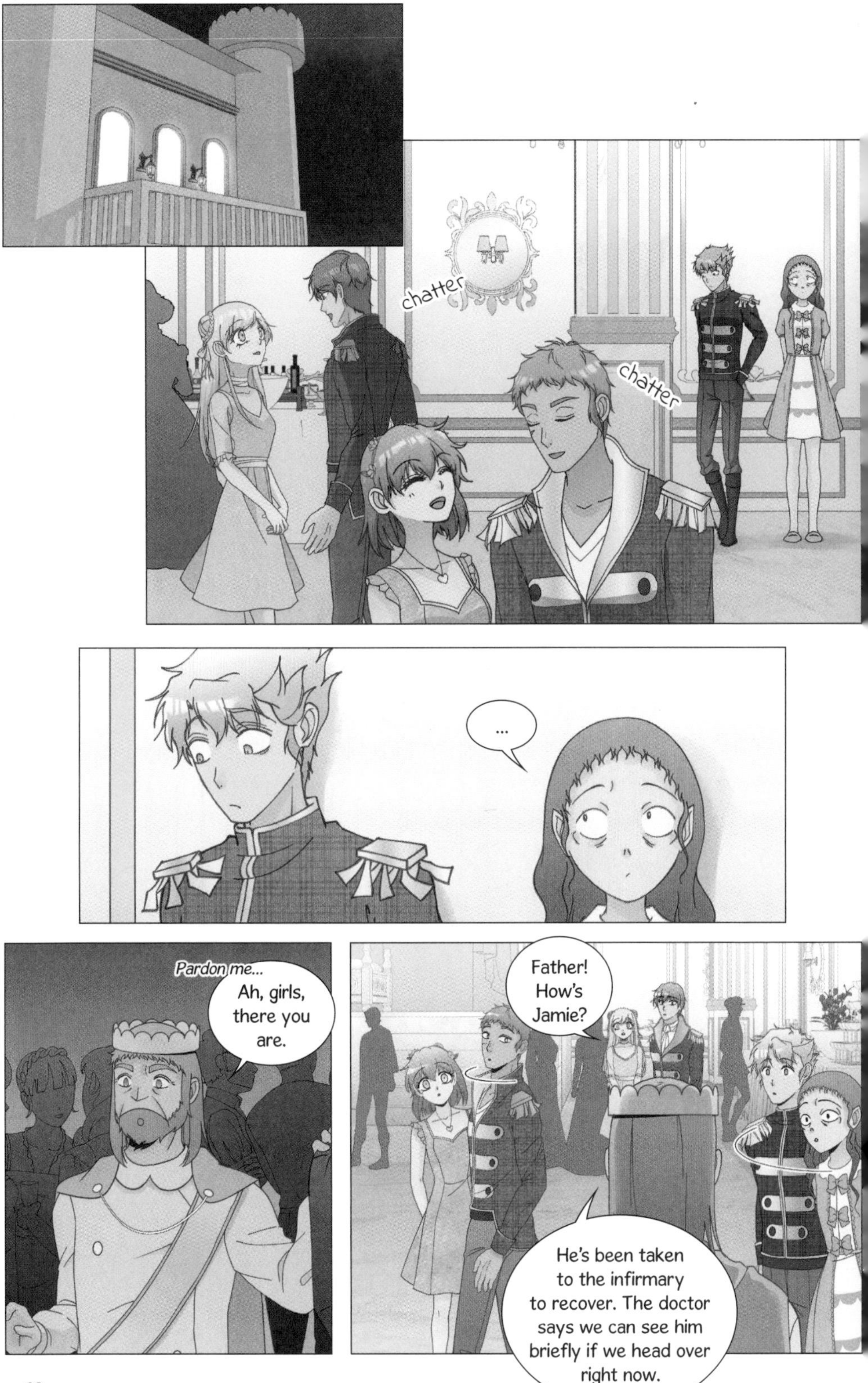
chatter
chatter
...
Pardon me...
Ah, girls, there you are.
Father! How's Jamie?
He's been taken to the infirmary to recover. The doctor says we can see him briefly if we head over right now.

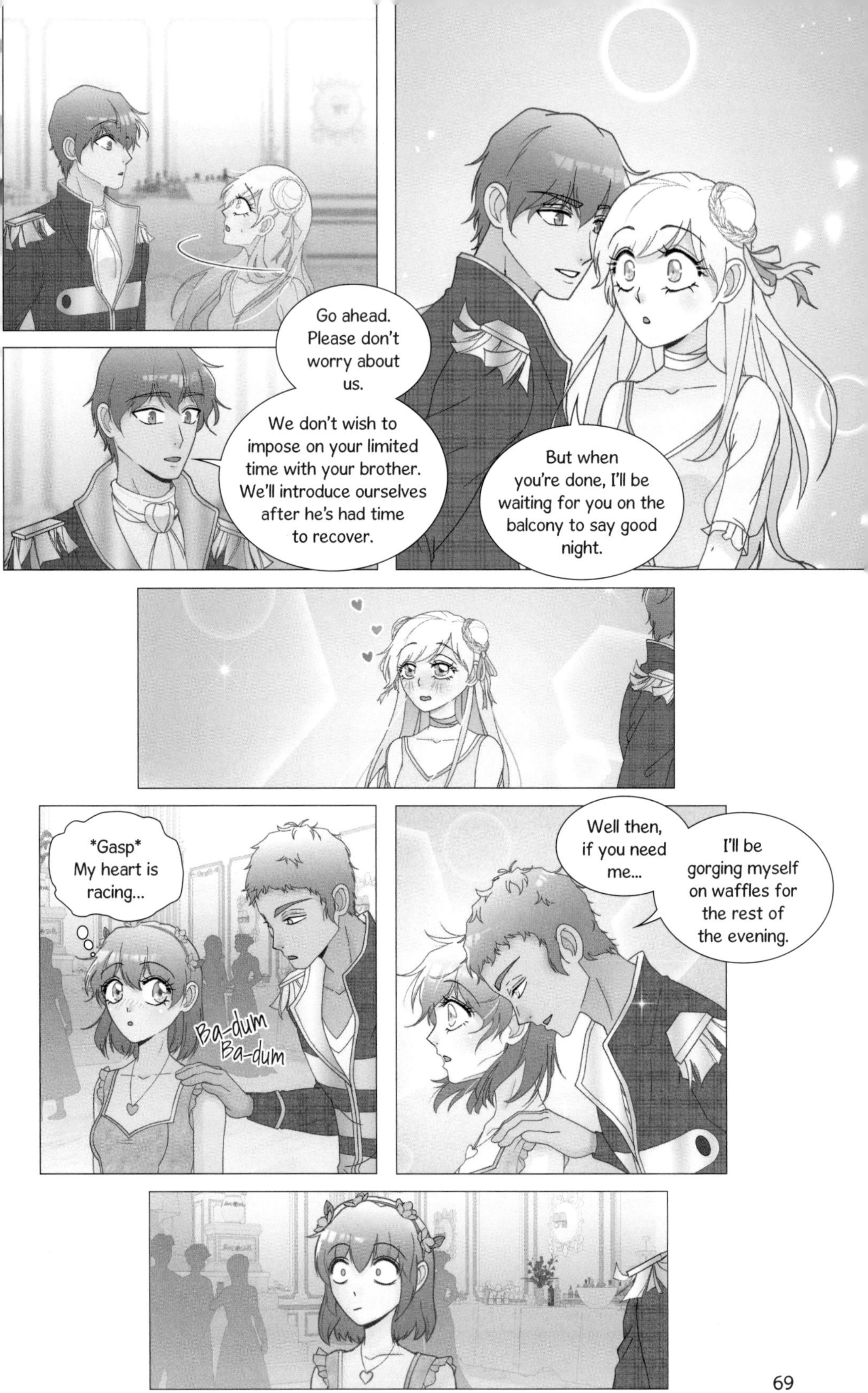
Go ahead. Please don't worry about us.
We don't wish to impose on your limited time with your brother. We'll introduce ourselves after he's had time to recover.
But when you're done, I'll be waiting for you on the balcony to say good night.
Gasp My heart is racing...
Ba-dum Ba-dum
Well then, if you need me...
I'll be gorging myself on waffles for the rest of the evening.

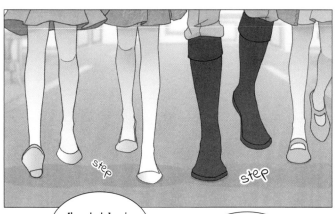

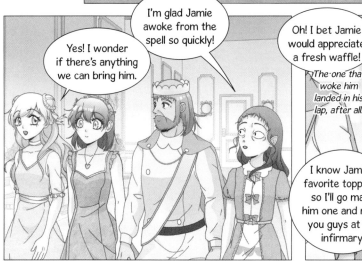

I'm glad Jamie awoke from the spell so quickly!

Yes! I wonder if there's anything we can bring him.

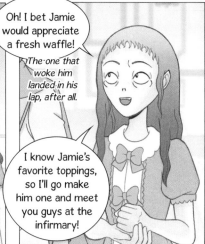

Oh! I bet Jamie would appreciate a fresh waffle!

The one that woke him landed in his lap, after all.

I know Jamie's favorite toppings, so I'll go make him one and meet you guys at the infirmary!

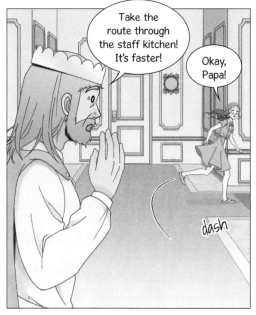

Take the route through the staff kitchen! It's faster!

Okay, Papa!

dash

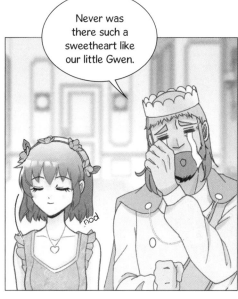

Never was there such a sweetheart like our little Gwen.

nod

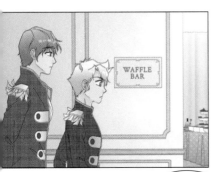

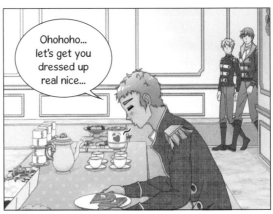

Ohohoho... let's get you dressed up real nice...

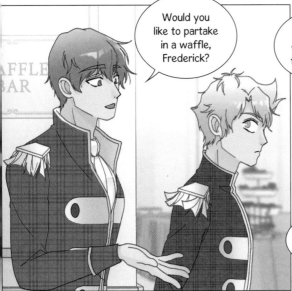

Would you like to partake in a waffle, Frederick?

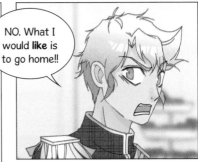

NO. What I would **like** is to go home!!

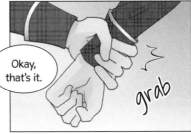

Okay, that's it.

grab

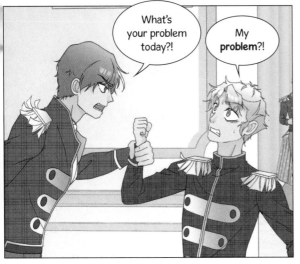

What's your problem today?!

My **problem**?!

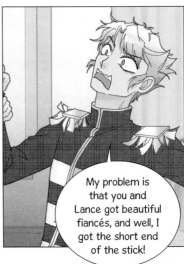

My problem is that you and Lance got beautiful fiancés, and well, I got the short end of the stick!

71

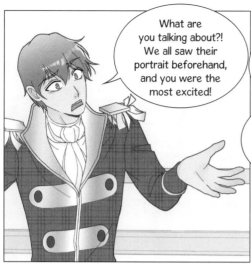

What are you talking about?! We all saw their portrait beforehand, and you were the most excited!

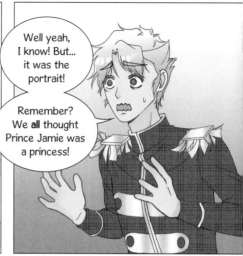

Well yeah, I know! But... it was the portrait!

Remember? We **all** thought Prince Jamie was a princess!

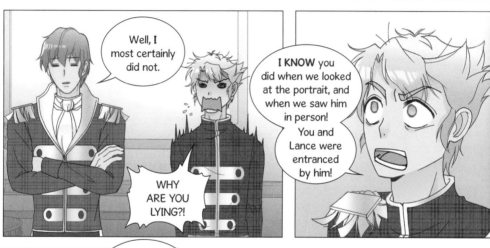

Well, **I** most certainly did not.

WHY ARE YOU LYING?!

I KNOW you did when we looked at the portrait, and when we saw him in person! You and Lance were entranced by him!

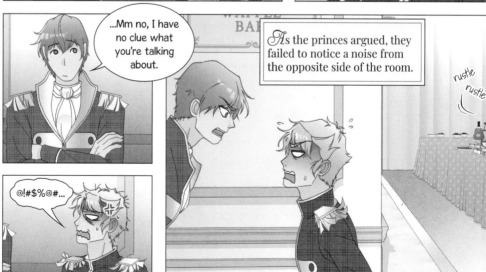

...Mm no, I have no clue what you're talking about.

As the princes argued, they failed to notice a noise from the opposite side of the room.

rustle
rustle

@!#$%@#...

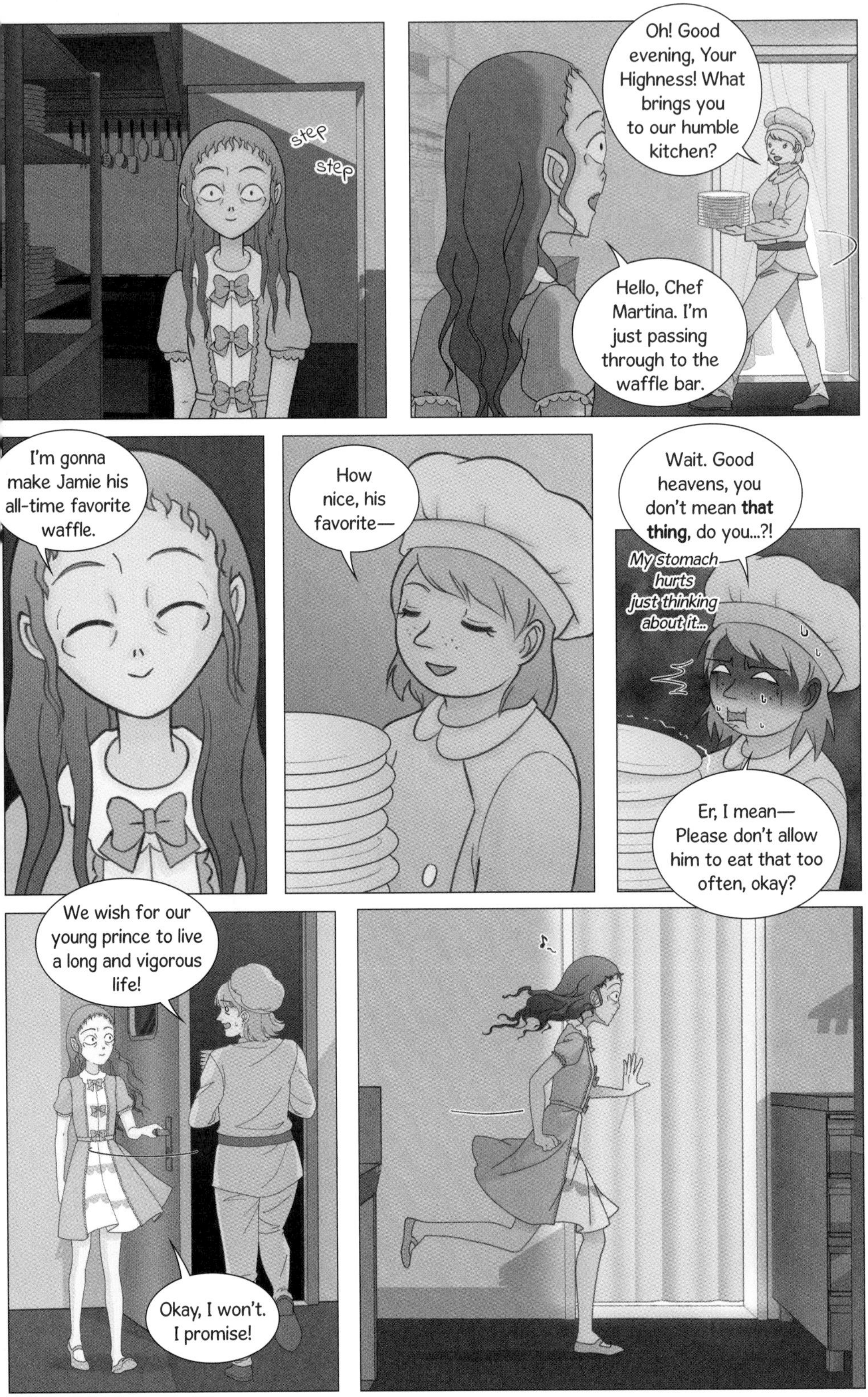
step
step
Oh! Good evening, Your Highness! What brings you to our humble kitchen?
Hello, Chef Martina. I'm just passing through to the waffle bar.
I'm gonna make Jamie his all-time favorite waffle.
How nice, his favorite—
Wait. Good heavens, you don't mean **that thing**, do you...?!
My stomach hurts just thinking about it...
Er, I mean— Please don't allow him to eat that too often, okay?
We wish for our young prince to live a long and vigorous life!
Okay, I won't. I promise!

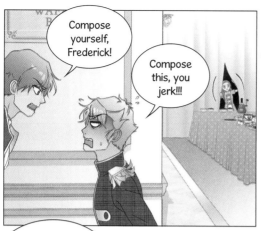

Compose yourself, Frederick!

Compose this, you jerk!!!

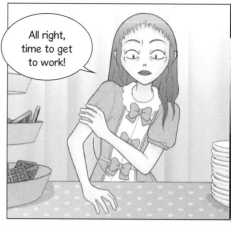

All right, time to get to work!

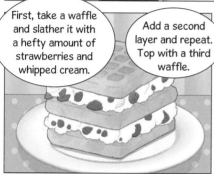

First, take a waffle and slather it with a hefty amount of strawberries and whipped cream.

Add a second layer and repeat. Top with a third waffle.

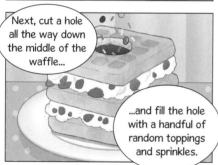

Next, cut a hole all the way down the middle of the waffle...

...and fill the hole with a handful of random toppings and sprinkles.

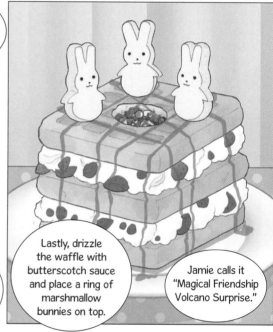

Lastly, drizzle the waffle with butterscotch sauce and place a ring of marshmallow bunnies on top.

Jamie calls it "Magical Friendship Volcano Surprise."

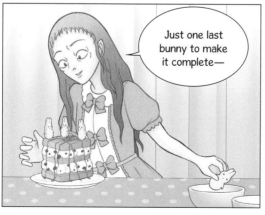

Just one last bunny to make it complete—

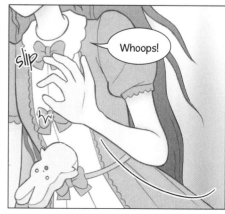

slip

Whoops!

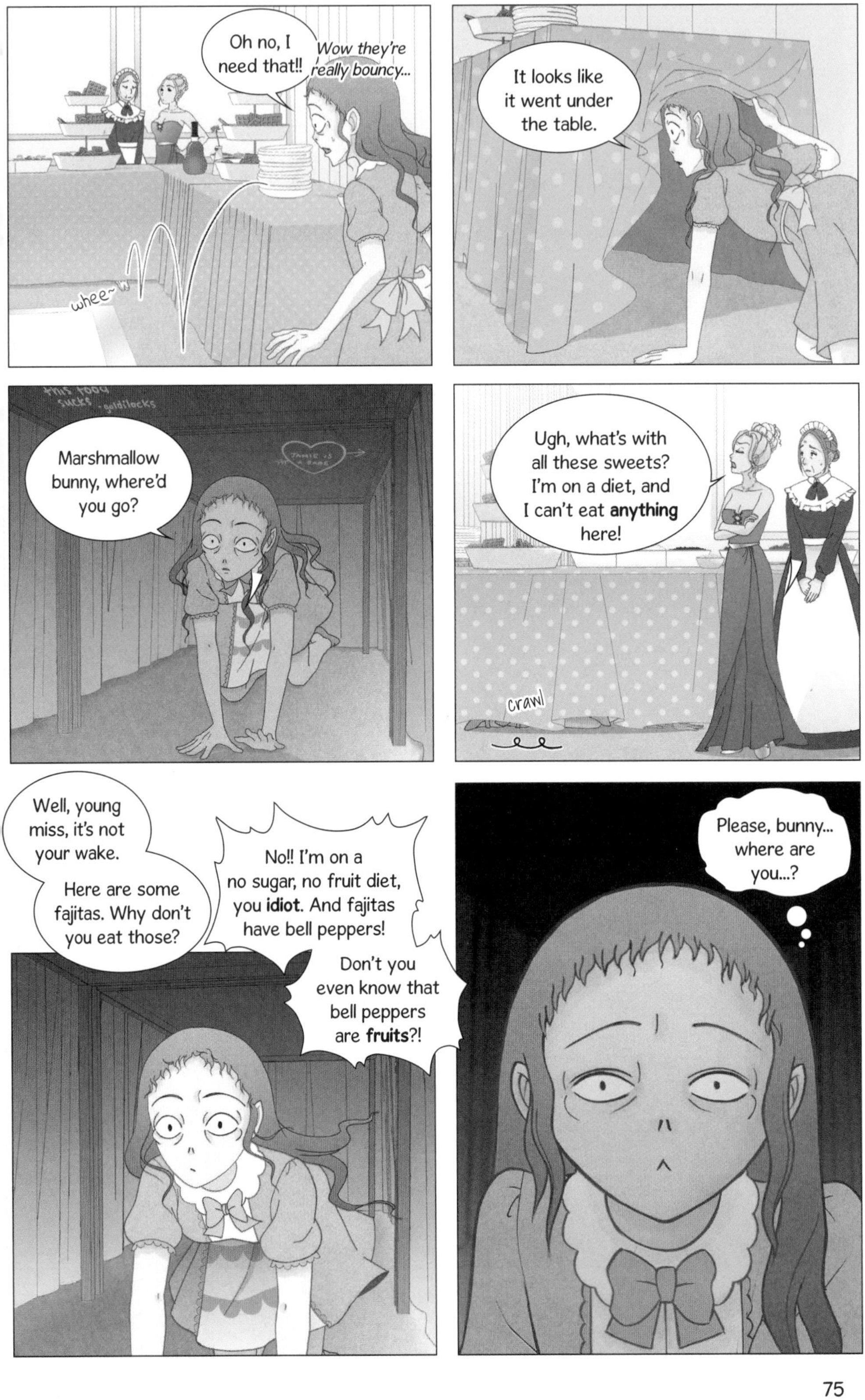
Oh no, I need that!!
Wow they're really bouncy...
whee~
It looks like it went under the table.
Marshmallow bunny, where'd you go?
Ugh, what's with all these sweets? I'm on a diet, and I can't eat **anything** here!
crawl
Well, young miss, it's not your wake.
Here are some fajitas. Why don't you eat those?
No!! I'm on a no sugar, no fruit diet, you **idiot**. And fajitas have bell peppers!
Don't you even know that bell peppers are **fruits**?!
Please, bunny... where are you...?

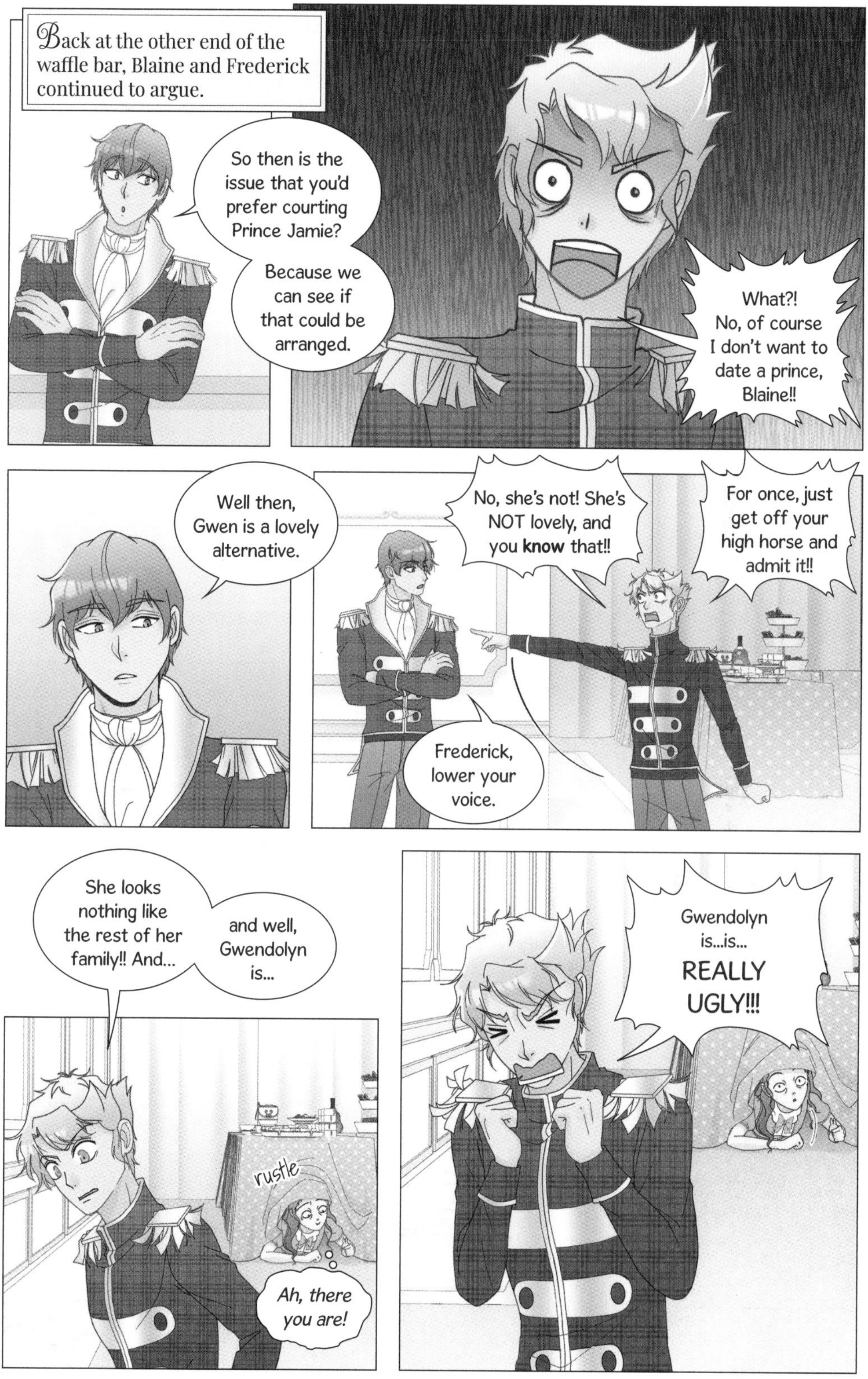
Back at the other end of the waffle bar, Blaine and Frederick continued to argue.
So then is the issue that you'd prefer courting Prince Jamie?
Because we can see if that could be arranged.
What?! No, of course I don't want to date a prince, Blaine!!
Well then, Gwen is a lovely alternative.
No, she's not! She's NOT lovely, and you **know** that!!
For once, just get off your high horse and admit it!!
Frederick, lower your voice.
She looks nothing like the rest of her family!! And...
and well, Gwendolyn is...
rustle
Ah, there you are!
Gwendolyn is...is... REALLY UGLY!!!

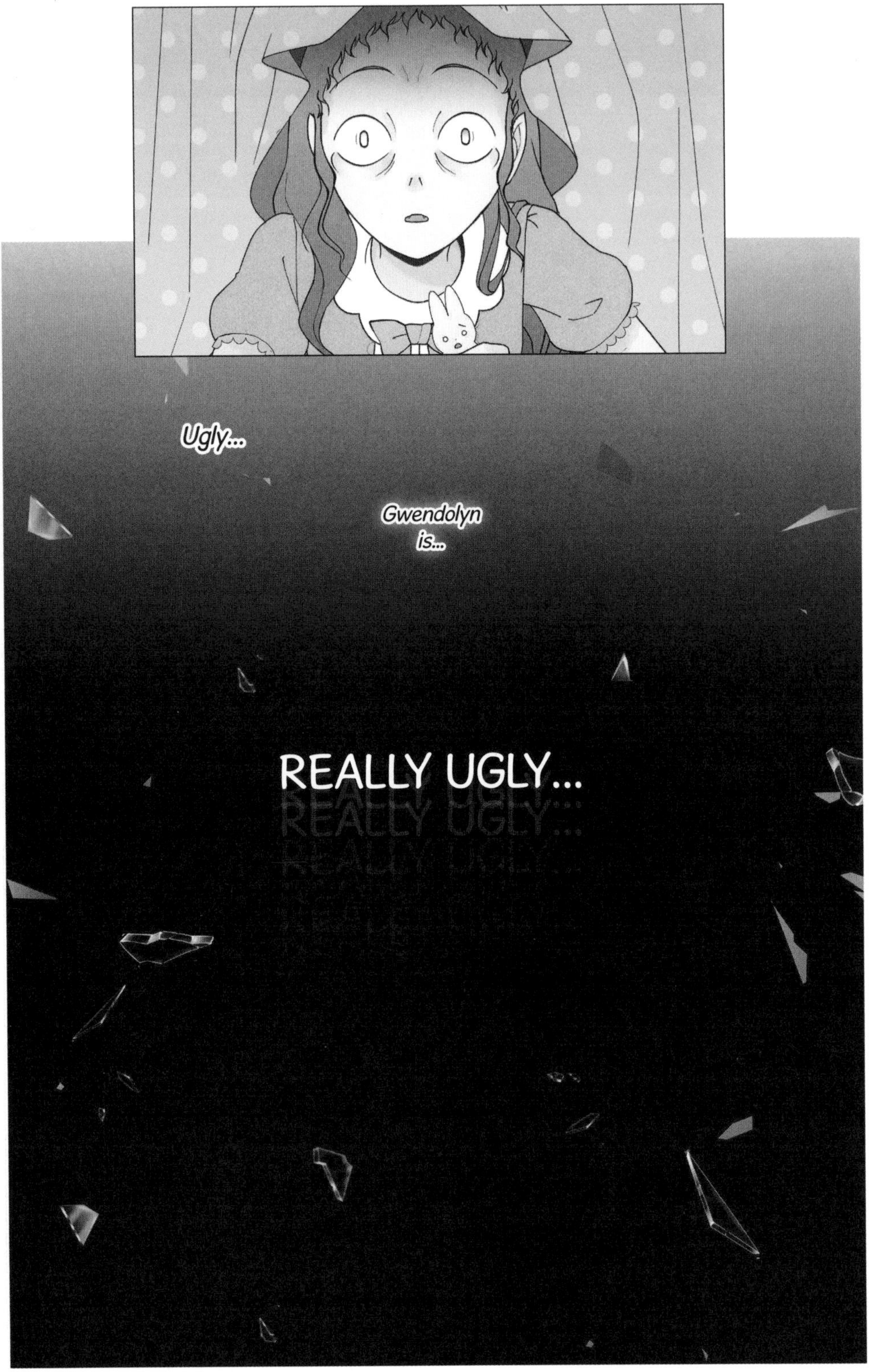
Ugly...
Gwendolyn is...
REALLY UGLY...

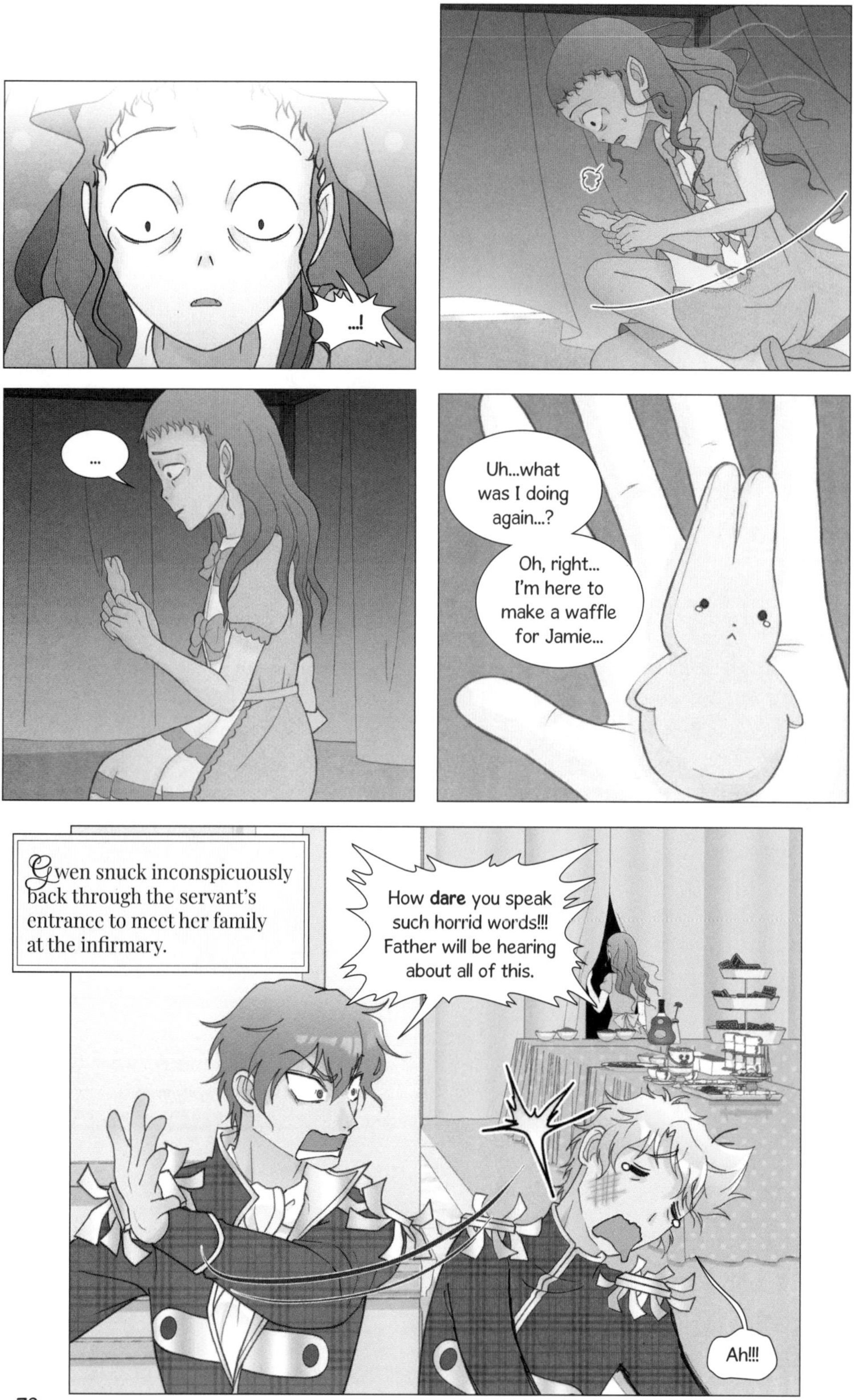
...!
...
Uh...what was I doing again...?
Oh, right... I'm here to make a waffle for Jamie...
Gwen snuck inconspicuously back through the servant's entrancc to mcct hcr family at the infirmary.
How **dare** you speak such horrid words!!! Father will be hearing about all of this.
Ah!!!

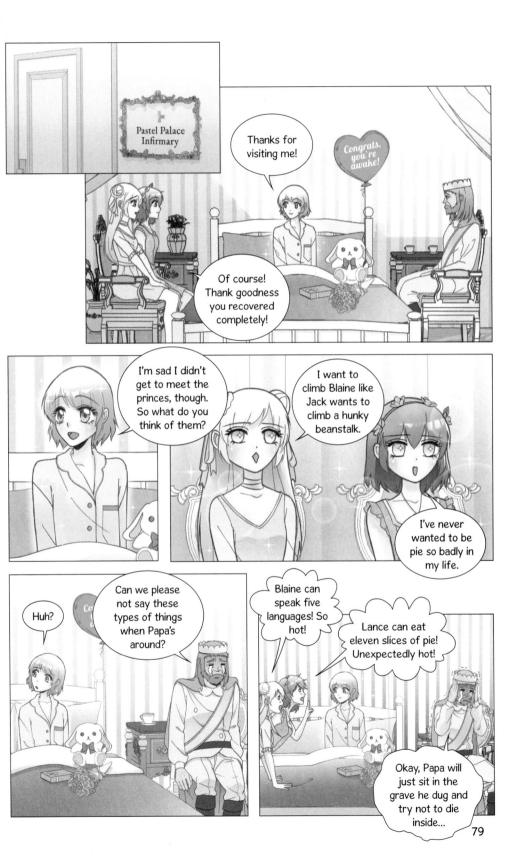

79

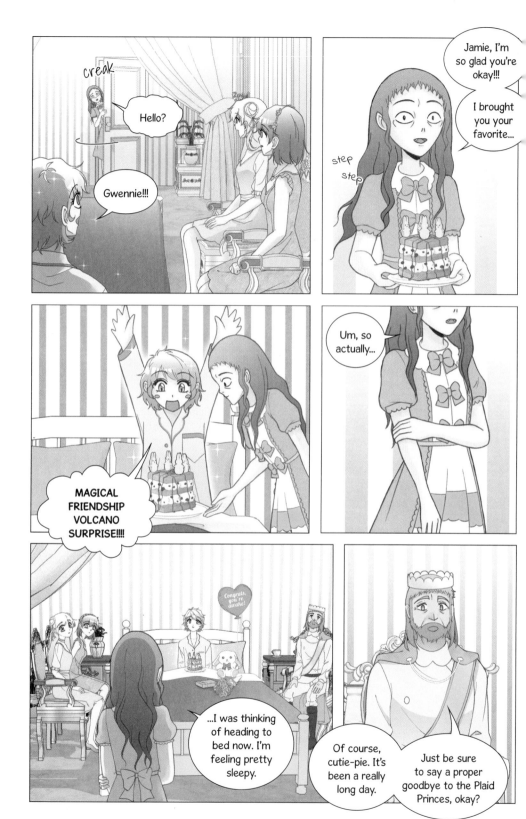

80

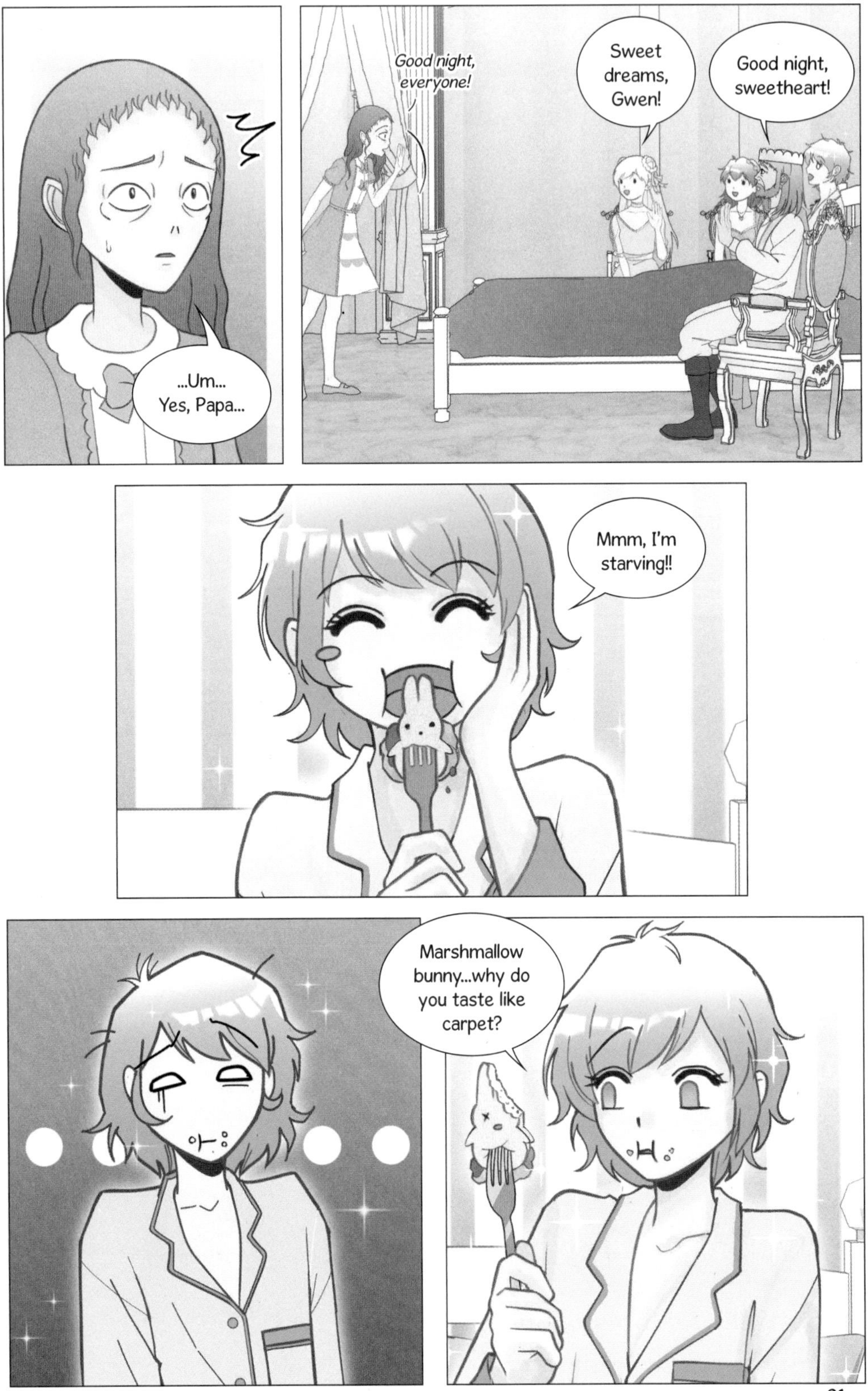
...Um...
Yes, Papa...
Good night, everyone!
Sweet dreams, Gwen!
Good night, sweetheart!
Mmm, I'm starving!!
Marshmallow bunny...why do you taste like carpet?

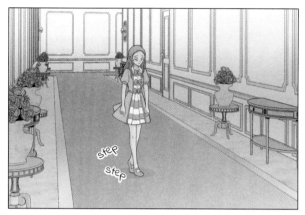

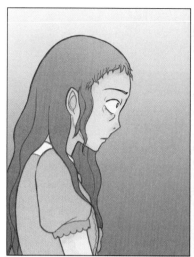

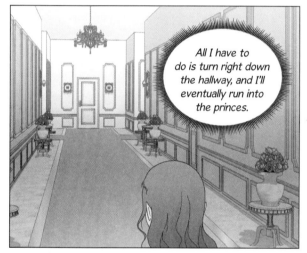

All I have to do is turn right down the hallway, and I'll eventually run into the princes.

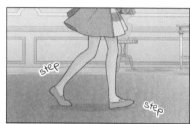

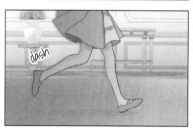

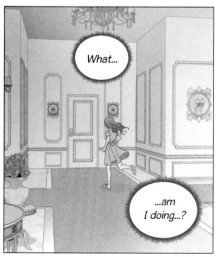

What...

...am I doing...?

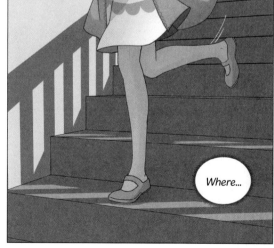

Where...

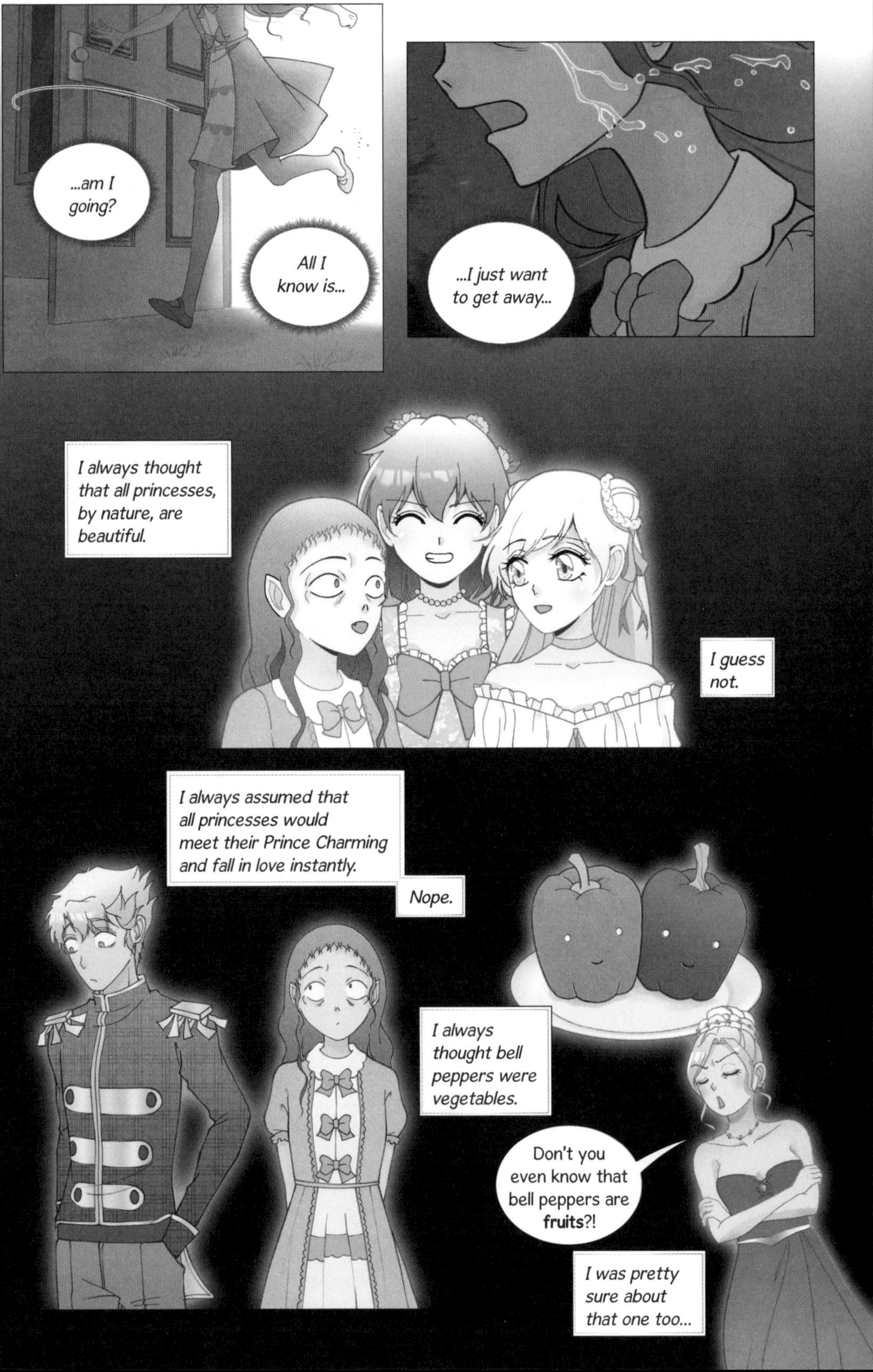
...am I going?
All I know is...
...I just want to get away...
I always thought that all princesses, by nature, are beautiful.
I guess not.
I always assumed that all princesses would meet their Prince Charming and fall in love instantly.
Nope.
I always thought bell peppers were vegetables.
Don't you even know that bell peppers are **fruits**?!
I was pretty sure about that one too...

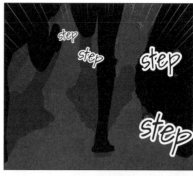

I've been so stupid...

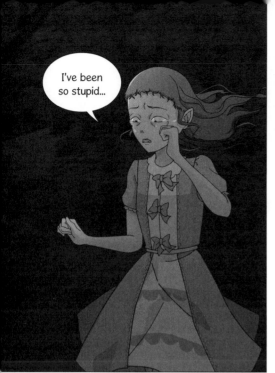

step
step
step
step

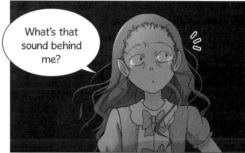

What's that sound behind me?

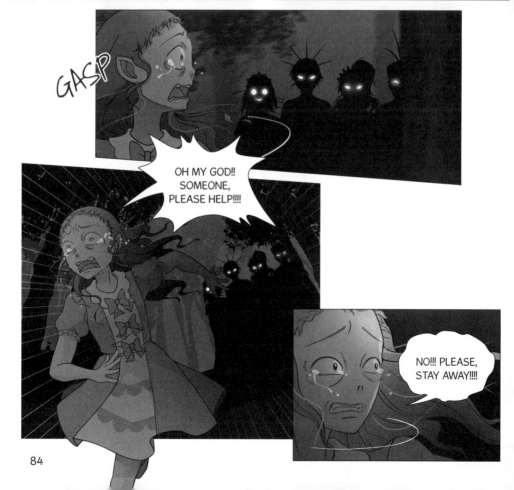

GASP

OH MY GOD!! SOMEONE, PLEASE HELP!!!!

NO!!! PLEASE, STAY AWAY!!!!

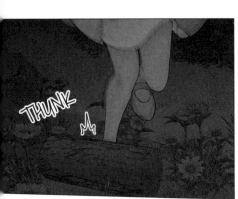

THUNK

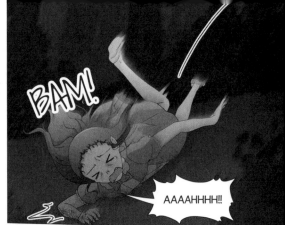

BAM!

AAAAHHHH!!

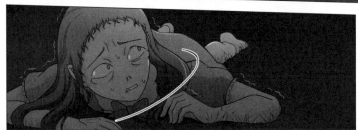

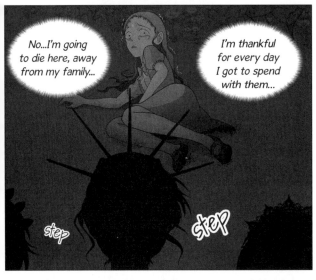

No...I'm going to die here, away from my family...

I'm thankful for every day I got to spend with them...

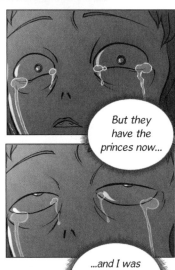

But they have the princes now...

...and I was just going to get in the way...

step step

Chapter

4

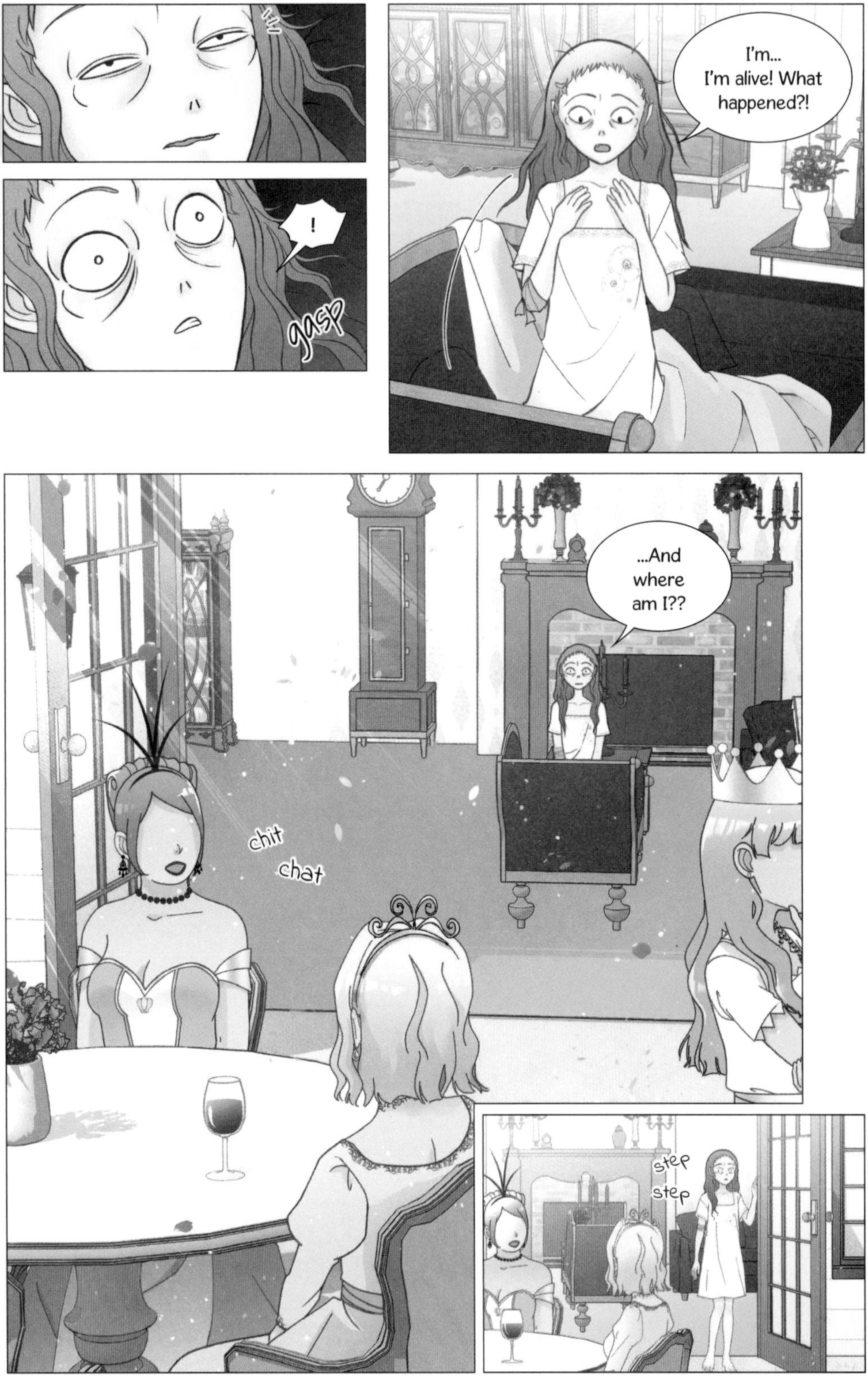
!
gasp
I'm...
I'm alive! What happened?!
...And where am I??
chit
chat
step
step

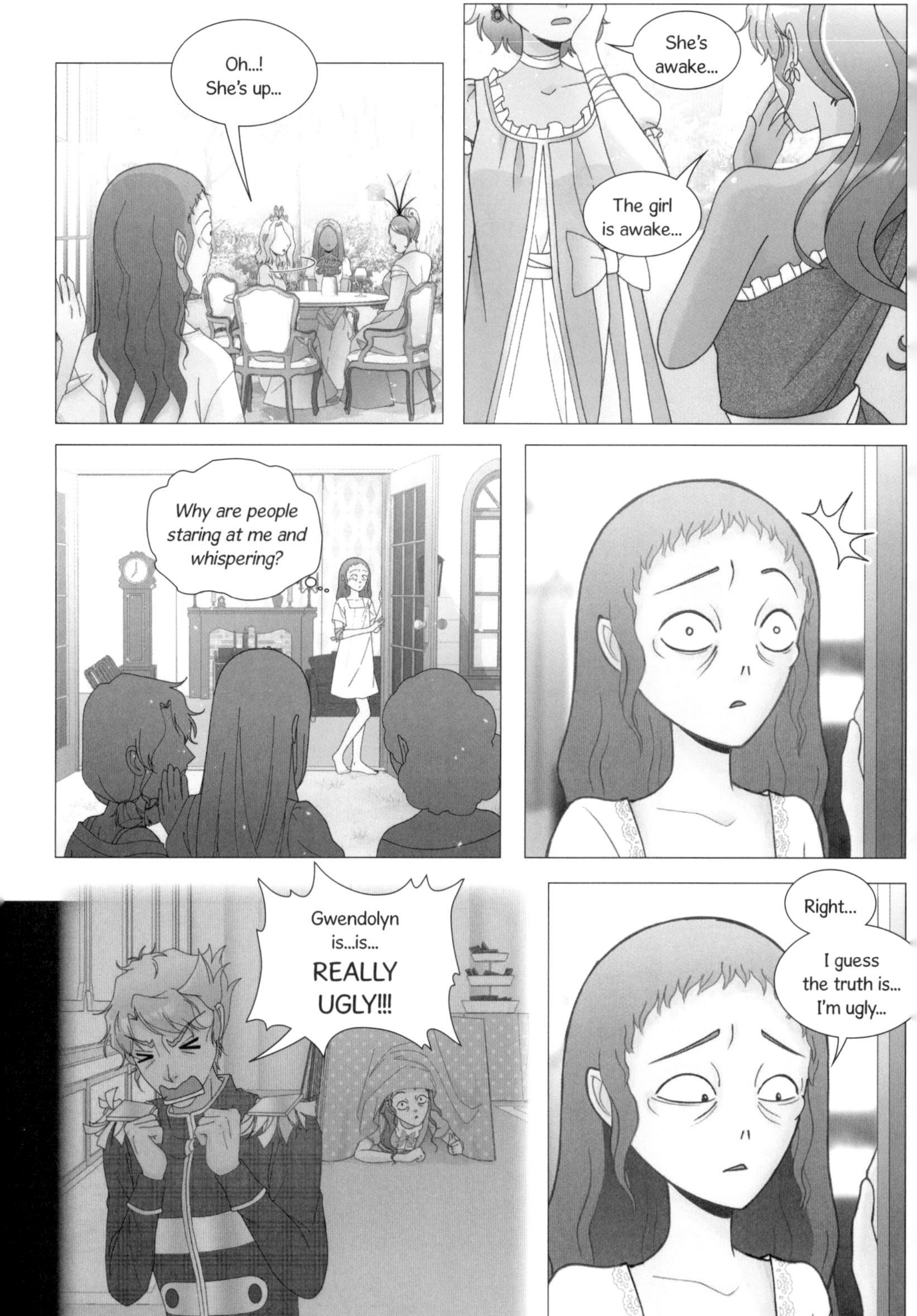

Oh...! She's up...
She's awake...
The girl is awake...
Why are people staring at me and whispering?
Gwendolyn is...is... REALLY UGLY!!!
Right...
I guess the truth is... I'm ugly...

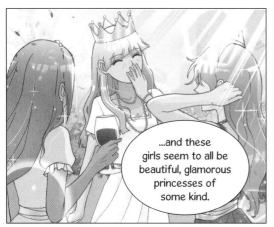

...and these girls seem to all be beautiful, glamorous princesses of some kind.

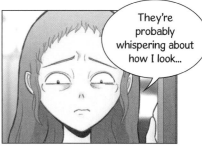

They're probably whispering about how I look...

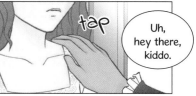

tap

Uh, hey there, kiddo.

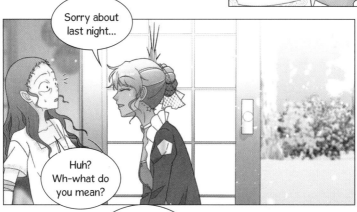

Sorry about last night...

Huh? Wh-what do you mean?

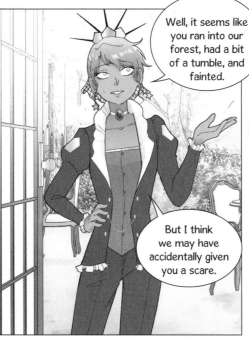

Well, it seems like you ran into our forest, had a bit of a tumble, and fainted.

But I think we may have accidentally given you a scare.

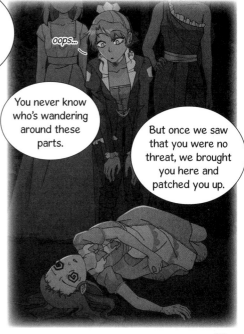

oops...

You never know who's wandering around these parts.

But once we saw that you were no threat, we brought you here and patched you up.

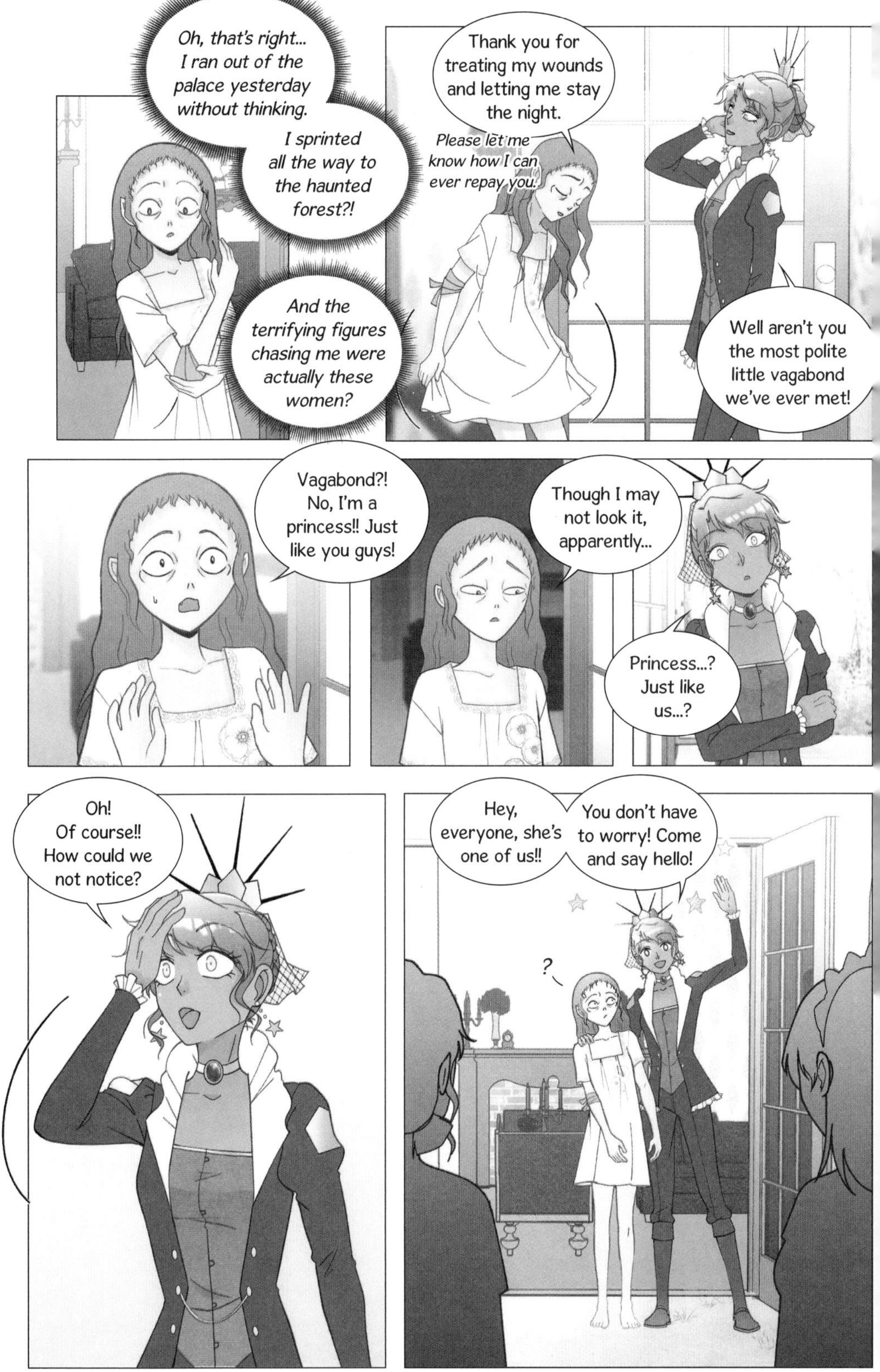
Oh, that's right... I ran out of the palace yesterday without thinking.
I sprinted all the way to the haunted forest?!
And the terrifying figures chasing me were actually these women?
Thank you for treating my wounds and letting me stay the night.
Please let me know how I can ever repay you.
Well aren't you the most polite little vagabond we've ever met!
Vagabond?! No, I'm a princess!! Just like you guys!
Though I may not look it, apparently...
Princess...? Just like us...?
Oh! Of course!! How could we not notice?
Hey, everyone, she's one of us!!
You don't have to worry! Come and say hello!
?

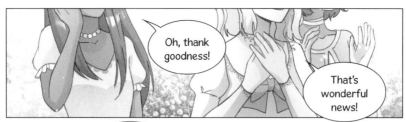

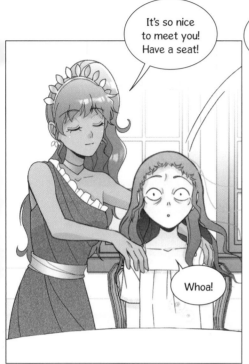

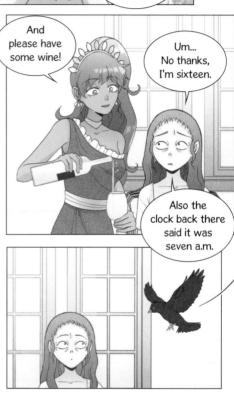

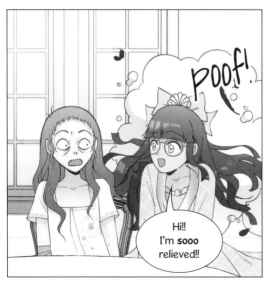

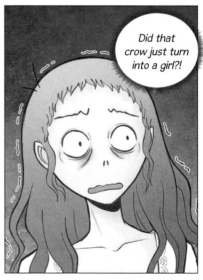

91

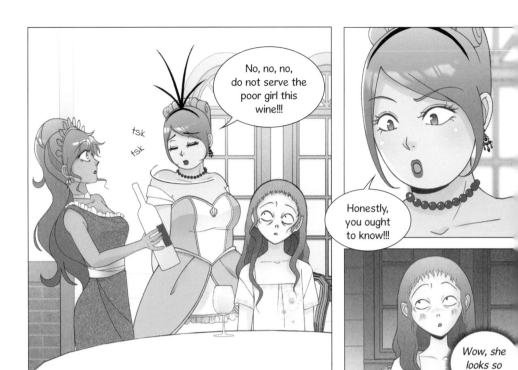

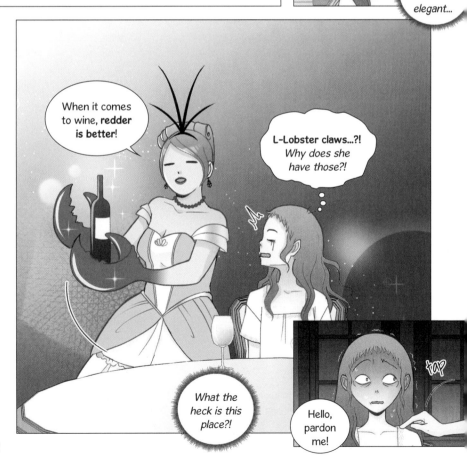

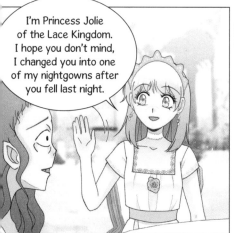

I'm Princess Jolie of the Lace Kingdom. I hope you don't mind, I changed you into one of my nightgowns after you fell last night.

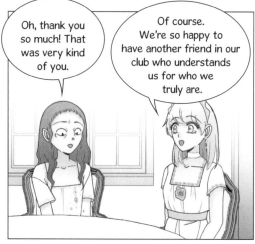

Oh, thank you so much! That was very kind of you.

Of course. We're so happy to have another friend in our club who understands us for who we truly are.

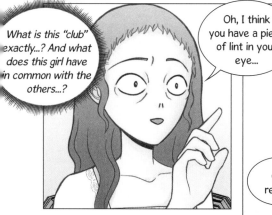

What is this "club" exactly...? And what does this girl have in common with the others...?

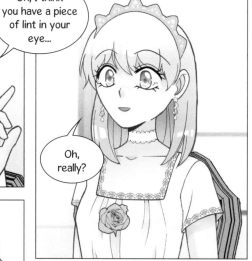

Oh, I think you have a piece of lint in your eye...

Oh, really?

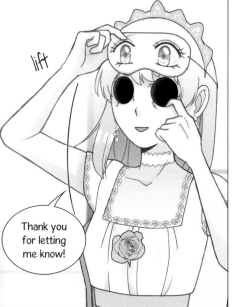

lift

Thank you for letting me know!

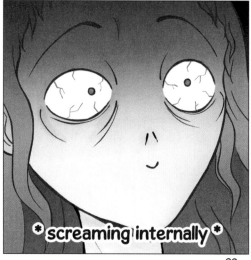

screaming internally

93

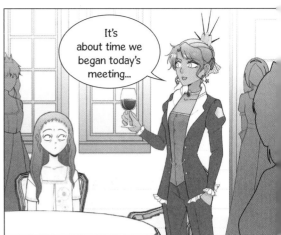

Ahem, may I please have everyone's attention?

clink

It's about time we began today's meeting...

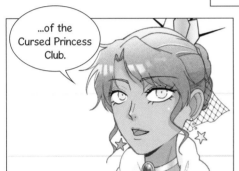

...of the Cursed Princess Club.

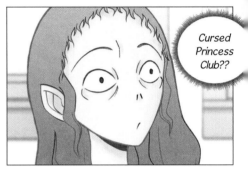

Cursed Princess Club??

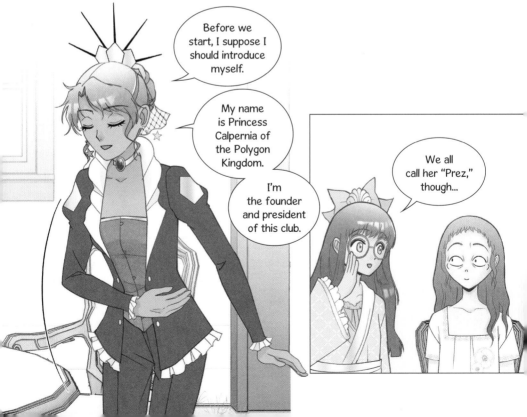

Before we start, I suppose I should introduce myself.

My name is Princess Calpernia of the Polygon Kingdom.

I'm the founder and president of this club.

We all call her "Prez," though...

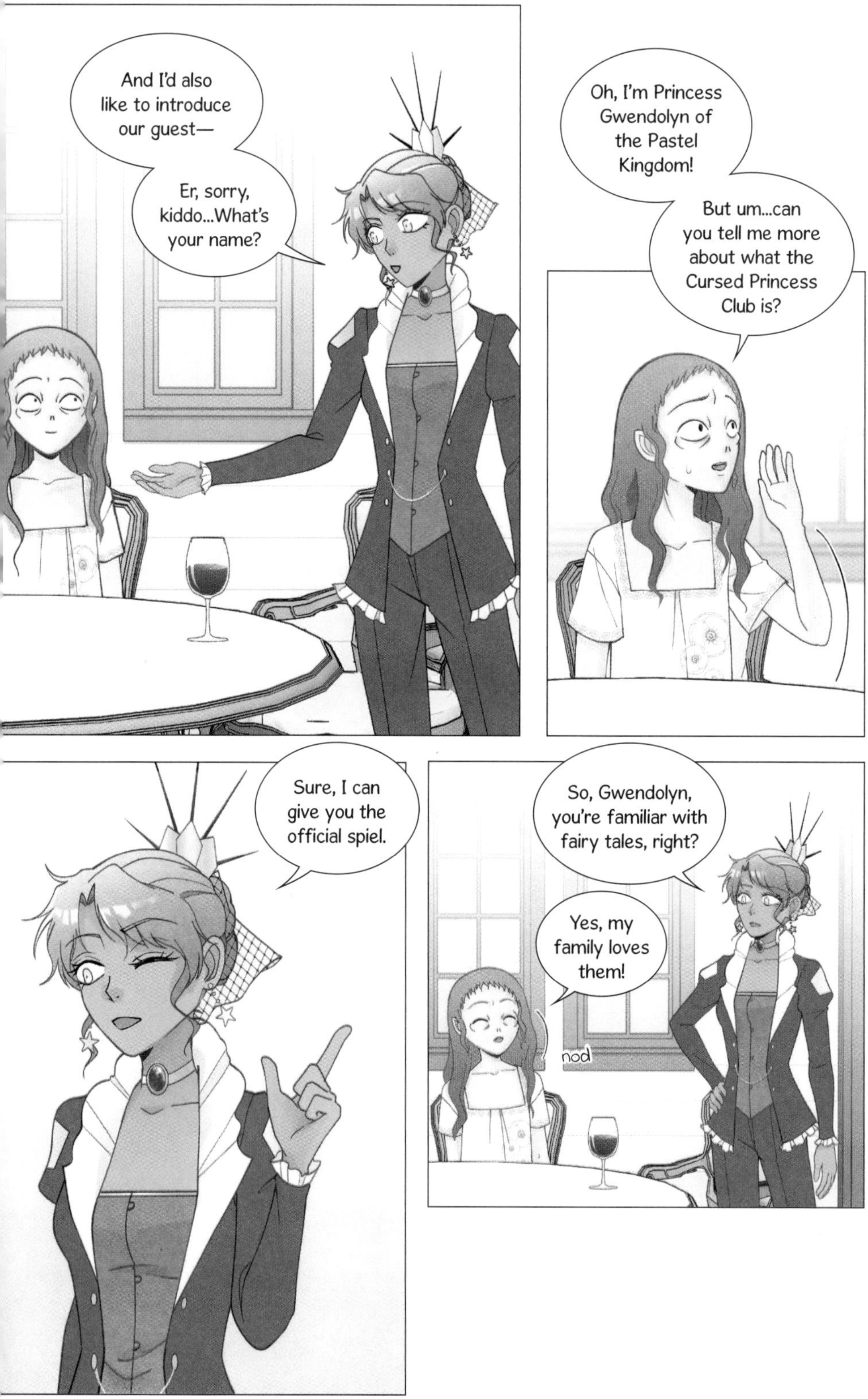
And I'd also like to introduce our guest—
Er, sorry, kiddo...What's your name?
Oh, I'm Princess Gwendolyn of the Pastel Kingdom!
But um...can you tell me more about what the Cursed Princess Club is?
Sure, I can give you the official spiel.
So, Gwendolyn, you're familiar with fairy tales, right?
Yes, my family loves them!
nod

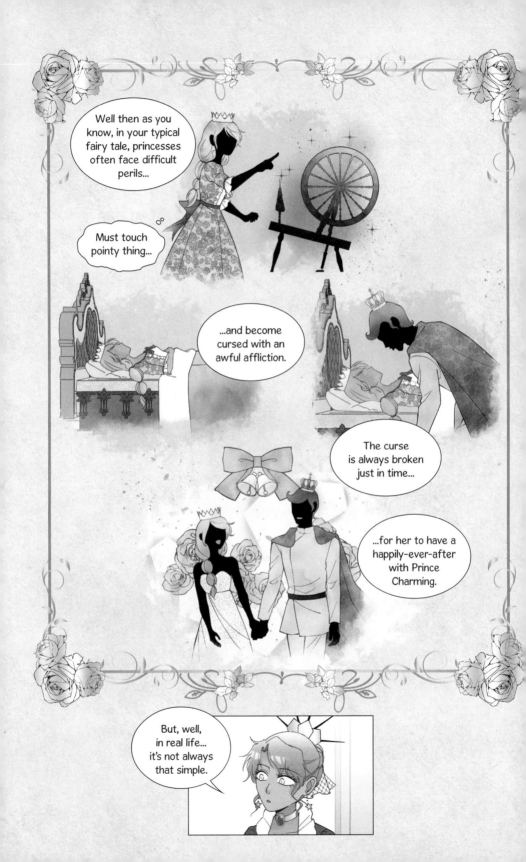

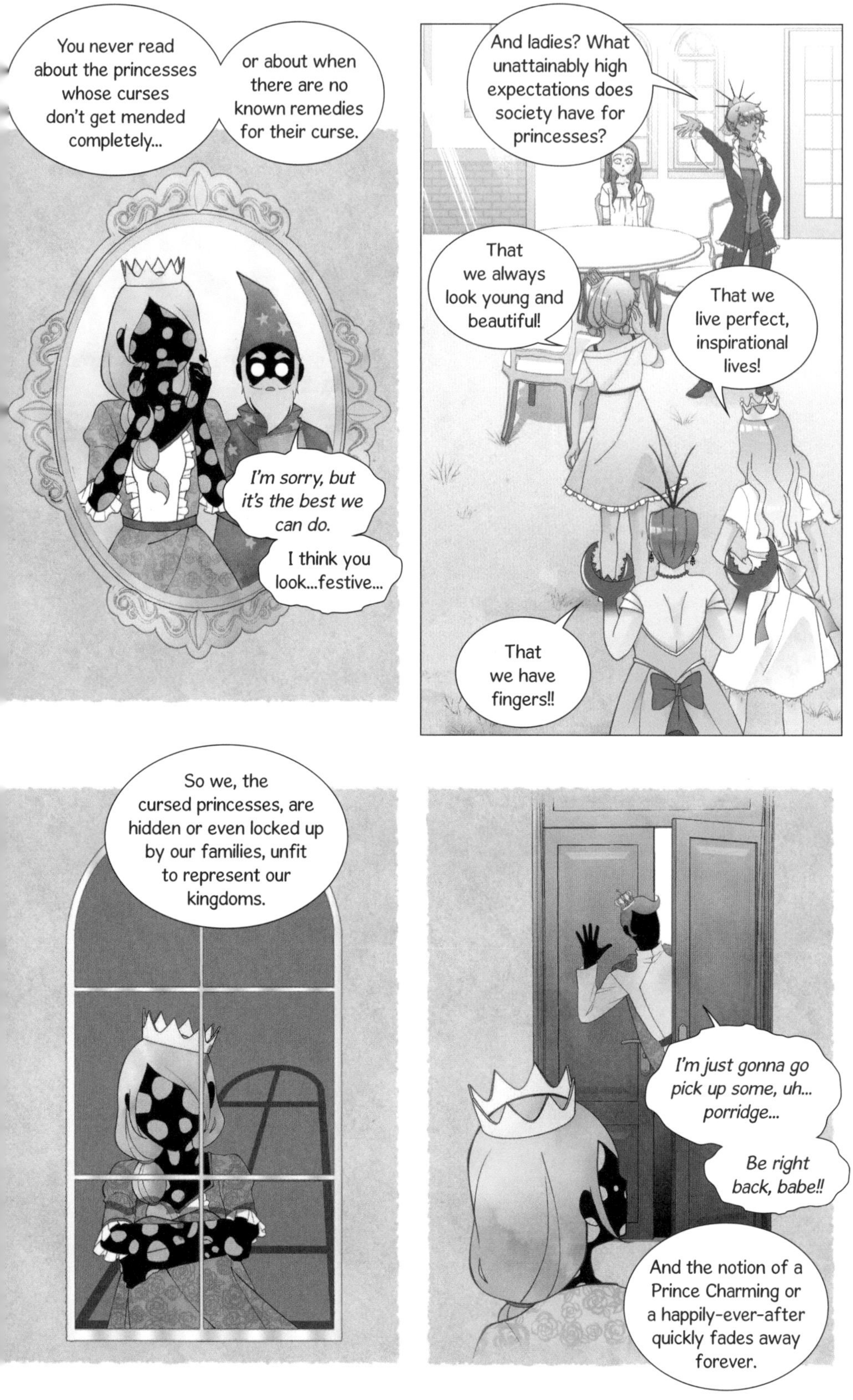
You never read about the princesses whose curses don't get mended completely...
or about when there are no known remedies for their curse.
I'm sorry, but it's the best we can do.
I think you look...festive...
And ladies? What unattainably high expectations does society have for princesses?
That we always look young and beautiful!
That we live perfect, inspirational lives!
That we have fingers!!
So we, the cursed princesses, are hidden or even locked up by our families, unfit to represent our kingdoms.
I'm just gonna go pick up some, uh... porridge...
Be right back, babe!!
And the notion of a Prince Charming or a happily-ever-after quickly fades away forever.

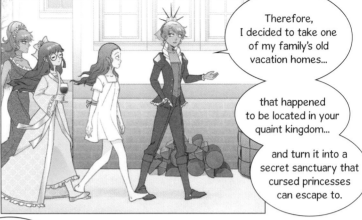

Therefore, I decided to take one of my family's old vacation homes...

that happened to be located in your quaint kingdom...

and turn it into a secret sanctuary that cursed princesses can escape to.

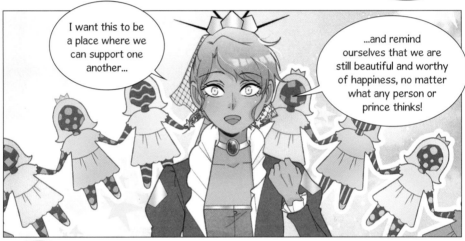

I want this to be a place where we can support one another...

...and remind ourselves that we are still beautiful and worthy of happiness, no matter what any person or prince thinks!

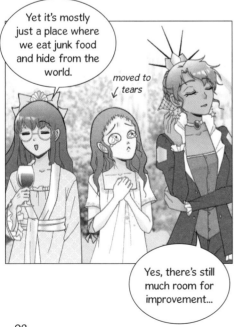

Yet it's mostly just a place where we eat junk food and hide from the world.

moved to tears

Yes, there's still much room for improvement...

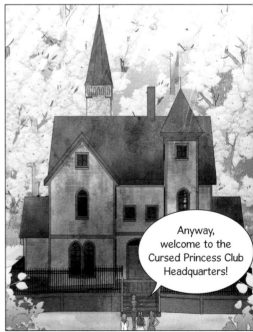

Anyway, welcome to the Cursed Princess Club Headquarters!

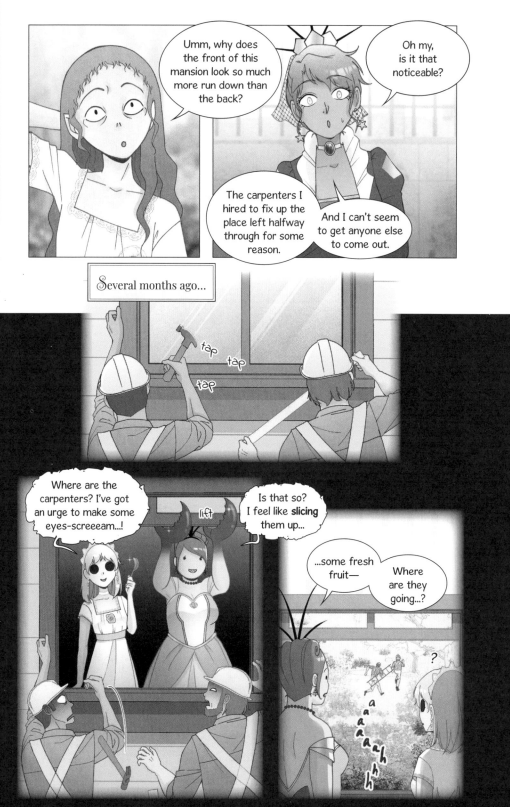

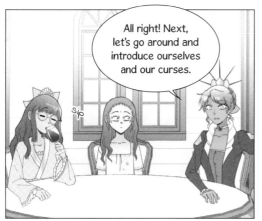

All right! Next, let's go around and introduce ourselves and our curses.

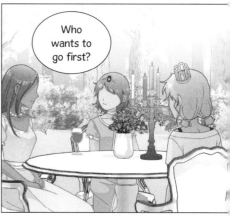

Who wants to go first?

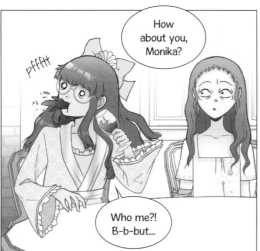

How about you, Monika?

Who me?! B-b-but...

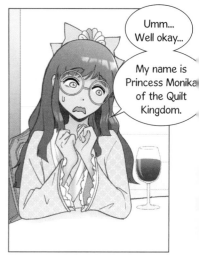

Umm... Well okay...

My name is Princess Monika of the Quilt Kingdom.

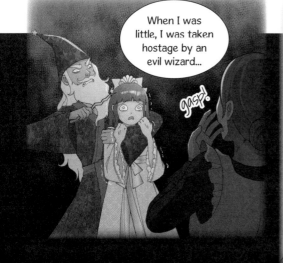

When I was little, I was taken hostage by an evil wizard...

gasp!

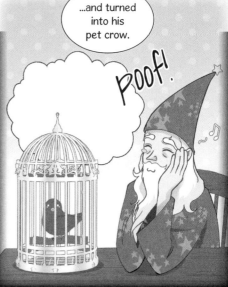

...and turned into his pet crow.

POOF!

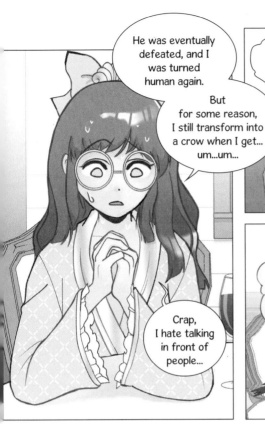

He was eventually defeated, and I was turned human again.

But for some reason, I still transform into a crow when I get... um...um...

Crap, I hate talking in front of people...

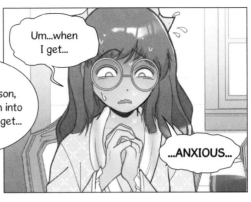

Um...when I get...

....ANXIOUS...

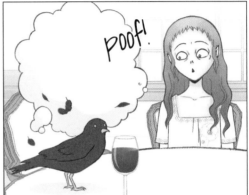

POOF!

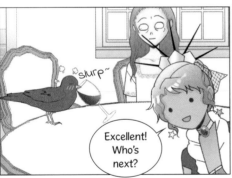

slurp~

Excellent! Who's next?

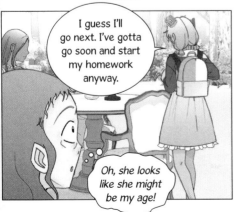

I guess I'll go next. I've gotta go soon and start my homework anyway.

Oh, she looks like she might be my age!

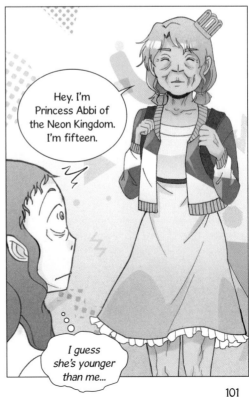

Hey. I'm Princess Abbi of the Neon Kingdom. I'm fifteen.

I guess she's younger than me...

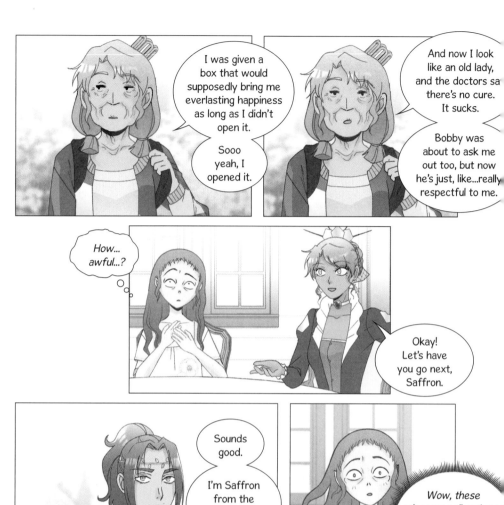

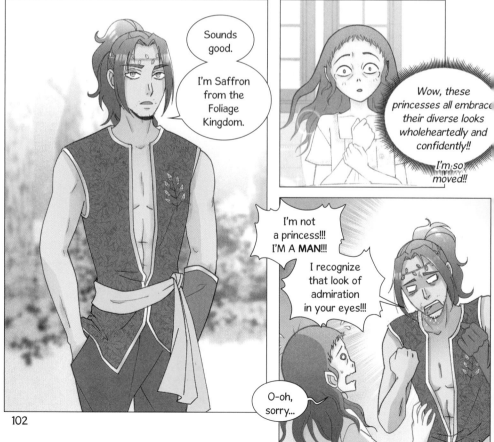

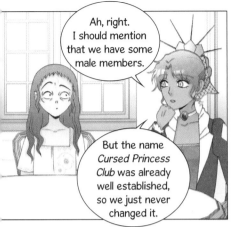

Ah, right. I should mention that we have some male members.

But the name *Cursed Princess Club* was already well established, so we just never changed it.

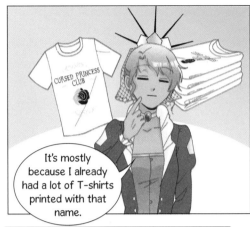

It's mostly because I already had a lot of T-shirts printed with that name.

CURSED PRINCESS CLUB

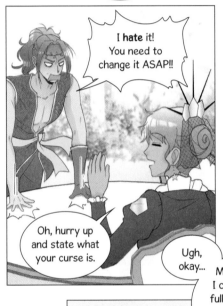

I **hate** it! You need to change it ASAP!!

Oh, hurry up and state what your curse is.

Ugh, okay...

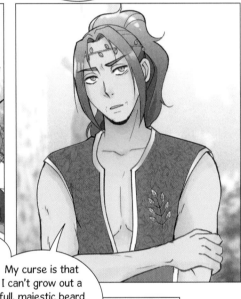

My curse is that I can't grow out a full, majestic beard like all the other men in my royal lineage.

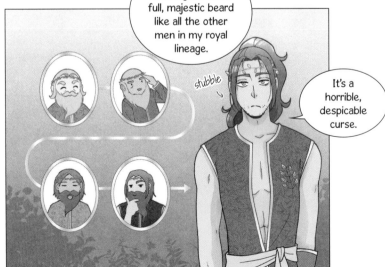

stubble

It's a horrible, despicable curse.

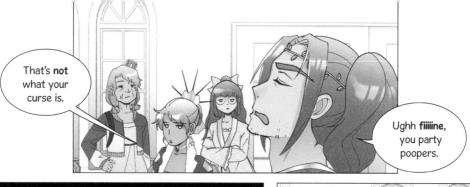

That's **not** what your curse is.

Ughh **fiiiine**, you party poopers.

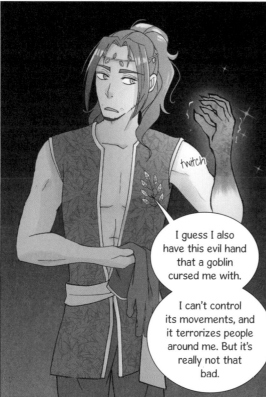

I guess I also have this evil hand that a goblin cursed me with.

I can't control its movements, and it terrorizes people around me. But it's really not that bad.

twitch

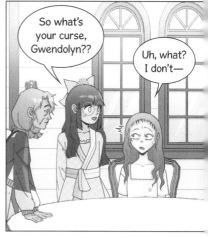

So what's your curse, Gwendolyn??

Uh, what? I don't—

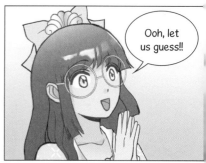

Ooh, let us guess!!

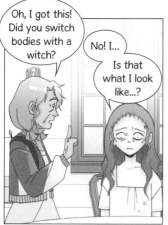

Oh, I got this! Did you switch bodies with a witch?

No! I...

Is that what I look like...?

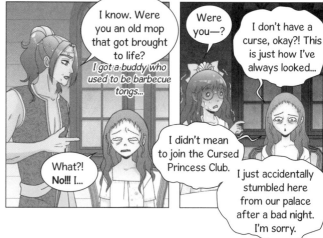

I know. Were you an old mop that got brought to life?
I got a buddy who used to be barbecue tongs...

What?! No!!! I...

Were you—?

I don't have a curse, okay?! This is just how I've always looked...

I didn't mean to join the Cursed Princess Club.

I just accidentally stumbled here from our palace after a bad night. I'm sorry.

104

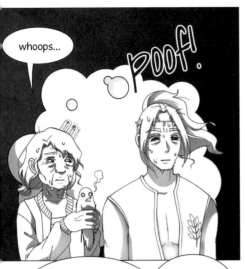

whoops...

Poof!

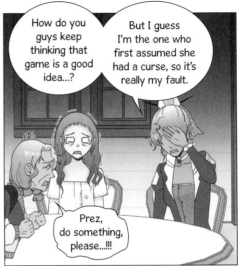

How do you guys keep thinking that game is a good idea...?

But I guess I'm the one who first assumed she had a curse, so it's really my fault.

Prez, do something, please...!!!

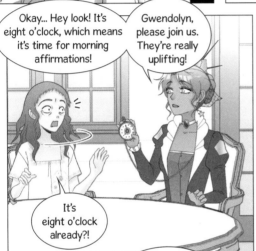

Okay... Hey look! It's eight o'clock, which means it's time for morning affirmations!

Gwendolyn, please join us. They're really uplifting!

It's eight o'clock already?!

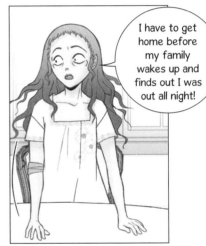

I have to get home before my family wakes up and finds out I was out all night!

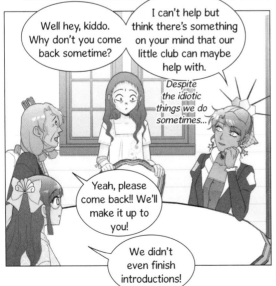

Well hey, kiddo. Why don't you come back sometime?

I can't help but think there's something on your mind that our little club can maybe help with.

Despite the idiotic things we do sometimes...

Yeah, please come back!! We'll make it up to you!

We didn't even finish introductions!

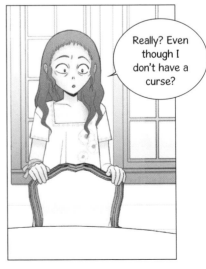

Really? Even though I don't have a curse?

105

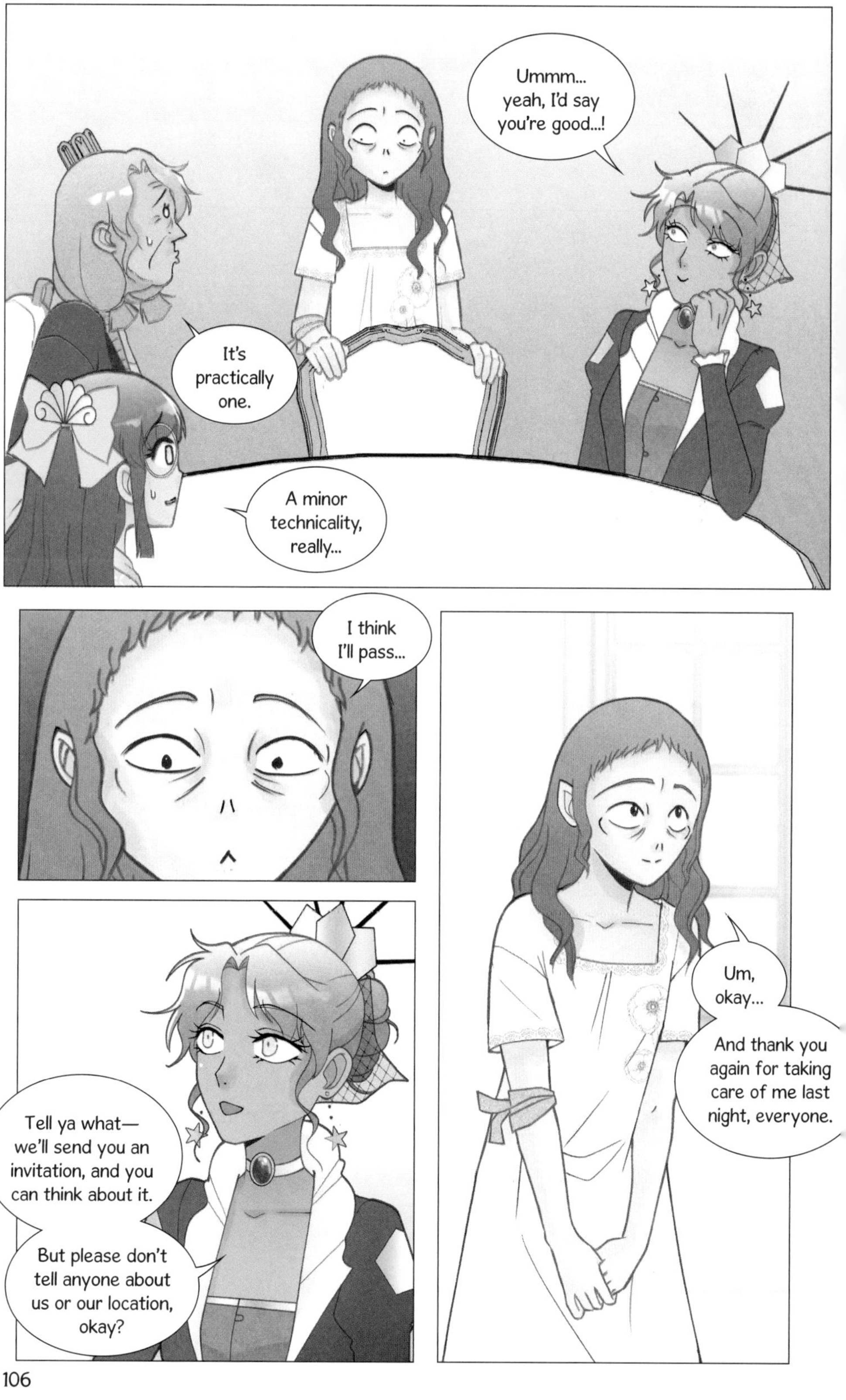
It's practically one.
A minor technicality, really...
Ummm... yeah, I'd say you're good...!
I think I'll pass...
Tell ya what— we'll send you an invitation, and you can think about it.
But please don't tell anyone about us or our location, okay?
Um, okay...
And thank you again for taking care of me last night, everyone.

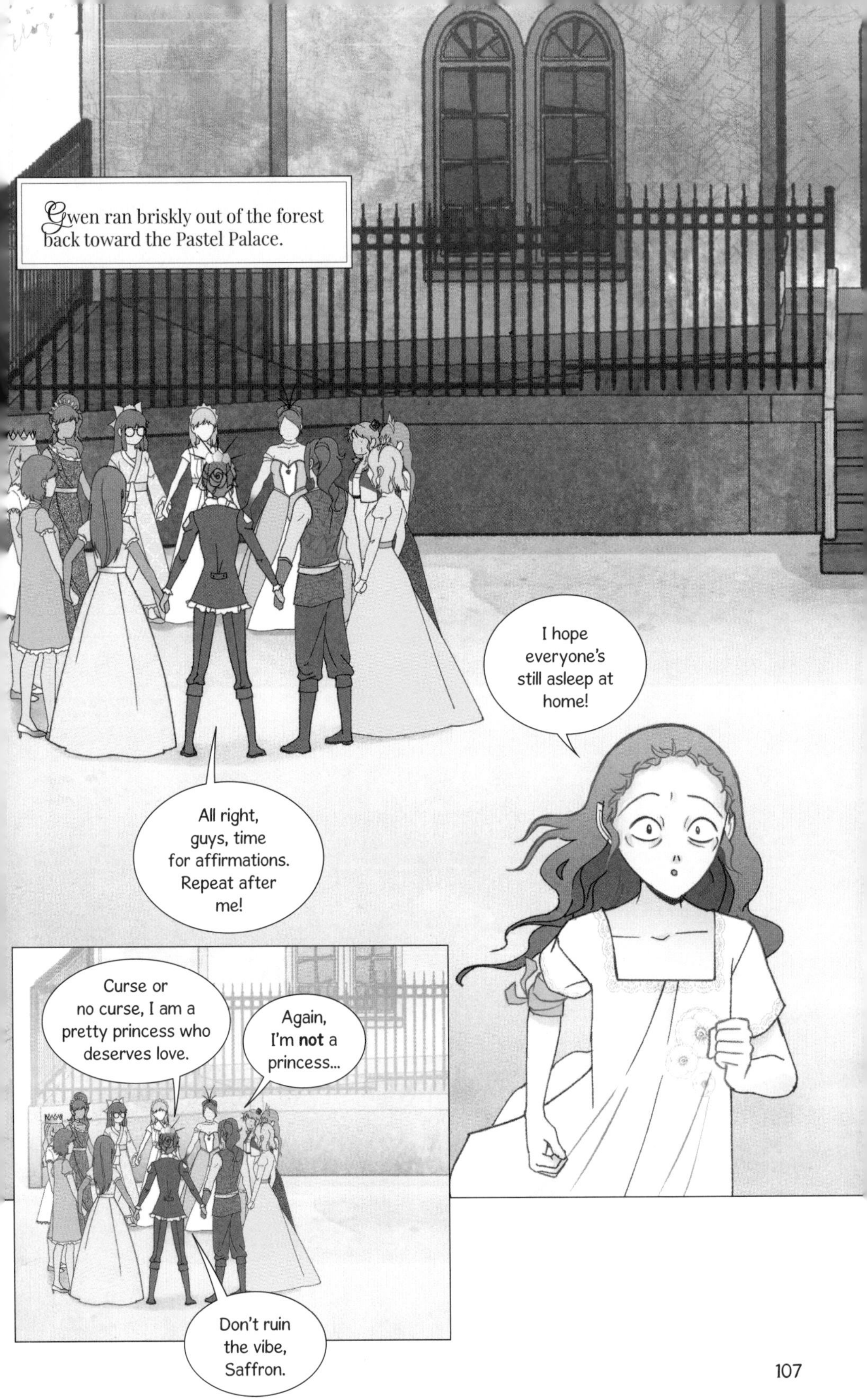
Gwen ran briskly out of the forest back toward the Pastel Palace.
I hope everyone's still asleep at home!
All right, guys, time for affirmations. Repeat after me!
Curse or no curse, I am a pretty princess who deserves love.
Again, I'm **not** a princess...
Don't ruin the vibe, Saffron.

Chapter

5

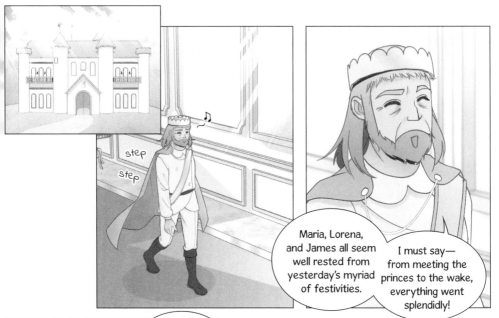

step

step

Maria, Lorena, and James all seem well rested from yesterday's myriad of festivities.

I must say—from meeting the princes to the wake, everything went splendidly!

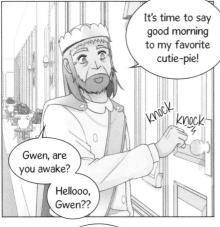

It's time to say good morning to my favorite cutie-pie!

knock knock

Gwen, are you awake?

Hellooo, Gwen??

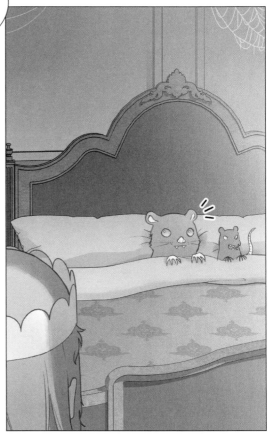

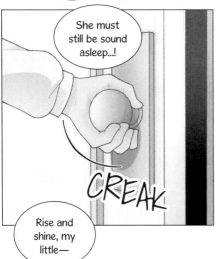

She must still be sound asleep...!

CREAK

Rise and shine, my little—

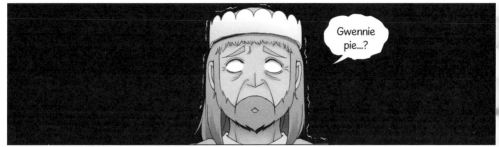

Gwennie pie...?

WHO TOOK MY BABY GIRL?!

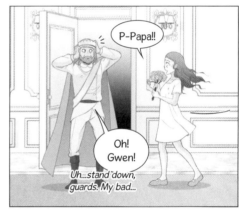

GUARDS!! MY BABY'S BEEN KIDNAPPED!!!

DEPLOY ALL TROOPS AND ARTILLERY **IMMEDIATELY**!!!

step

step

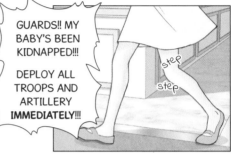

P-Papa!!

Oh! Gwen!

Uh...stand down, guards. My bad...

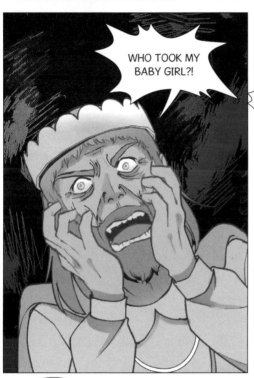

Where were you, sweetie??

I...I woke up really early this morning, so I went out and gathered some wildflowers from the garden...

I can't believe I'm lying to Papa! I'm sorry!!

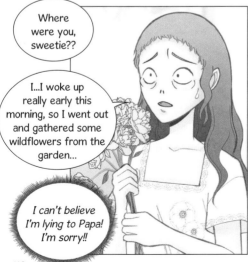

Ooh, my little early bird! It's just like you to do something adorable like that!

You had me worried, though!

That's also such an adorable new nightgown!

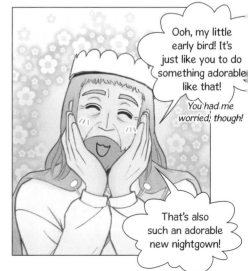

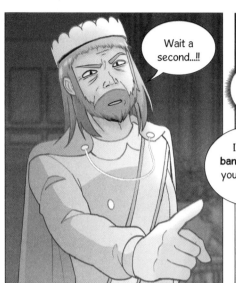

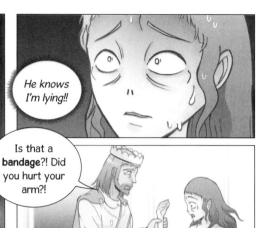

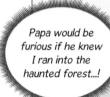

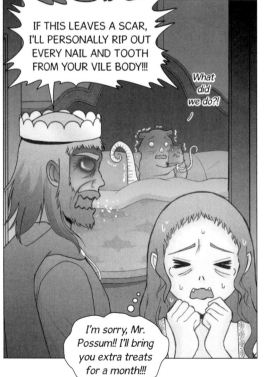

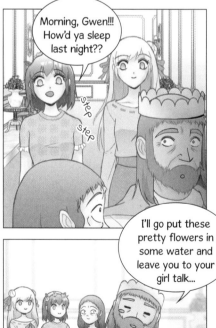

111

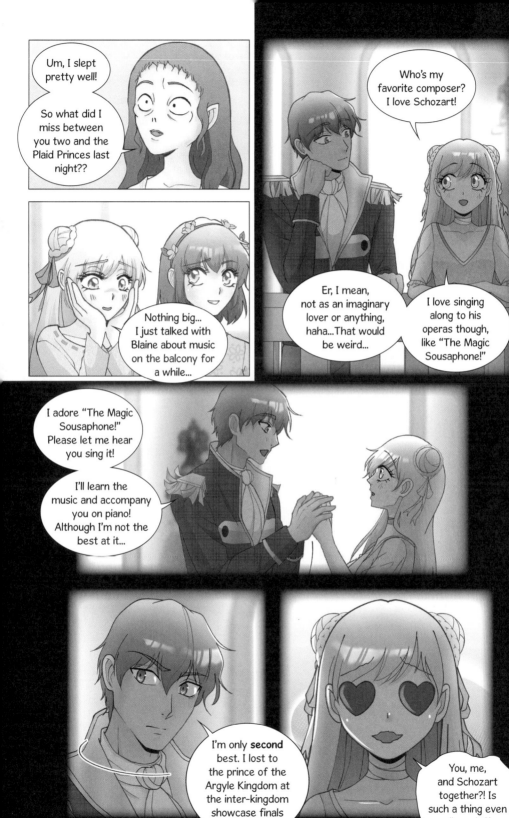

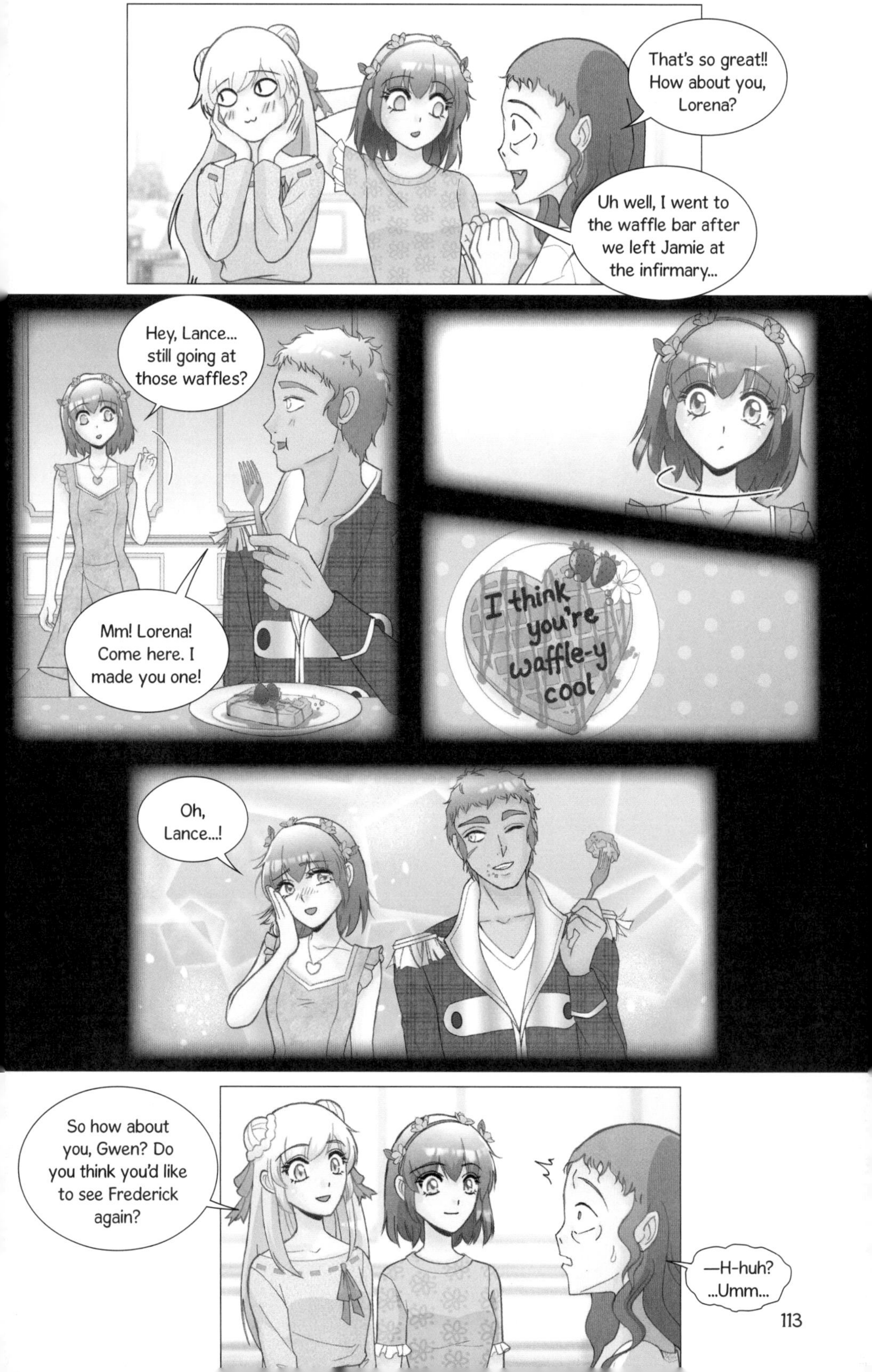
That's so great!! How about you, Lorena?
Uh well, I went to the waffle bar after we left Jamie at the infirmary...
Hey, Lance... still going at those waffles?
Mm! Lorena! Come here. I made you one!
I think you're waffle-y cool
Oh, Lance...!
So how about you, Gwen? Do you think you'd like to see Frederick again?
—H-huh? ...Umm...

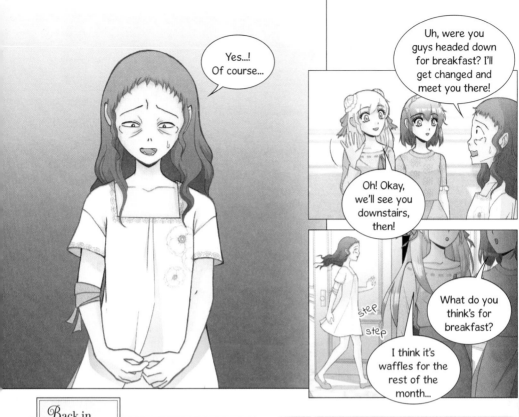

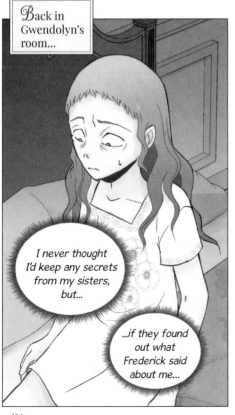

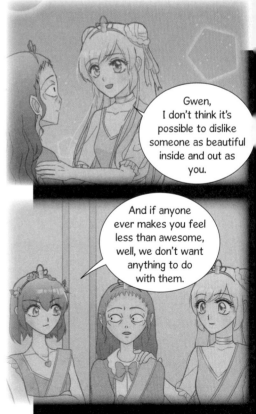

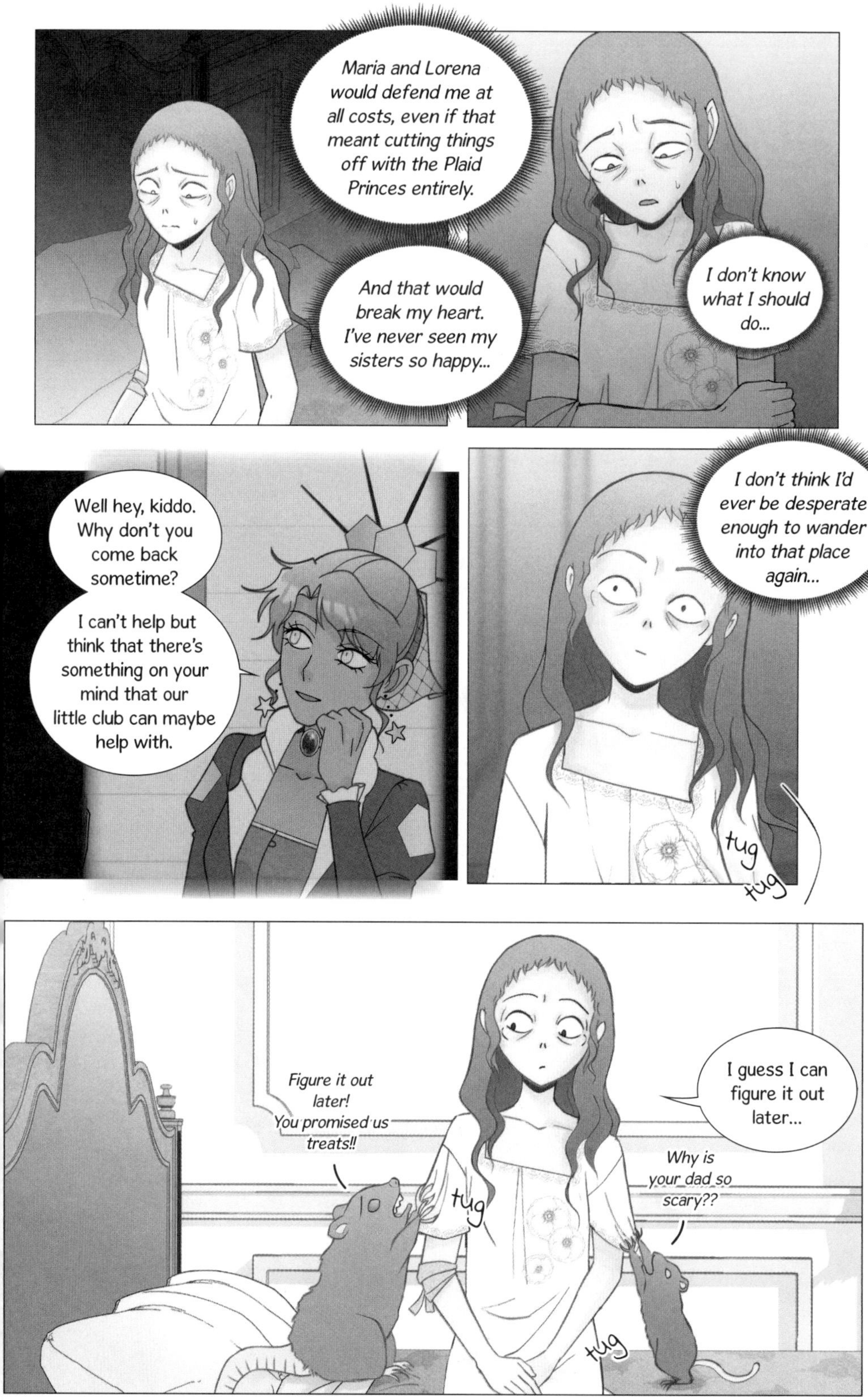

Maria and Lorena would defend me at all costs, even if that meant cutting things off with the Plaid Princes entirely.
And that would break my heart. I've never seen my sisters so happy...
I don't know what I should do...
Well hey, kiddo. Why don't you come back sometime?
I can't help but think that there's something on your mind that our little club can maybe help with.
I don't think I'd ever be desperate enough to wander into that place again...
tug
tug
Figure it out later! You promised us treats!!
tug
Why is your dad so scary??
I guess I can figure it out later...
tug

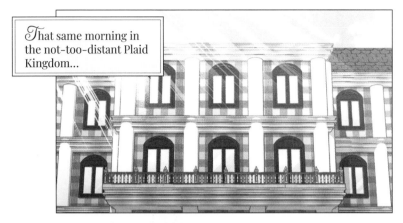

That same morning in the not-too-distant Plaid Kingdom...

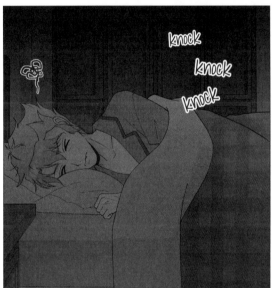

knock

knock

knock

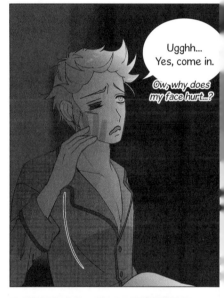

Ugghh... Yes, come in.

Ow, why does my face hurt...?

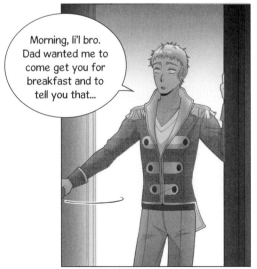

Morning, li'l bro. Dad wanted me to come get you for breakfast and to tell you that...

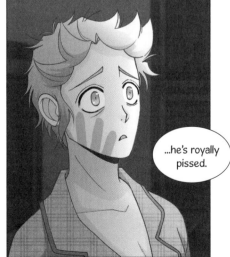

...he's royally pissed.

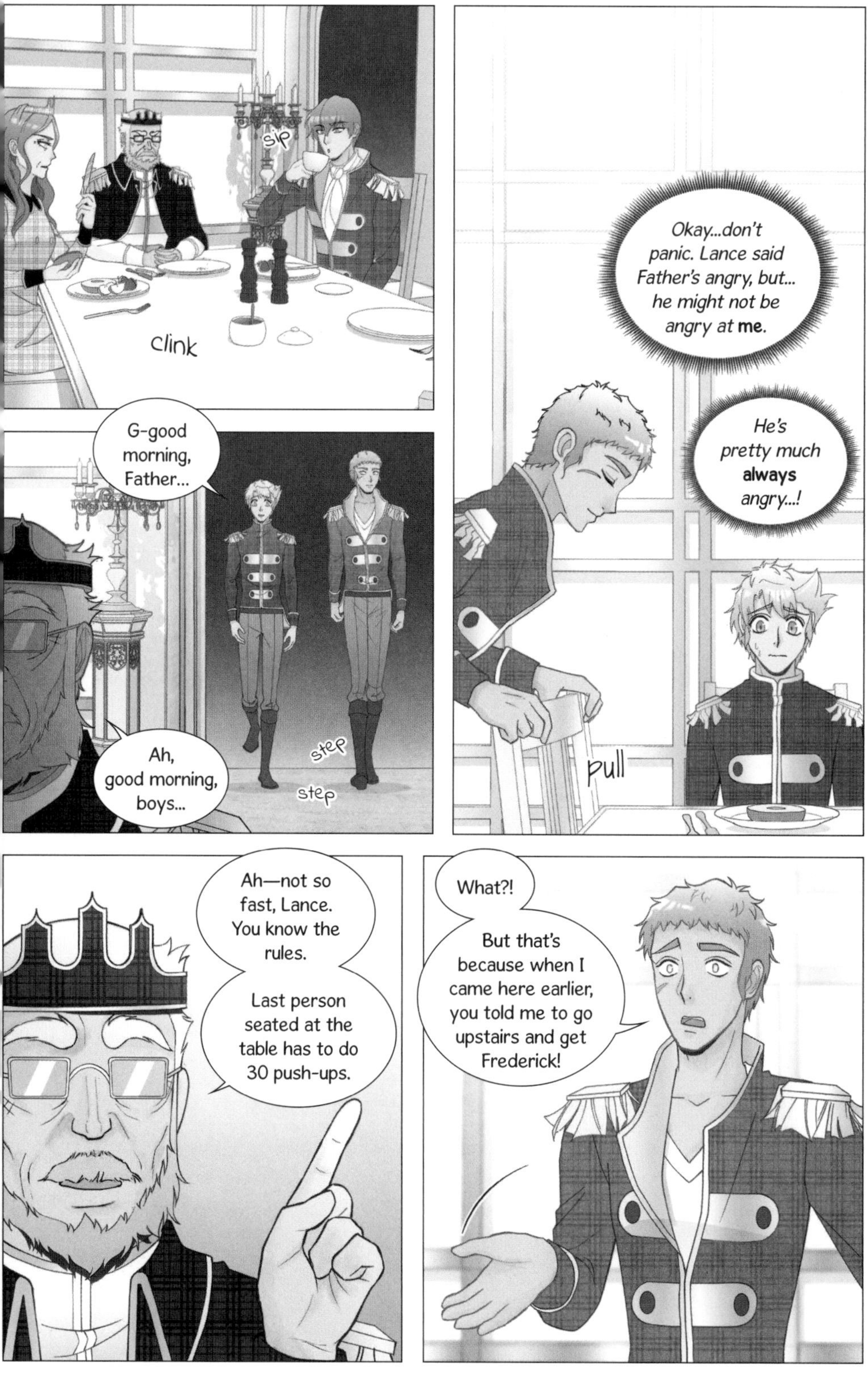
sip
clink
G-good morning, Father...
Ah, good morning, boys...
step
step
Okay...don't panic. Lance said Father's angry, but... he might not be angry at **me**.
He's pretty much **always** angry...!
pull
Ah—not so fast, Lance. You know the rules.
Last person seated at the table has to do 30 push-ups.
What?!
But that's because when I came here earlier, you told me to go upstairs and get Frederick!

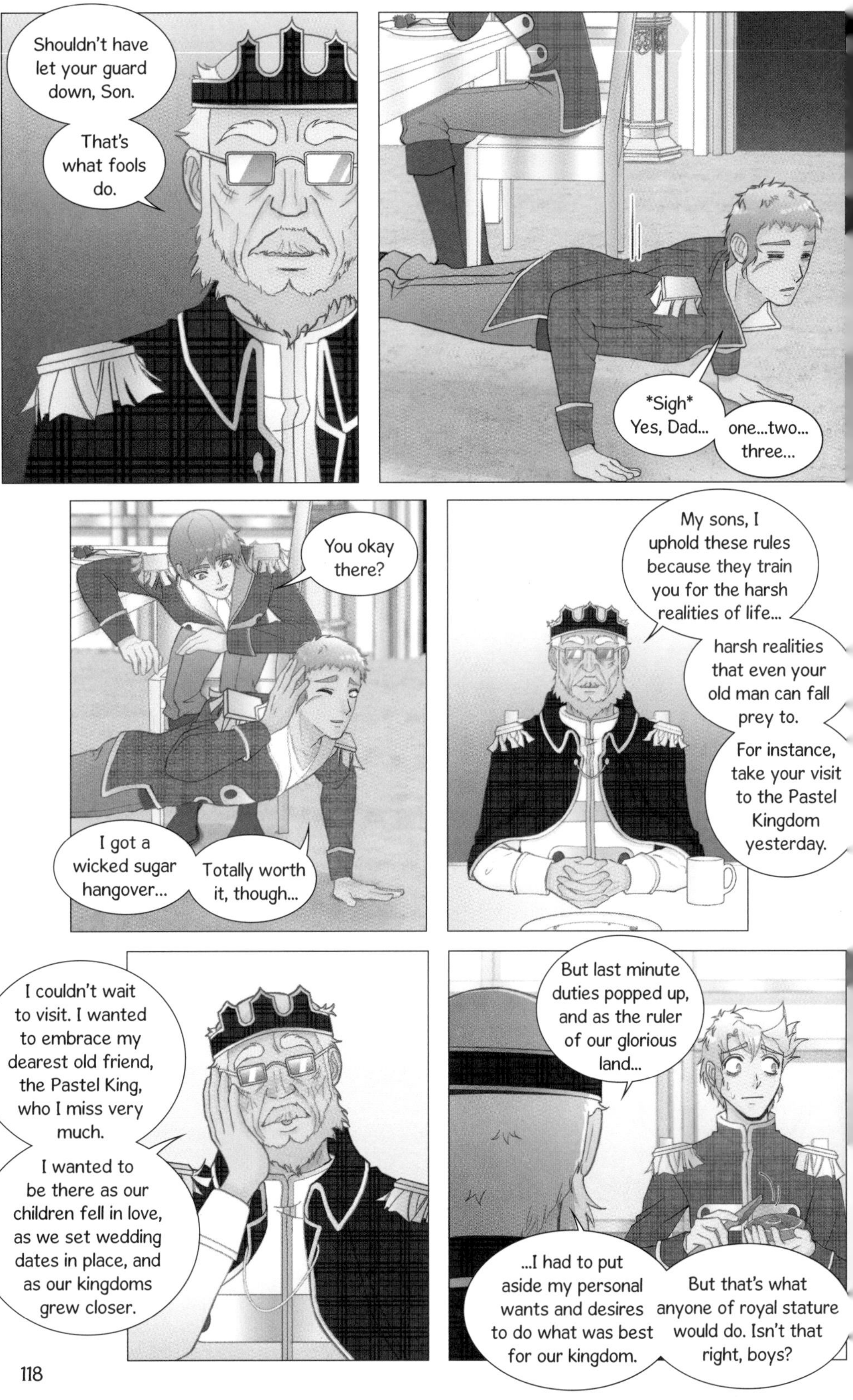
Shouldn't have let your guard down, Son.
That's what fools do.
Sigh Yes, Dad...
one...two... three...
You okay there?
I got a wicked sugar hangover...
Totally worth it, though...
My sons, I uphold these rules because they train you for the harsh realities of life...
harsh realities that even your old man can fall prey to.
For instance, take your visit to the Pastel Kingdom yesterday.
I couldn't wait to visit. I wanted to embrace my dearest old friend, the Pastel King, who I miss very much.
I wanted to be there as our children fell in love, as we set wedding dates in place, and as our kingdoms grew closer.
But last minute duties popped up, and as the ruler of our glorious land...
...I had to put aside my personal wants and desires to do what was best for our kingdom.
But that's what anyone of royal stature would do. Isn't that right, boys?

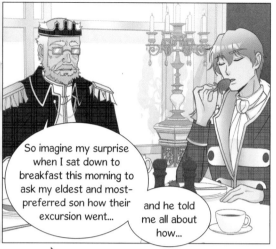

So imagine my surprise when I sat down to breakfast this morning to ask my eldest and most-preferred son how their excursion went...

and he told me all about how...

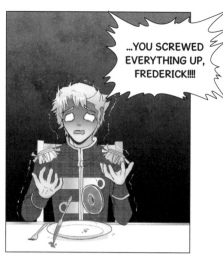

...YOU SCREWED EVERYTHING UP, FREDERICK!!!!

...you wasted months of planning, and now the Pastel King thinks I'm **hesitant** about uniting our kingdoms!!!

I let my guard down, and YOU—my stupid, selfish worm of a son—made a **fool** out of ME!!

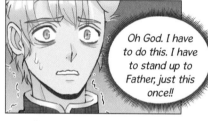

Oh God. I have to do this. I have to stand up to Father, just this once!!

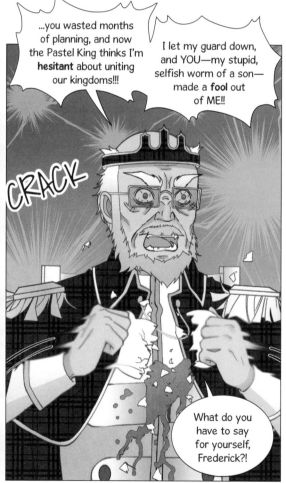

CRACK

What do you have to say for yourself, Frederick?!

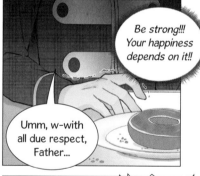

Be strong!!! Your happiness depends on it!!

Umm, w-with all due respect, Father...

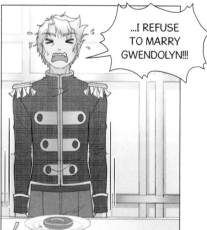

...I REFUSE TO MARRY GWENDOLYN!!!

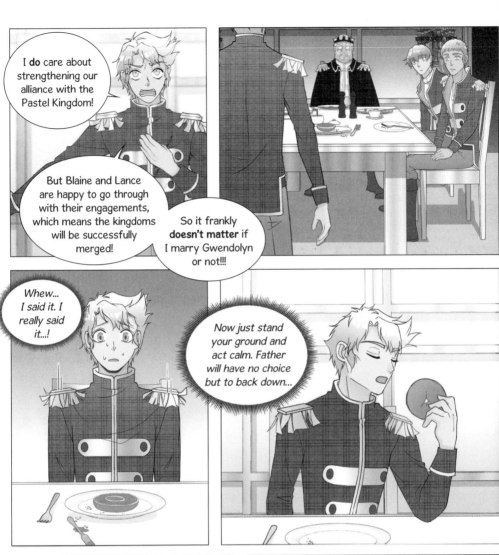

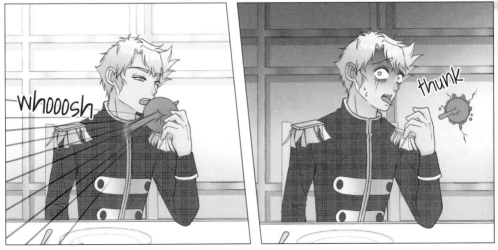

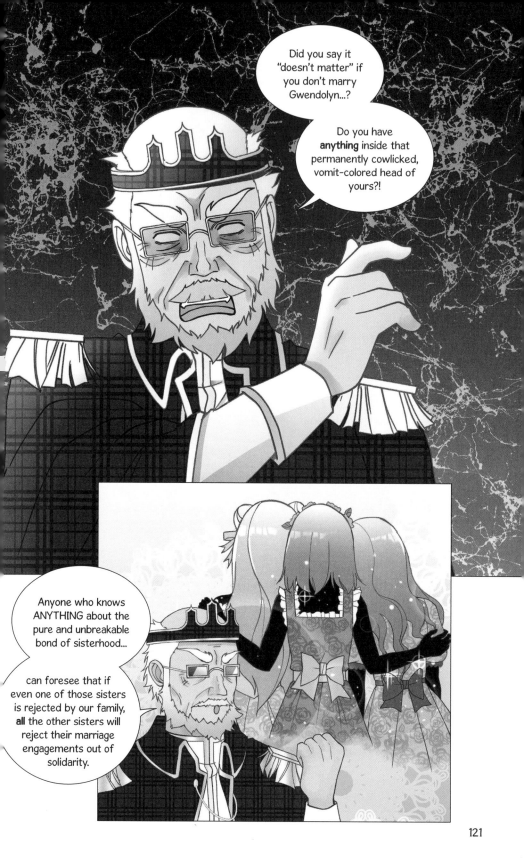

121

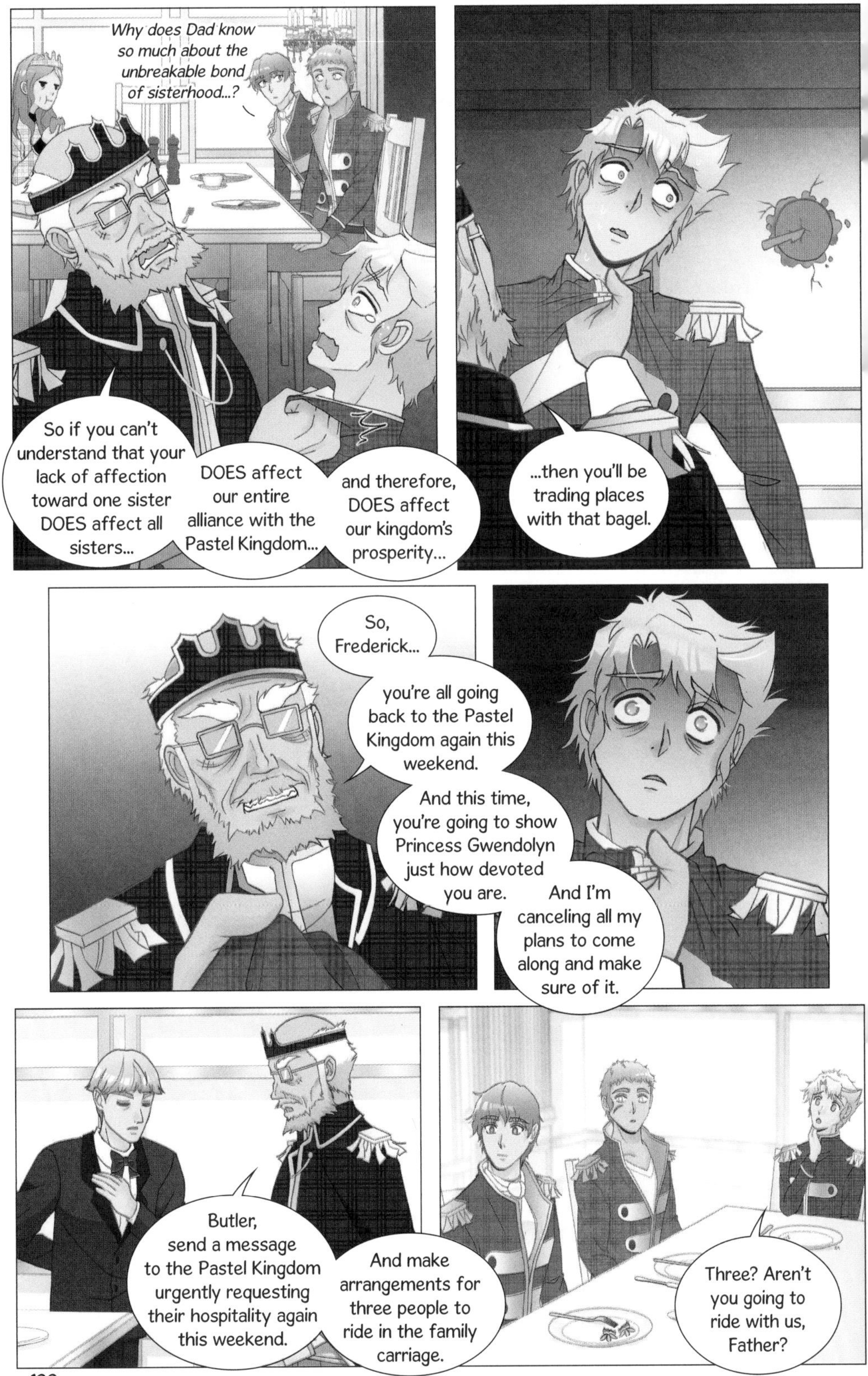
Why does Dad know so much about the unbreakable bond of sisterhood...?
So if you can't understand that your lack of affection toward one sister DOES affect all sisters...
DOES affect our entire alliance with the Pastel Kingdom...
and therefore, DOES affect our kingdom's prosperity...
...then you'll be trading places with that bagel.
So, Frederick...
you're all going back to the Pastel Kingdom again this weekend.
And this time, you're going to show Princess Gwendolyn just how devoted you are.
And I'm canceling all my plans to come along and make sure of it.
Butler, send a message to the Pastel Kingdom urgently requesting their hospitality again this weekend.
And make arrangements for three people to ride in the family carriage.
Three? Aren't you going to ride with us, Father?

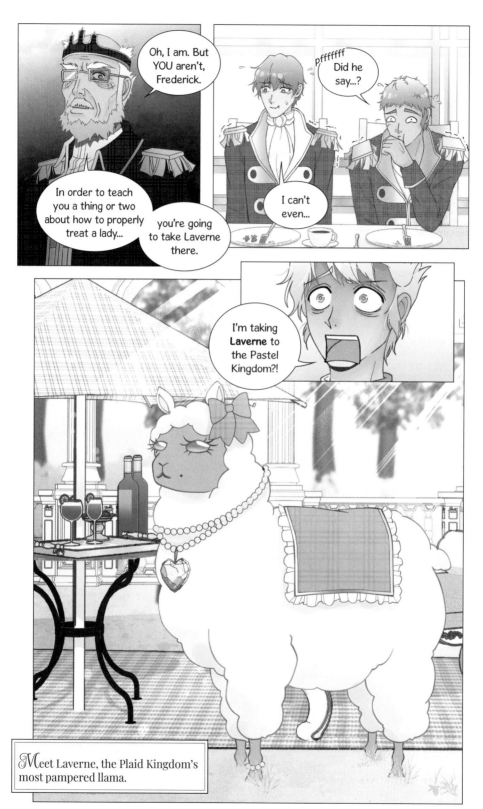

Meet Laverne, the Plaid Kingdom's most pampered llama.

Chapter

6

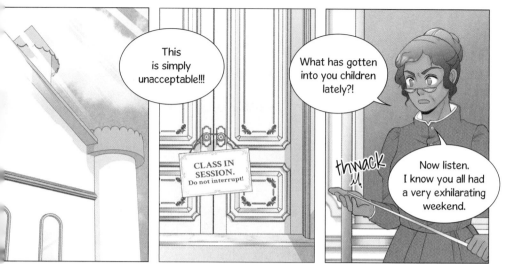

This is simply unacceptable!!!

What has gotten into you children lately?!

CLASS IN SESSION.
Do not interrupt!

thwack

Now listen. I know you all had a very exhilarating weekend.

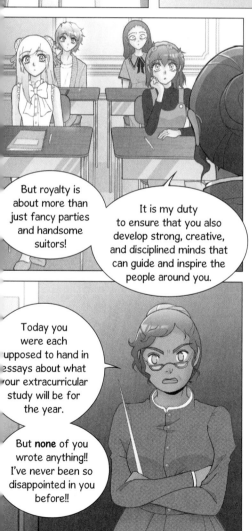

But royalty is about more than just fancy parties and handsome suitors!

It is my duty to ensure that you also develop strong, creative, and disciplined minds that can guide and inspire the people around you.

Today you were each supposed to hand in essays about what your extracurricular study will be for the year.

But **none** of you wrote anything!! I've never been so disappointed in you before!!

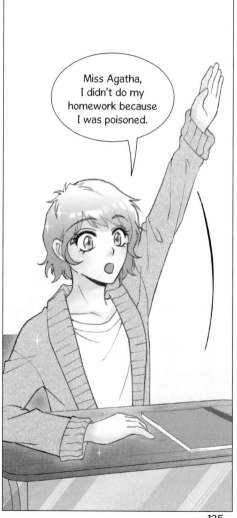

Miss Agatha, I didn't do my homework because I was poisoned.

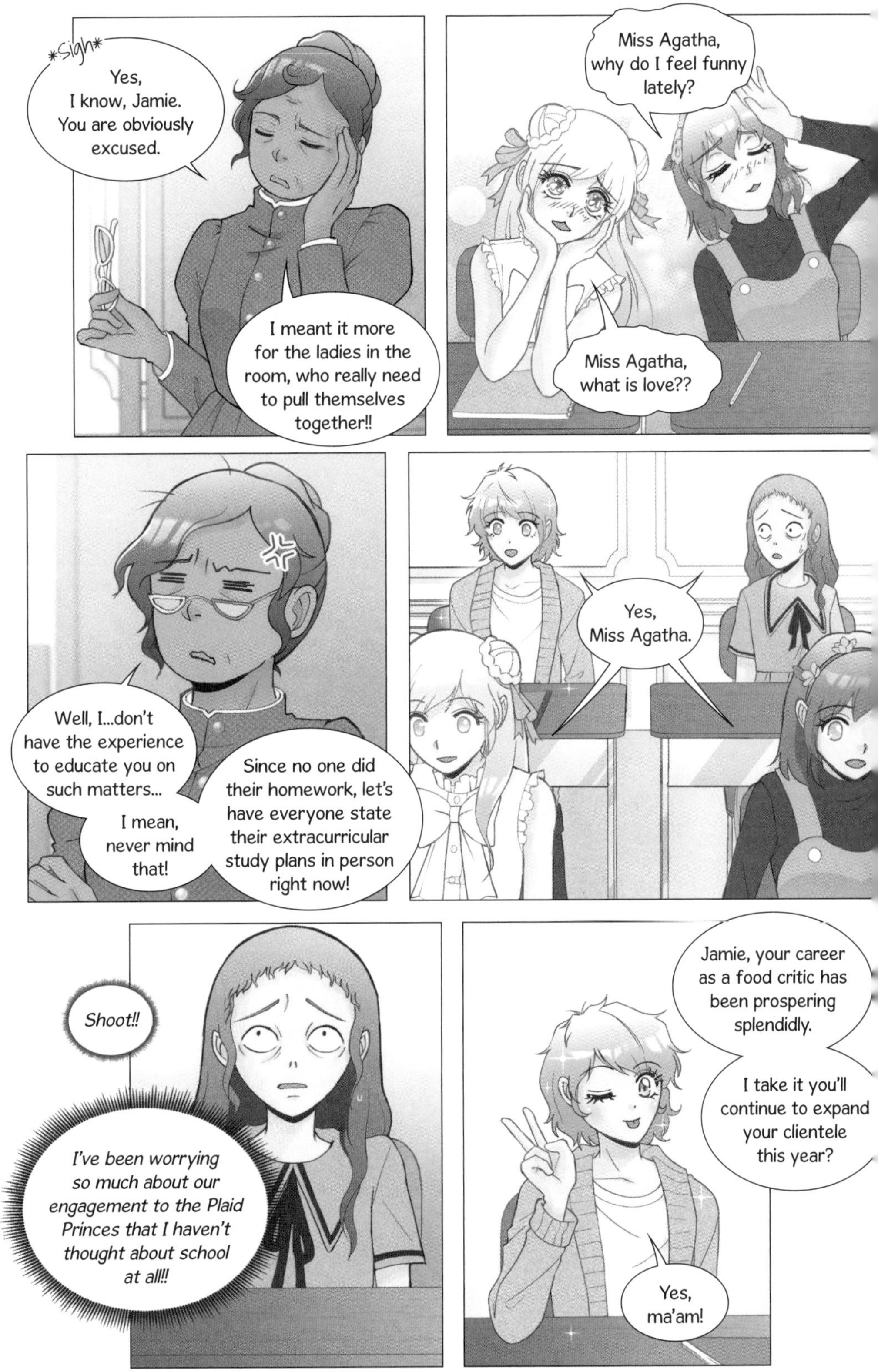
Sigh
Yes, I know, Jamie. You are obviously excused.
I meant it more for the ladies in the room, who really need to pull themselves together!!
Miss Agatha, why do I feel funny lately?
Miss Agatha, what is love??
Well, I...don't have the experience to educate you on such matters...
I mean, never mind that!
Since no one did their homework, let's have everyone state their extracurricular study plans in person right now!
Yes, Miss Agatha.
Shoot!!
I've been worrying so much about our engagement to the Plaid Princes that I haven't thought about school at all!!
Jamie, your career as a food critic has been prospering splendidly.
I take it you'll continue to expand your clientele this year?
Yes, ma'am!

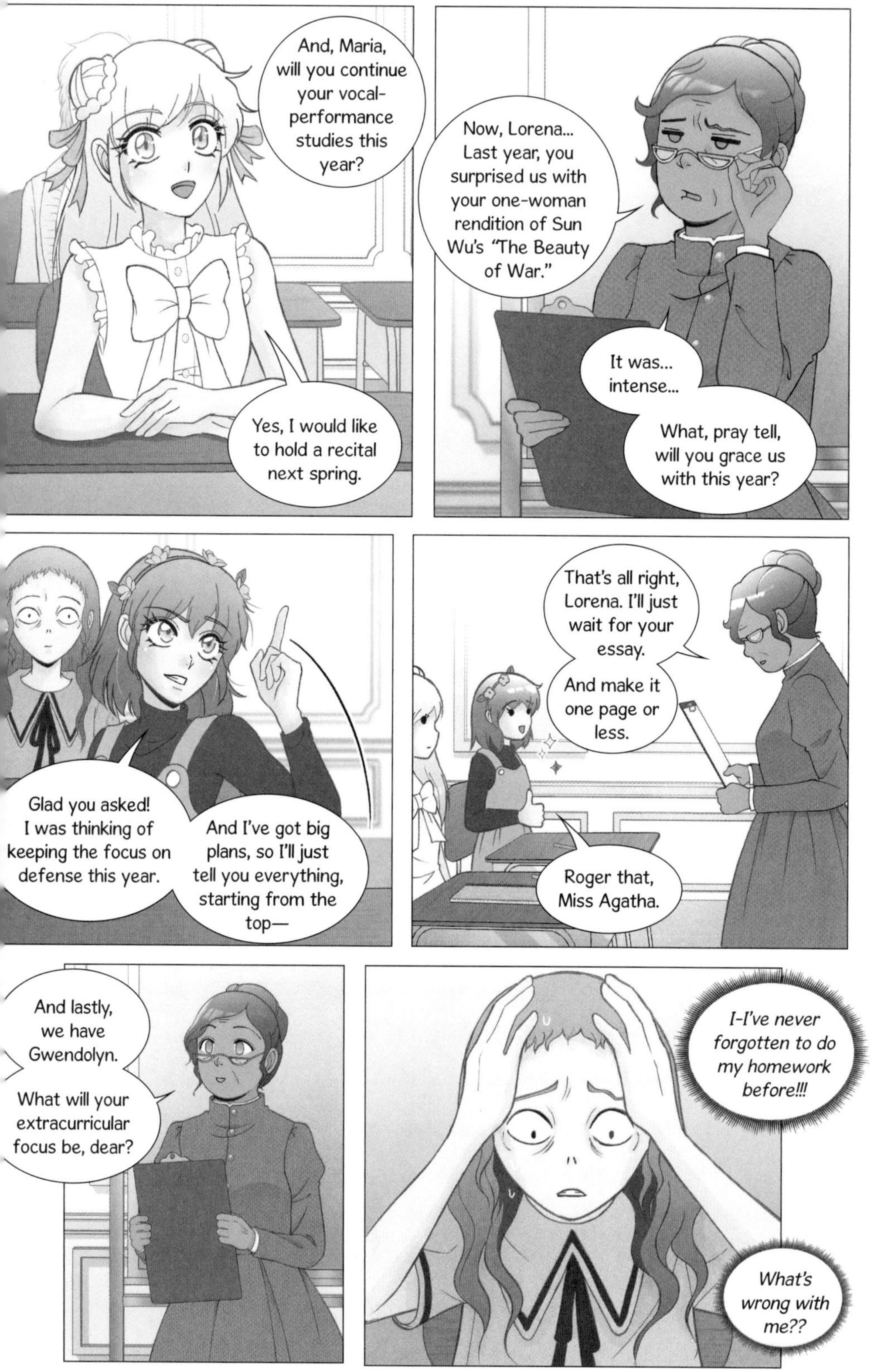

And, Maria, will you continue your vocal-performance studies this year?
Yes, I would like to hold a recital next spring.
Now, Lorena... Last year, you surprised us with your one-woman rendition of Sun Wu's "The Beauty of War."
It was... intense...
What, pray tell, will you grace us with this year?
Glad you asked! I was thinking of keeping the focus on defense this year.
And I've got big plans, so I'll just tell you everything, starting from the top—
That's all right, Lorena. I'll just wait for your essay.
And make it one page or less.
Roger that, Miss Agatha.
And lastly, we have Gwendolyn.
What will your extracurricular focus be, dear?
I-I've never forgotten to do my homework before!!!
What's wrong with me??

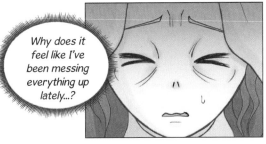

Why does it feel like I've been messing everything up lately...?

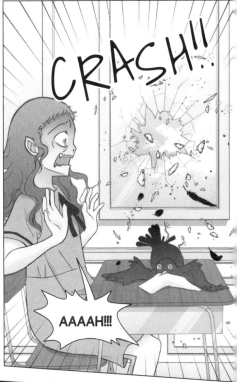

CRASH!!!

AAAAH!!!

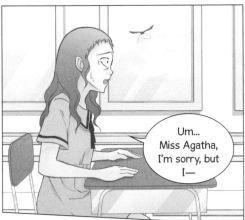

Um...
Miss Agatha,
I'm sorry, but
I—

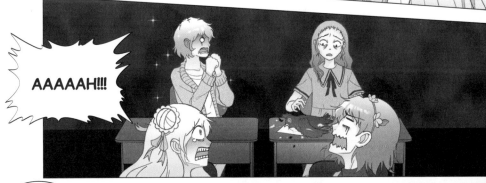

AAAAAH!!!

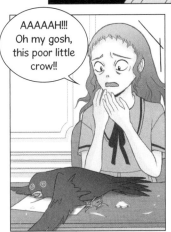

AAAAAH!!!
Oh my gosh,
this poor little
crow!!

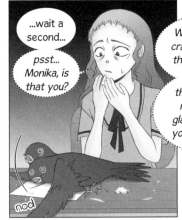

...wait a
second...

psst...
Monika, is
that you?

nod

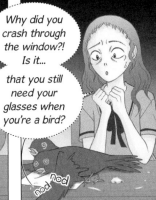

Why did you
crash through
the window?!
Is it...

that you still
need your
glasses when
you're a bird?

nod nod

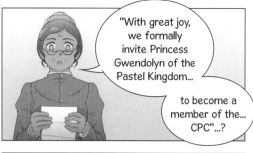

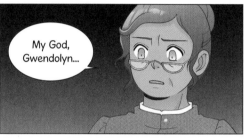

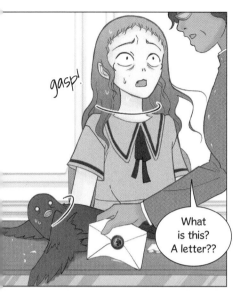

"With great joy, we formally invite Princess Gwendolyn of the Pastel Kingdom...

to become a member of the... CPC"...?

My God, Gwendolyn...

What is this? A letter??

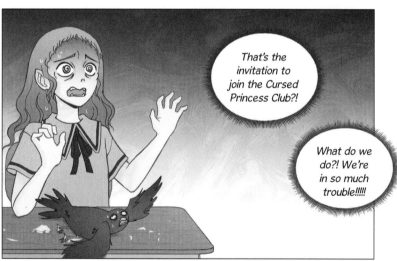

That's the invitation to join the Cursed Princess Club?!

What do we do?! We're in so much trouble!!!!!

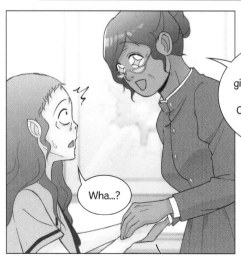

You **brilliant** girl!! You were accepted into **the** CPC?! The Cosmopolitan Princess Conservatory?!

That's the utmost renowned institution, exclusively open to only the most refined and elite princesses!!

Wha...?

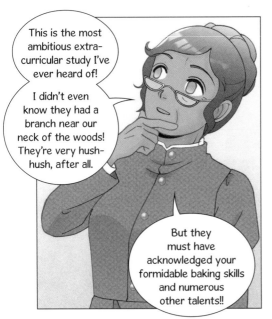

This is the most ambitious extra-curricular study I've ever heard of!

I didn't even know they had a branch near our neck of the woods! They're very hush-hush, after all.

But they must have acknowledged your formidable baking skills and numerous other talents!!

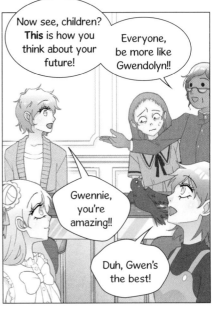

Now see, children? **This** is how you think about your future!

Everyone, be more like Gwendolyn!!

Gwennie, you're amazing!!

Duh, Gwen's the best!

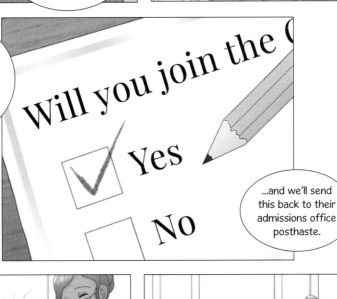

So I'll just confirm that you'll be attending their initiation ceremony this Friday at twilight...

Will you join the (

☑ Yes

☐ No

...and we'll send this back to their admissions office posthaste.

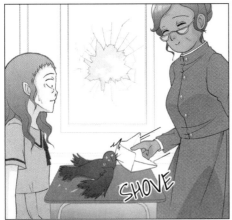

SHOVE

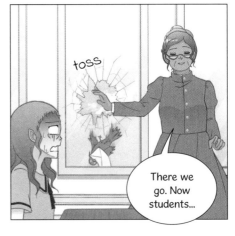

toss

There we go. Now students...

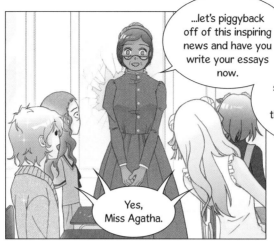

...let's piggyback off of this inspiring news and have you write your essays now.

After all, nothing strengthens one's intentions better than putting pen to paper.

Yes, Miss Agatha.

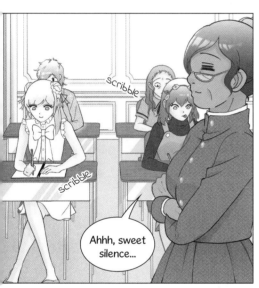

scribble

scribble

Ahhh, sweet silence...

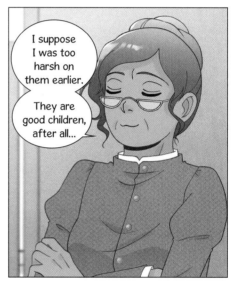

I suppose I was too harsh on them earlier.

They are good children, after all...

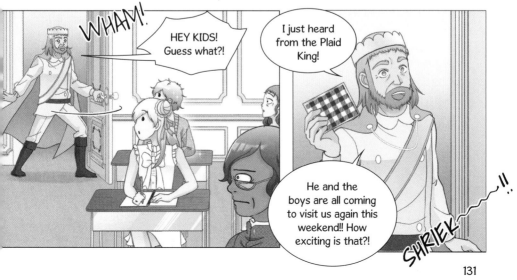

WHAM!

HEY KIDS! Guess what?!

I just heard from the Plaid King!

He and the boys are all coming to visit us again this weekend!! How exciting is that?!

SHRIEK!!

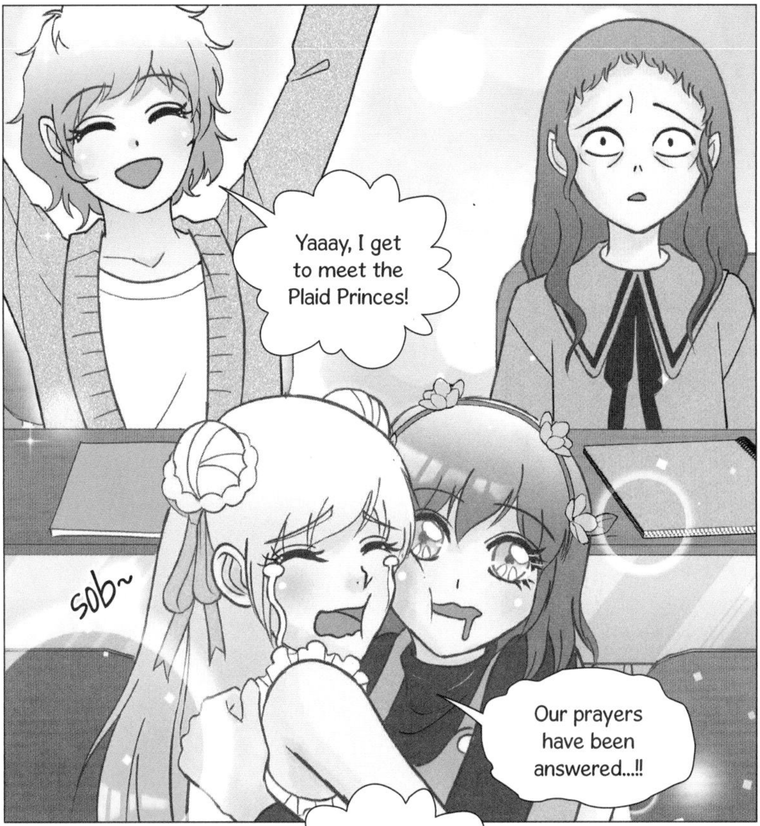
Yaaay, I get to meet the Plaid Princes!
sob~
Our prayers have been answered...!!
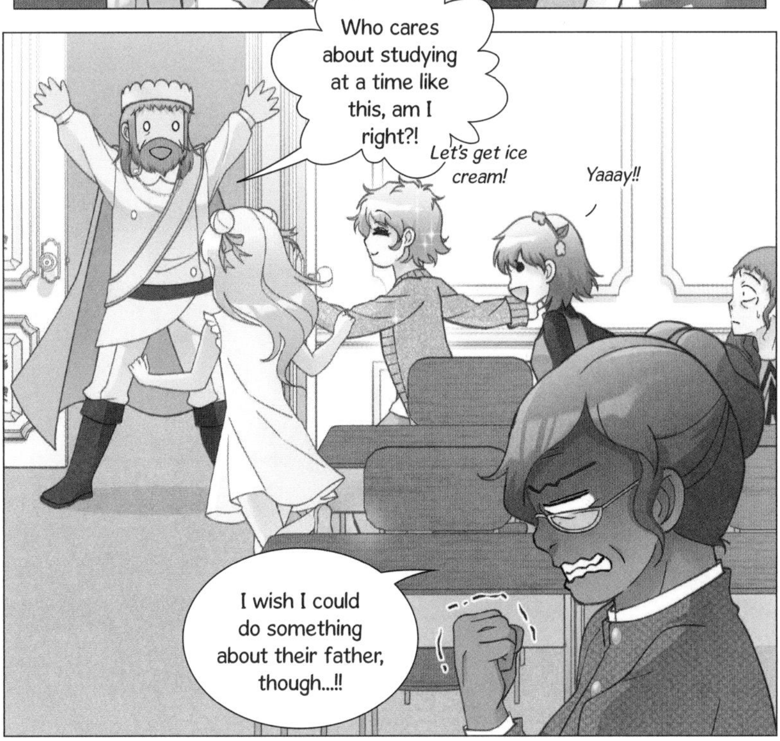
Who cares about studying at a time like this, am I right?!
Let's get ice cream!
Yaaay!!
I wish I could do something about their father, though...!!

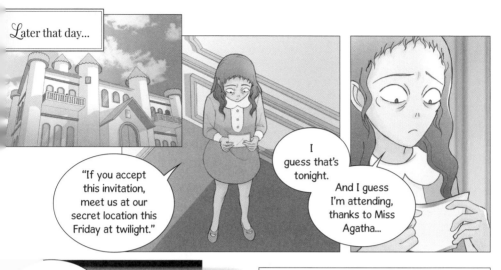

Later that day...

"If you accept this invitation, meet us at our secret location this Friday at twilight."

I guess that's tonight.

And I guess I'm attending, thanks to Miss Agatha...

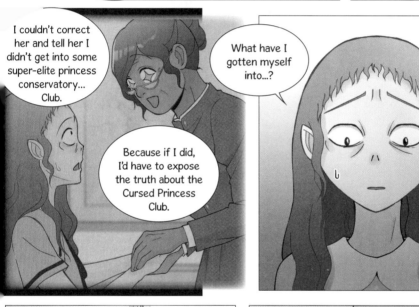

I couldn't correct her and tell her I didn't get into some super-elite princess conservatory... Club.

Because if I did, I'd have to expose the truth about the Cursed Princess Club.

What have I gotten myself into...?

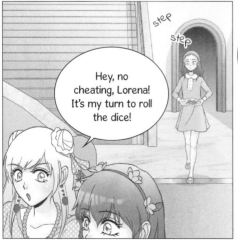

step

step

Hey, no cheating, Lorena! It's my turn to roll the dice!

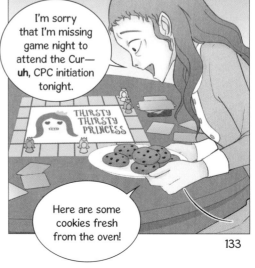

I'm sorry that I'm missing game night to attend the Cur— uh, CPC initiation tonight.

THIRSTY THIRSTY PRINCESS

Here are some cookies fresh from the oven!

133

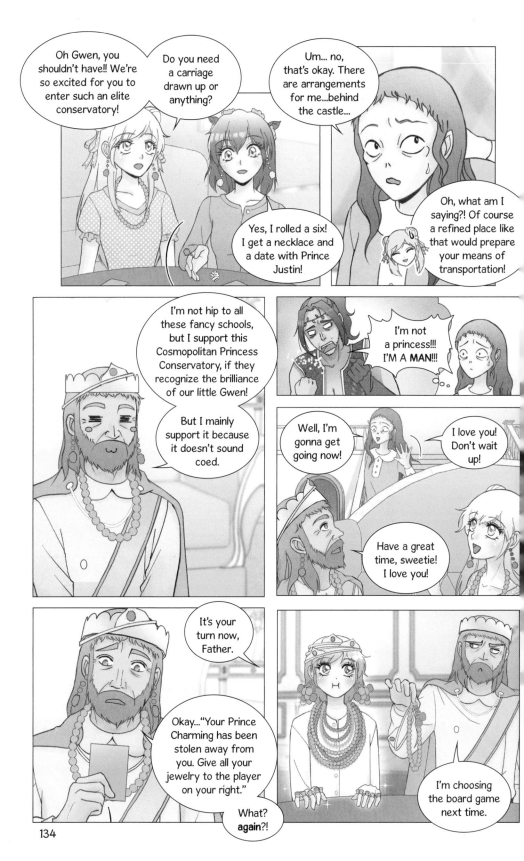

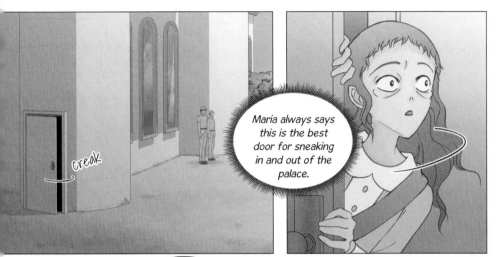

Maria always says this is the best door for sneaking in and out of the palace.

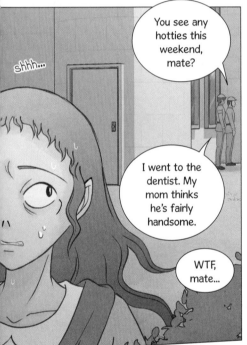

You see any hotties this weekend, mate?

I went to the dentist. My mom thinks he's fairly handsome.

WTF, mate...

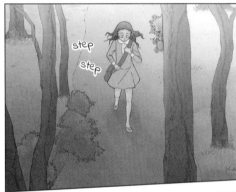

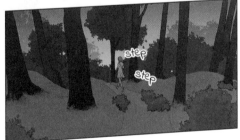

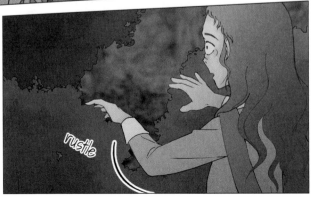

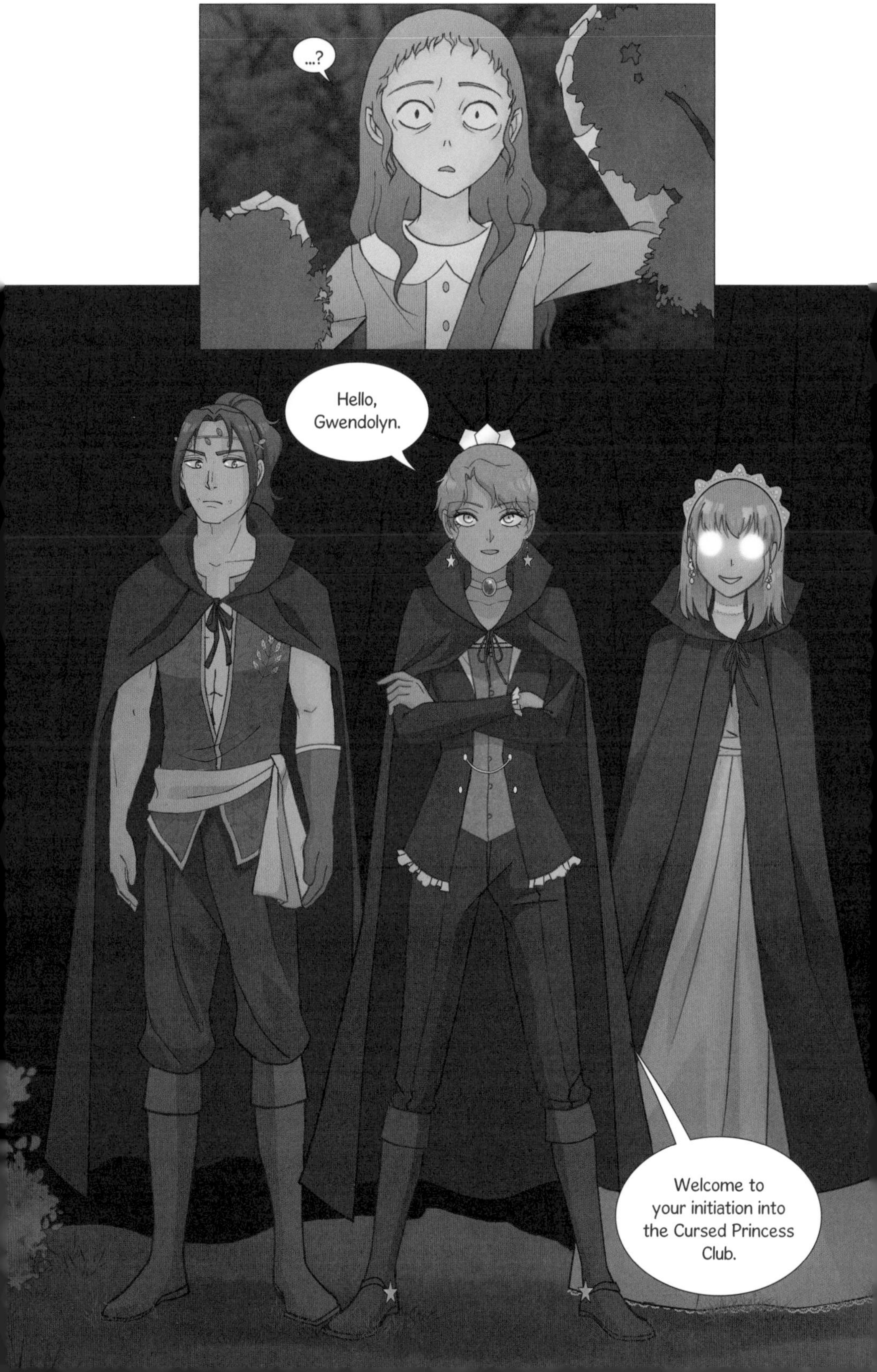
...?
Hello, Gwendolyn.
Welcome to your initiation into the Cursed Princess Club.

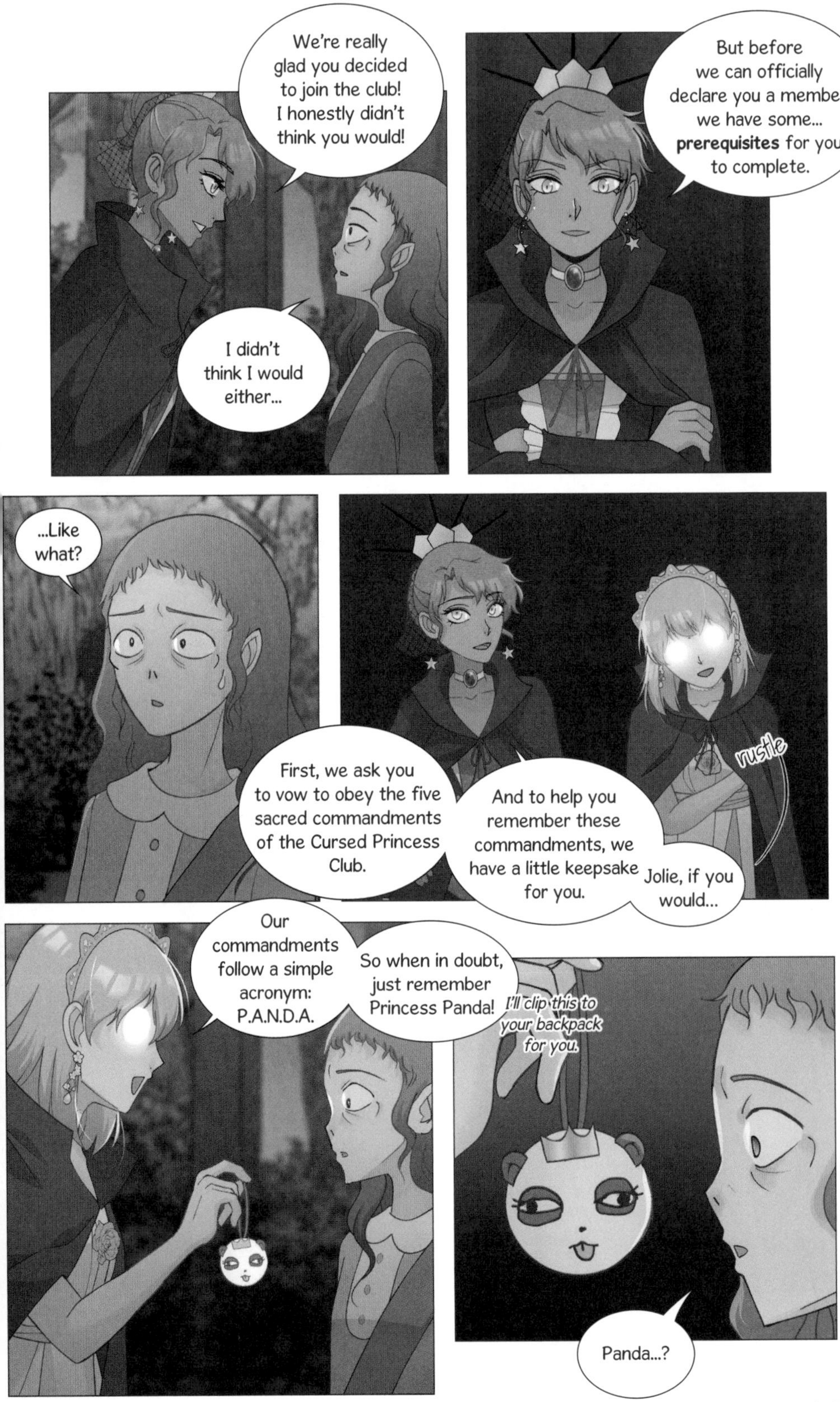

We're really glad you decided to join the club! I honestly didn't think you would!
I didn't think I would either...
But before we can officially declare you a member, we have some... **prerequisites** for you to complete.
...Like what?
First, we ask you to vow to obey the five sacred commandments of the Cursed Princess Club.
And to help you remember these commandments, we have a little keepsake for you.
rustle
Jolie, if you would...
Our commandments follow a simple acronym: P.A.N.D.A.
So when in doubt, just remember Princess Panda!
I'll clip this to your backpack for you.
Panda...?

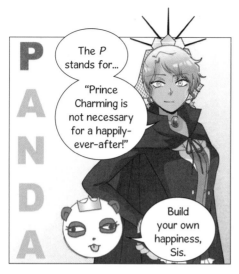

The *P* stands for...

"Prince Charming is not necessary for a happily-ever-after!"

Build your own happiness, Sis.

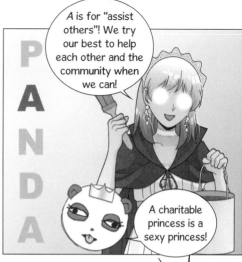

A is for "assist others"! We try our best to help each other and the community when we can!

A charitable princess is a sexy princess!

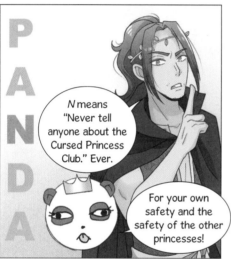

N means "Never tell anyone about the Cursed Princess Club." Ever.

For your own safety and the safety of the other princesses!

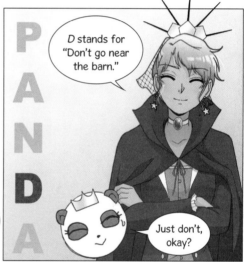

D stands for "Don't go near the barn."

Just don't, okay?

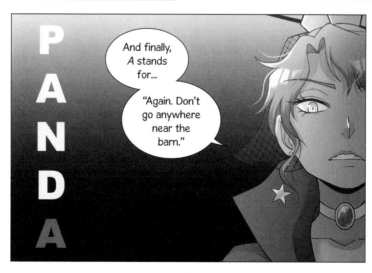

And finally, *A* stands for...

"Again. Don't go anywhere near the barn."

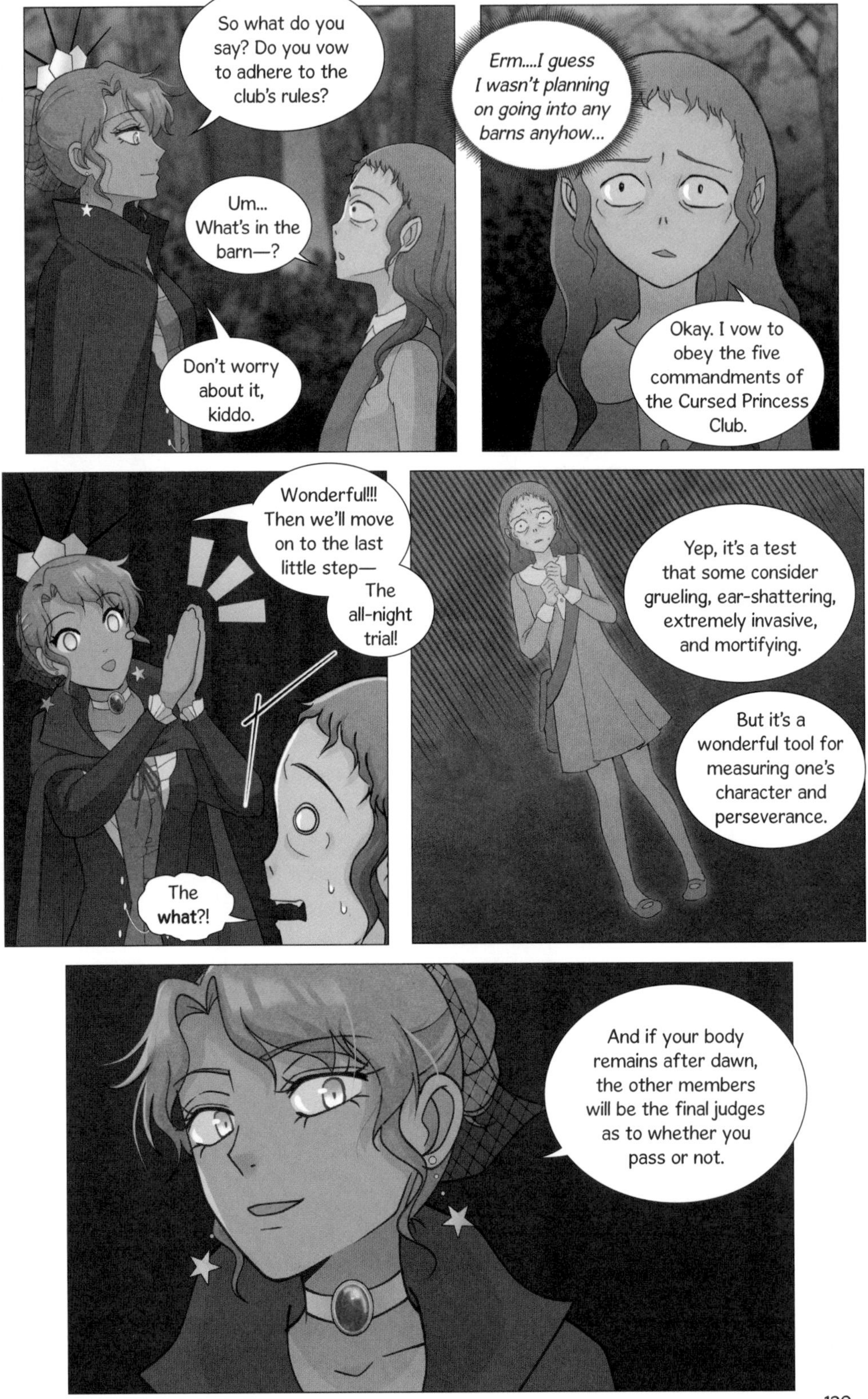
So what do you say? Do you vow to adhere to the club's rules?
Um... What's in the barn—?
Don't worry about it, kiddo.
Erm....I guess I wasn't planning on going into any barns anyhow...
Okay. I vow to obey the five commandments of the Cursed Princess Club.
Wonderful!!! Then we'll move on to the last little step—
The all-night trial!
The **what**?!
Yep, it's a test that some consider grueling, ear-shattering, extremely invasive, and mortifying.
But it's a wonderful tool for measuring one's character and perseverance.
And if your body remains after dawn, the other members will be the final judges as to whether you pass or not.

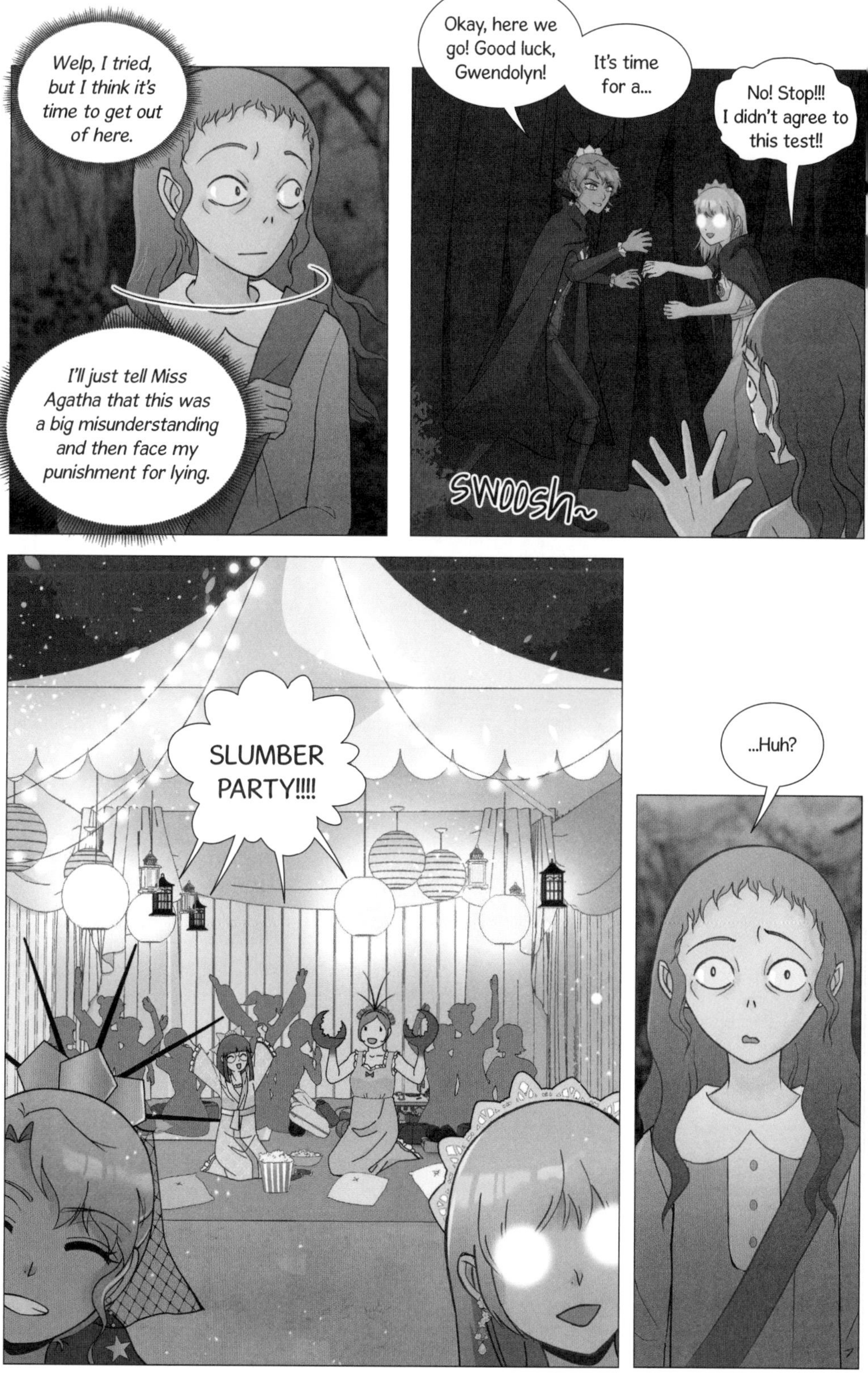
Welp, I tried, but I think it's time to get out of here.
I'll just tell Miss Agatha that this was a big misunderstanding and then face my punishment for lying.
Okay, here we go! Good luck, Gwendolyn!
It's time for a...
No! Stop!!! I didn't agree to this test!!
SWOOSH~
SLUMBER PARTY!!!!
...Huh?

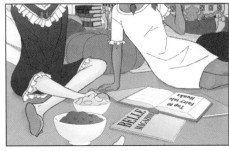

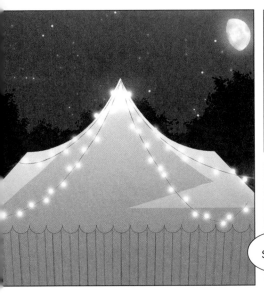

Sooo...

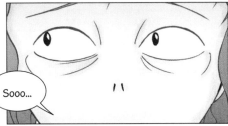

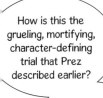

How is this the grueling, mortifying, character-defining trial that Prez described earlier?

This is just a normal slumber party...

Wearing the nightgown she brought to return to Jolie

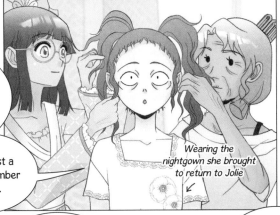

Well, those were actual complaints. Most were verbatim out of Saffron's mouth.

He just really hates slumber parties.

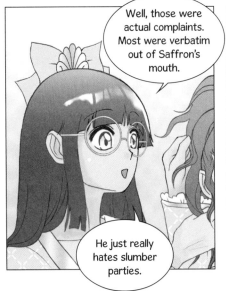

But slumber parties **are** truly a great test of one's character.

You can learn a lot about someone through all the laughter, stupid games, and lack of sleep.

Really?

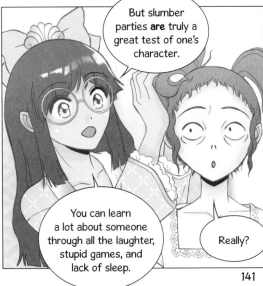

141

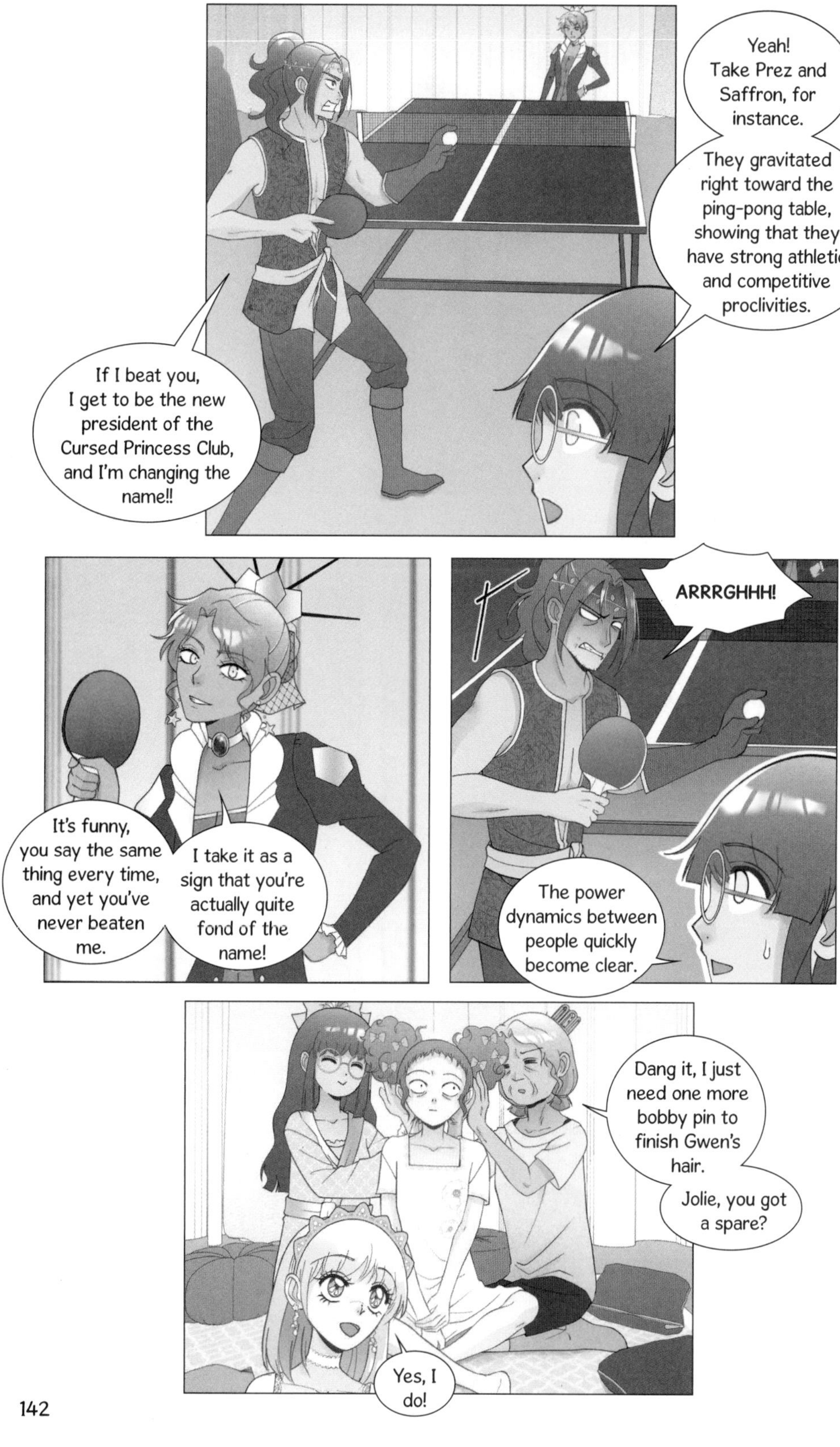
Yeah! Take Prez and Saffron, for instance.
They gravitated right toward the ping-pong table, showing that they have strong athletic and competitive proclivities.
If I beat you, I get to be the new president of the Cursed Princess Club, and I'm changing the name!!
It's funny, you say the same thing every time, and yet you've never beaten me.
I take it as a sign that you're actually quite fond of the name!
ARRRGHHH!
The power dynamics between people quickly become clear.
Dang it, I just need one more bobby pin to finish Gwen's hair.
Jolie, you got a spare?
Yes, I do!

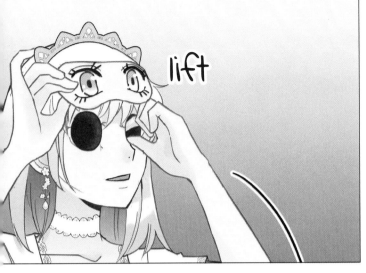

lift

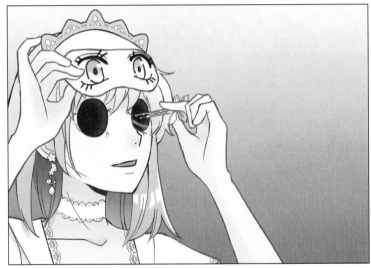

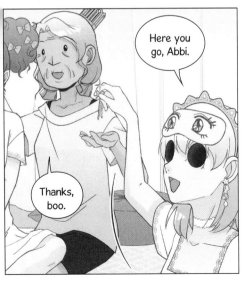

Here you go, Abbi.

Thanks, boo.

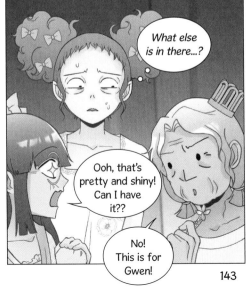

What else is in there...?

Ooh, that's pretty and shiny! Can I have it??

No! This is for Gwen!

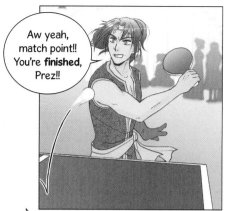

Aw yeah, match point!! You're **finished**, Prez!!

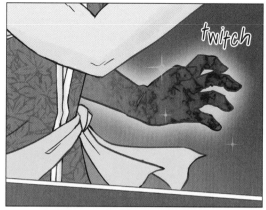

twitch

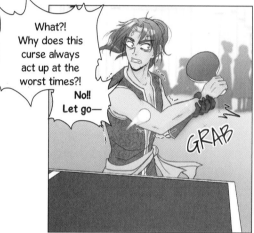

What?! Why does this curse always act up at the worst times?!

No!! Let go—

GRAB

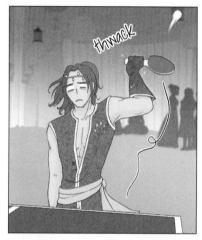

thwack

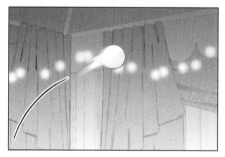

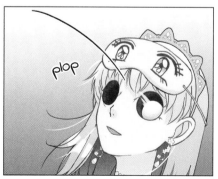

plop

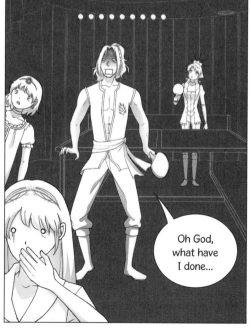

Oh God, what have I done...

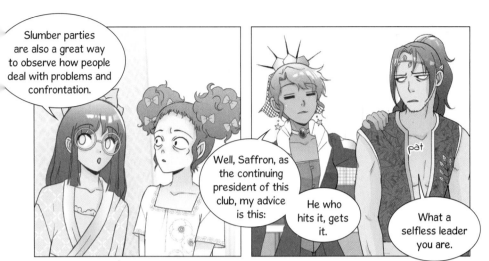

Slumber parties are also a great way to observe how people deal with problems and confrontation.

Well, Saffron, as the continuing president of this club, my advice is this:

He who hits it, gets it.

What a selfless leader you are.

pat

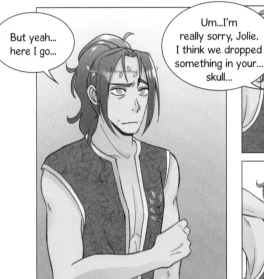

But yeah... here I go...

Um...I'm really sorry, Jolie. I think we dropped something in your... skull...

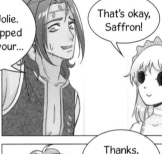

That's okay, Saffron!

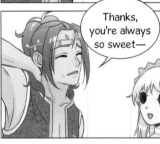

Thanks, you're always so sweet—

But you'll have to get it out yourself.

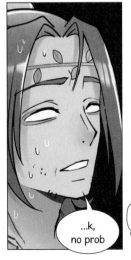

...k, no prob

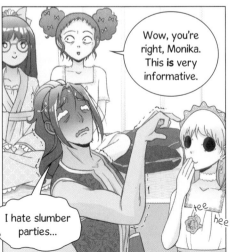

Wow, you're right, Monika. This **is** very informative.

I hate slumber parties...

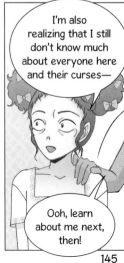

I'm also realizing that I still don't know much about everyone here and their curses—

Ooh, learn about me next, then!

tee hee

145

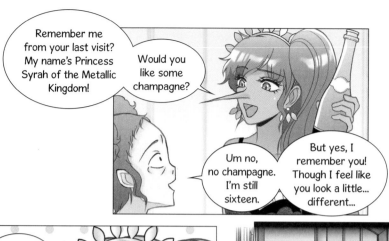

Remember me from your last visit? My name's Princess Syrah of the Metallic Kingdom!

Would you like some champagne?

Um no, no champagne. I'm still sixteen.

But yes, I remember you! Though I feel like you look a little... different...

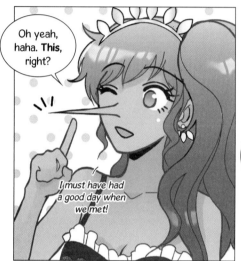

Oh yeah, haha. **This**, right?

I must have had a good day when we met!

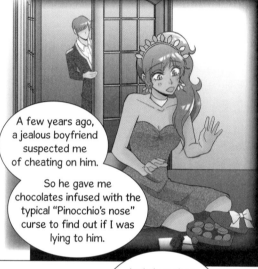

A few years ago, a jealous boyfriend suspected me of cheating on him.

So he gave me chocolates infused with the typical "Pinocchio's nose" curse to find out if I was lying to him.

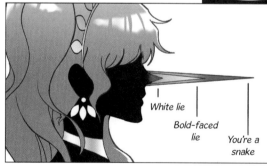

And since then, every time I tell a lie, my nose grows in proportion to the severity of the untruthfulness.

But it always eventually returns to its normal size.

White lie

Bold-faced lie

You're a snake

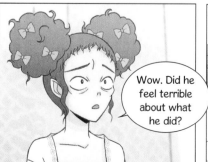

Wow. Did he feel terrible about what he did?

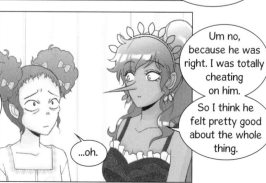

...oh.

Um no, because he was right. I was totally cheating on him.

So I think he felt pretty good about the whole thing.

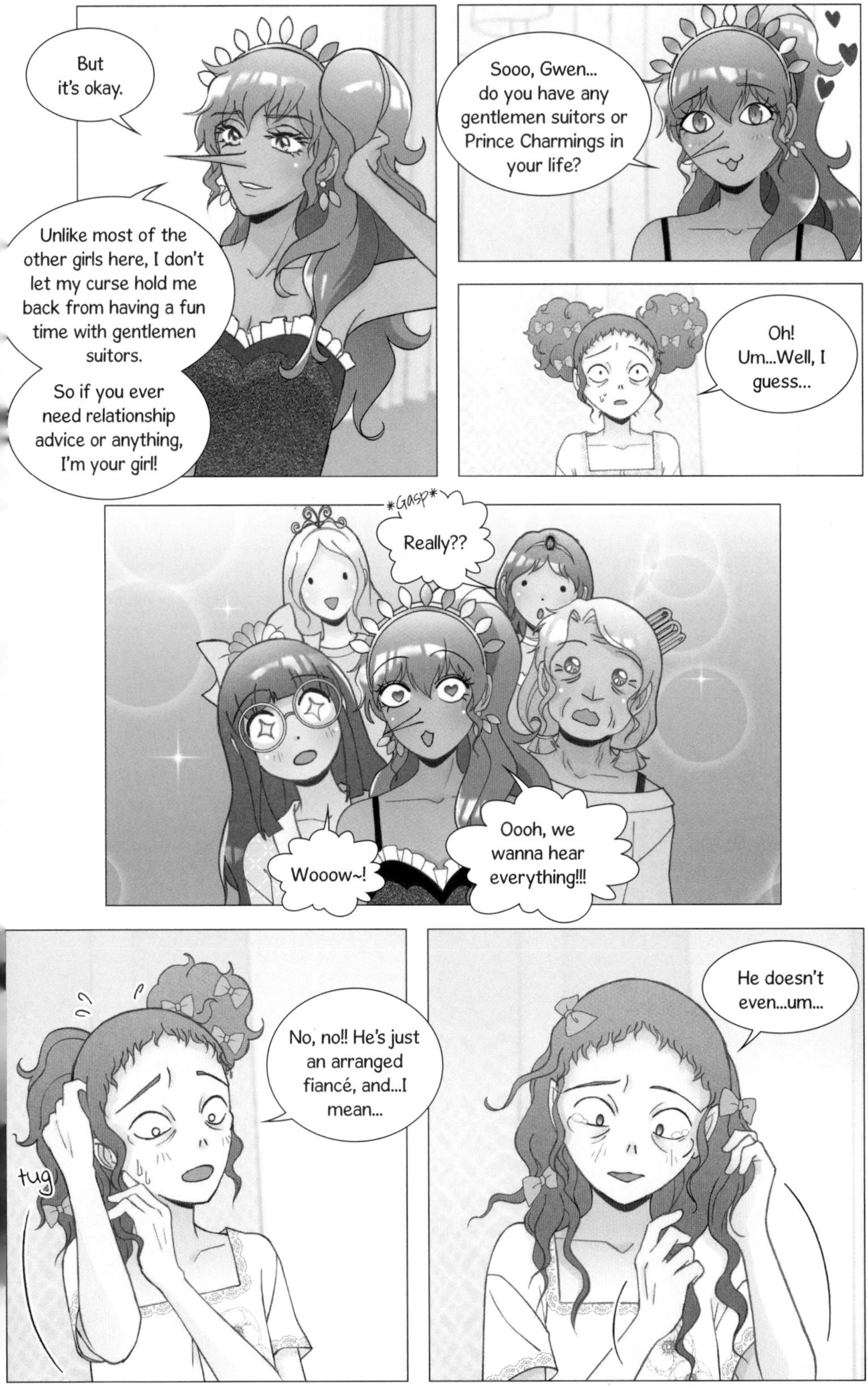
But it's okay.
Unlike most of the other girls here, I don't let my curse hold me back from having a fun time with gentlemen suitors.
So if you ever need relationship advice or anything, I'm your girl!
Sooo, Gwen... do you have any gentlemen suitors or Prince Charmings in your life?
Oh! Um...Well, I guess...
Gasp
Really??
Wooow~!
Oooh, we wanna hear everything!!!
tug
No, no!! He's just an arranged fiancé, and...I mean...
He doesn't even...um...

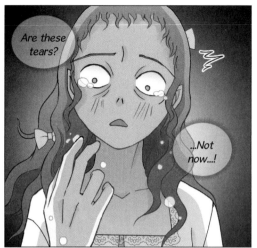

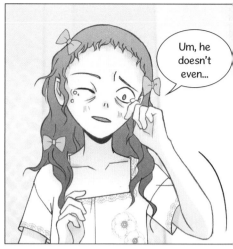

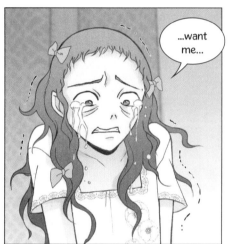

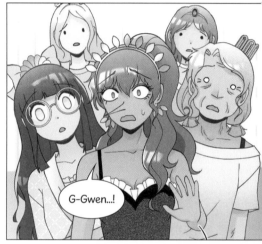

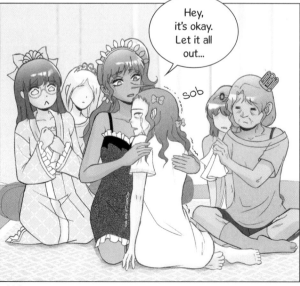

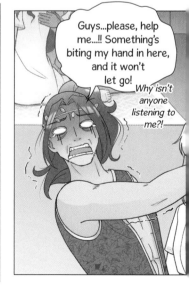

148

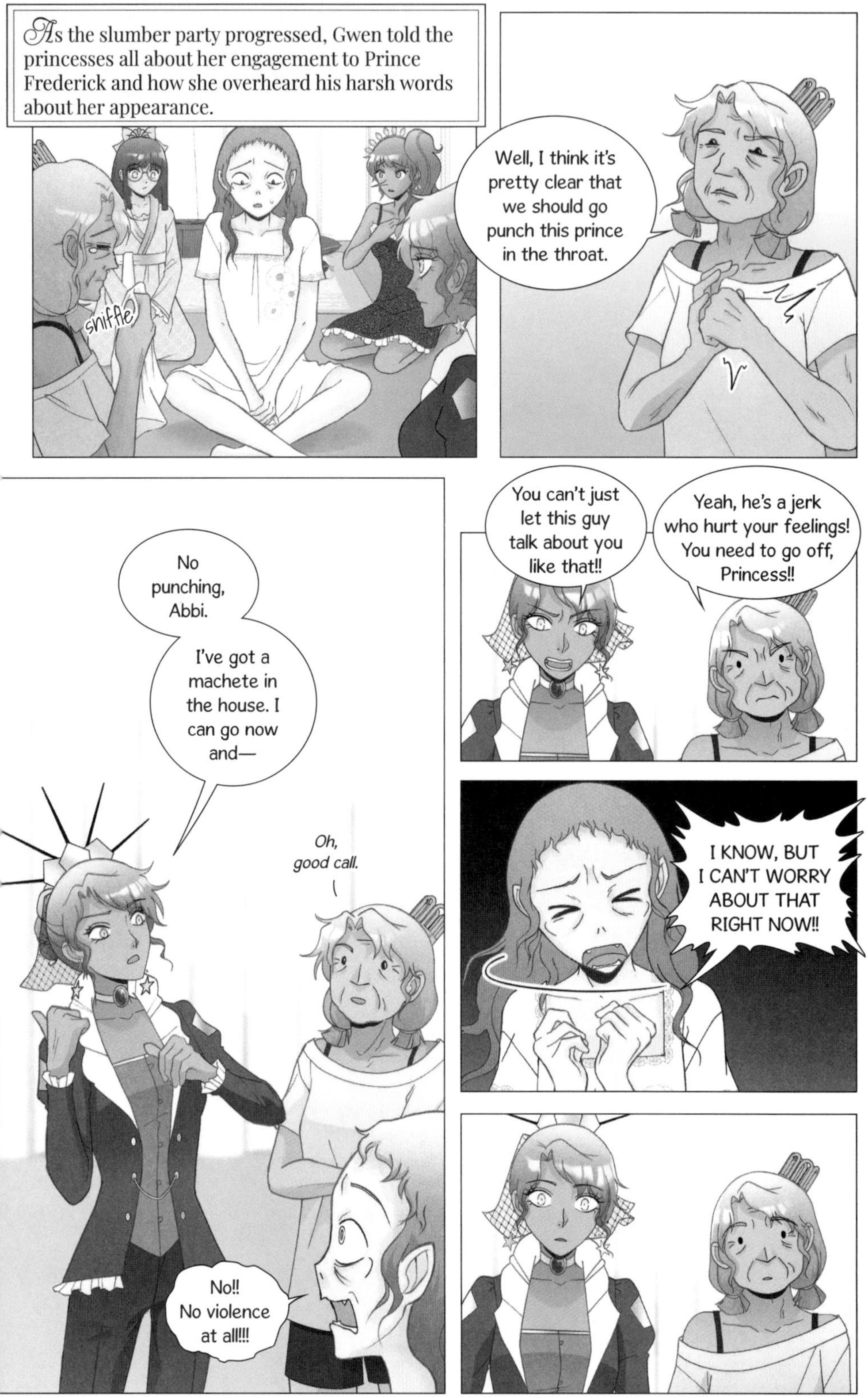
As the slumber party progressed, Gwen told the princesses all about her engagement to Prince Frederick and how she overheard his harsh words about her appearance.
sniffle
Well, I think it's pretty clear that we should go punch this prince in the throat.
No punching, Abbi.
I've got a machete in the house. I can go now and—
Oh, good call.
No!! No violence at all!!!
You can't just let this guy talk about you like that!!
Yeah, he's a jerk who hurt your feelings! You need to go off, Princess!!
I KNOW, BUT I CAN'T WORRY ABOUT THAT RIGHT NOW!!

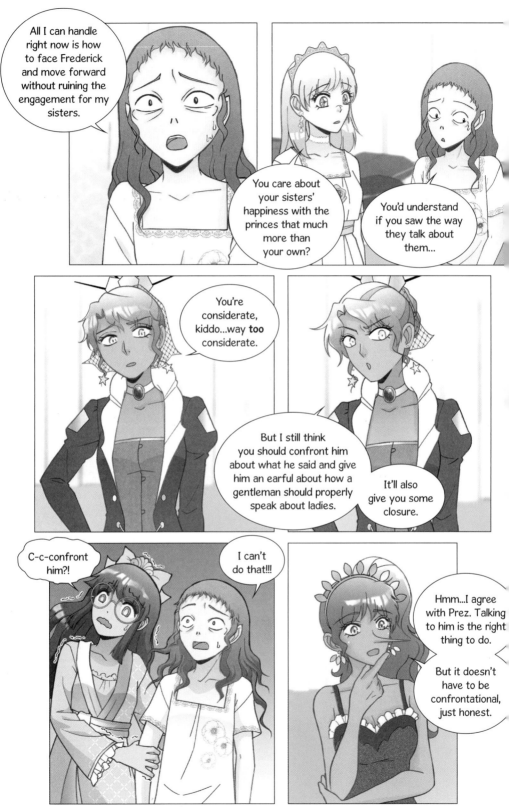

150

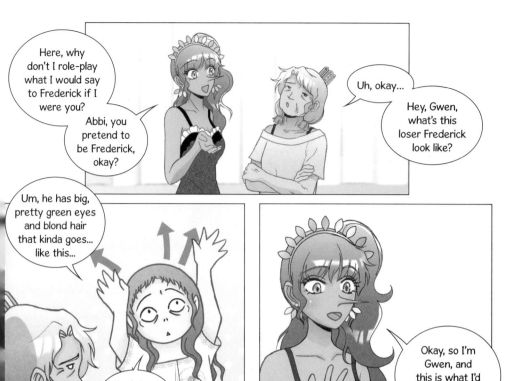

Here, why don't I role-play what I would say to Frederick if I were you?

Abbi, you pretend to be Frederick, okay?

Uh, okay...

Hey, Gwen, what's this loser Frederick look like?

Um, he has big, pretty green eyes and blond hair that kinda goes... like this...

And then it goes like... that way...?

What...?

Okay, so I'm Gwen, and this is what I'd say once I ran into Frederick.

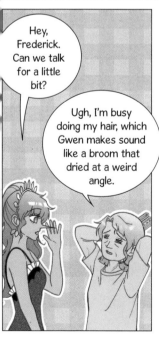

Hey, Frederick. Can we talk for a little bit?

Ugh, I'm busy doing my hair, which Gwen makes sound like a broom that dried at a weird angle.

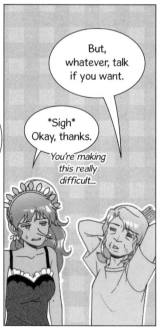

But, whatever, talk if you want.

Sigh Okay, thanks.

You're making this really difficult...

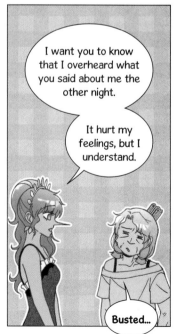

I want you to know that I overheard what you said about me the other night.

It hurt my feelings, but I understand.

Busted...

151

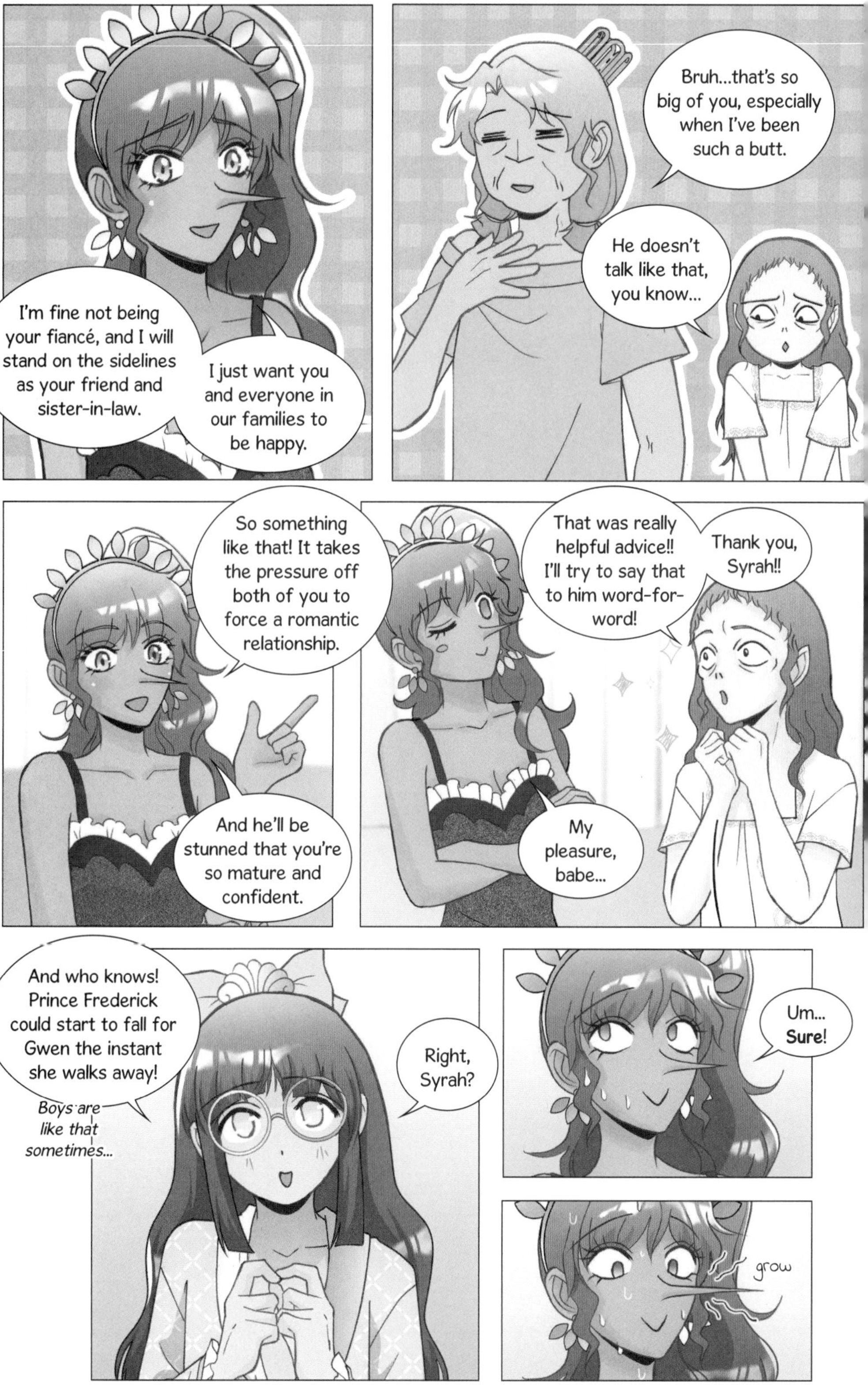
I'm fine not being your fiancé, and I will stand on the sidelines as your friend and sister-in-law.
I just want you and everyone in our families to be happy.
Bruh...that's so big of you, especially when I've been such a butt.
He doesn't talk like that, you know...
So something like that! It takes the pressure off both of you to force a romantic relationship.
And he'll be stunned that you're so mature and confident.
That was really helpful advice!! I'll try to say that to him word-for-word!
Thank you, Syrah!!
My pleasure, babe...
And who knows! Prince Frederick could start to fall for Gwen the instant she walks away!
Boys are like that sometimes...
Right, Syrah?
Um... **Sure**!
grow

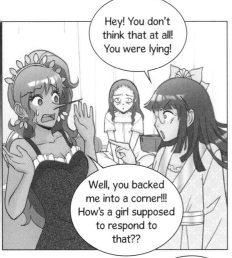

Hey! You don't think that at all! You were lying!

Well, you backed me into a corner!!! How's a girl supposed to respond to that??

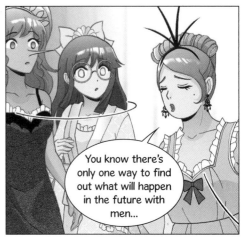

You know there's only one way to find out what will happen in the future with men...

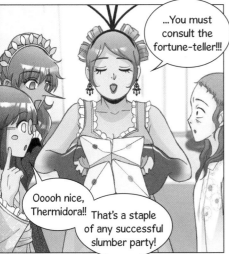

...You must consult the fortune-teller!!!

Ooooh nice, Thermidora!! That's a staple of any successful slumber party!

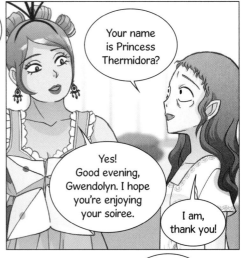

Your name is Princess Thermidora?

Yes! Good evening, Gwendolyn. I hope you're enjoying your soiree.

I am, thank you!

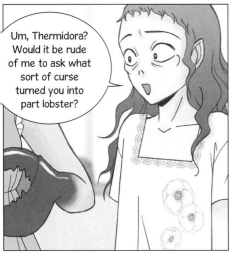

Um, Thermidora? Would it be rude of me to ask what sort of curse turned you into part lobster?

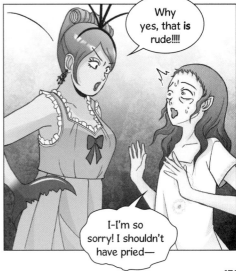

Why yes, that **is** rude!!!!

I-I'm so sorry! I shouldn't have pried—

153

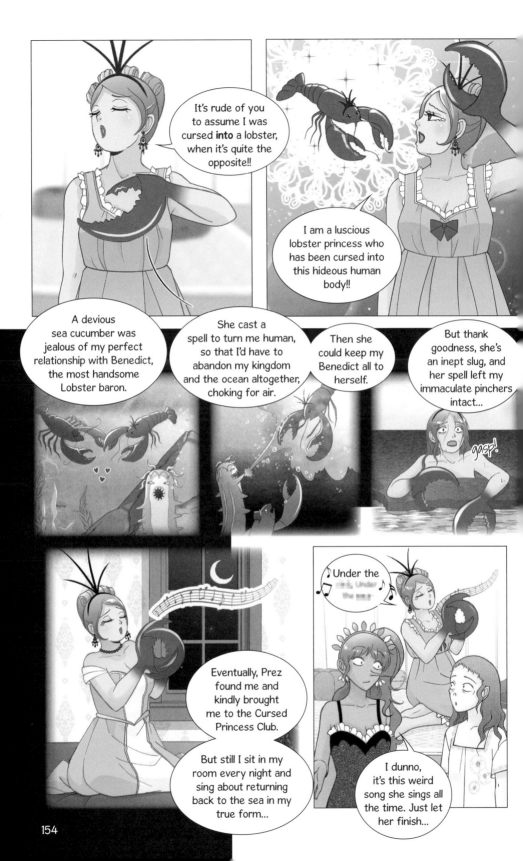

154

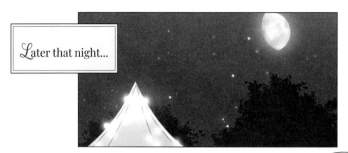

It's fortune-telling time, everyone!!

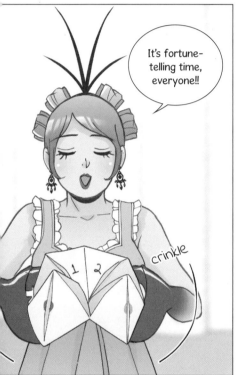

crinkle

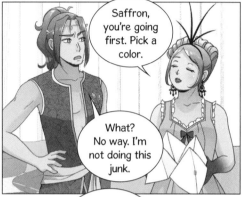

Saffron, you're going first. Pick a color.

What? No way. I'm not doing this junk.

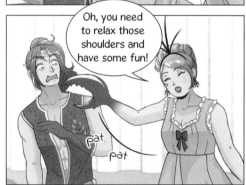

Oh, you need to relax those shoulders and have some fun!

pat pat

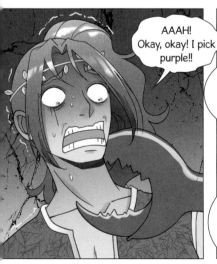

AAAH! Okay, okay! I pick purple!!

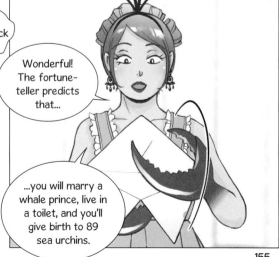

Wonderful! The fortune-teller predicts that...

...you will marry a whale prince, live in a toilet, and you'll give birth to 89 sea urchins.

155

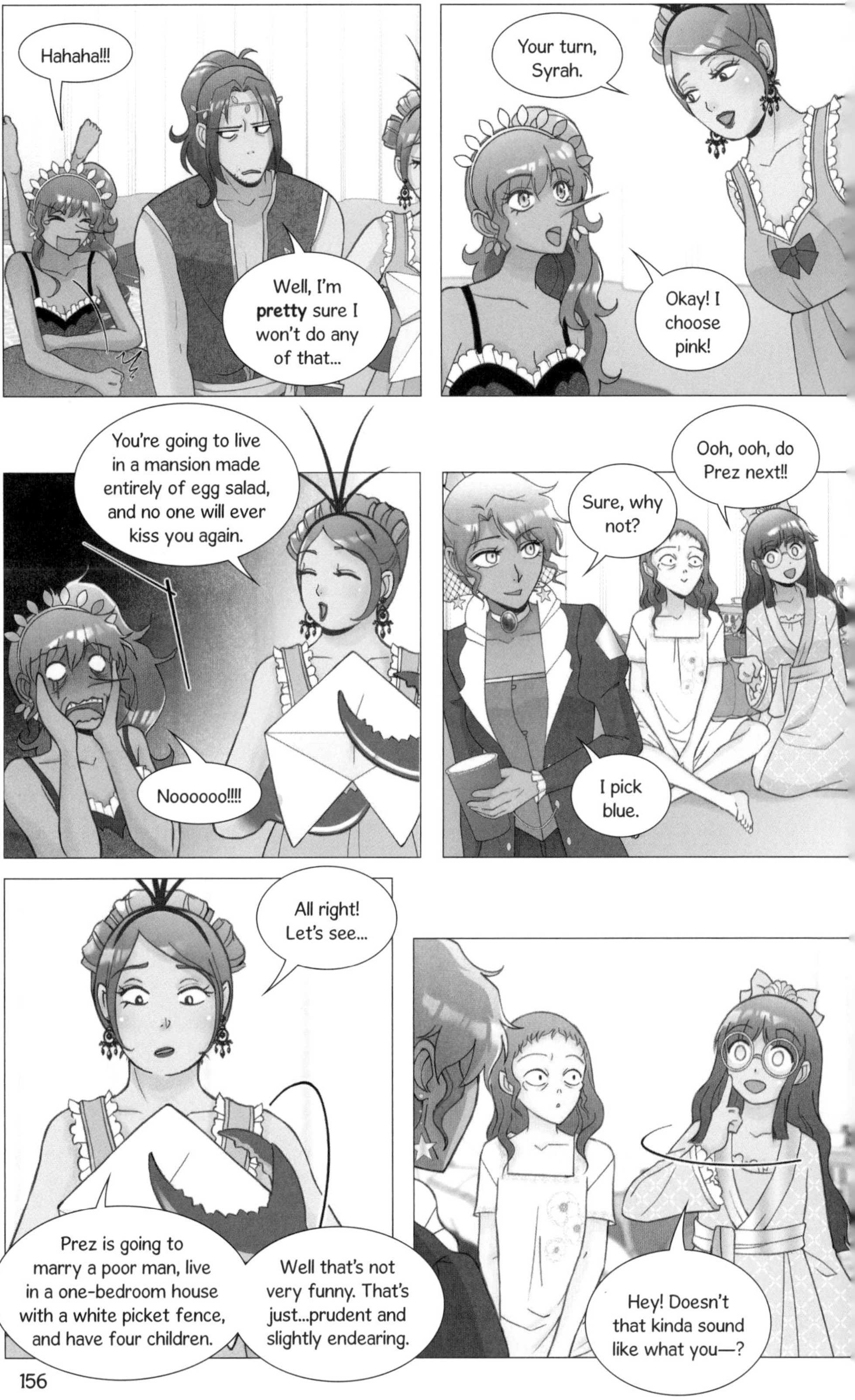
Hahaha!!!
Well, I'm **pretty** sure I won't do any of that...
Your turn, Syrah.
Okay! I choose pink!
You're going to live in a mansion made entirely of egg salad, and no one will ever kiss you again.
Noooooo!!!!
Sure, why not?
Ooh, ooh, do Prez next!!
I pick blue.
All right! Let's see...
Prez is going to marry a poor man, live in a one-bedroom house with a white picket fence, and have four children.
Well that's not very funny. That's just...prudent and slightly endearing.
Hey! Doesn't that kinda sound like what you—?

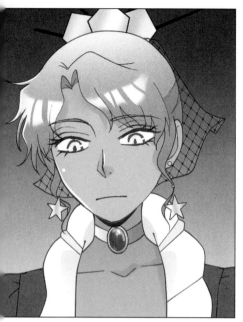

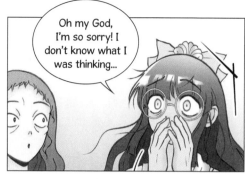

Oh my God, I'm so sorry! I don't know what I was thinking...

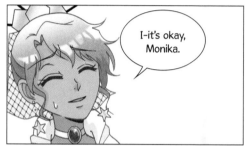

I-it's okay, Monika.

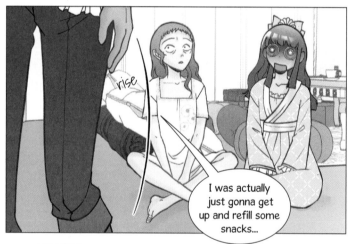

rise

I was actually just gonna get up and refill some snacks...

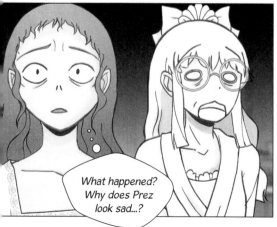

What happened? Why does Prez look sad...?

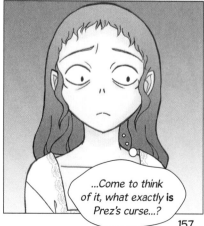

...Come to think of it, what exactly **is** Prez's curse...?

157

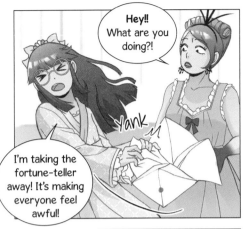

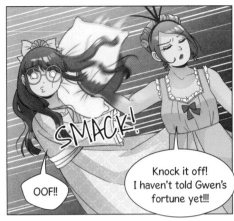

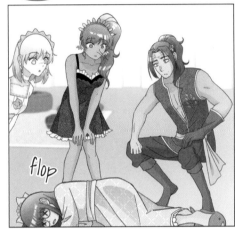

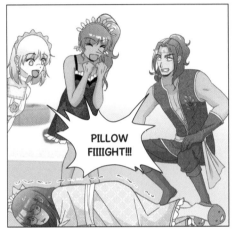

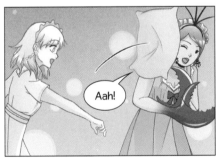

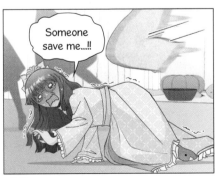

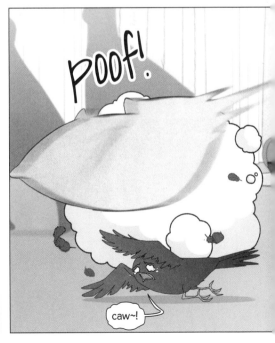

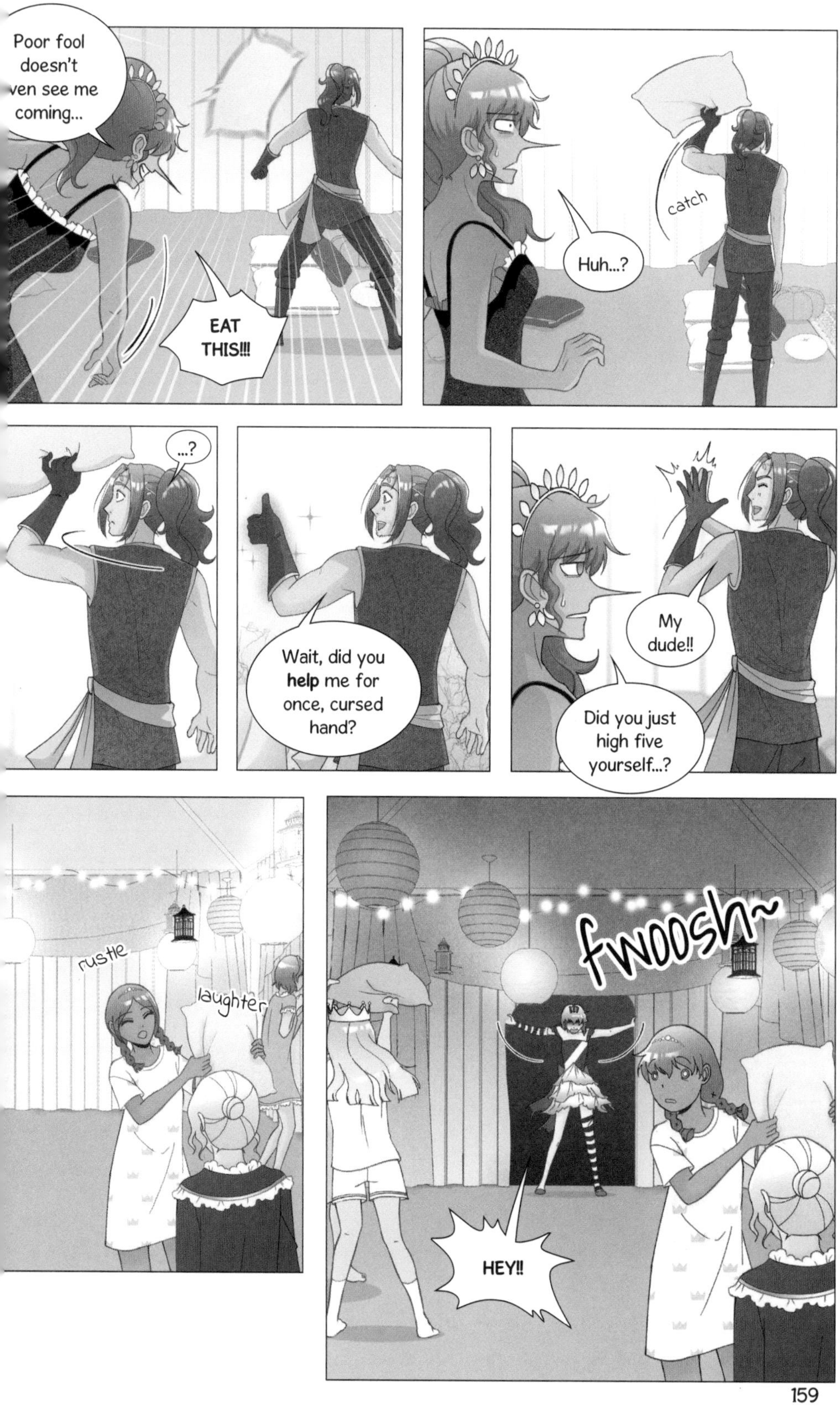
Poor fool doesn't ven see me coming...
EAT THIS!!!
Huh...?
catch
...?
Wait, did you **help** me for once, cursed hand?
My dude!!
Did you just high five yourself...?
rustle
laughter
fwoosh~
HEY!!

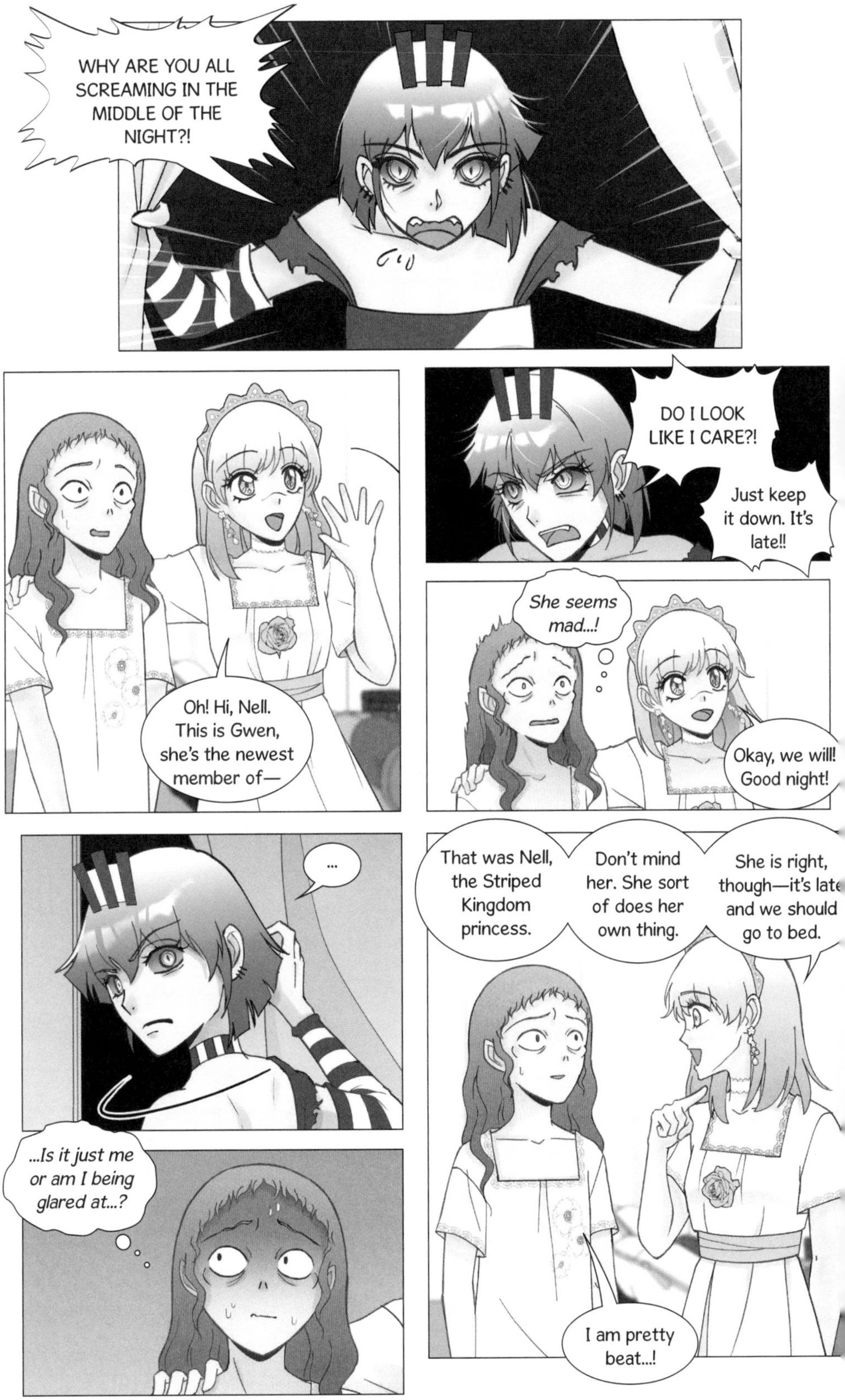
WHY ARE YOU ALL SCREAMING IN THE MIDDLE OF THE NIGHT?!
Oh! Hi, Nell. This is Gwen, she's the newest member of—
DO I LOOK LIKE I CARE?!
Just keep it down. It's late!!
She seems mad...!
Okay, we will! Good night!
...
...Is it just me or am I being glared at...?
That was Nell, the Striped Kingdom princess.
Don't mind her. She sort of does her own thing.
She is right, though—it's late and we should go to bed.
I am pretty beat...!

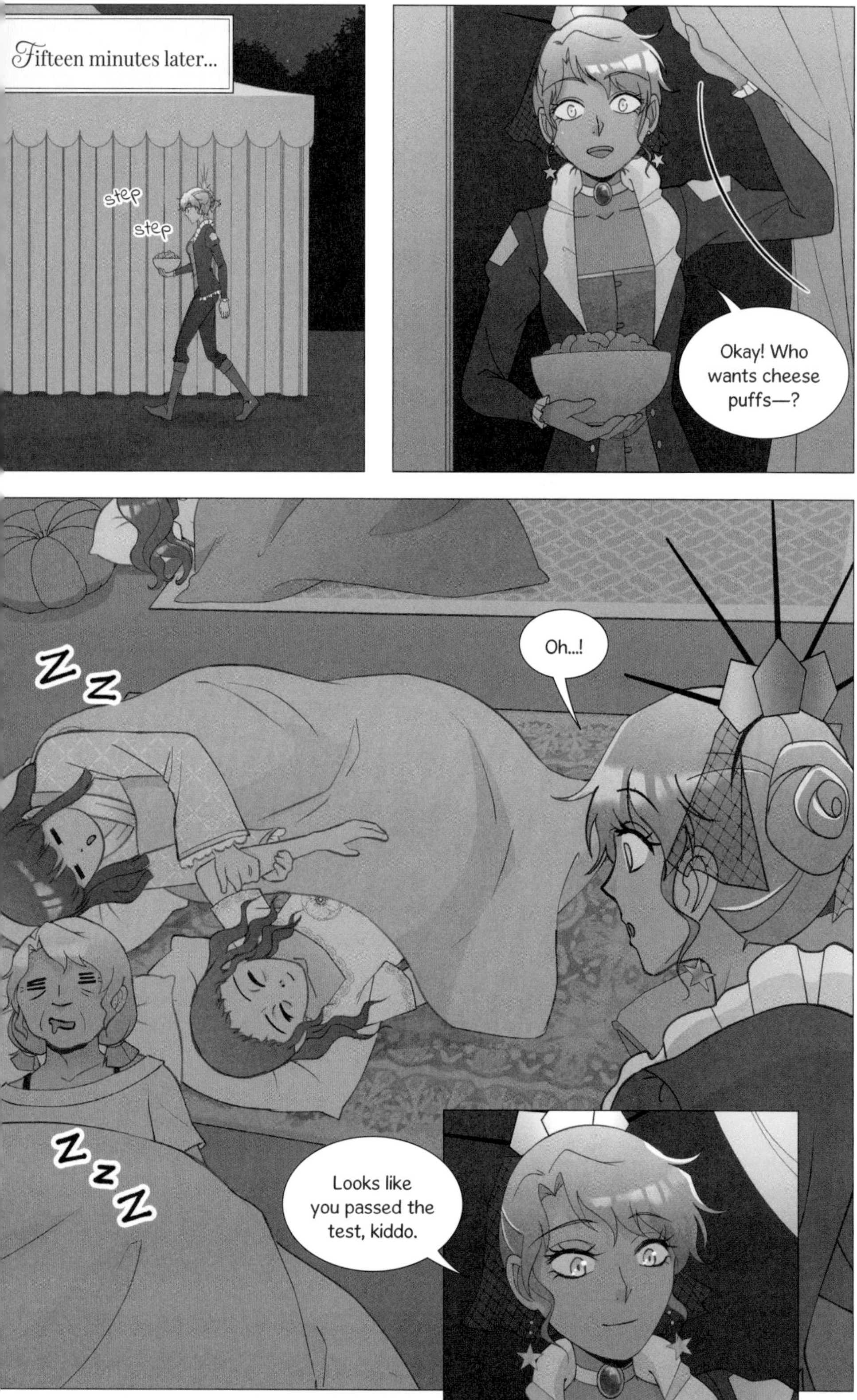
Fifteen minutes later...
step
step
Okay! Who wants cheese puffs—?
Z Z
Oh...!
Z Z Z
Looks like you passed the test, kiddo.

Chapter

7

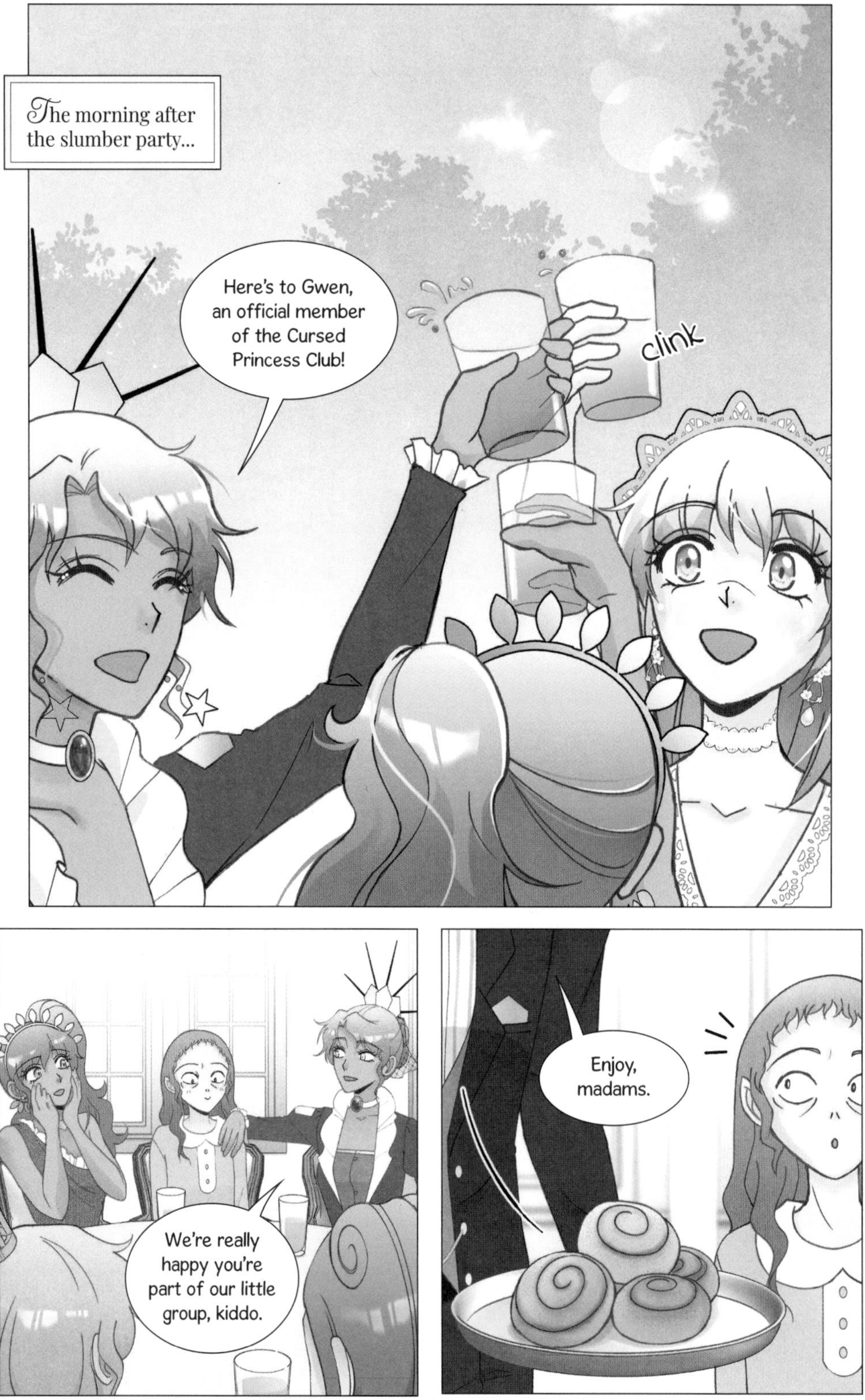
The morning after the slumber party...
Here's to Gwen, an official member of the Cursed Princess Club!
clink
We're really happy you're part of our little group, kiddo.
Enjoy, madams.

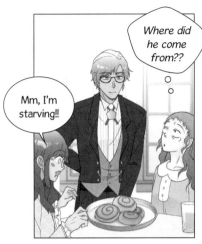

Mm, I'm starving!!

Where did he come from??

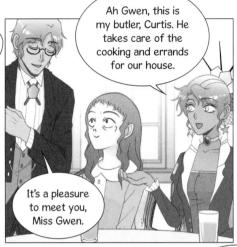

Ah Gwen, this is my butler, Curtis. He takes care of the cooking and errands for our house.

It's a pleasure to meet you, Miss Gwen.

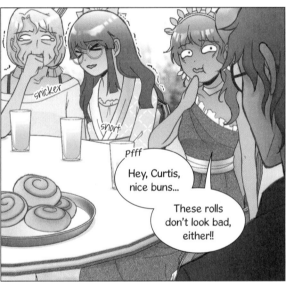

snicker

snort

Pfff

Hey, Curtis, nice buns...

These rolls don't look bad, either!!

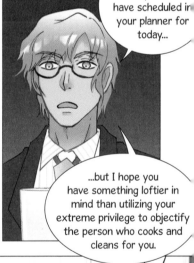

I don't know what you ladies have scheduled in your planner for today...

...but I hope you have something loftier in mind than utilizing your extreme privilege to objectify the person who cooks and cleans for you.

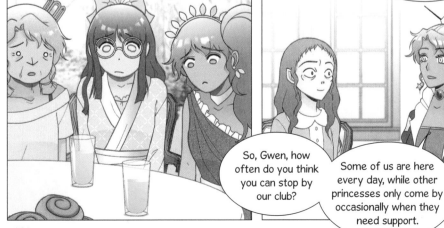

So, Gwen, how often do you think you can stop by our club?

Some of us are here every day, while other princesses only come by occasionally when they need support.

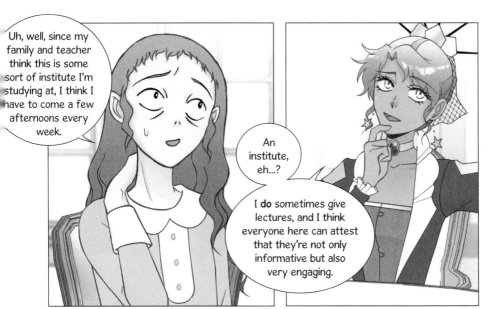

Uh, well, since my family and teacher think this is some sort of institute I'm studying at, I think I have to come a few afternoons every week.

An institute, eh...?

I **do** sometimes give lectures, and I think everyone here can attest that they're not only informative but also very engaging.

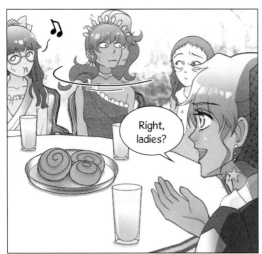

Right, ladies?

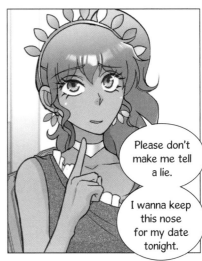

Please don't make me tell a lie.

I wanna keep this nose for my date tonight.

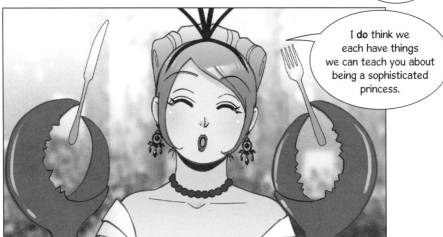

I **do** think we each have things we can teach you about being a sophisticated princess.

165

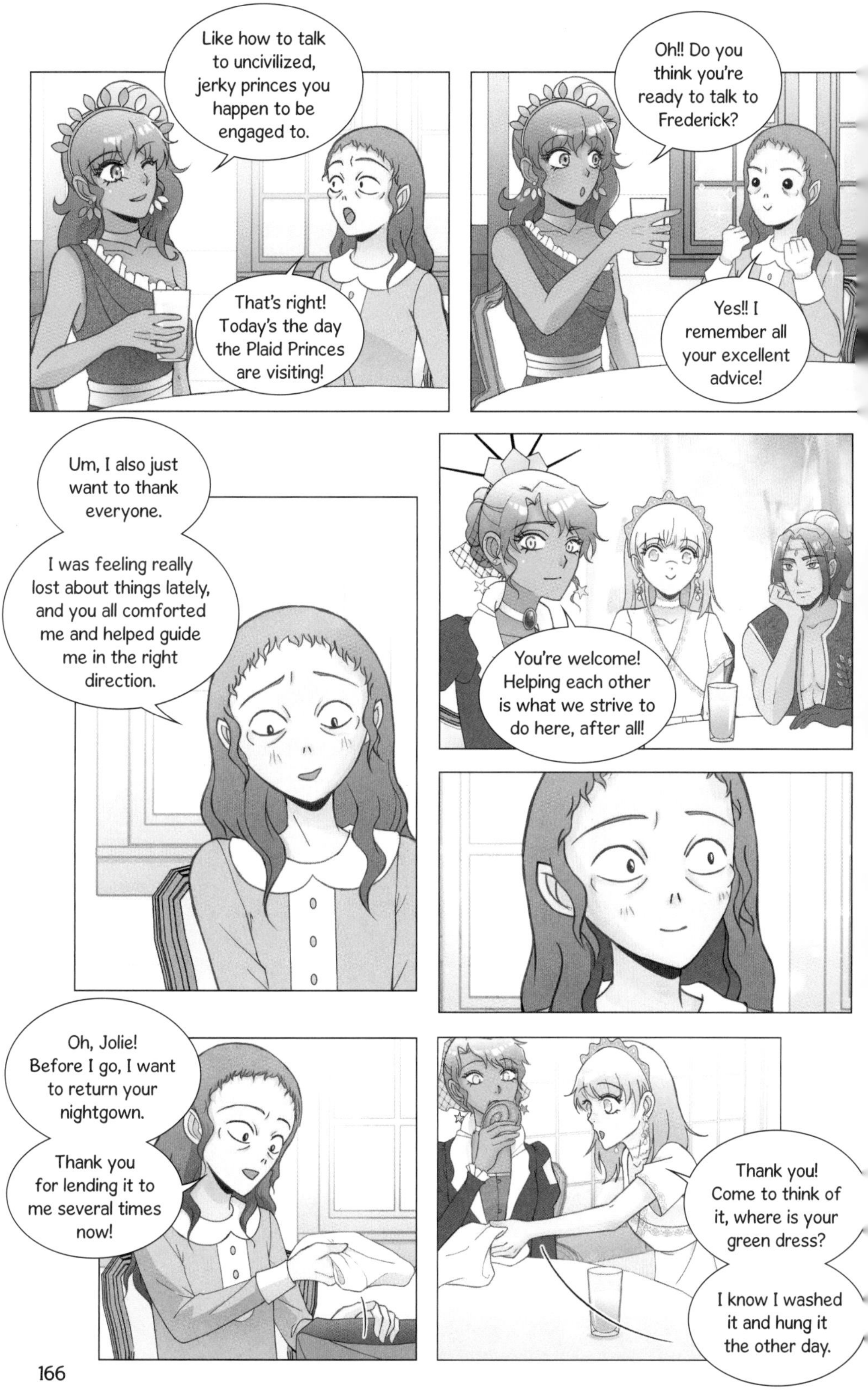
Like how to talk to uncivilized, jerky princes you happen to be engaged to.
That's right! Today's the day the Plaid Princes are visiting!
Oh!! Do you think you're ready to talk to Frederick?
Yes!! I remember all your excellent advice!
Um, I also just want to thank everyone.
I was feeling really lost about things lately, and you all comforted me and helped guide me in the right direction.
You're welcome! Helping each other is what we strive to do here, after all!
Oh, Jolie! Before I go, I want to return your nightgown.
Thank you for lending it to me several times now!
Thank you! Come to think of it, where is your green dress?
I know I washed it and hung it the other day.

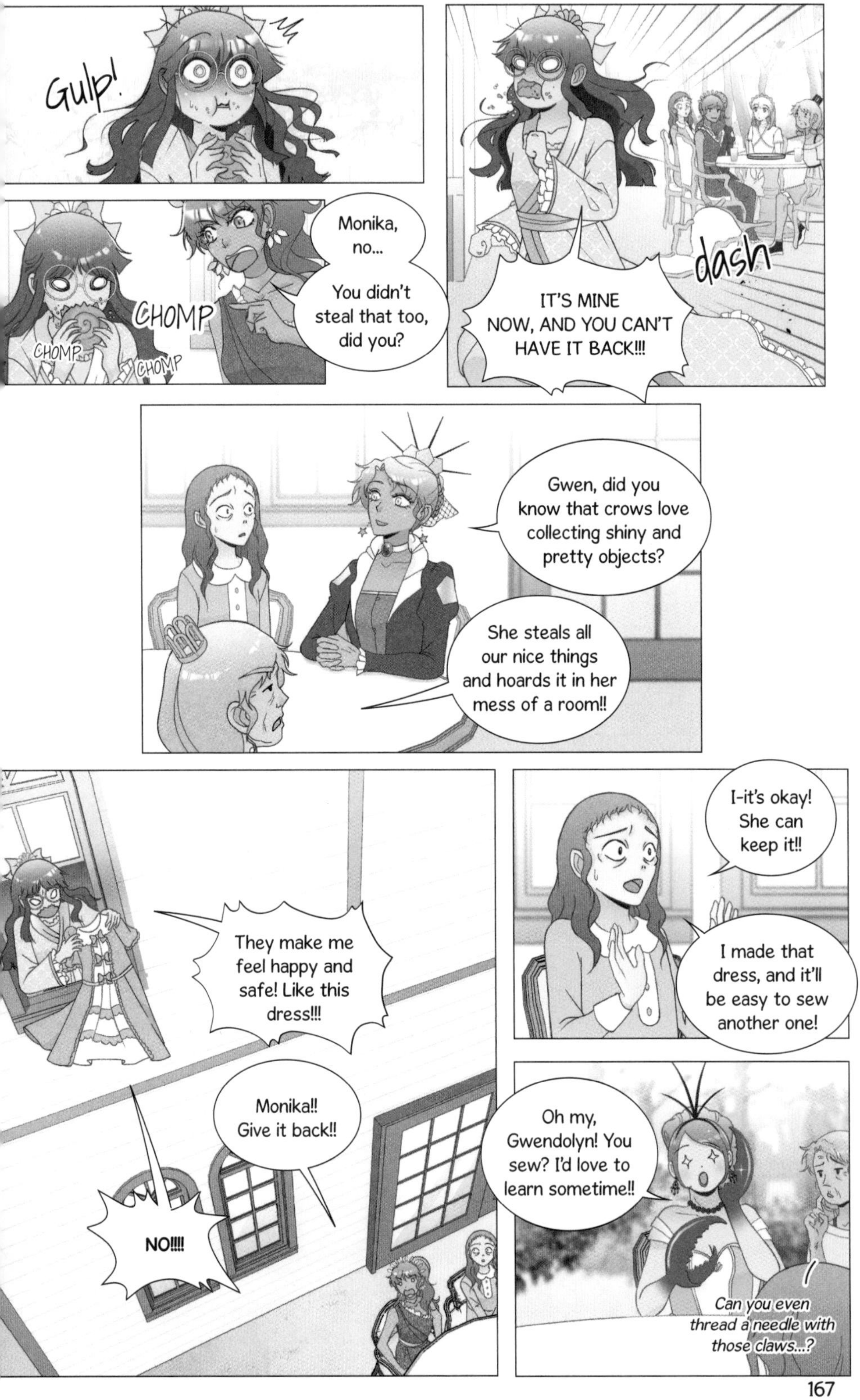
Gulp!
Monika,
no...
You didn't steal that too, did you?
CHOMP
CHOMP
CHOMP
IT'S MINE NOW, AND YOU CAN'T HAVE IT BACK!!!
dash
Gwen, did you know that crows love collecting shiny and pretty objects?
She steals all our nice things and hoards it in her mess of a room!!
They make me feel happy and safe! Like this dress!!!
Monika!! Give it back!!
NO!!!!
I-it's okay! She can keep it!!
I made that dress, and it'll be easy to sew another one!
Oh my, Gwendolyn! You sew? I'd love to learn sometime!!
Can you even thread a needle with those claws...?

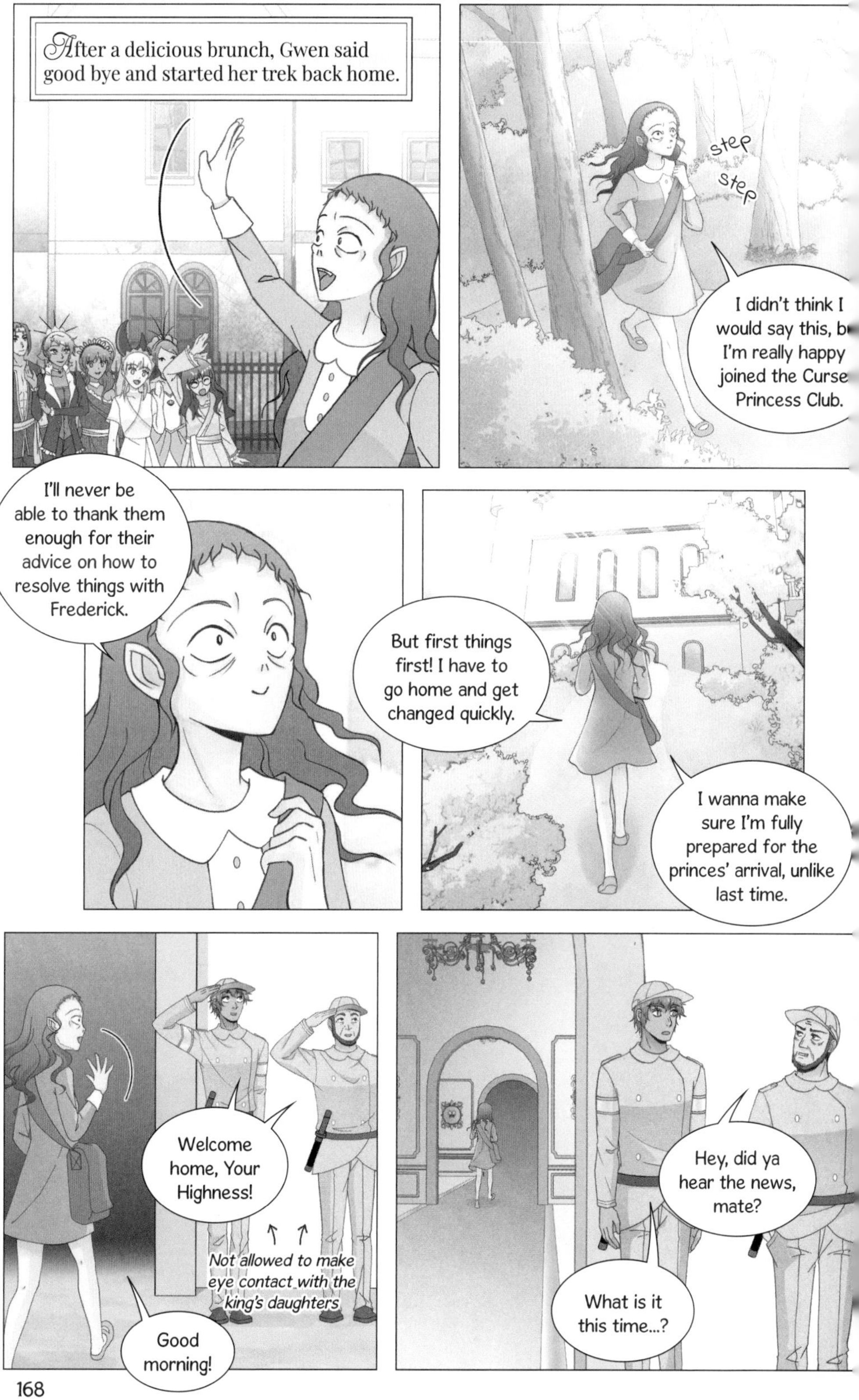
After a delicious brunch, Gwen said good bye and started her trek back home.
step
step
I didn't think I would say this, b
I'm really happy
joined the Curse
Princess Club.
I'll never be able to thank them enough for their advice on how to resolve things with Frederick.
But first things first! I have to go home and get changed quickly.
I wanna make sure I'm fully prepared for the princes' arrival, unlike last time.
Welcome home, Your Highness!
Not allowed to make eye contact with the king's daughters
Good morning!
Hey, did ya hear the news, mate?
What is it this time...?

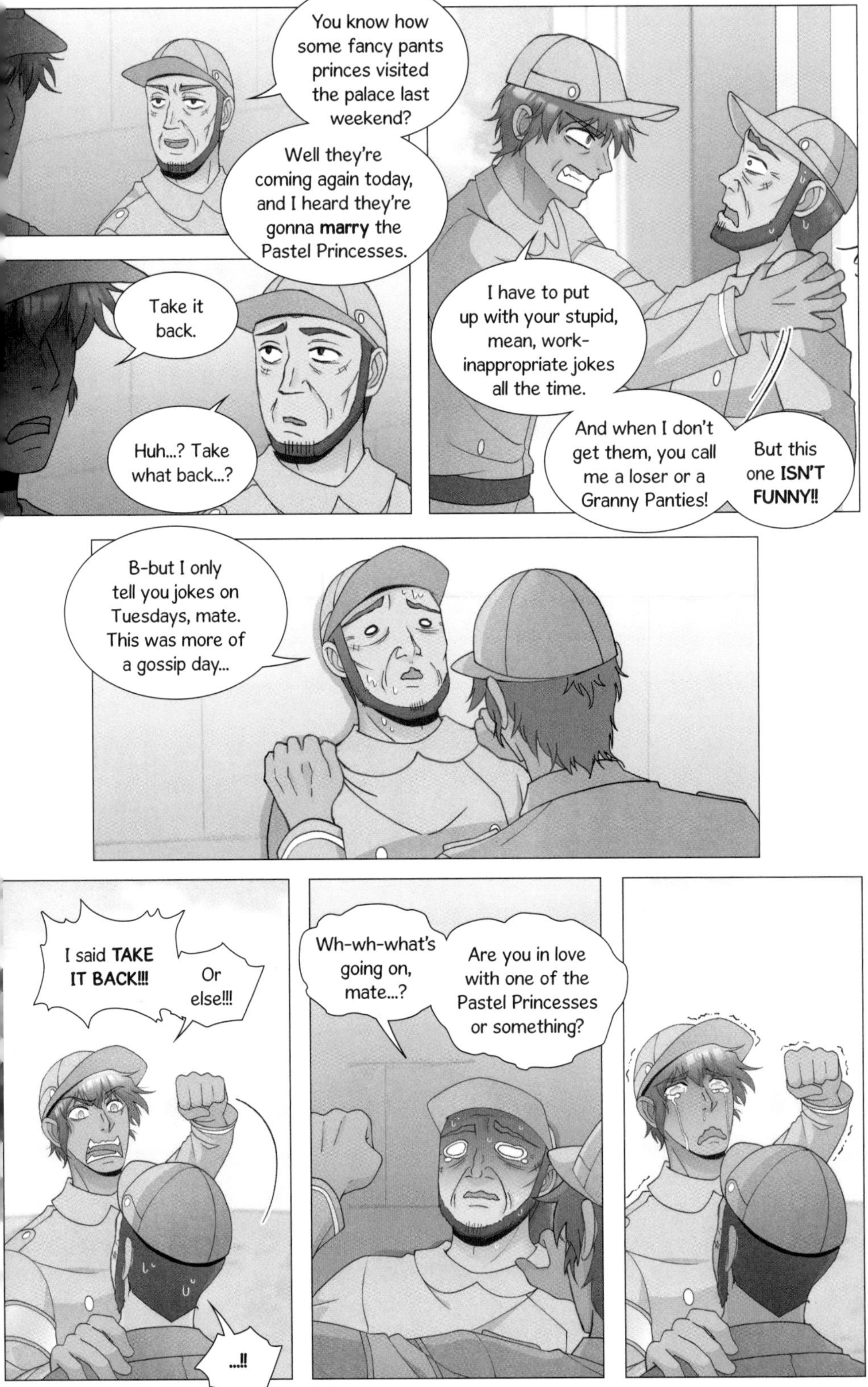

You know how some fancy pants princes visited the palace last weekend?
Well they're coming again today, and I heard they're gonna **marry** the Pastel Princesses.
Take it back.
Huh...? Take what back...?
I have to put up with your stupid, mean, work-inappropriate jokes all the time.
And when I don't get them, you call me a loser or a Granny Panties!
But this one **ISN'T FUNNY!!**
B-but I only tell you jokes on Tuesdays, mate. This was more of a gossip day...
I said **TAKE IT BACK!!!**
Or else!!!
...!!
Wh-wh-what's going on, mate...?
Are you in love with one of the Pastel Princesses or something?

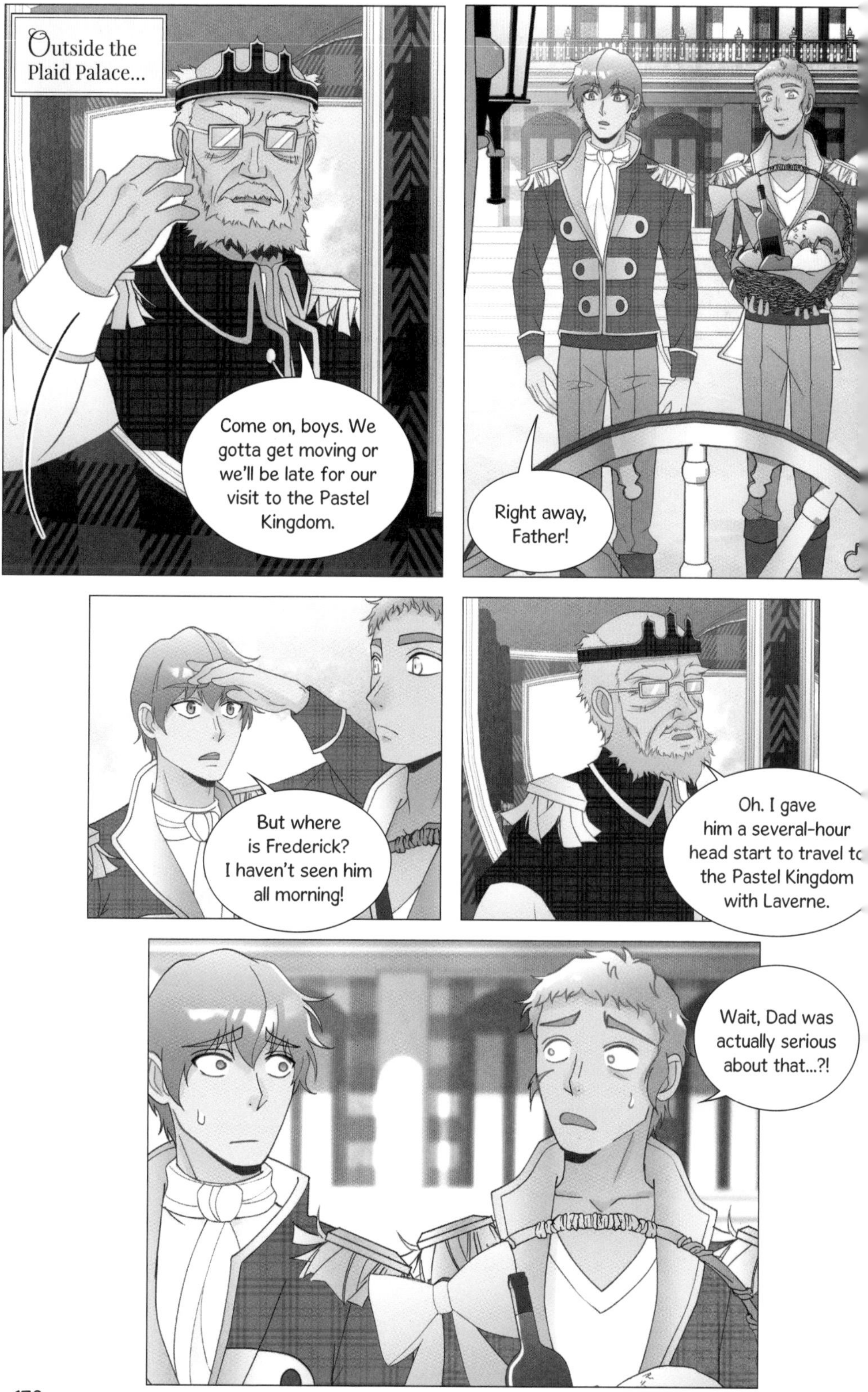
Outside the Plaid Palace...
Come on, boys. We gotta get moving or we'll be late for our visit to the Pastel Kingdom.
Right away, Father!
But where is Frederick? I haven't seen him all morning!
Oh. I gave him a several-hour head start to travel to the Pastel Kingdom with Laverne.
Wait, Dad was actually serious about that...?!

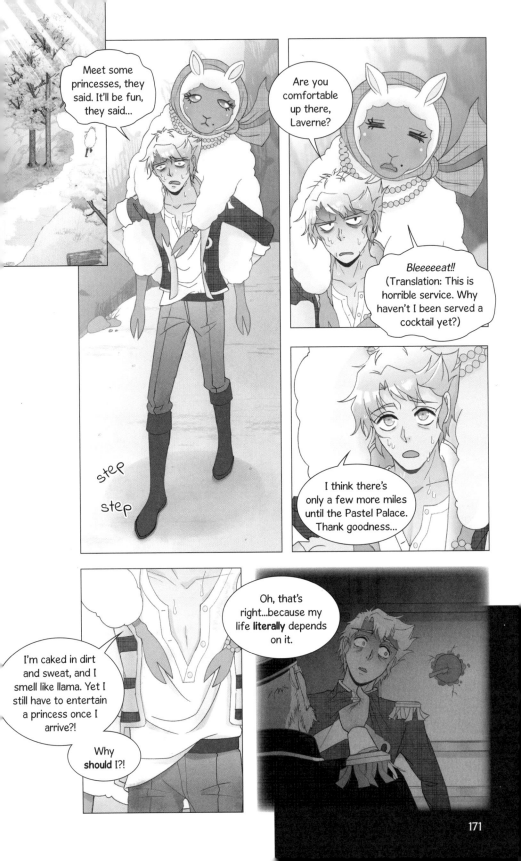

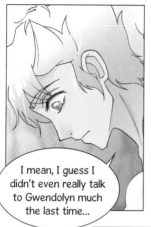
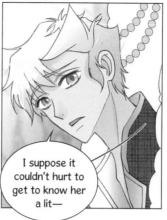
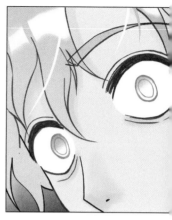

I mean, I guess I didn't even really talk to Gwendolyn much the last time...

I suppose it couldn't hurt to get to know her a lit—

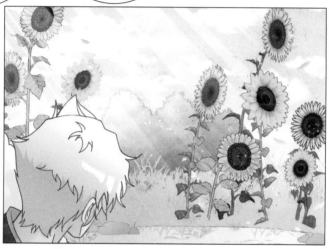

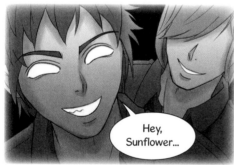

Hey, Sunflower...

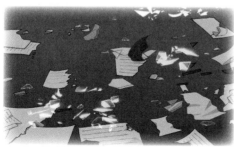

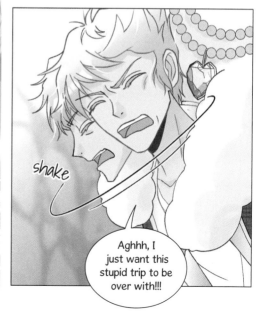

shake

Aghhh, I just want this stupid trip to be over with!!!

172

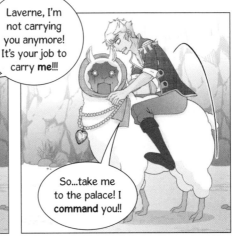

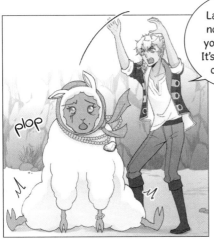

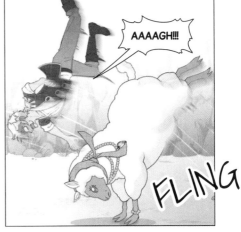

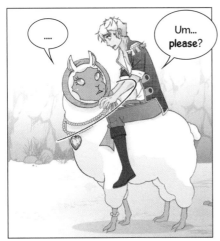

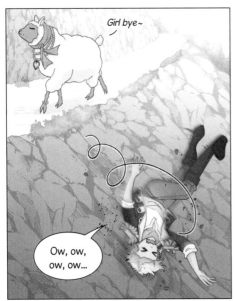

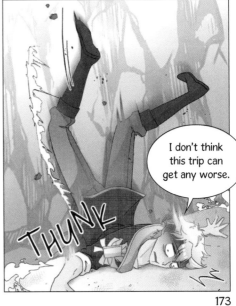

173

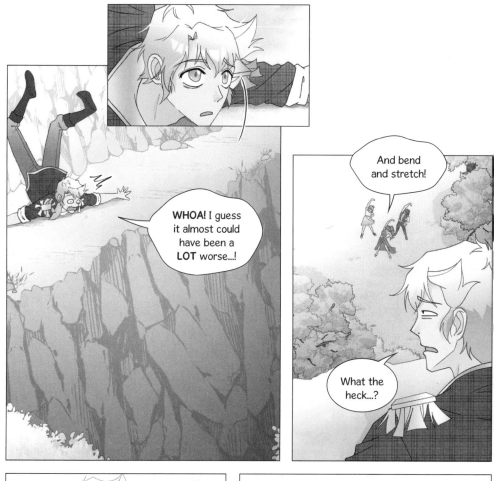

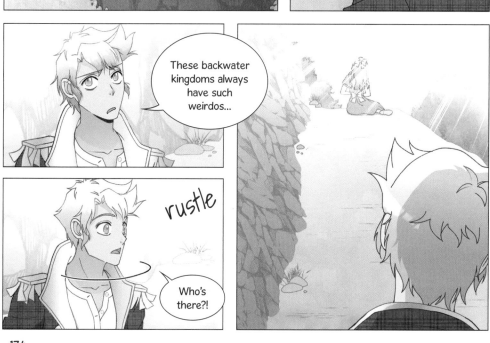

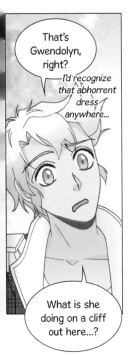

That's Gwendolyn, right?

I'd recognize that abhorrent dress anywhere...

What is she doing on a cliff out here...?

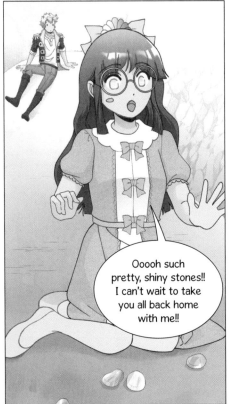

Ooooh such pretty, shiny stones!! I can't wait to take you all back home with me!!

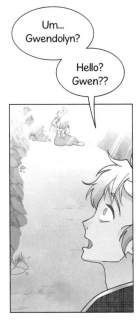

Um... Gwendolyn?

Hello? Gwen??

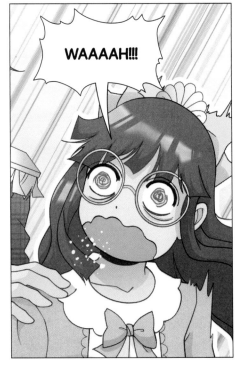

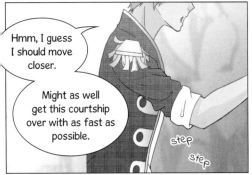

Hmm, I guess I should move closer.

Might as well get this courtship over with as fast as possible.

step
step

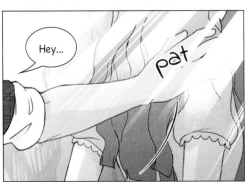

Hey...

pat

WAAAAH!!!

175

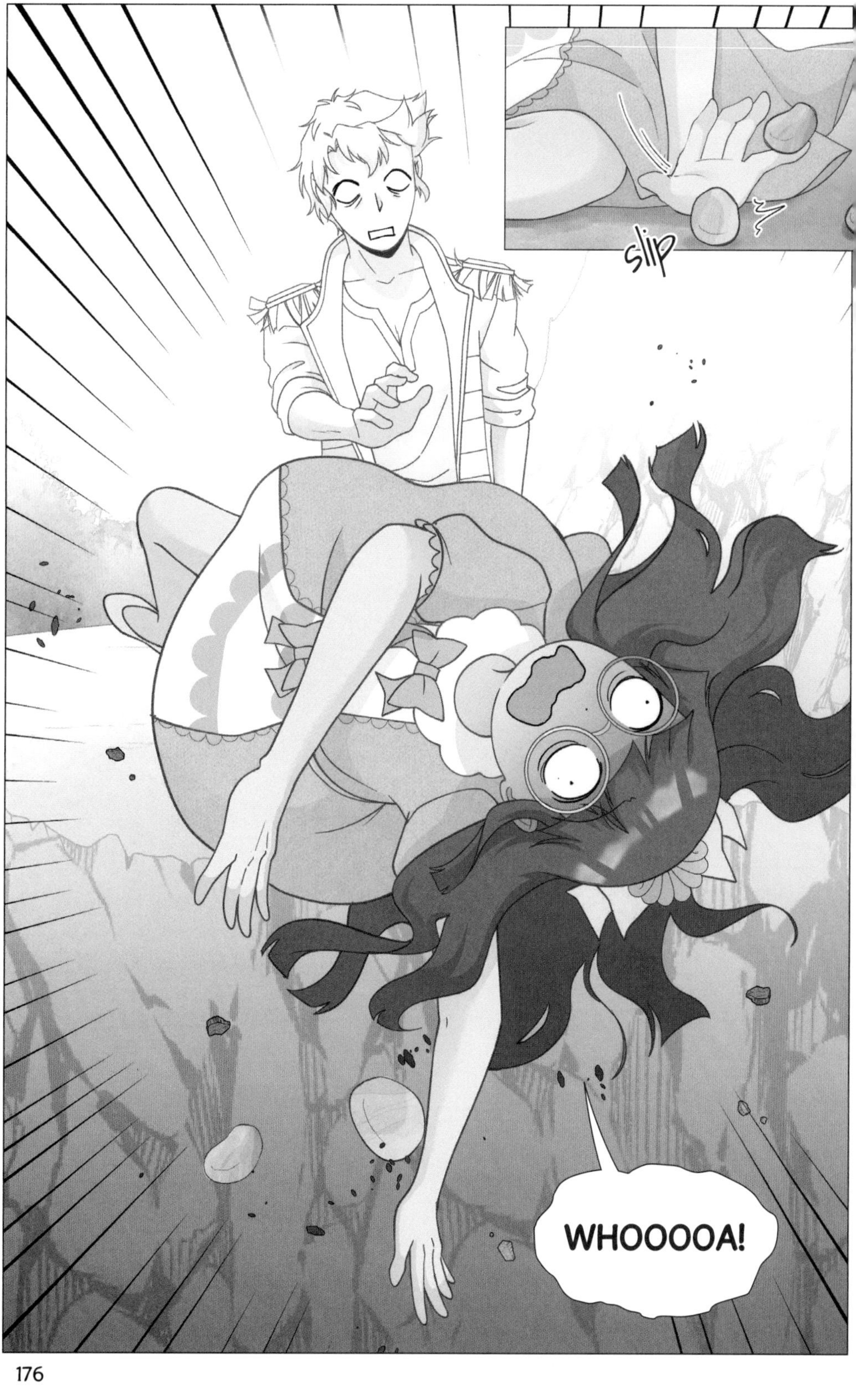
slip
WHOOOOA!

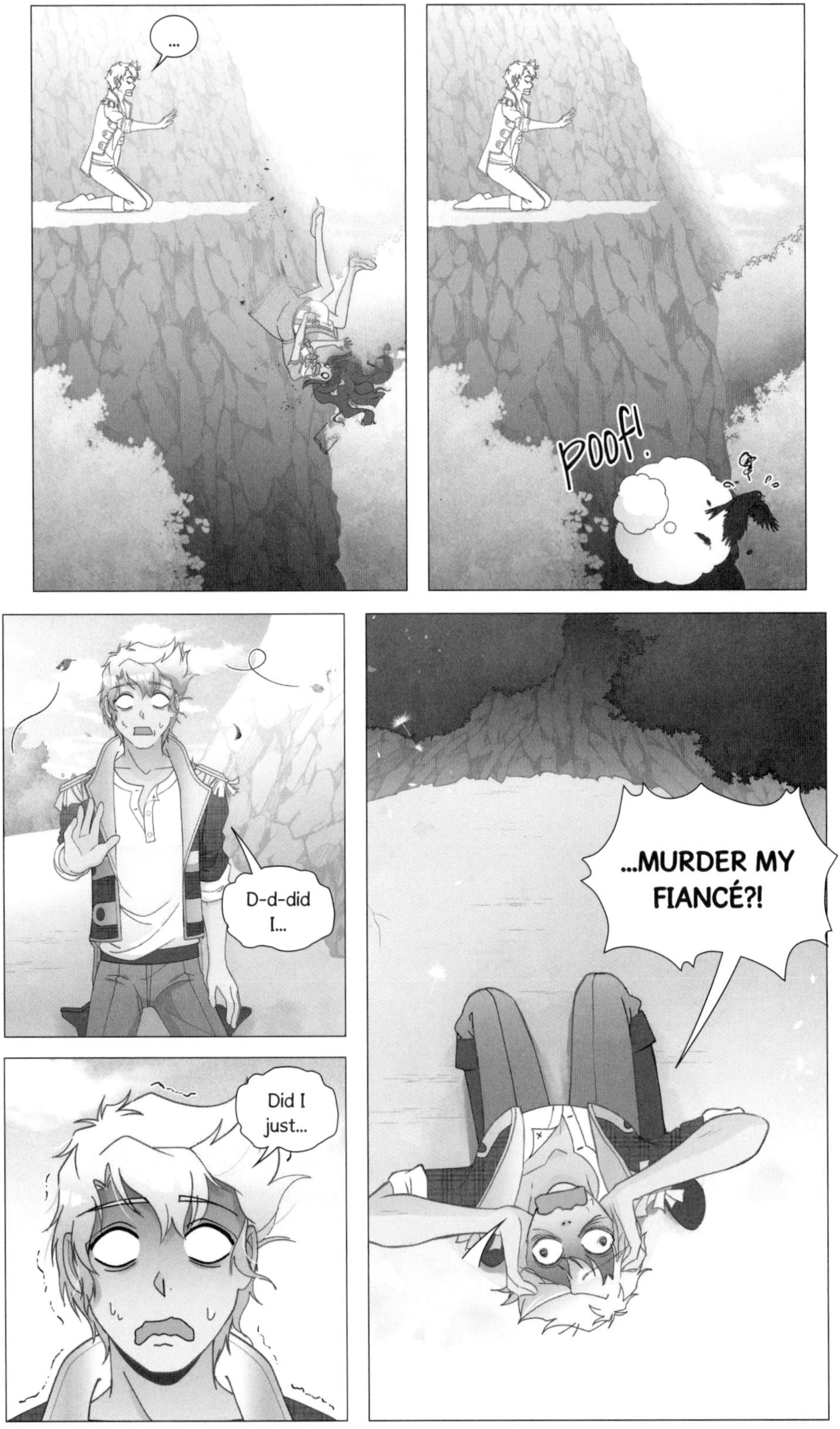
...
POOF!
D-d-did I...
Did I just...
...MURDER MY FIANCÉ?!

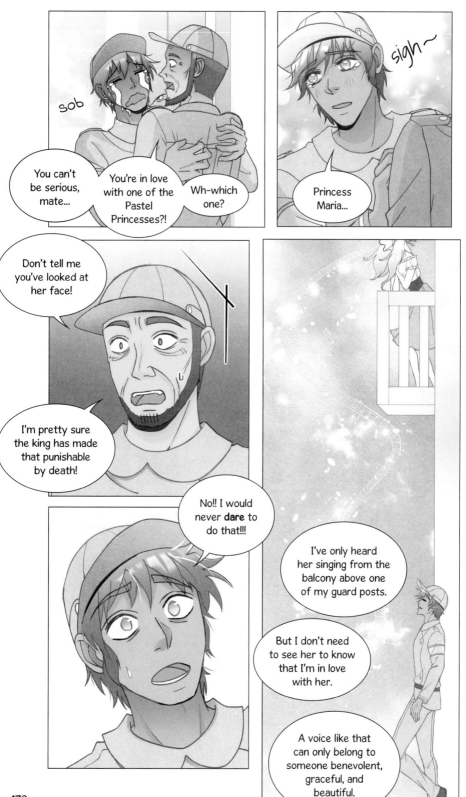

I had it in my ten-year plan to gradually rise up the ranks and eventually ask the king for her hand in marriage.

But I guess I'll just have to speak to him now and demand that he cancel Princess Maria's engagement!

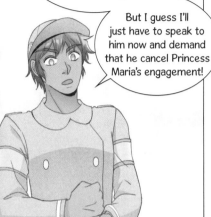

Okay, hold up... You think the king would cancel his daughter's engagement to an incredibly rich, hot, and powerful prince...

and hand her over to a shabby **guard** that he personally underpays?

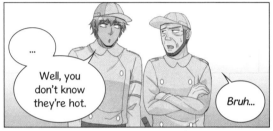

...

Well, you don't know they're hot.

Bruh...

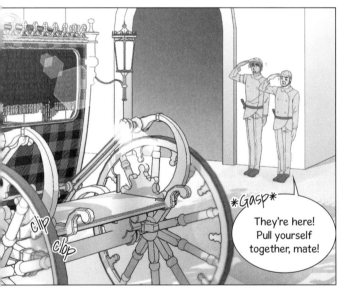

clip

clop

Gasp

They're here! Pull yourself together, mate!

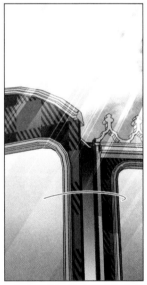

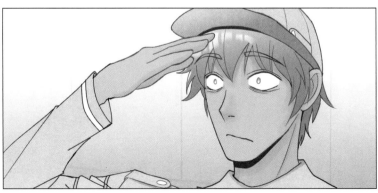

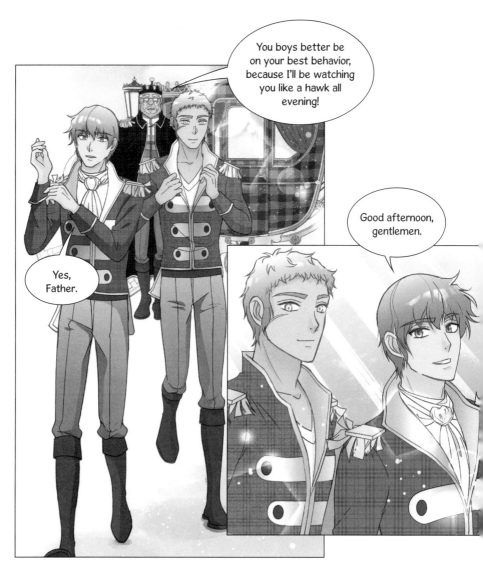

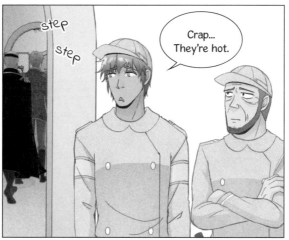

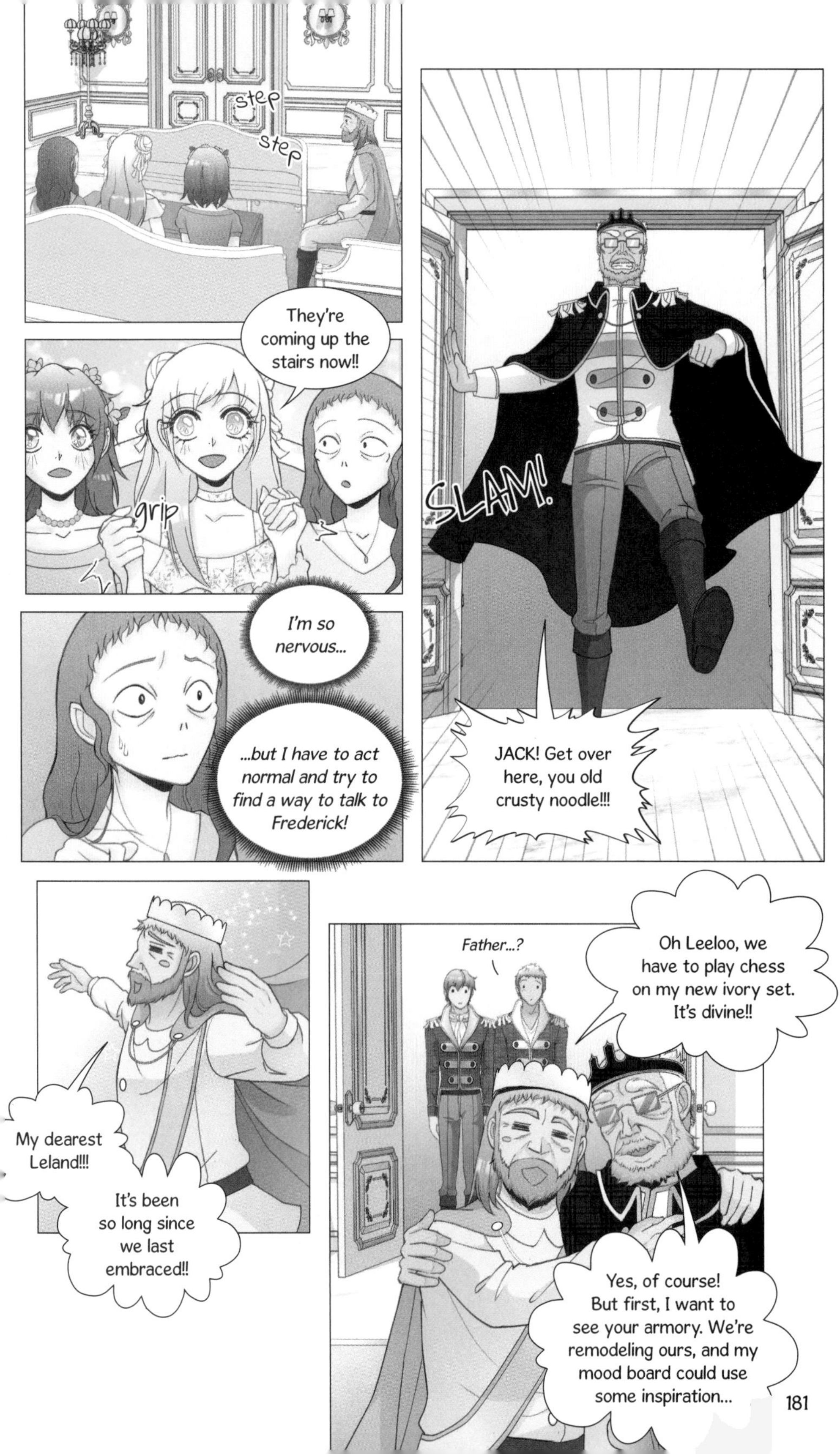
step
step
They're coming up the stairs now!!
grip
I'm so nervous...
...but I have to act normal and try to find a way to talk to Frederick!
SLAM!
JACK! Get over here, you old crusty noodle!!!
My dearest Leland!!!
It's been so long since we last embraced!!
Father...?
Oh Leeloo, we have to play chess on my new ivory set. It's divine!!
Yes, of course! But first, I want to see your armory. We're remodeling ours, and my mood board could use some inspiration...

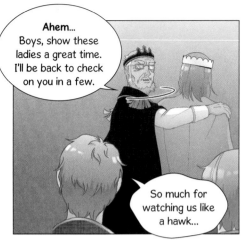

Ahem... Boys, show these ladies a great time. I'll be back to check on you in a few.

So much for watching us like a hawk...

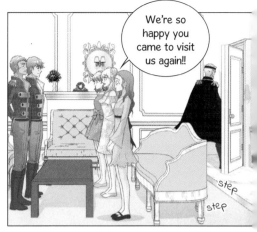

We're so happy you came to visit us again!!

step
step

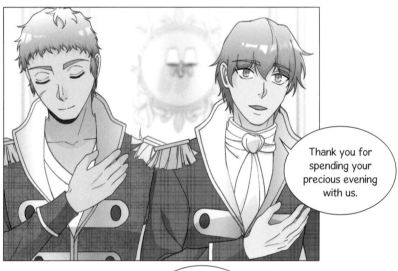

Thank you for spending your precious evening with us.

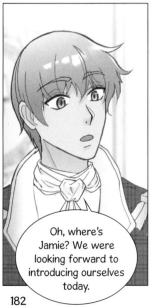

Oh, where's Jamie? We were looking forward to introducing ourselves today.

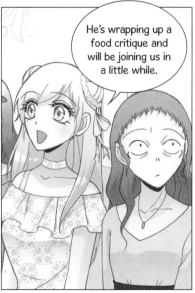

He's wrapping up a food critique and will be joining us in a little while.

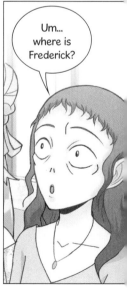

Um... where is Frederick?

182

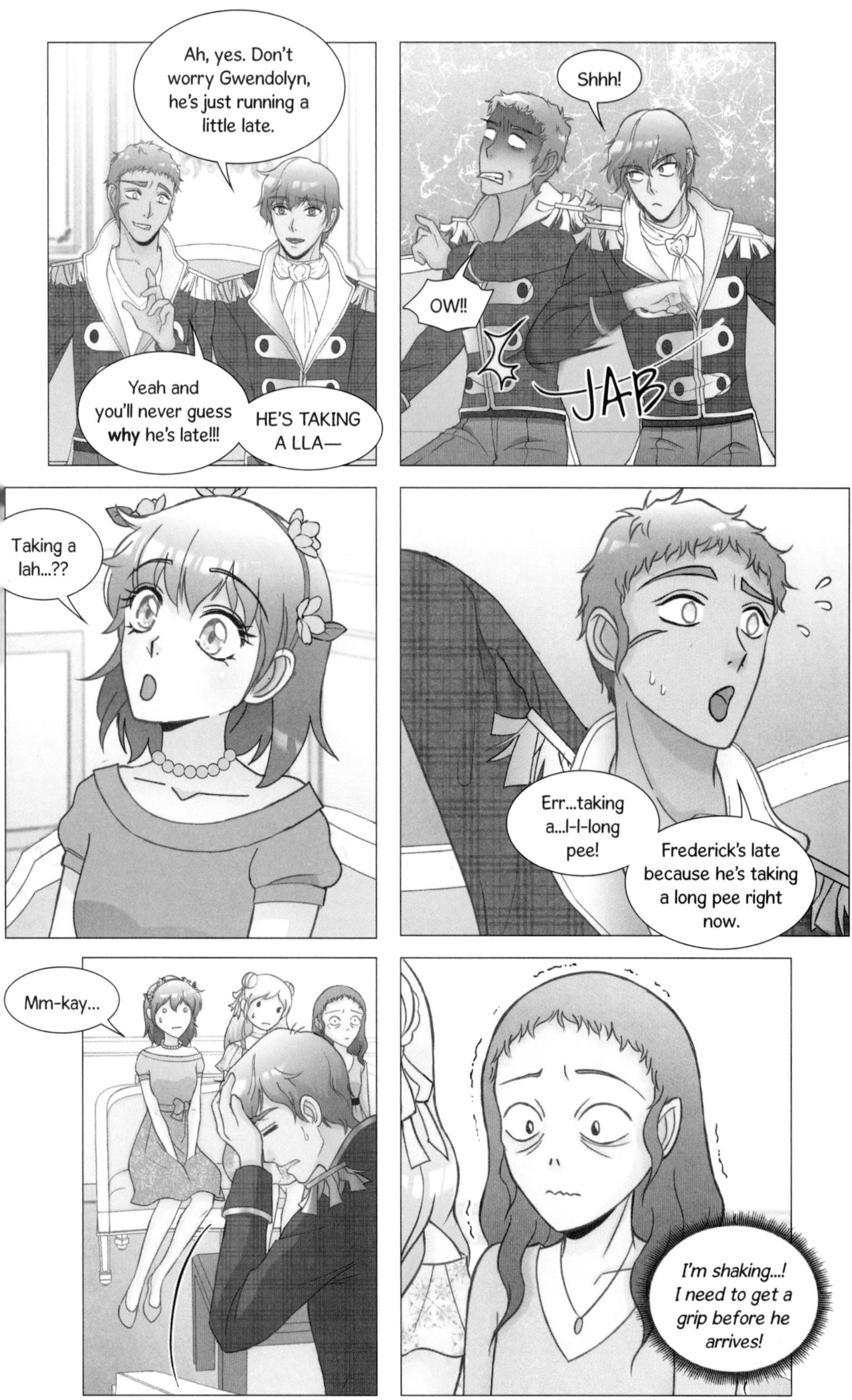

Ah, yes. Don't worry Gwendolyn, he's just running a little late.
Yeah and you'll never guess **why** he's late!!!
HE'S TAKING A LLA—
Shhh!
OW!!
JAB
Taking a lah...??
Err...taking a...l-l-long pee!
Frederick's late because he's taking a long pee right now.
Mm-kay...
I'm shaking...! I need to get a grip before he arrives!

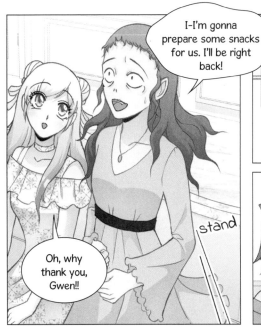

I-I'm gonna prepare some snacks for us. I'll be right back!

stand

Oh, why thank you, Gwen!!

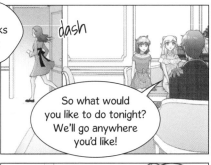

dash

So what would you like to do tonight? We'll go anywhere you'd like!

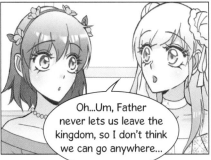

Oh...Um, Father never lets us leave the kingdom, so I don't think we can go anywhere...

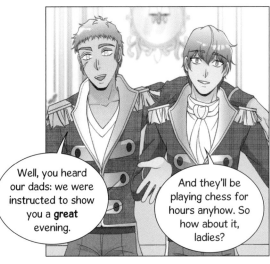

Well, you heard our dads: we were instructed to show you a **great** evening.

And they'll be playing chess for hours anyhow. So how about it, ladies?

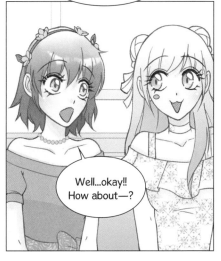

Well...okay!! How about—?

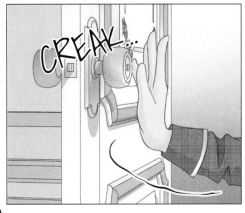

CREAK...

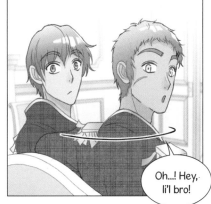

Oh...! Hey, li'l bro!

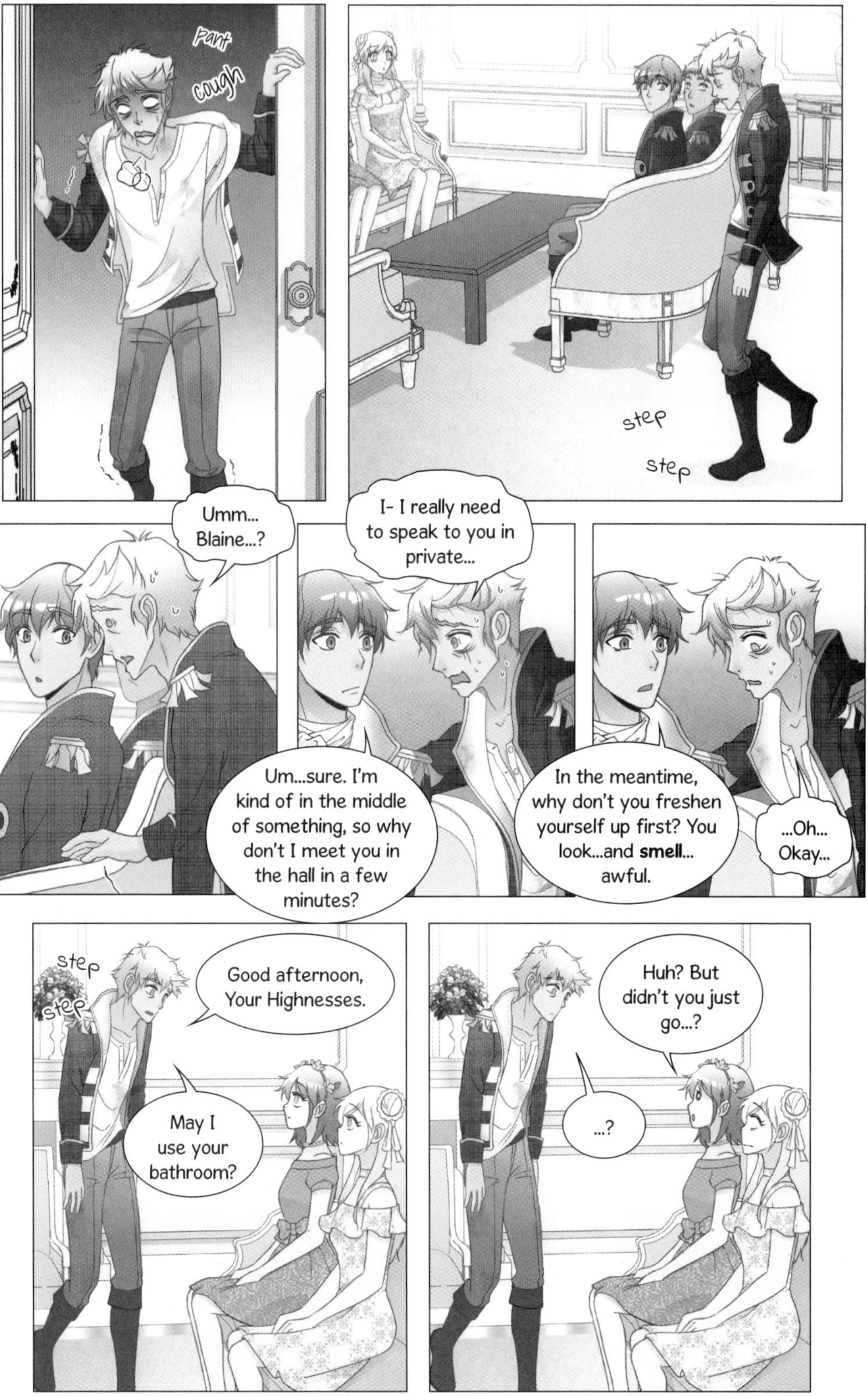
pant
cough
step
step
Umm... Blaine...?
I- I really need to speak to you in private...
Um...sure. I'm kind of in the middle of something, so why don't I meet you in the hall in a few minutes?
In the meantime, why don't you freshen yourself up first? You look...and **smell**... awful.
...Oh... Okay...
step
step
Good afternoon, Your Highnesses.
May I use your bathroom?
Huh? But didn't you just go...?
...?

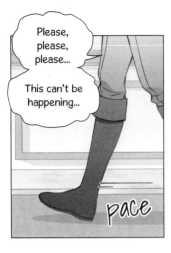

Please, please, please...

This can't be happening...

pace

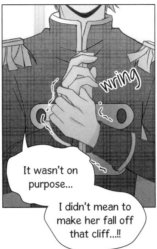

wring

It wasn't on purpose...

I didn't mean to make her fall off that cliff...!!

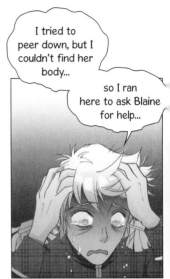

I tried to peer down, but I couldn't find her body...

so I ran here to ask Blaine for help...

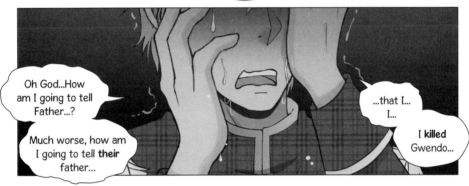

Oh God...How am I going to tell Father...?

Much worse, how am I going to tell **their** father...

...that I... I...

I **killed** Gwendo...

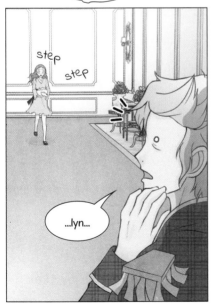

step

step

...lyn...

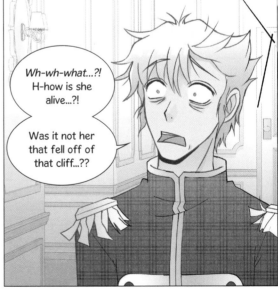

Wh-wh-what...?! H-how is she alive...?!

Was it not her that fell off of that cliff...??

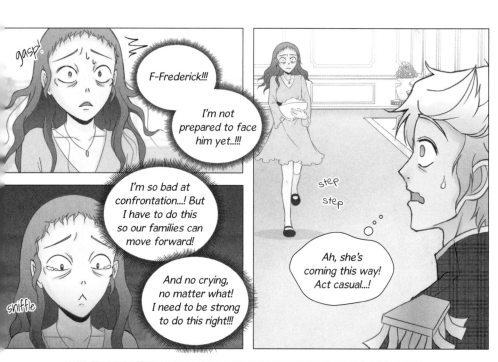

gasp!

F-Frederick!!!

I'm not prepared to face him yet..!!!

sniffle

I'm so bad at confrontation...! But I have to do this so our families can move forward!

And no crying, no matter what! I need to be strong to do this right!!!

step
step

Ah, she's coming this way! Act casual...!

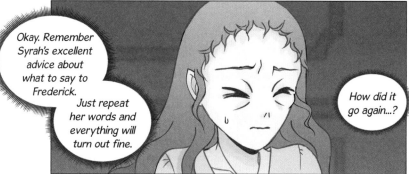

Okay. Remember Syrah's excellent advice about what to say to Frederick.

Just repeat her words and everything will turn out fine.

How did it go again...?

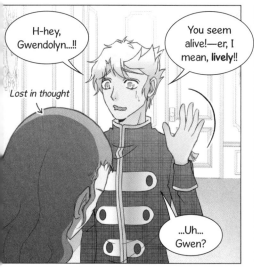

H-hey, Gwendolyn...!!

You seem alive!—er, I mean, **lively**!!

Lost in thought

...Uh... Gwen?

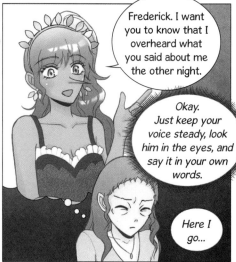

Frederick. I want you to know that I overheard what you said about me the other night.

Okay. Just keep your voice steady, look him in the eyes, and say it in your own words.

Here I go...

187

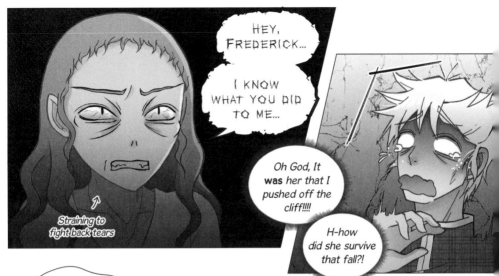

HEY, FREDERICK...

I KNOW WHAT YOU DID TO ME...

Straining to fight back tears

Oh God, It **was** her that I pushed off the cliff!!!!

H-how did she survive that fall?!

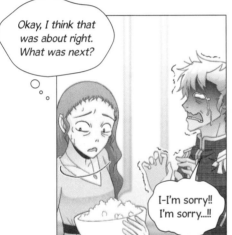

Okay, I think that was about right. What was next?

I-I'm sorry!! I'm sorry...!!

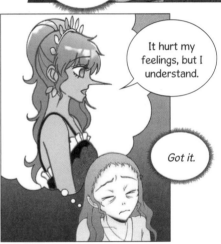

It hurt my feelings, but I understand.

Got it.

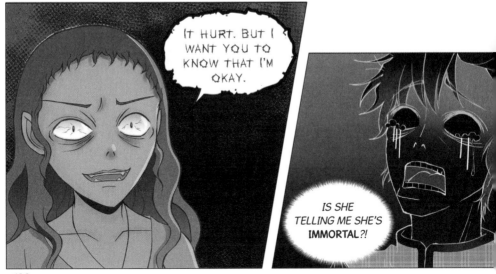

IT HURT. BUT I WANT YOU TO KNOW THAT I'M OKAY.

IS SHE TELLING ME SHE'S **IMMORTAL**?!

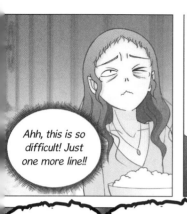

Ahh, this is so difficult! Just one more line!!

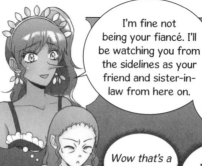

I'm fine not being your fiancé. I'll be watching you from the sidelines as your friend and sister-in-law from here on.

I just want you and everyone in our families to be happy.

Wow that's a mouthful.

Just keep it short and get it over with...!!

inhale~

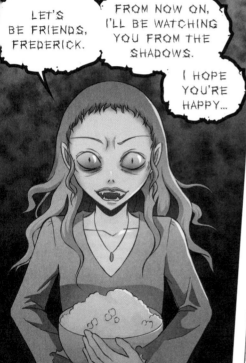

LET'S BE FRIENDS, FREDERICK.

FROM NOW ON, I'LL BE WATCHING YOU FROM THE SHADOWS.

I HOPE YOU'RE HAPPY...

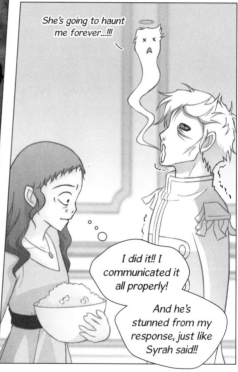

She's going to haunt me forever...!!!

I did it!! I communicated it all properly!

And he's stunned from my response, just like Syrah said!!

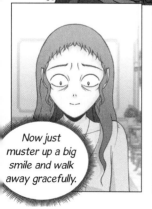

Now just muster up a big smile and walk away gracefully.

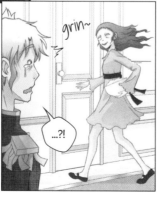

grin~

....?!

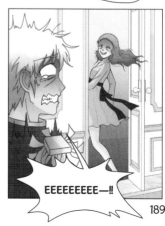

EEEEEEEEE—!!

189

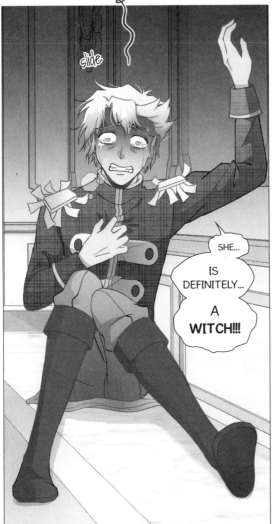

slide

SHE...

IS DEFINITELY...

A WITCH!!!

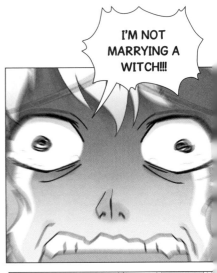

I'M NOT MARRYING A WITCH!!!

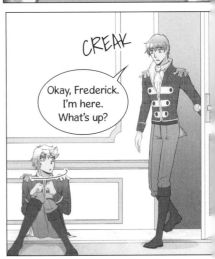

CREAK

Okay, Frederick. I'm here. What's up?

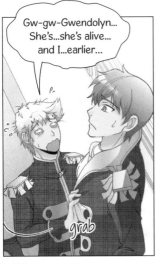

Gw-gw-Gwendolyn... She's...she's alive... and I...earlier...

grab

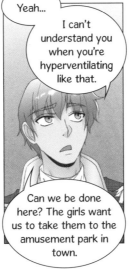

Yeah...

I can't understand you when you're hyperventilating like that.

Can we be done here? The girls want us to take them to the amusement park in town.

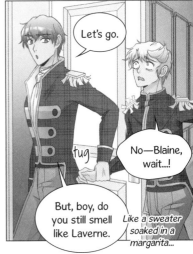

Let's go.

tug

No—Blaine, wait...!

But, boy, do you still smell like Laverne.

Like a sweater soaked in a margarita...

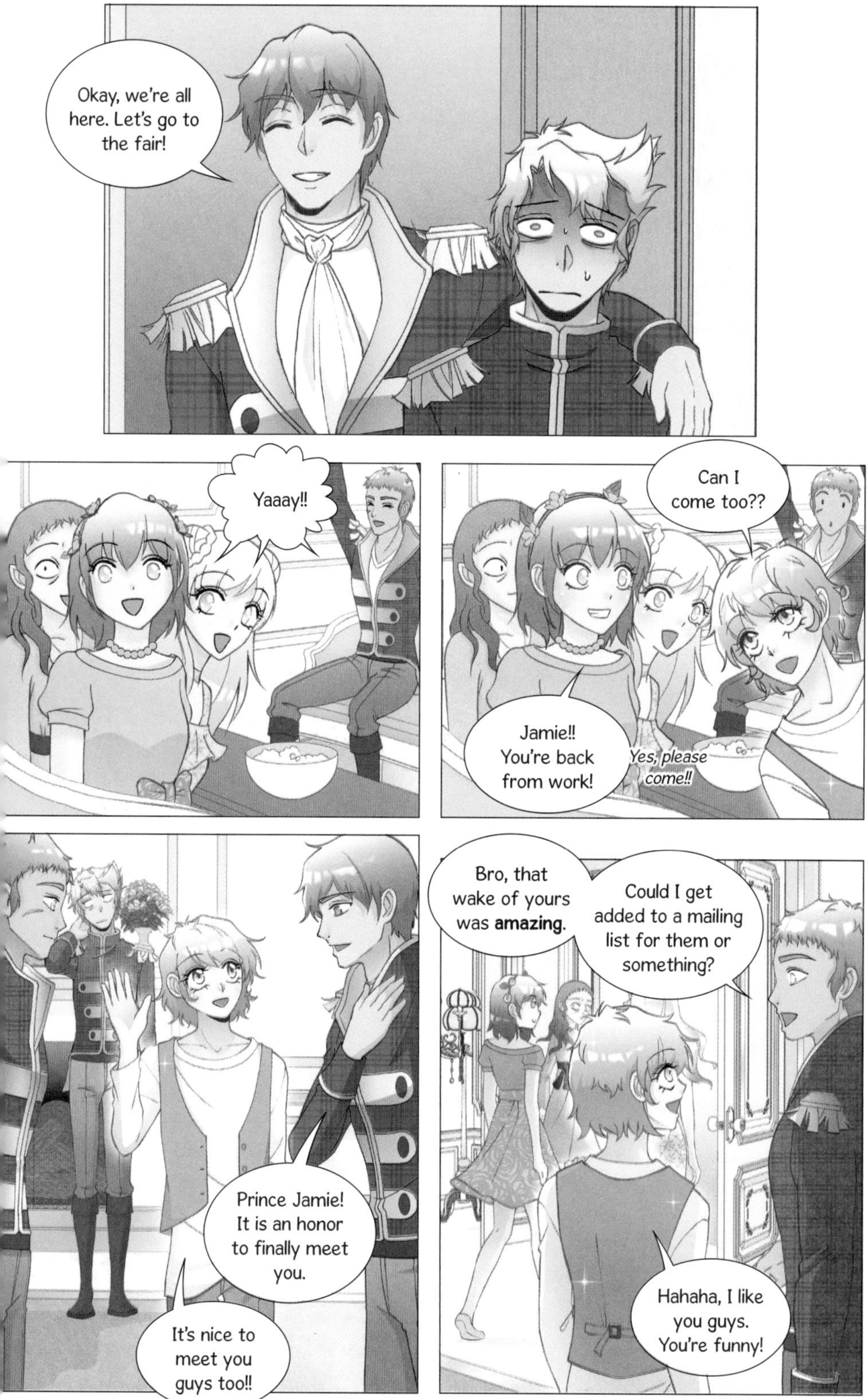
Okay, we're all here. Let's go to the fair!
Yaaay!!
Can I come too??
Jamie!! You're back from work!
Yes, please come!!
Prince Jamie! It is an honor to finally meet you.
It's nice to meet you guys too!!
Bro, that wake of yours was **amazing**.
Could I get added to a mailing list for them or something?
Hahaha, I like you guys. You're funny!

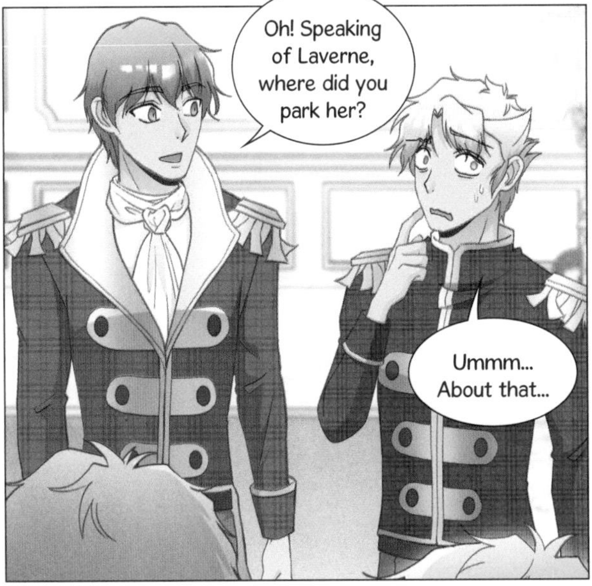
Oh! Speaking of Laverne, where did you park her?
Ummm... About that...

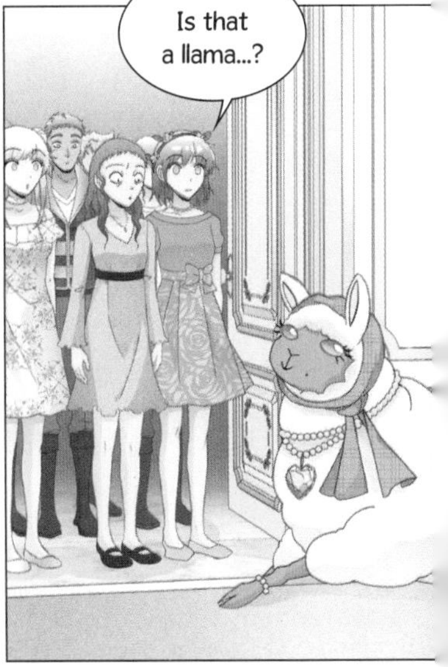
Is that a llama...?

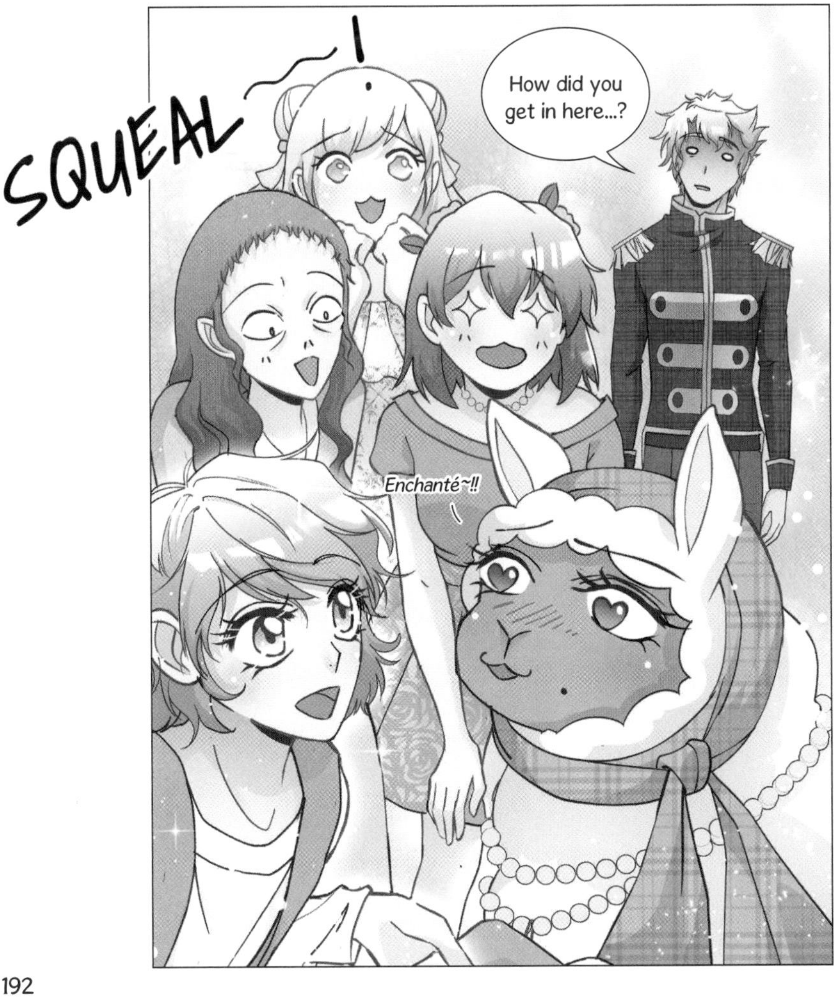
SQUEAL~!
How did you get in here...?
Enchanté~!!

Chapter

8

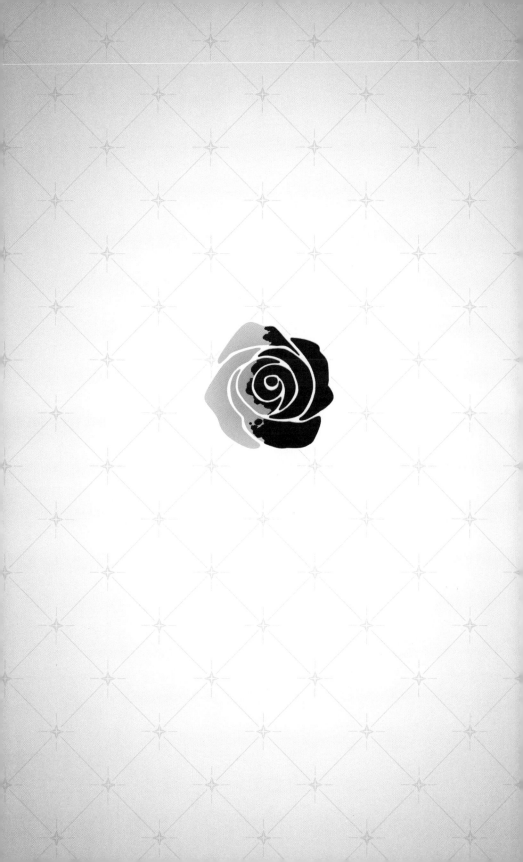

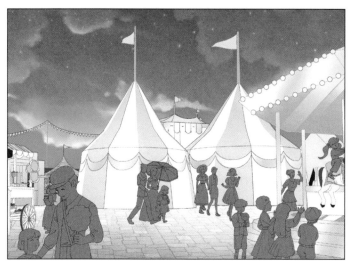

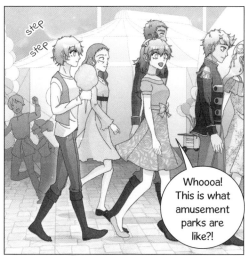

Whoooa! This is what amusement parks are like?!

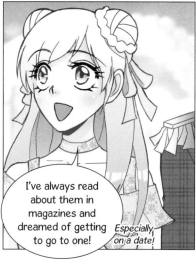

I've always read about them in magazines and dreamed of getting to go to one!

Especially on a date!

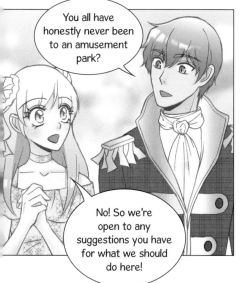

You all have honestly never been to an amusement park?

No! So we're open to any suggestions you have for what we should do here!

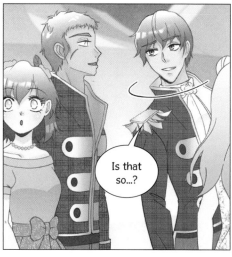

Is that so...?

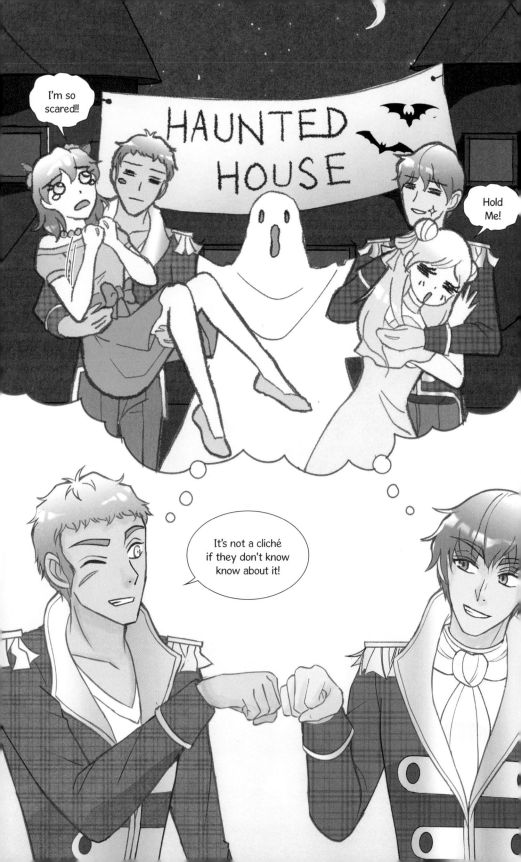

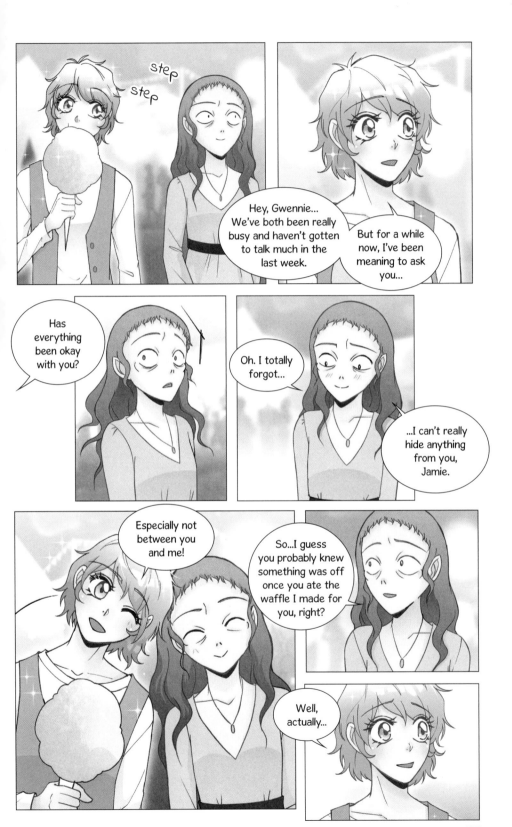

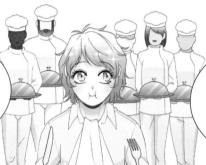

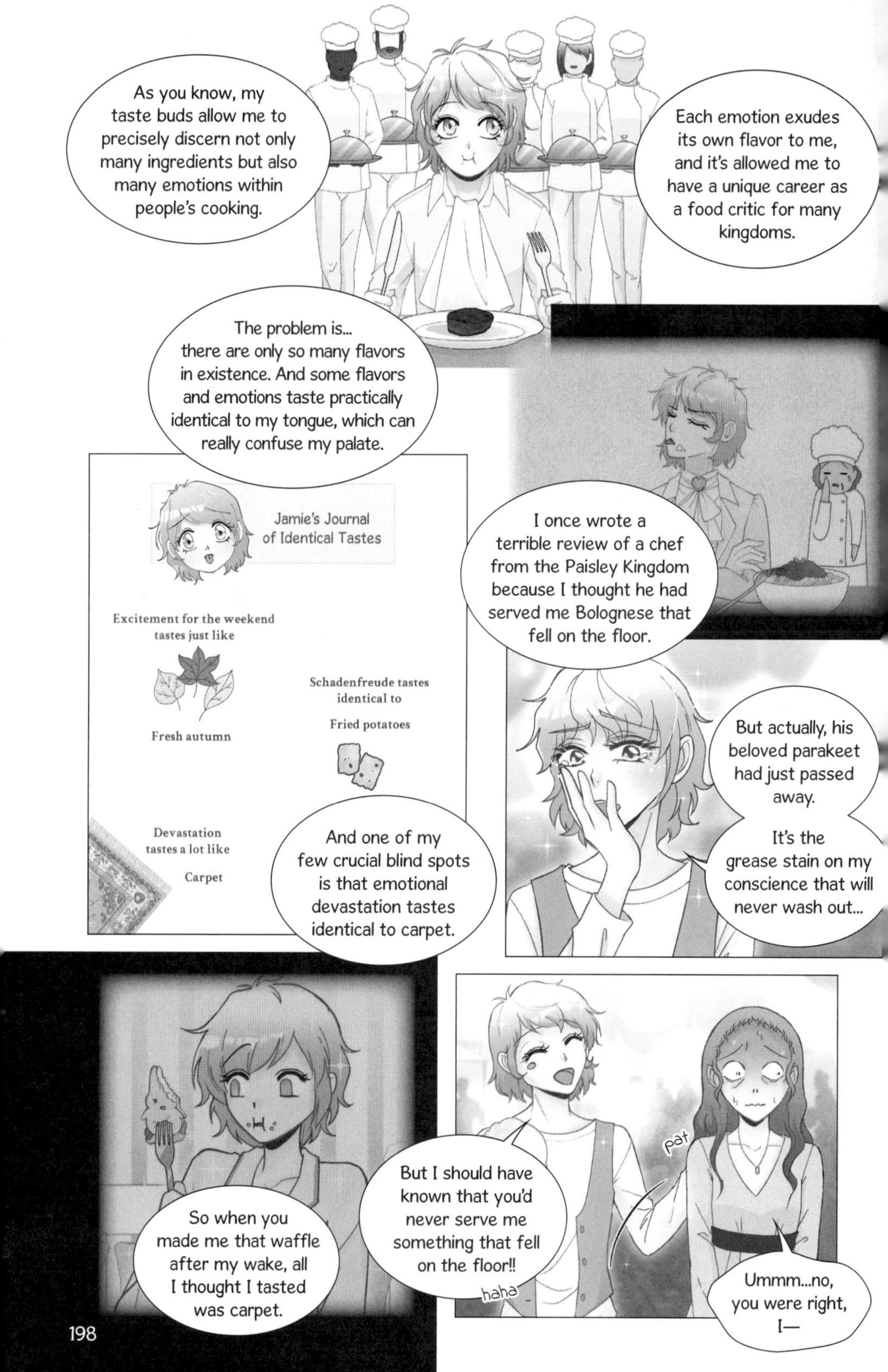

As you know, my taste buds allow me to precisely discern not only many ingredients but also many emotions within people's cooking.

Each emotion exudes its own flavor to me, and it's allowed me to have a unique career as a food critic for many kingdoms.

The problem is... there are only so many flavors in existence. And some flavors and emotions taste practically identical to my tongue, which can really confuse my palate.

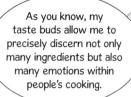

Jamie's Journal of Identical Tastes

Excitement for the weekend tastes just like

Fresh autumn

Schadenfreude tastes identical to

Fried potatoes

Devastation tastes a lot like

Carpet

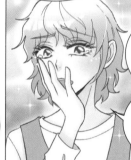

I once wrote a terrible review of a chef from the Paisley Kingdom because I thought he had served me Bolognese that fell on the floor.

But actually, his beloved parakeet had just passed away.

It's the grease stain on my conscience that will never wash out...

And one of my few crucial blind spots is that emotional devastation tastes identical to carpet.

So when you made me that waffle after my wake, all I thought I tasted was carpet.

But I should have known that you'd never serve me something that fell on the floor!!

haha

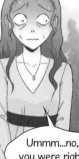

pat

Ummm...no, you were right, I—

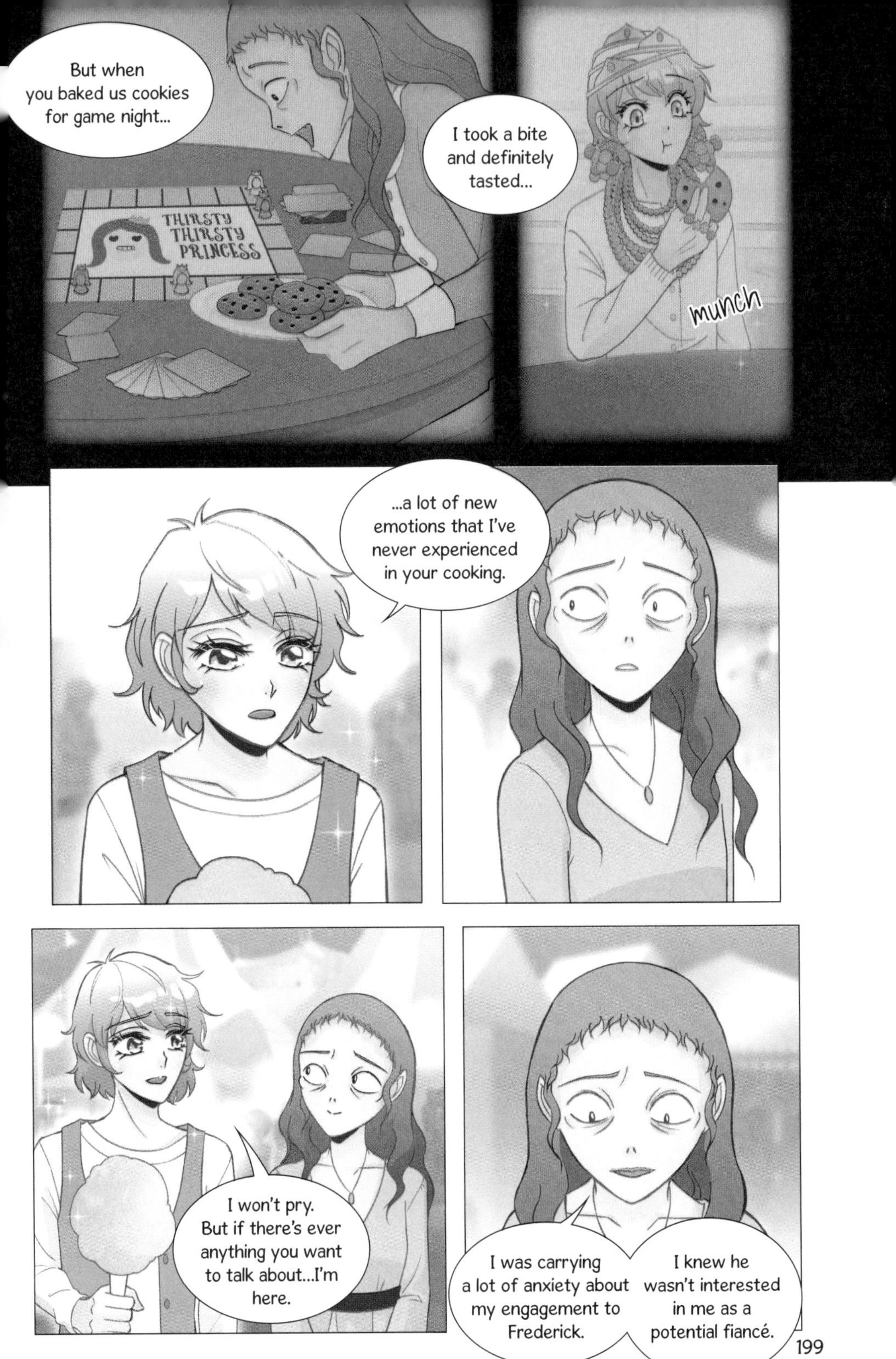
But when you baked us cookies for game night...
THIRSTY THIRSTY PRINCESS
I took a bite and definitely tasted...
munch
...a lot of new emotions that I've never experienced in your cooking.
I won't pry. But if there's ever anything you want to talk about...I'm here.
I was carrying a lot of anxiety about my engagement to Frederick.
I knew he wasn't interested in me as a potential fiancé.

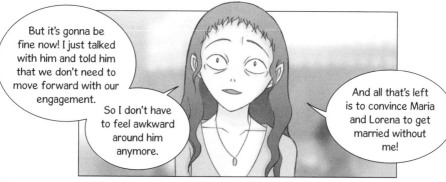

But it's gonna be fine now! I just talked with him and told him that we don't need to move forward with our engagement.

So I don't have to feel awkward around him anymore.

And all that's left is to convince Maria and Lorena to get married without me!

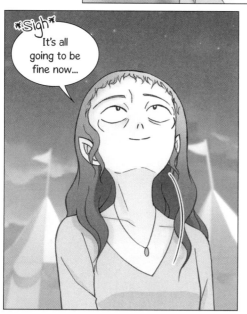

Sigh
It's all going to be fine now...

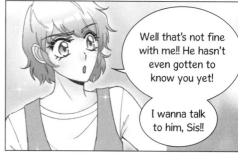

Well that's not fine with me!! He hasn't even gotten to know you yet!

I wanna talk to him, Sis!!

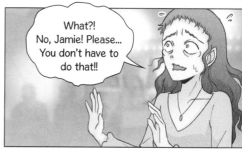

What?! No, Jamie! Please... You don't have to do that!!

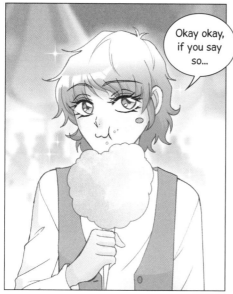

Okay okay, if you say so...

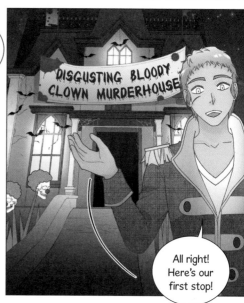

DISGUSTING BLOODY CLOWN MURDERHOUSE

All right! Here's our first stop!

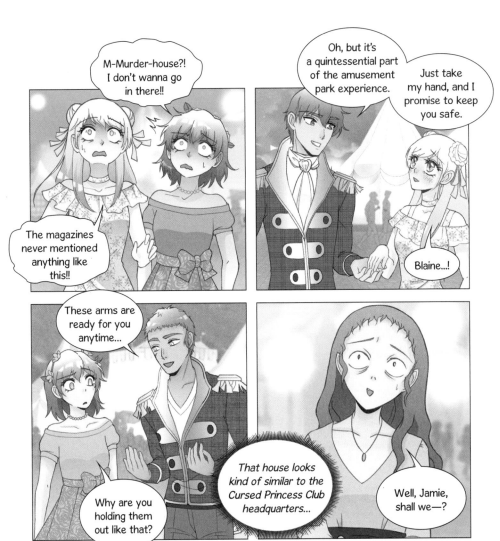

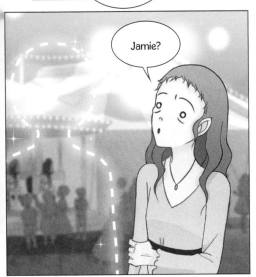

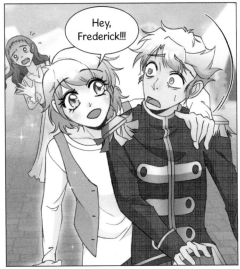

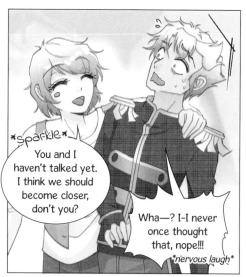

sparkle

You and I haven't talked yet. I think we should become closer, don't you?

Wha—? I-I never once thought that, nope!!!

nervous laugh

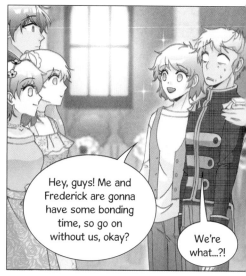

Hey, guys! Me and Frederick are gonna have some bonding time, so go on without us, okay?

We're what...?!

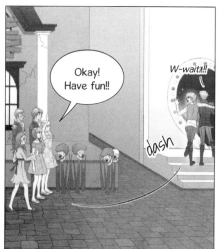

Okay! Have fun!!

W-wait?!!

dash

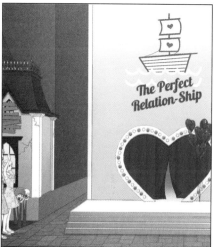

The Perfect Relation-Ship

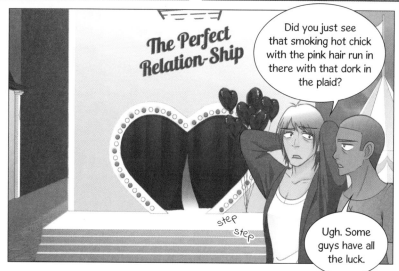

The Perfect Relation-Ship

Did you just see that smoking hot chick with the pink hair run in there with that dork in the plaid?

step step

Ugh. Some guys have all the luck.

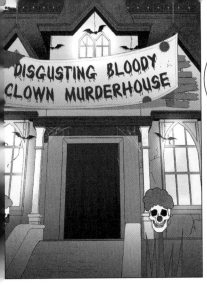

DISGUSTING BLOODY CLOWN MURDERHOUSE

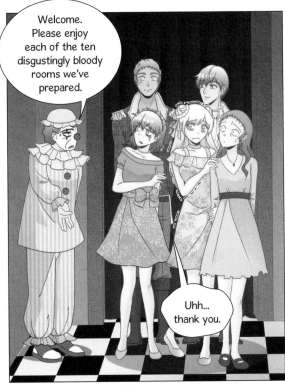

Welcome. Please enjoy each of the ten disgustingly bloody rooms we've prepared.

Uhh... thank you.

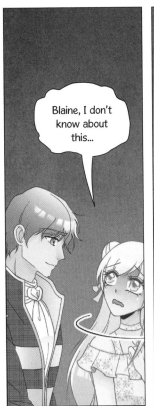

Blaine, I don't know about this...

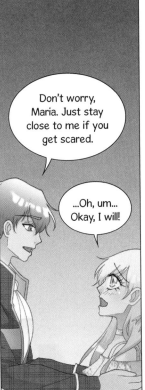

Don't worry, Maria. Just stay close to me if you get scared.

...Oh, um... Okay, I will!

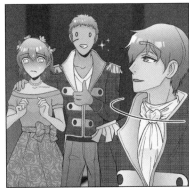

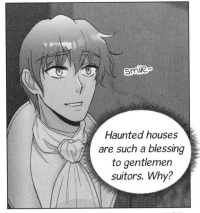

smile~

Haunted houses are such a blessing to gentlemen suitors. Why?

203

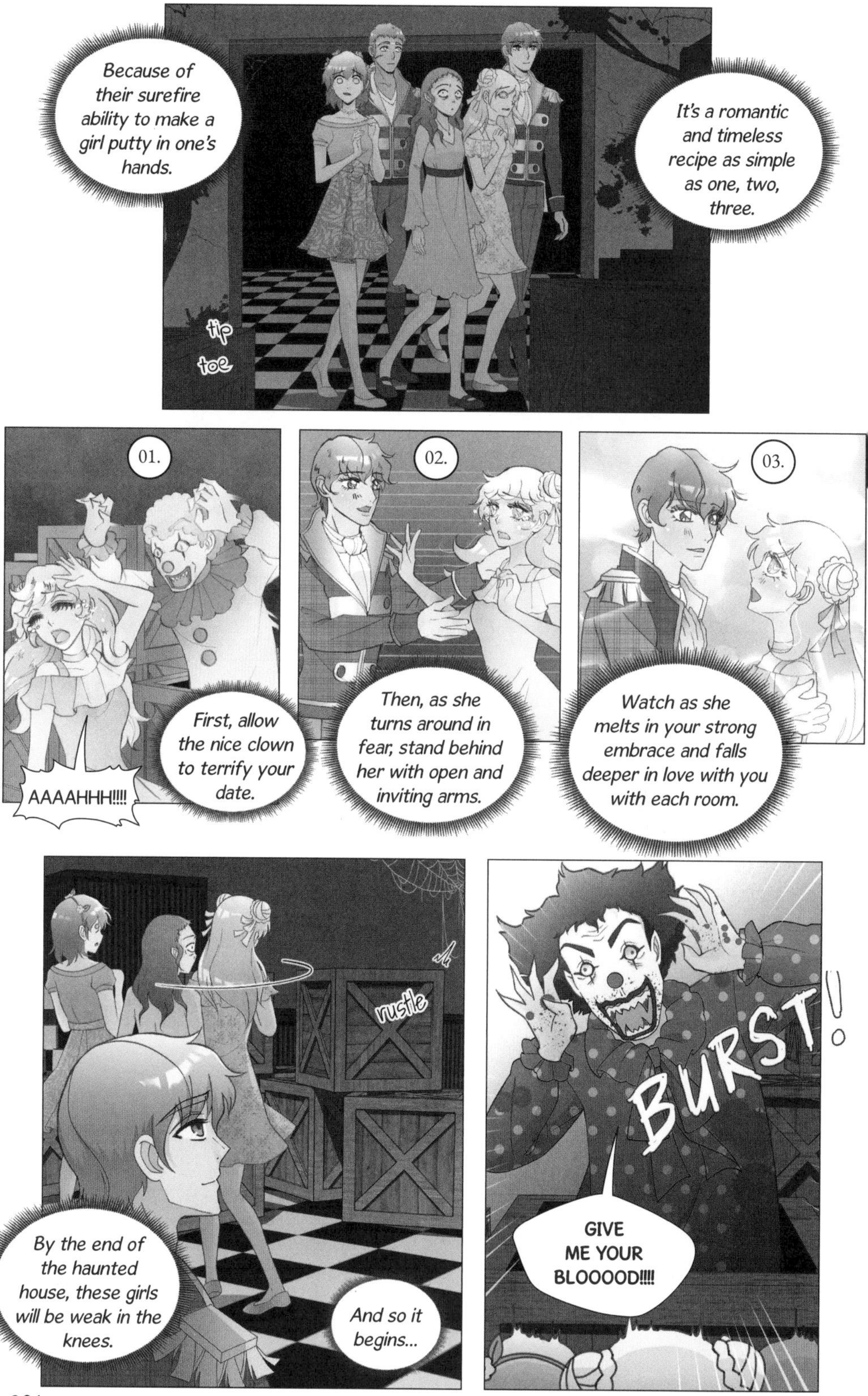

Because of their surefire ability to make a girl putty in one's hands.
tip
toe
It's a romantic and timeless recipe as simple as one, two, three.
01.
AAAAHHH!!!!
First, allow the nice clown to terrify your date.
02.
Then, as she turns around in fear, stand behind her with open and inviting arms.
03.
Watch as she melts in your strong embrace and falls deeper in love with you with each room.
rustle
By the end of the haunted house, these girls will be weak in the knees.
And so it begins...
BURST!
GIVE ME YOUR BLOOOOD!!!!

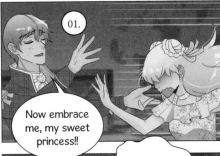

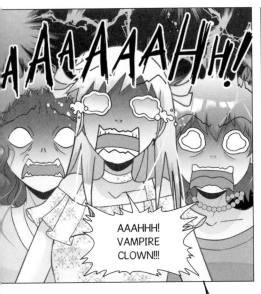

AAAHHH! VAMPIRE CLOWN!!!

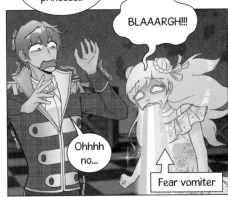

01.

Now embrace me, my sweet princess!!

BLAAARGH!!!

Ohhhh no...

Fear vomiter

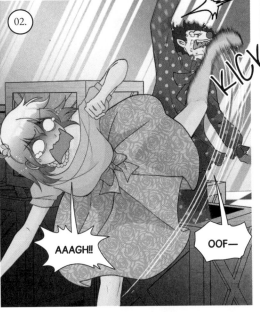

02.

KICK

AAAGH!!

OOF—

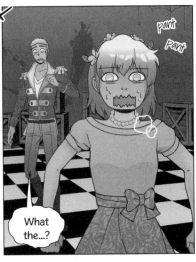

pant
pant

What the...?

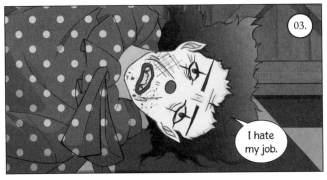

03.

I hate my job.

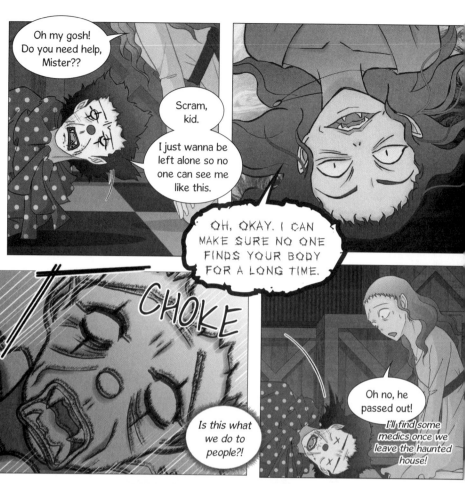

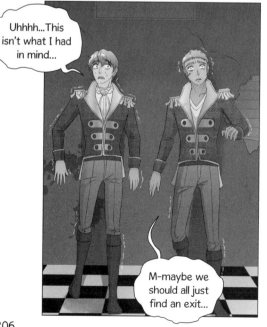

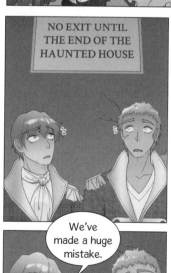

206

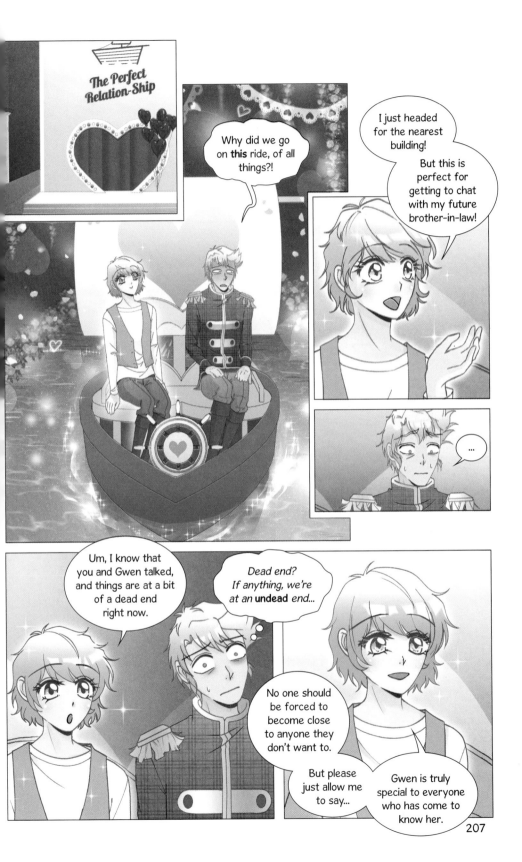

207

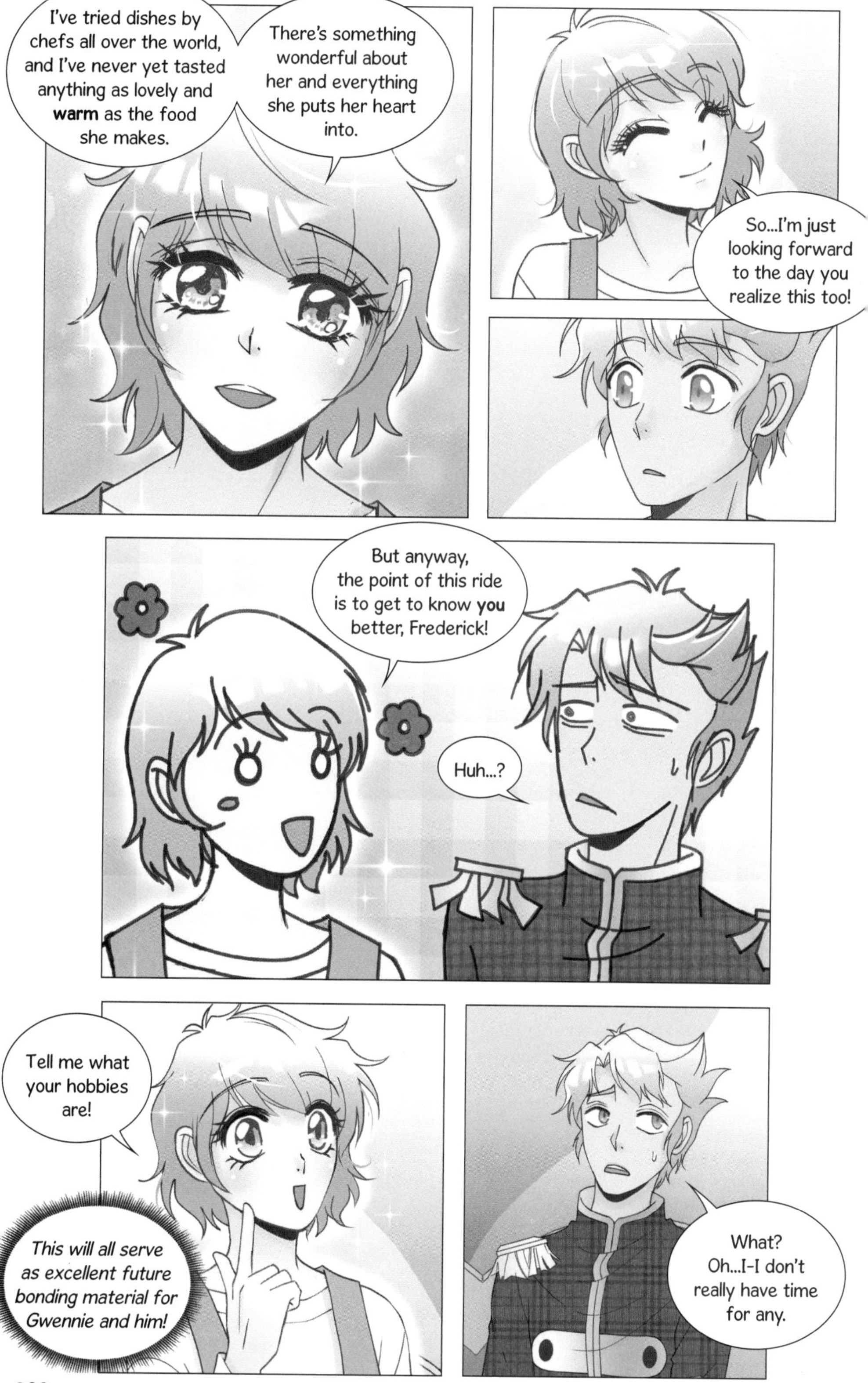
I've tried dishes by chefs all over the world, and I've never yet tasted anything as lovely and **warm** as the food she makes.
There's something wonderful about her and everything she puts her heart into.
So...I'm just looking forward to the day you realize this too!
But anyway, the point of this ride is to get to know **you** better, Frederick!
Huh...?
Tell me what your hobbies are!
This will all serve as excellent future bonding material for Gwennie and him!
What? Oh...I-I don't really have time for any.

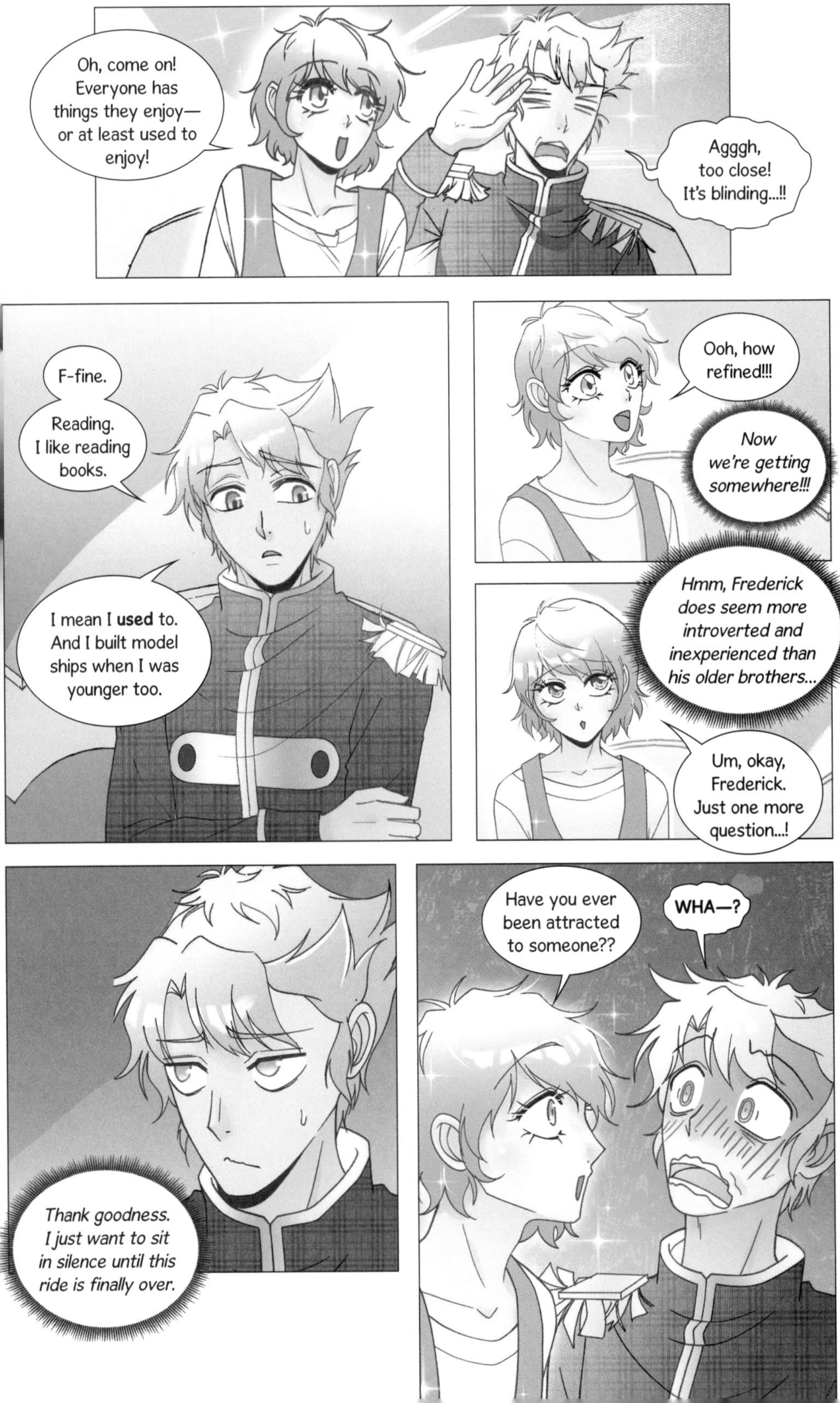
Oh, come on! Everyone has things they enjoy— or at least used to enjoy!
Agggh, too close! It's blinding...!!
F-fine.
Reading. I like reading books.
I mean I **used** to. And I built model ships when I was younger too.
Ooh, how refined!!!
Now we're getting somewhere!!!
Hmm, Frederick does seem more introverted and inexperienced than his older brothers...
Um, okay, Frederick. Just one more question...!
Thank goodness. I just want to sit in silence until this ride is finally over.
Have you ever been attracted to someone??
WHA—?

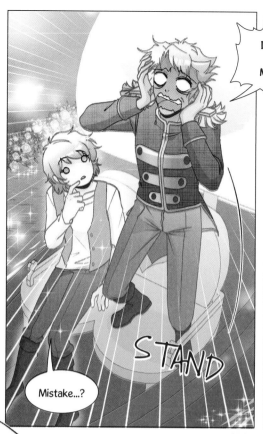

IT WAS AN HONEST MISTAKE!!!!!!

STAND

Mistake...?

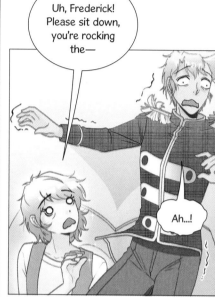

Uh, Frederick! Please sit down, you're rocking the—

Ah...!

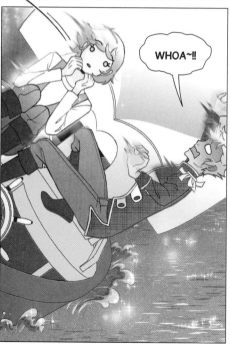

WHOA~!!

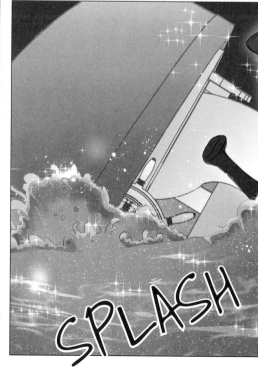

SPLASH

Chapter

9

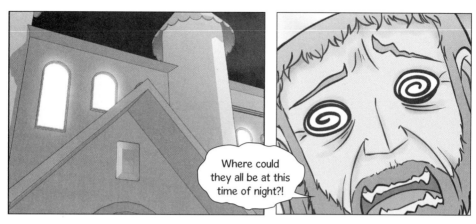

Where could they all be at this time of night?!

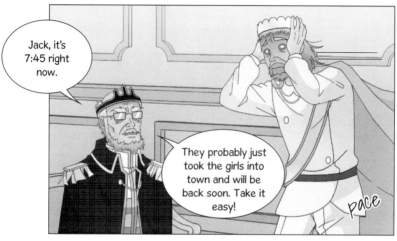

Jack, it's 7:45 right now.

They probably just took the girls into town and will be back soon. Take it easy!

PACE

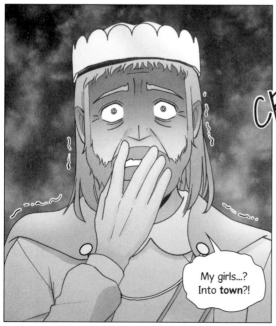

My girls...? Into **town**?!

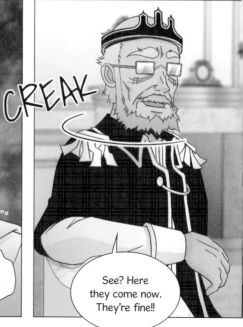

CREAK

See? Here they come now. They're fine!!

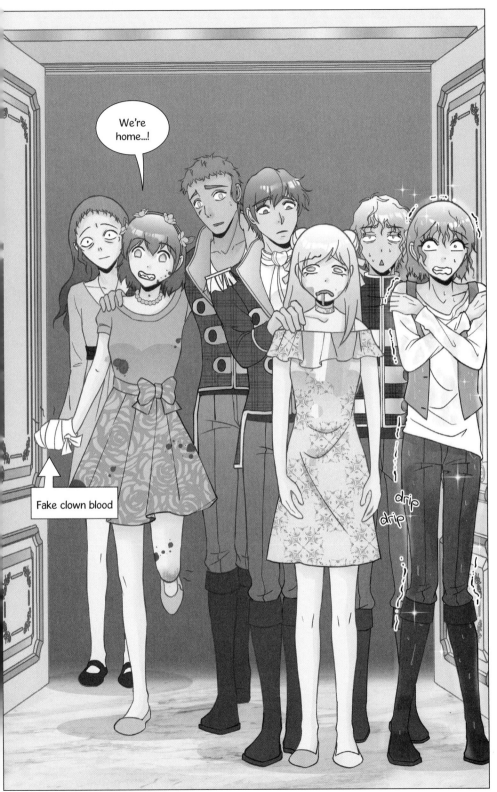

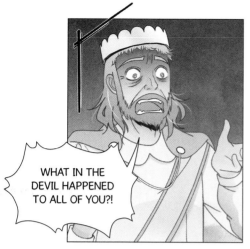

WHAT IN THE DEVIL HAPPENED TO ALL OF YOU?!

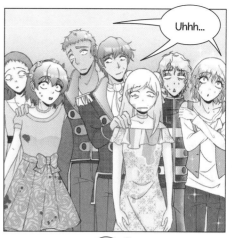

Uhhh...

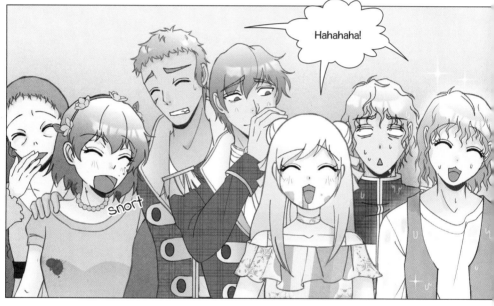

Hahahaha!

snort

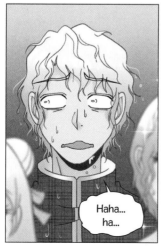

Haha... ha...

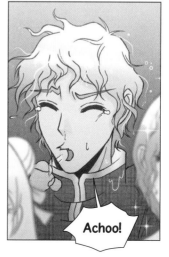

Achoo!

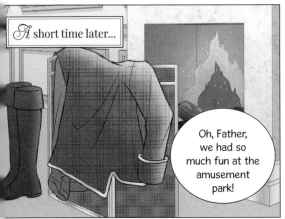

A short time later...

Oh, Father, we had so much fun at the amusement park!

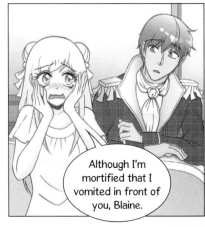

Although I'm mortified that I vomited in front of you, Blaine.

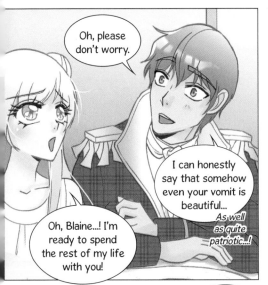

Oh, please don't worry.

I can honestly say that somehow even your vomit is beautiful...

As well as quite patriotic...!

Oh, Blaine...! I'm ready to spend the rest of my life with you!

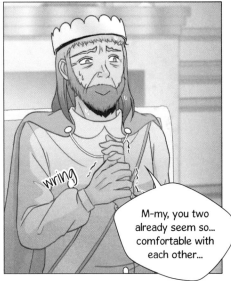

wring

M-my, you two already seem so... comfortable with each other...

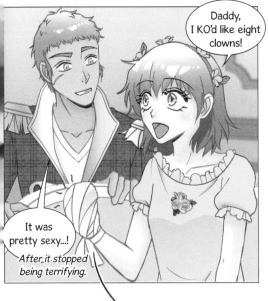

Daddy, I KO'd like eight clowns!

It was pretty sexy...!

After it stopped being terrifying.

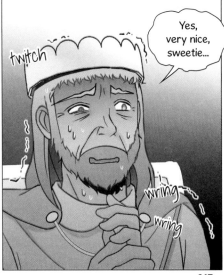

twitch

Yes, very nice, sweetie...

wring

wring

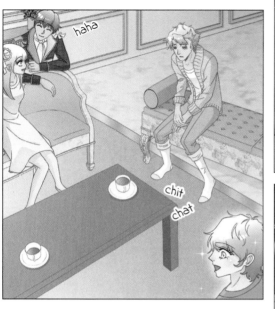

haha

chit
chat

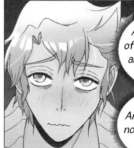

Ugggh, somehow this trip to the Pastel Kingdom was even worse than the first one.

I had an exhausting journey with Laverne, then that horrific encounter with Gwendolyn.

And to top it all off, I fell into filthy amusement park water.

And of course, now I'm feeling sick too.

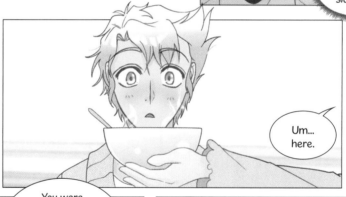

Um... here.

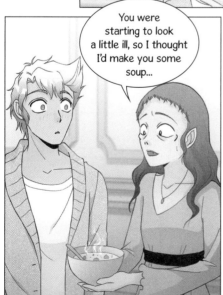

You were starting to look a little ill, so I thought I'd make you some soup...

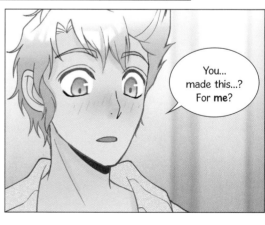

You... made this...? For **me**?

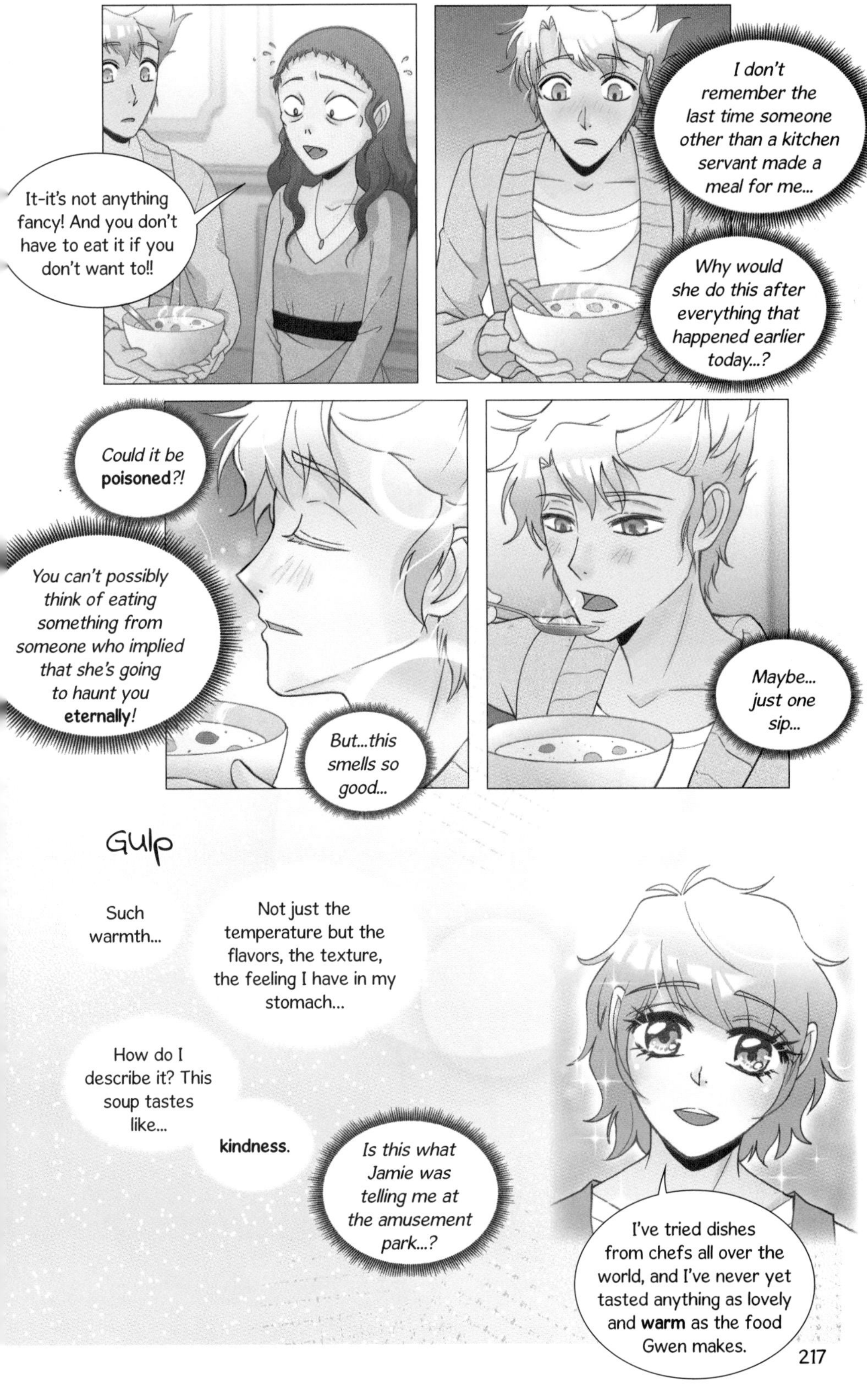
It-it's not anything fancy! And you don't have to eat it if you don't want to!!
I don't remember the last time someone other than a kitchen servant made a meal for me...
Why would she do this after everything that happened earlier today...?
Could it be **poisoned**?!
You can't possibly think of eating something from someone who implied that she's going to haunt you **eternally**!
But...this smells so good...
Maybe... just one sip...
Gulp
Such warmth...
Not just the temperature but the flavors, the texture, the feeling I have in my stomach...
How do I describe it? This soup tastes like...
kindness.
Is this what Jamie was telling me at the amusement park...?
I've tried dishes from chefs all over the world, and I've never yet tasted anything as lovely and **warm** as the food Gwen makes.

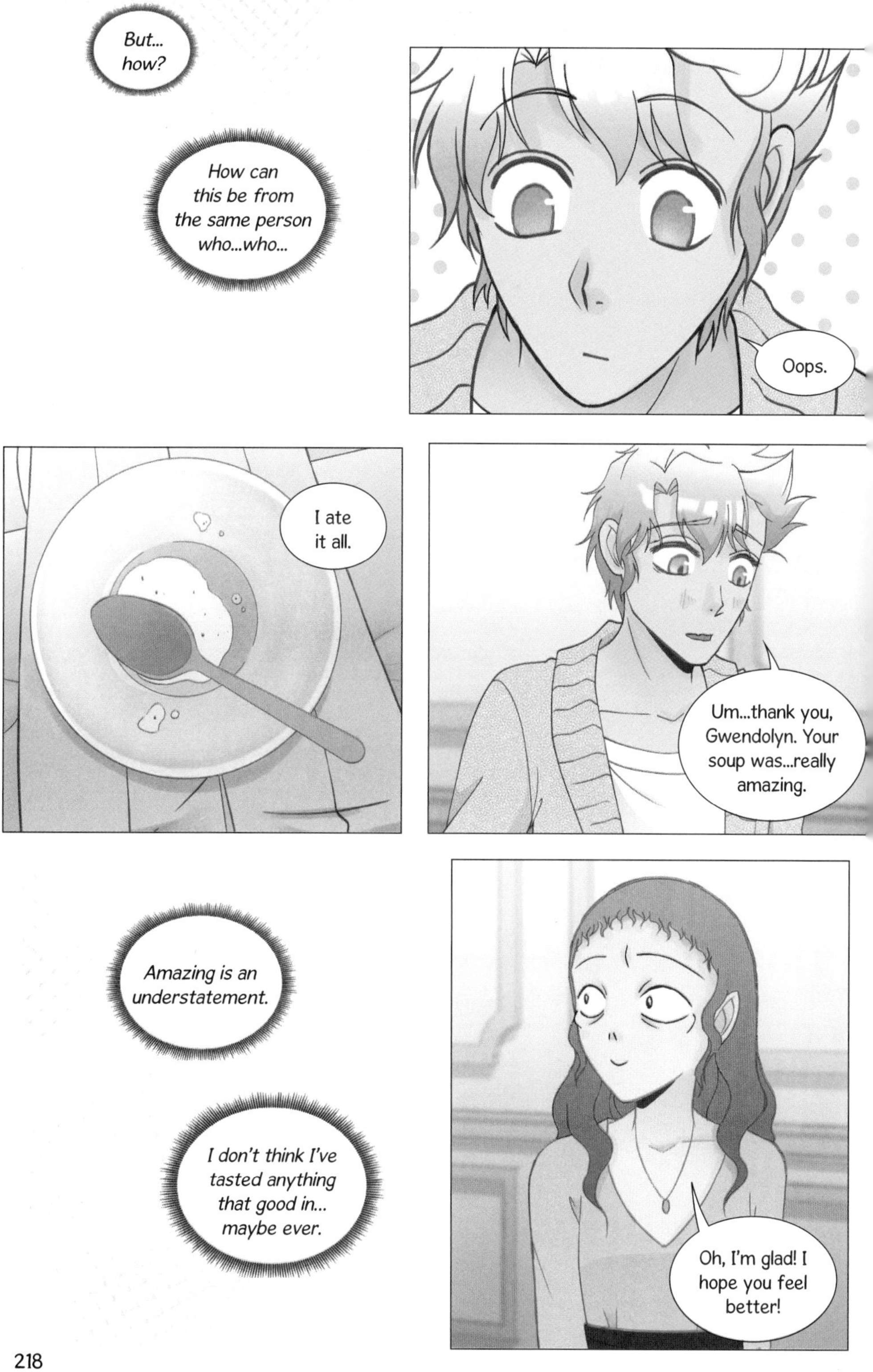
But... how?
How can this be from the same person who...who...
Oops.
I ate it all.
Um...thank you, Gwendolyn. Your soup was...really amazing.
Amazing is an understatement.
I don't think I've tasted anything that good in... maybe ever.
Oh, I'm glad! I hope you feel better!

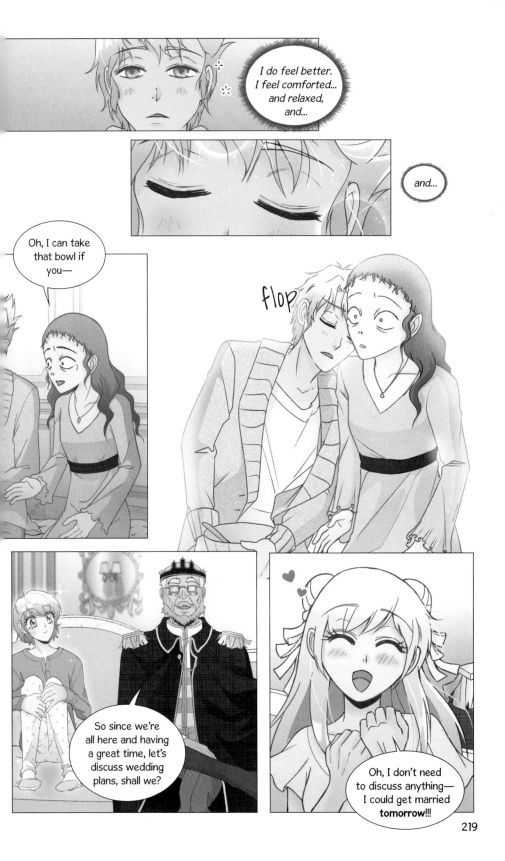

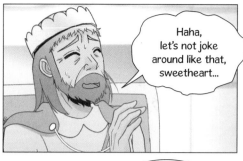

Haha, let's not joke around like that, sweetheart...

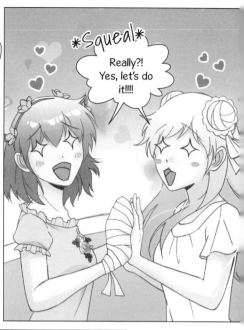

Squeal

Really?! Yes, let's do it!!!!

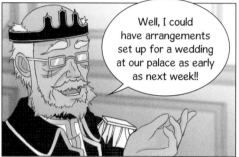

Well, I could have arrangements set up for a wedding at our palace as early as next week!!

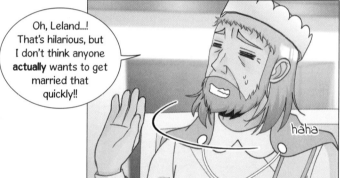

Oh, Leland...! That's hilarious, but I don't think anyone **actually** wants to get married that quickly!!

haha

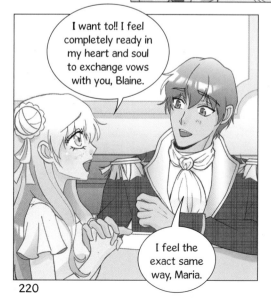

I want to!! I feel completely ready in my heart and soul to exchange vows with you, Blaine.

I feel the exact same way, Maria.

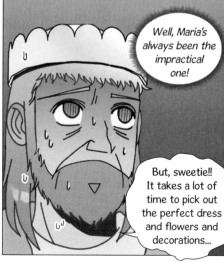

Well, Maria's always been the impractical one!

But, sweetie!! It takes a lot of time to pick out the perfect dress and flowers and decorations...

220

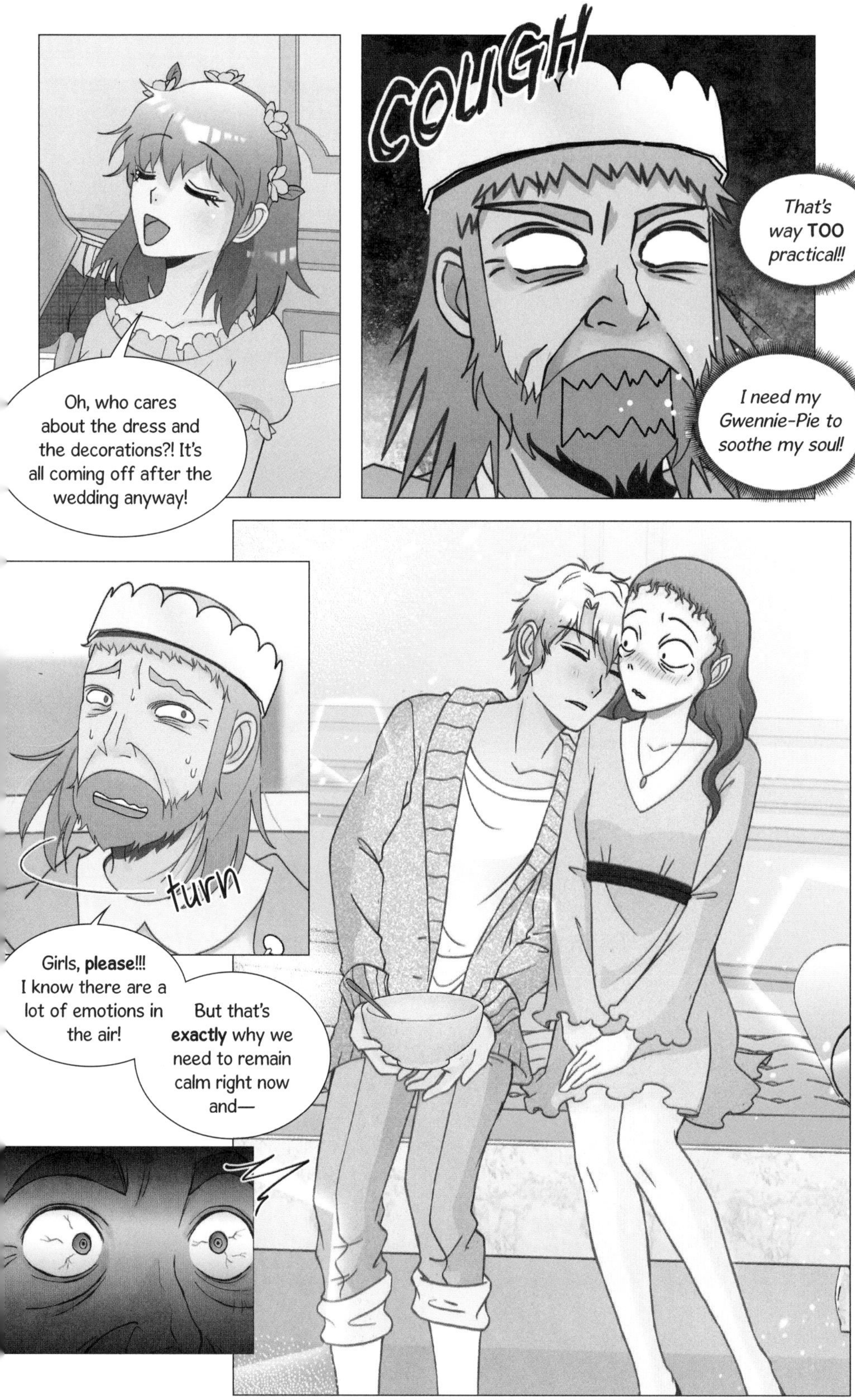

Oh, who cares about the dress and the decorations?! It's all coming off after the wedding anyway!
COUGH
That's way TOO practical!!
I need my Gwennie-Pie to soothe my soul!
turn
Girls, please!!! I know there are a lot of emotions in the air!
But that's exactly why we need to remain calm right now and—

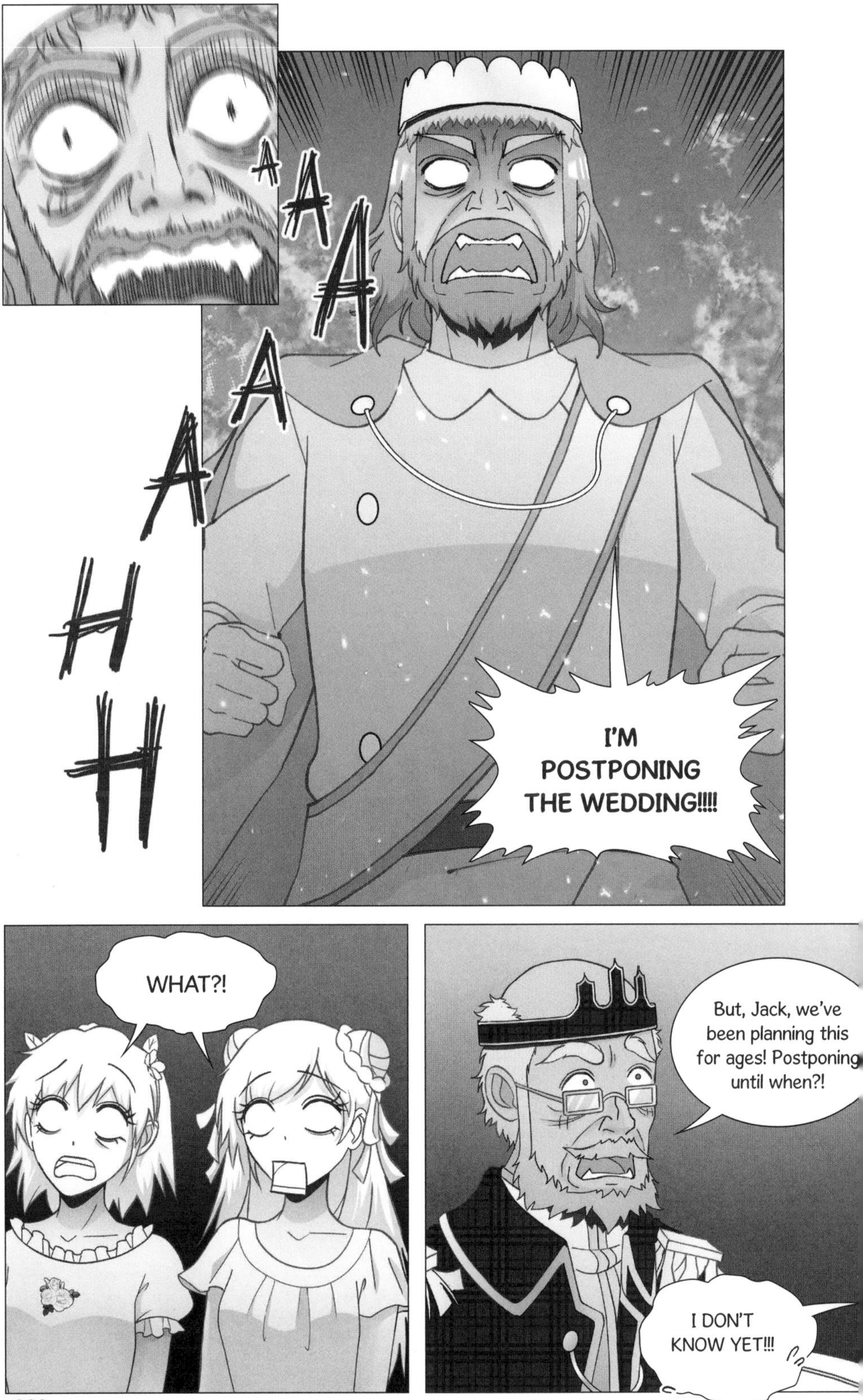
AAAAAHH
I'M POSTPONING THE WEDDING!!!!
WHAT?!
But, Jack, we've been planning this for ages! Postponing until when?!
I DON'T KNOW YET!!!

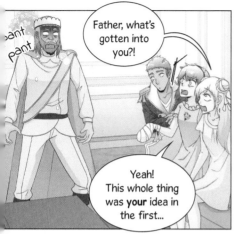

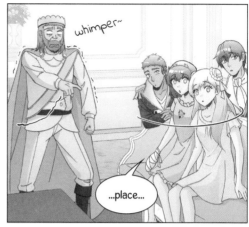

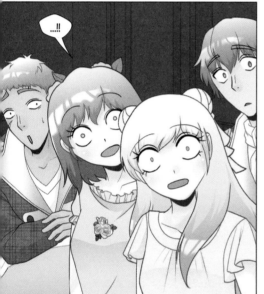

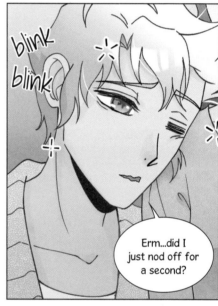

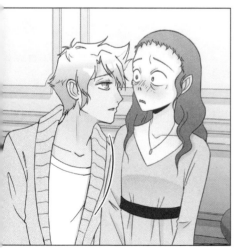

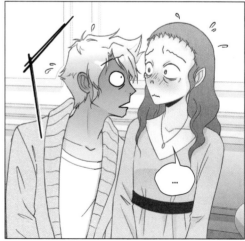

223

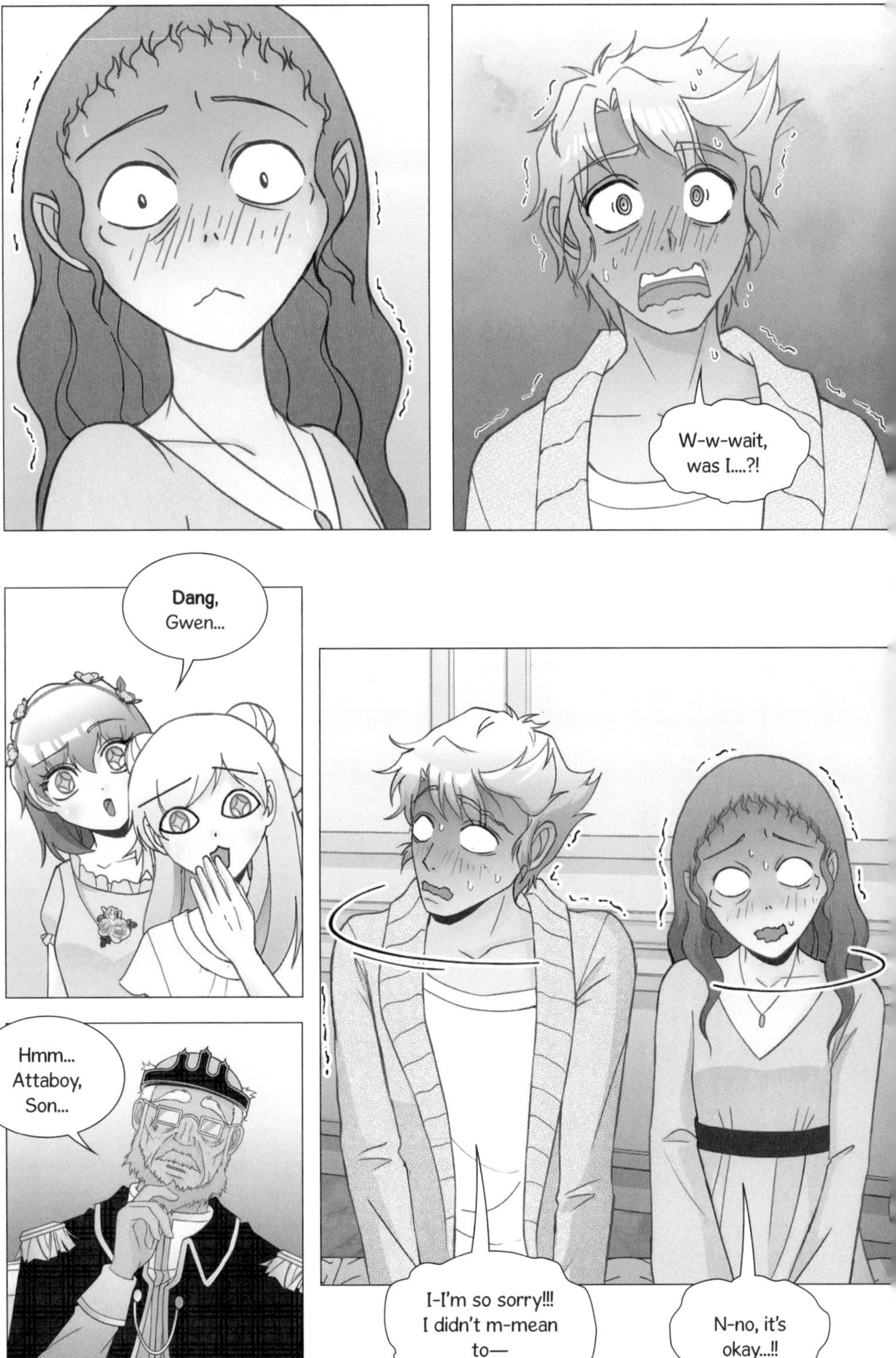
W-w-wait,
was I....?!
Dang,
Gwen...
Hmm...
Attaboy,
Son...
I-I'm so sorry!!!
I didn't m-mean
to—
N-no, it's
okay...!!

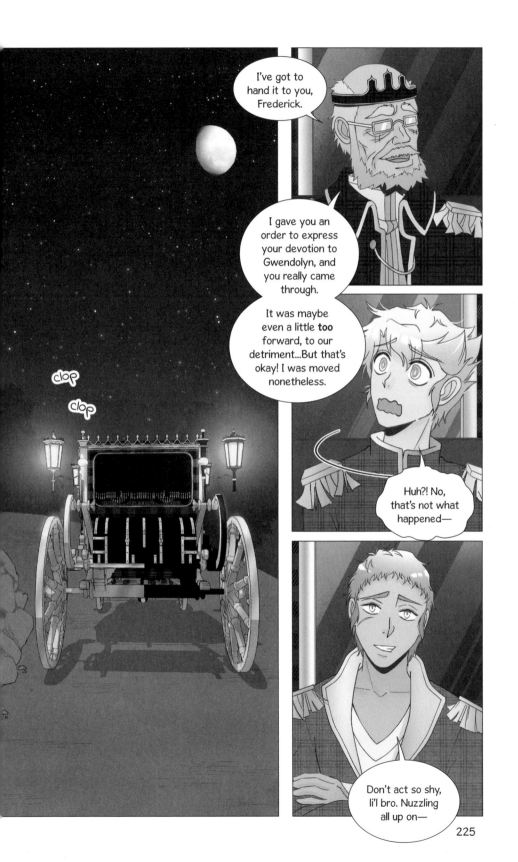

225

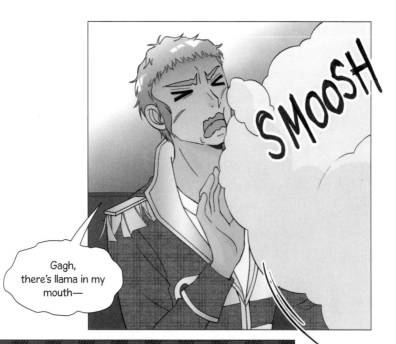

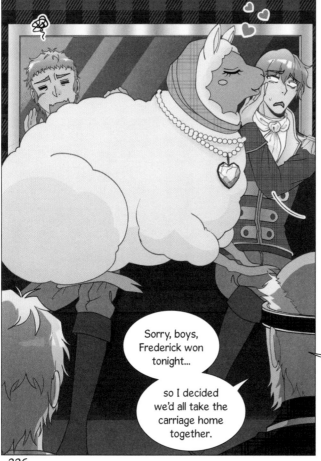

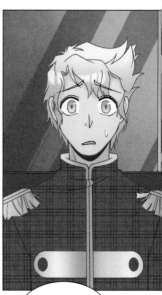

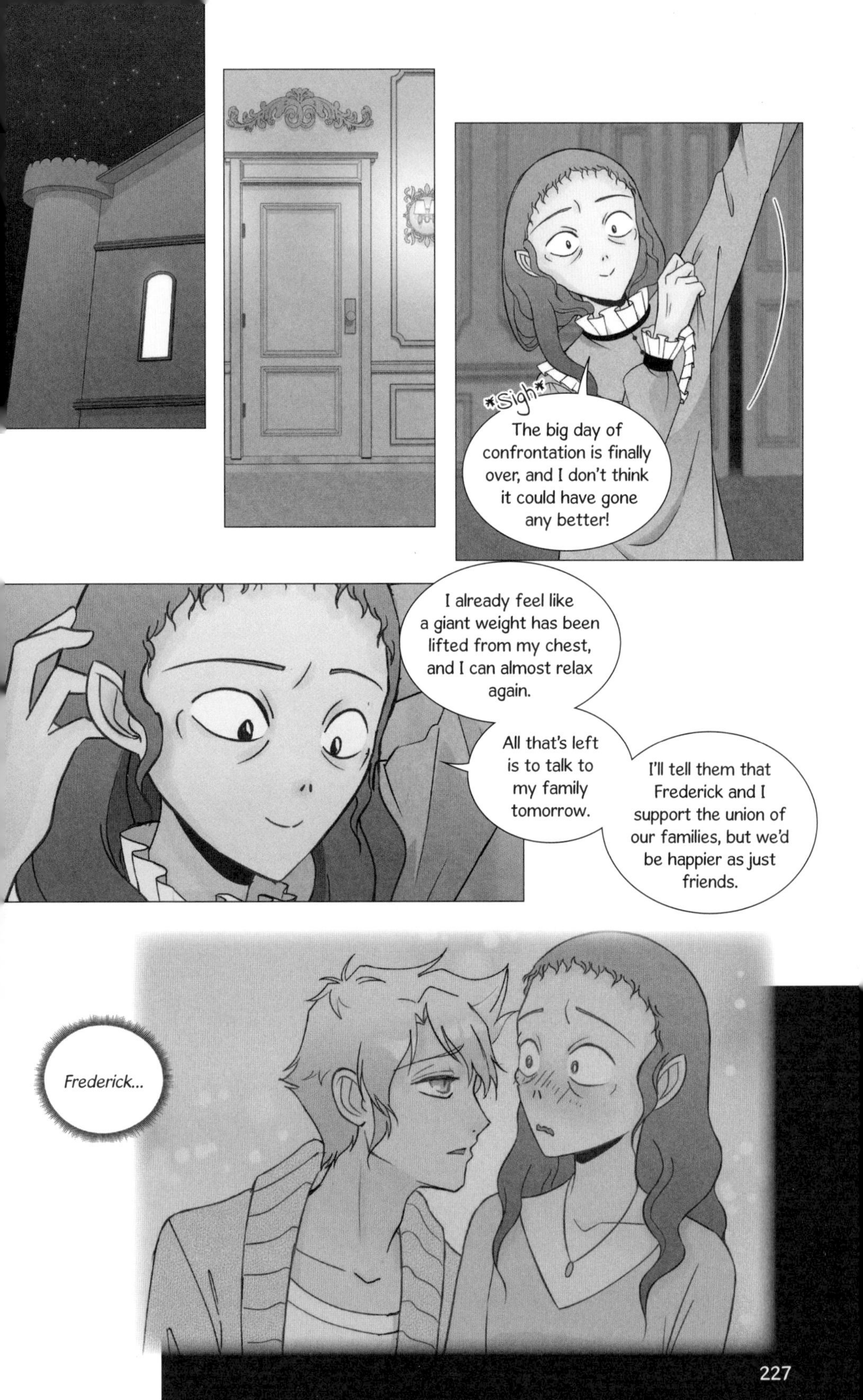
Sigh
The big day of confrontation is finally over, and I don't think it could have gone any better!
I already feel like a giant weight has been lifted from my chest, and I can almost relax again.
All that's left is to talk to my family tomorrow.
I'll tell them that Frederick and I support the union of our families, but we'd be happier as just friends.
Frederick...

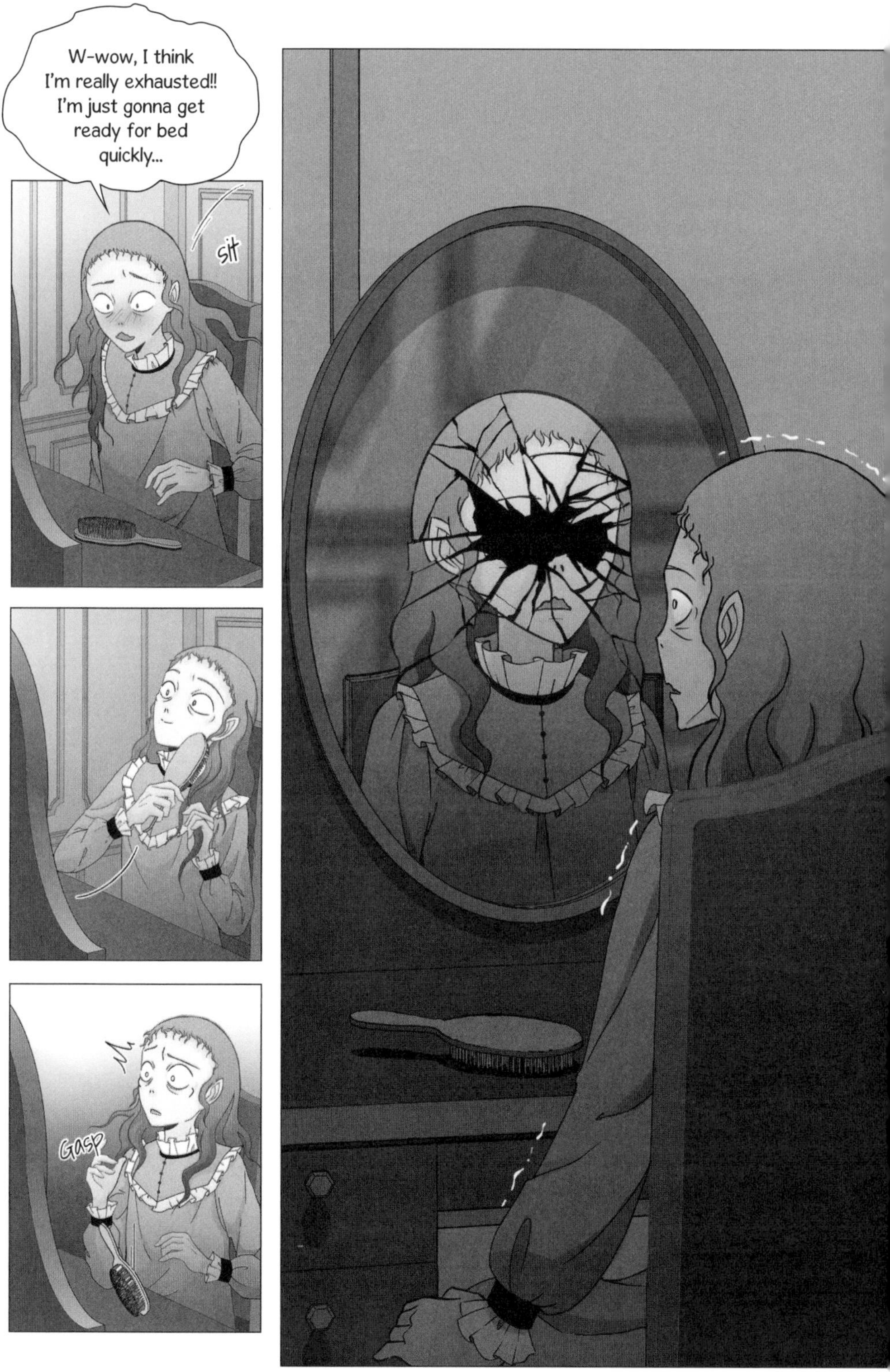
W-wow, I think I'm really exhausted!! I'm just gonna get ready for bed quickly...
sit
Gasp

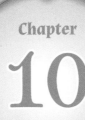

Chapter

10

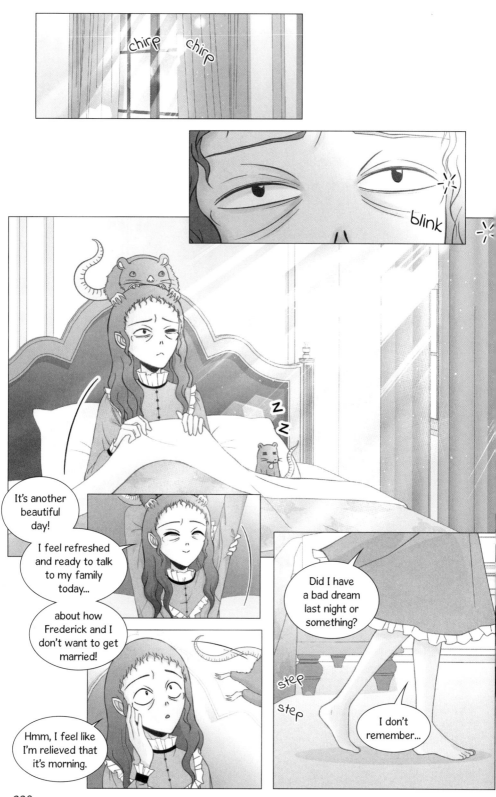

chirp   chirp

blink

z
z

It's another beautiful day!

I feel refreshed and ready to talk to my family today...

about how Frederick and I don't want to get married!

Hmm, I feel like I'm relieved that it's morning.

Did I have a bad dream last night or something?

step

step

I don't remember...

230

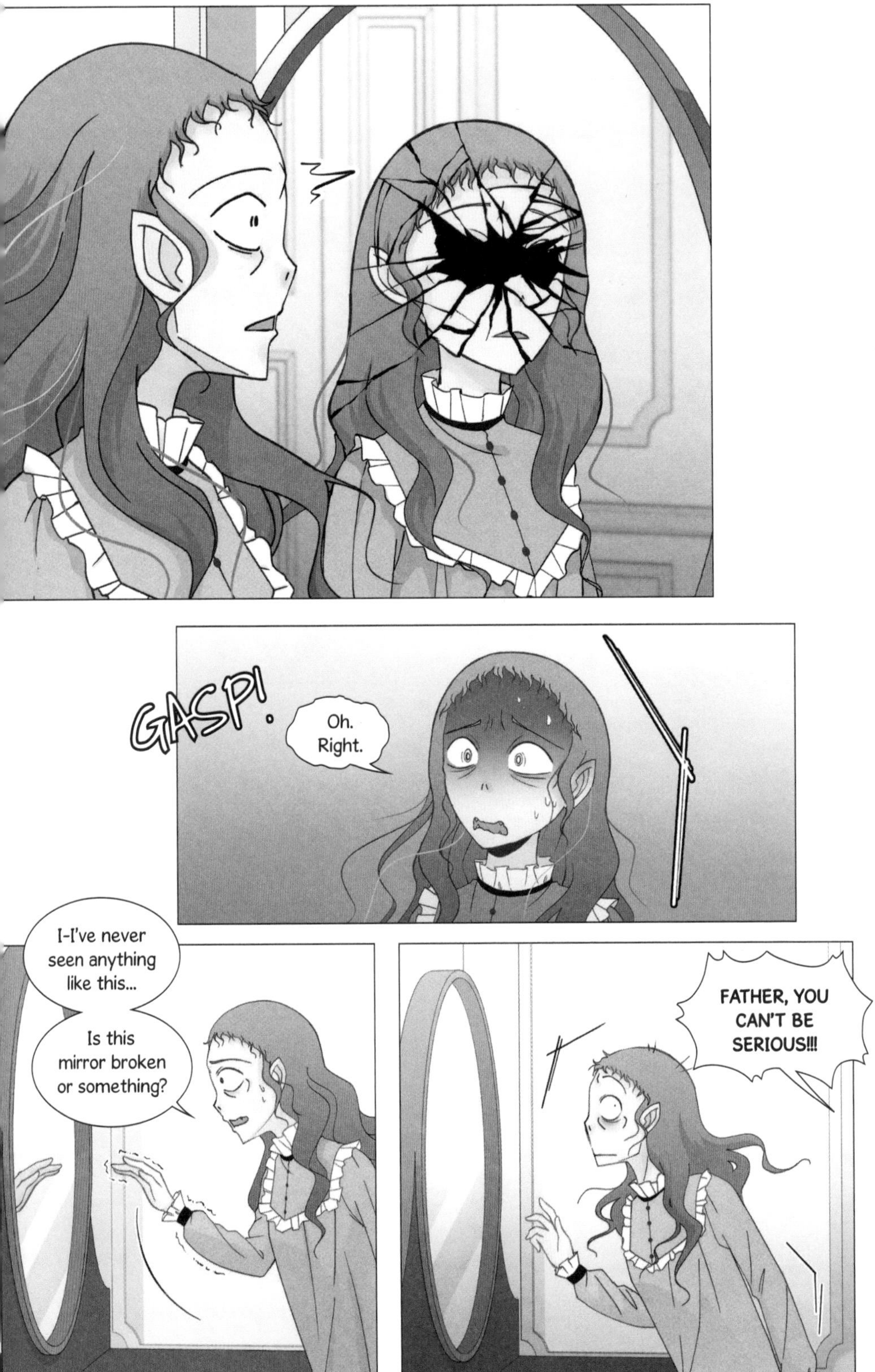
GASP!
Oh. Right.
I-I've never seen anything like this...
Is this mirror broken or something?
FATHER, YOU CAN'T BE SERIOUS!!!

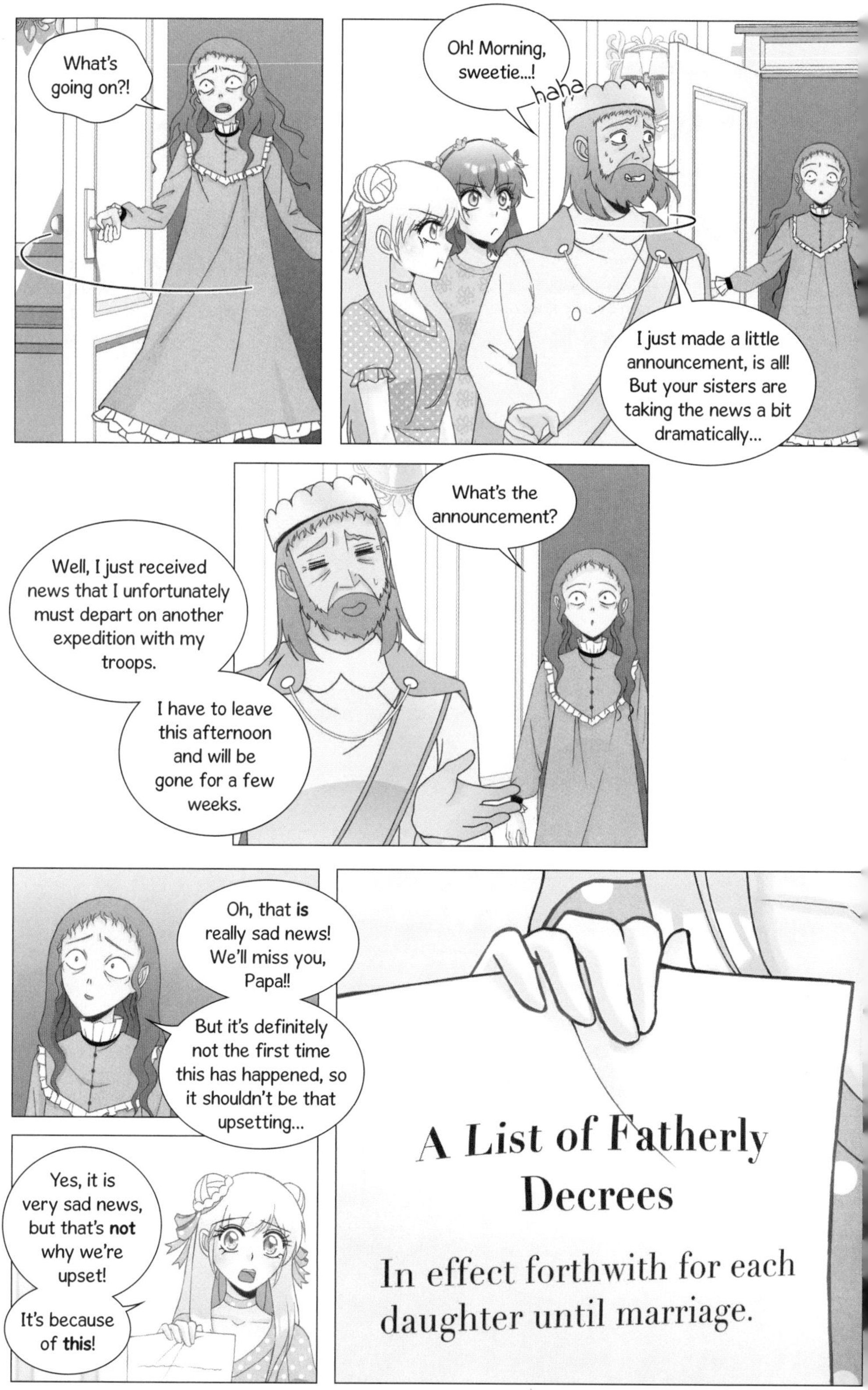
What's going on?!
Oh! Morning, sweetie...!
haha
I just made a little announcement, is all! But your sisters are taking the news a bit dramatically...
What's the announcement?
Well, I just received news that I unfortunately must depart on another expedition with my troops.
I have to leave this afternoon and will be gone for a few weeks.
Oh, that **is** really sad news! We'll miss you, Papa!!
But it's definitely not the first time this has happened, so it shouldn't be that upsetting...
Yes, it is very sad news, but that's **not** why we're upset!
It's because of **this**!
A List of Fatherly Decrees
In effect forthwith for each daughter until marriage.

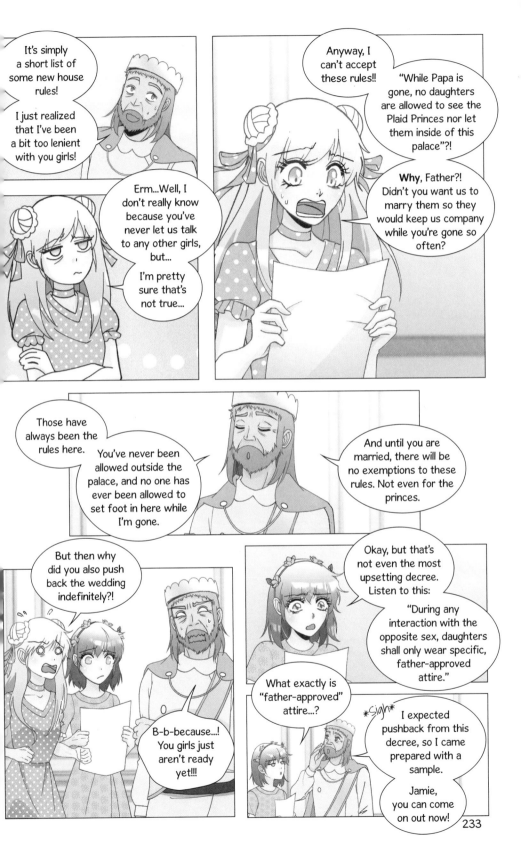

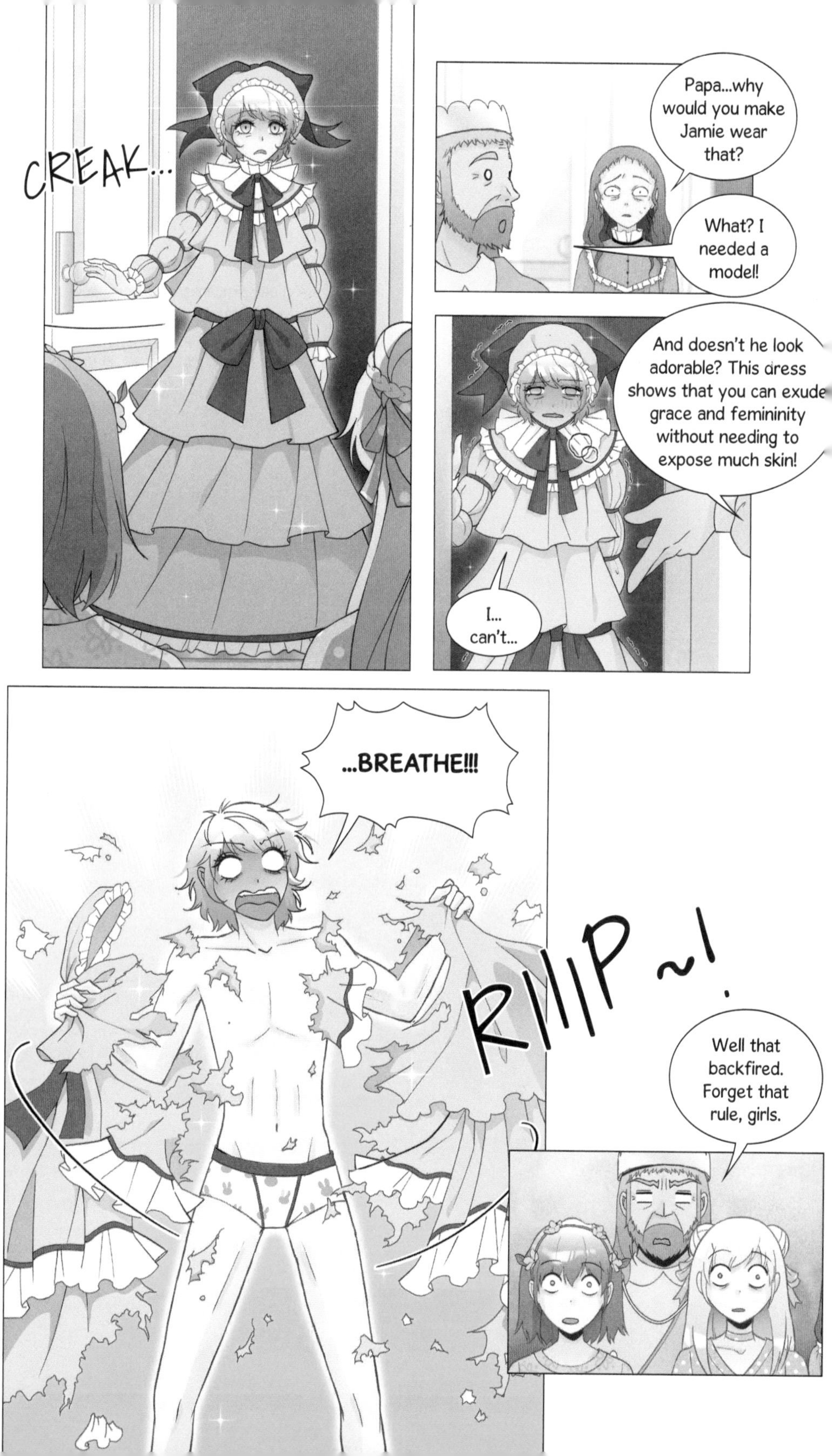
CREAK...
Papa...why would you make Jamie wear that?
What? I needed a model!
And doesn't he look adorable? This dress shows that you can exude grace and femininity without needing to expose much skin!
I... can't...
...BREATHE!!!
RIIIP~!
Well that backfired. Forget that rule, girls.

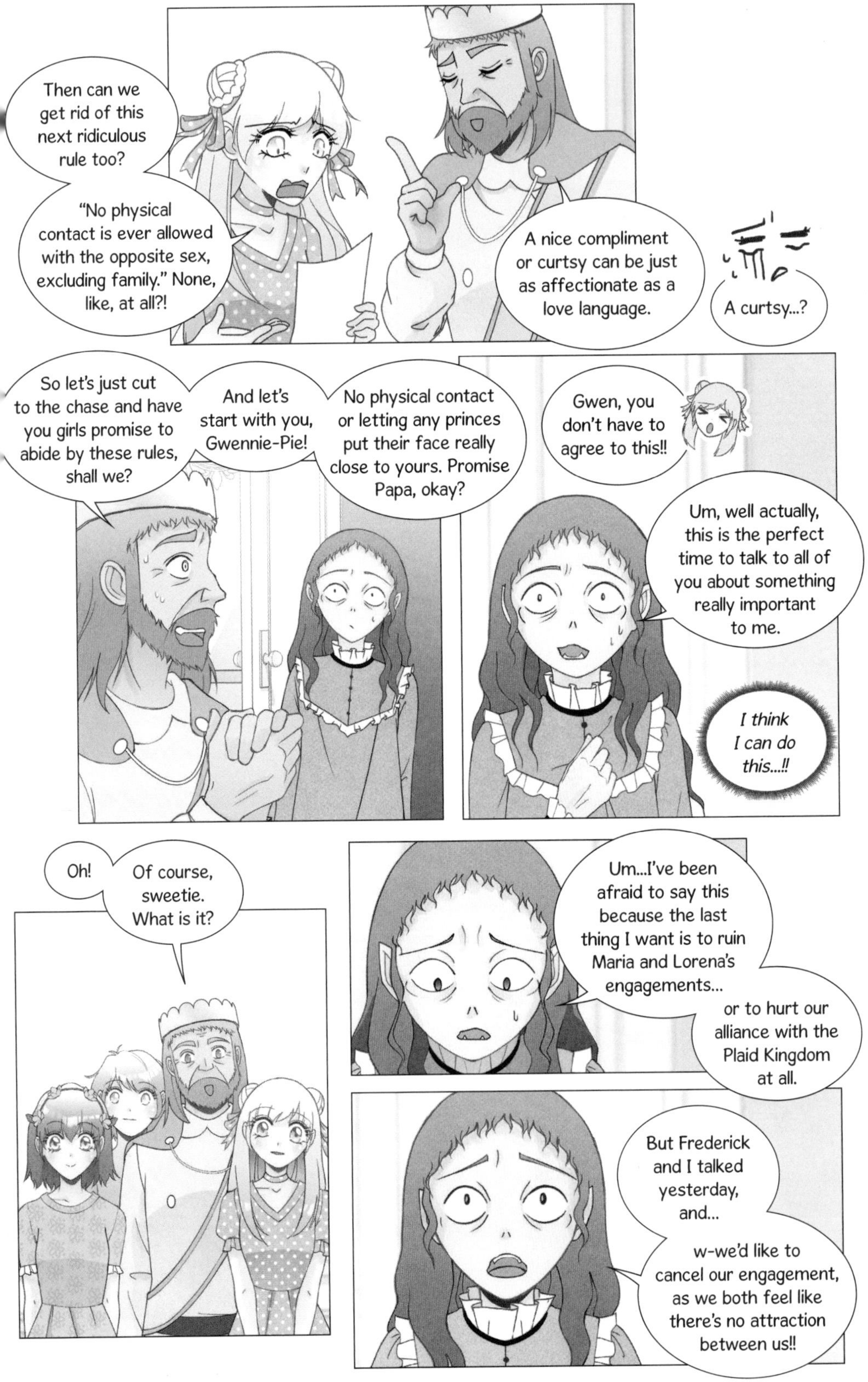

Then can we get rid of this next ridiculous rule too?
"No physical contact is ever allowed with the opposite sex, excluding family." None, like, at all?!
A nice compliment or curtsy can be just as affectionate as a love language.
A curtsy...?
So let's just cut to the chase and have you girls promise to abide by these rules, shall we?
And let's start with you, Gwennie-Pie!
No physical contact or letting any princes put their face really close to yours. Promise Papa, okay?
Gwen, you don't have to agree to this!!
Um, well actually, this is the perfect time to talk to all of you about something really important to me.
I think I can do this...!!
Oh!
Of course, sweetie. What is it?
Um...I've been afraid to say this because the last thing I want is to ruin Maria and Lorena's engagements...
or to hurt our alliance with the Plaid Kingdom at all.
But Frederick and I talked yesterday, and...
w-we'd like to cancel our engagement, as we both feel like there's no attraction between us!!

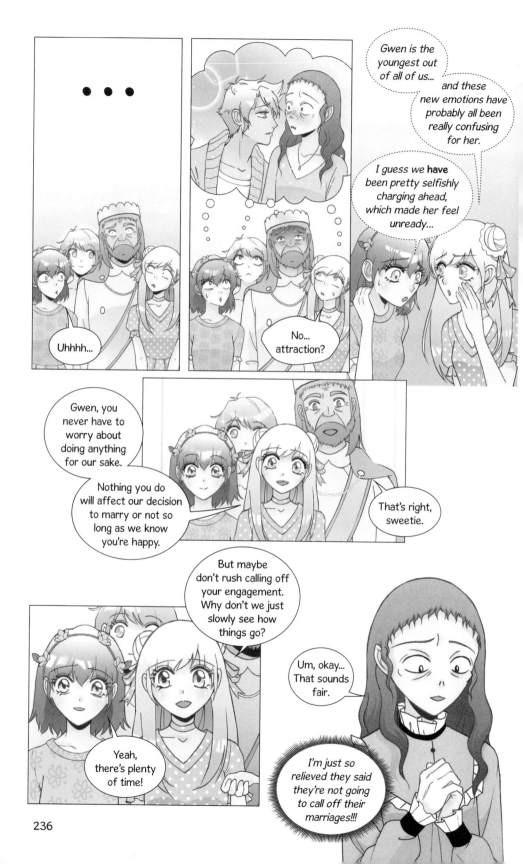

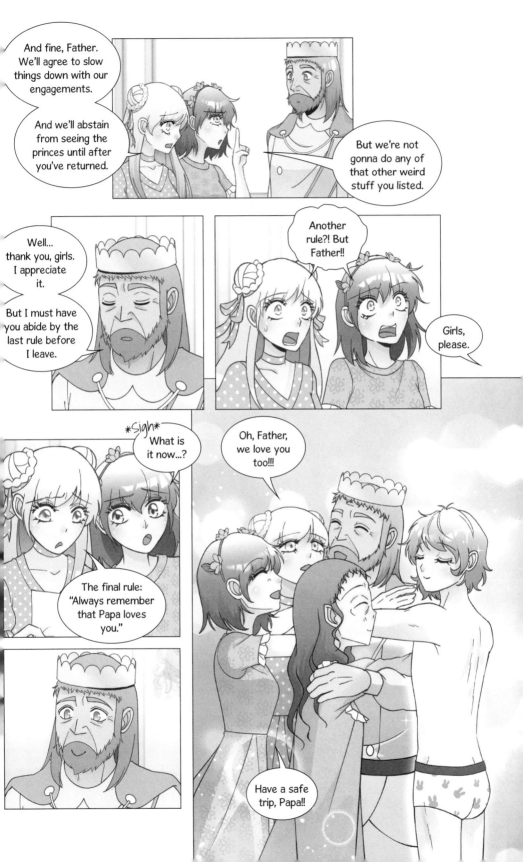

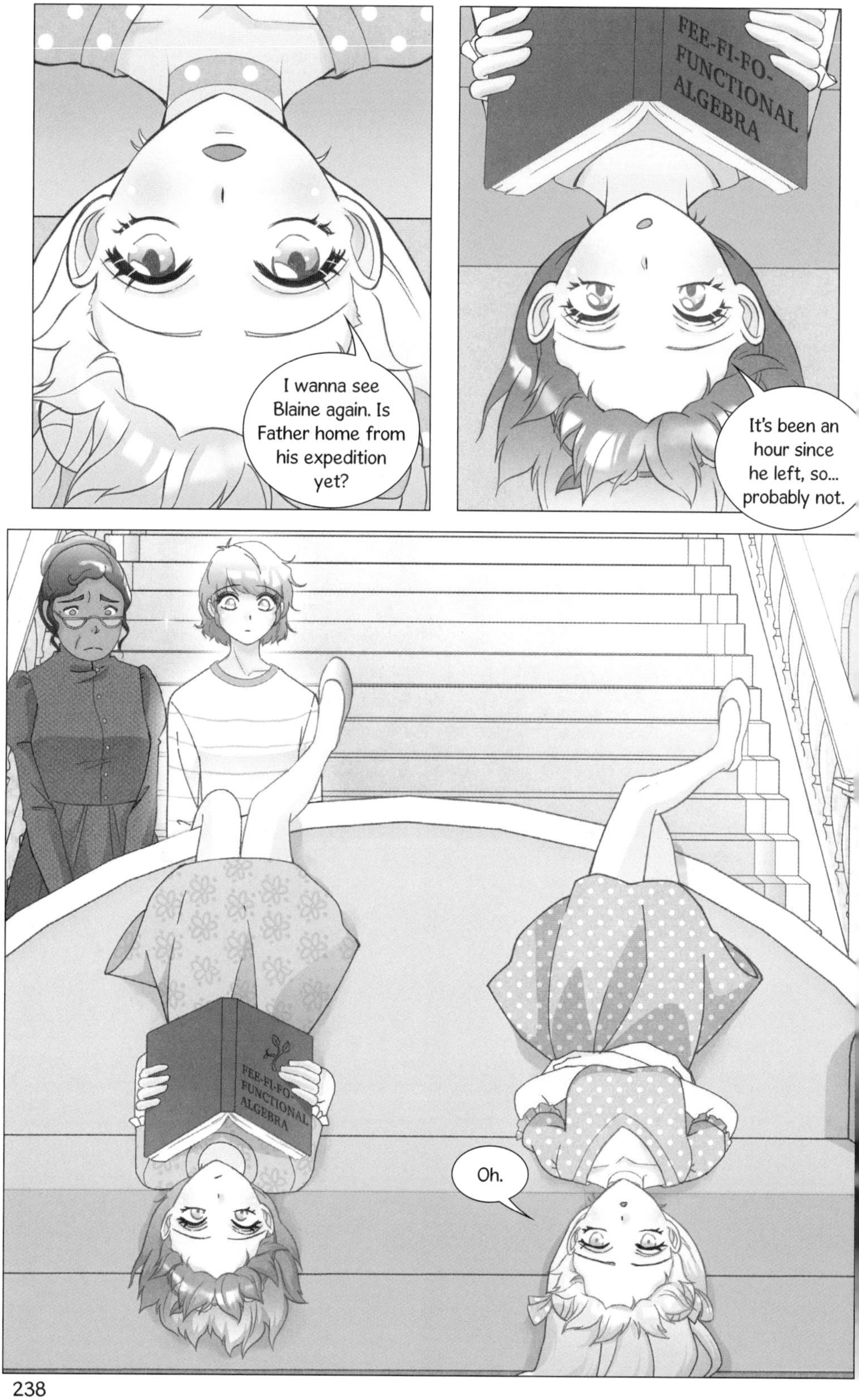
I wanna see Blaine again. Is Father home from his expedition yet?
FEE-FI-FO-FUNCTIONAL ALGEBRA
It's been an hour since he left, so... probably not.
FEE-FI-FO-FUNCTIONAL ALGEBRA
Oh.

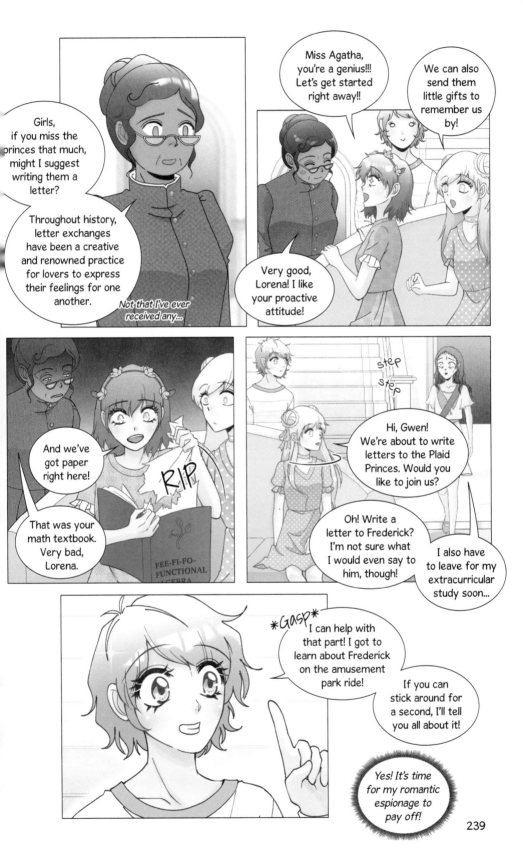

239

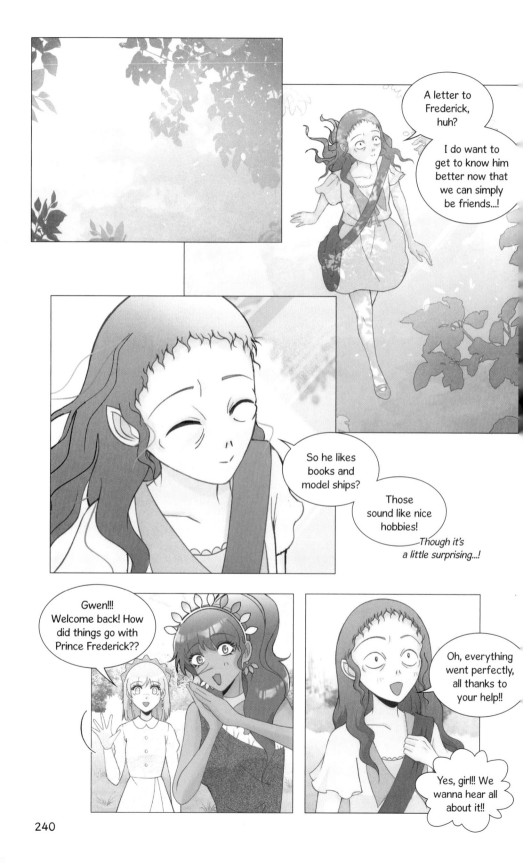

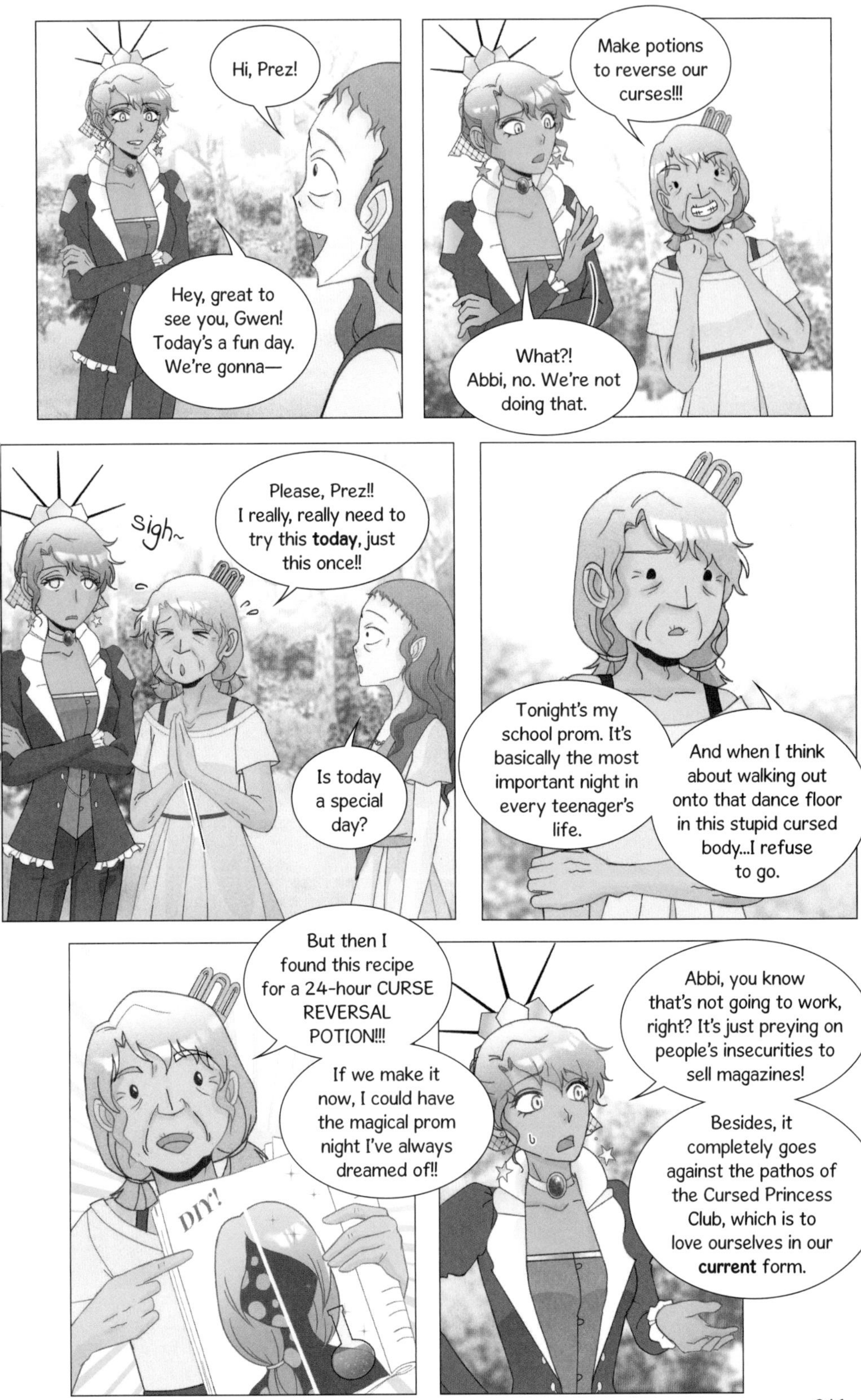
Hi, Prez!
Hey, great to see you, Gwen! Today's a fun day. We're gonna—
Make potions to reverse our curses!!!
What?! Abbi, no. We're not doing that.
sigh~
Please, Prez!! I really, really need to try this **today**, just this once!!
Is today a special day?
Tonight's my school prom. It's basically the most important night in every teenager's life.
And when I think about walking out onto that dance floor in this stupid cursed body...I refuse to go.
But then I found this recipe for a 24-hour CURSE REVERSAL POTION!!!
If we make it now, I could have the magical prom night I've always dreamed of!!
DIY!
Abbi, you know that's not going to work, right? It's just preying on people's insecurities to sell magazines!
Besides, it completely goes against the pathos of the Cursed Princess Club, which is to love ourselves in our **current** form.

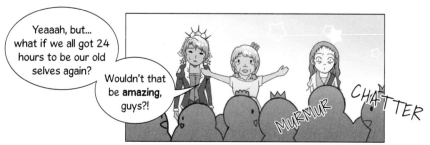

Yeaaah, but... what if we all got 24 hours to be our old selves again?

Wouldn't that be **amazing**, guys?!

MURMUR

CHATTER

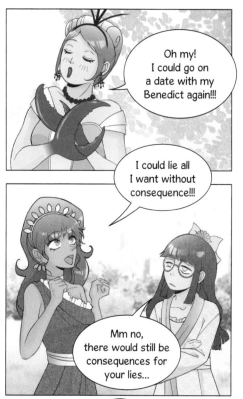

Oh my! I could go on a date with my Benedict again!!!

I could lie all I want without consequence!!!

Mm no, there would still be consequences for your lies...

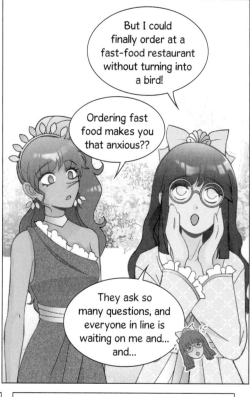

But I could finally order at a fast-food restaurant without turning into a bird!

Ordering fast food makes you that anxious??

They ask so many questions, and everyone in line is waiting on me and... and...

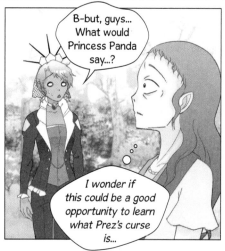

B-but, guys... What would Princess Panda say...?

I wonder if this could be a good opportunity to learn what Prez's curse is...

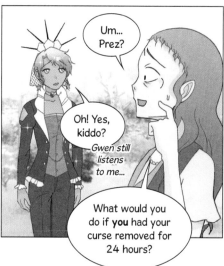

Um... Prez?

Oh! Yes, kiddo?

Gwen still listens to me...

What would you do if **you** had your curse removed for 24 hours?

242

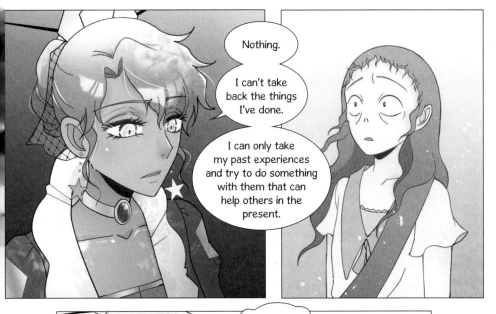

Nothing.

I can't take back the things I've done.

I can only take my past experiences and try to do something with them that can help others in the present.

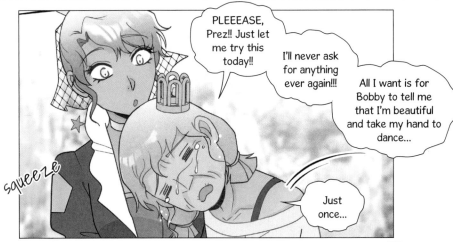

PLEEEASE, Prez!! Just let me try this today!!

I'll never ask for anything ever again!!!

All I want is for Bobby to tell me that I'm beautiful and take my hand to dance...

Just once...

squeeze

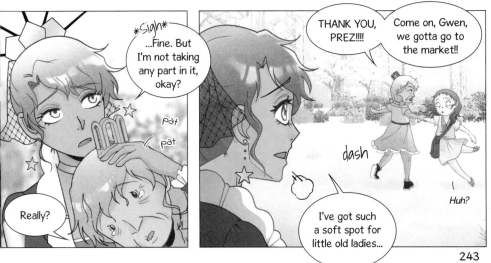

sigh
...Fine. But I'm not taking any part in it, okay?

pat
pat

Really?

THANK YOU, PREZ!!!!

Come on, Gwen, we gotta go to the market!!

dash

Huh?

I've got such a soft spot for little old ladies...

243

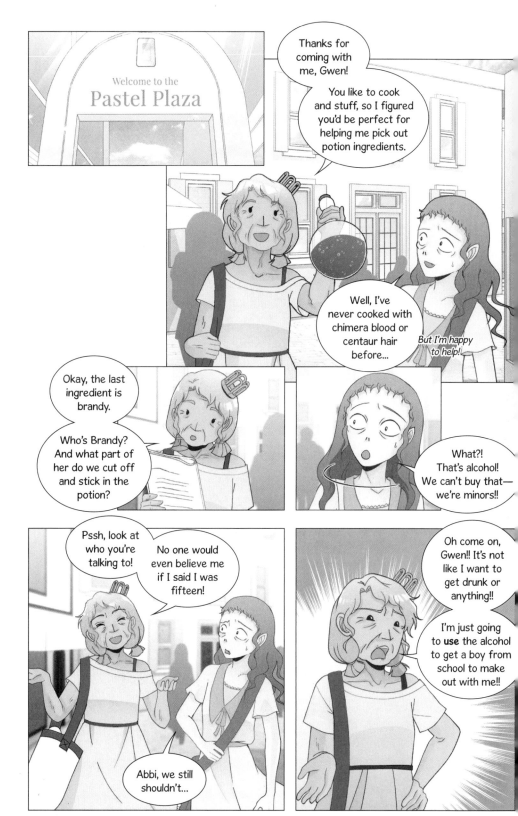

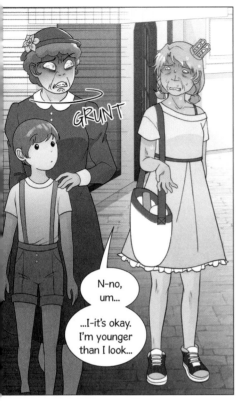

GRUNT

N-no, um...

...I-it's okay. I'm younger than I look...

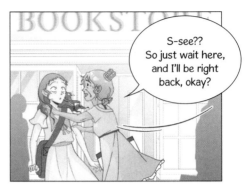

BOOKSTORE

S-see?? So just wait here, and I'll be right back, okay?

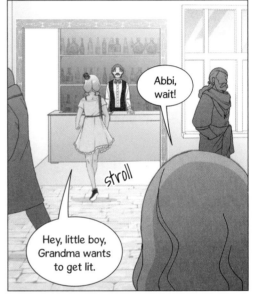

Abbi, wait!

stroll

Hey, little boy, Grandma wants to get lit.

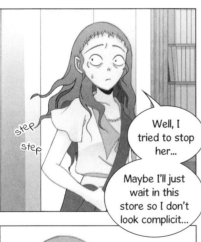

step
step

Well, I tried to stop her...

Maybe I'll just wait in this store so I don't look complicit...

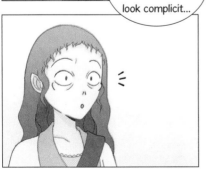

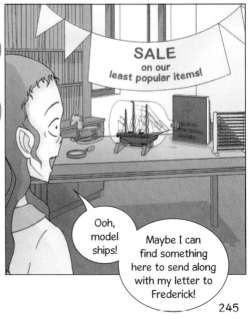

SALE
on our least popular items!

Ooh, model ships!

Maybe I can find something here to send along with my letter to Frederick!

245

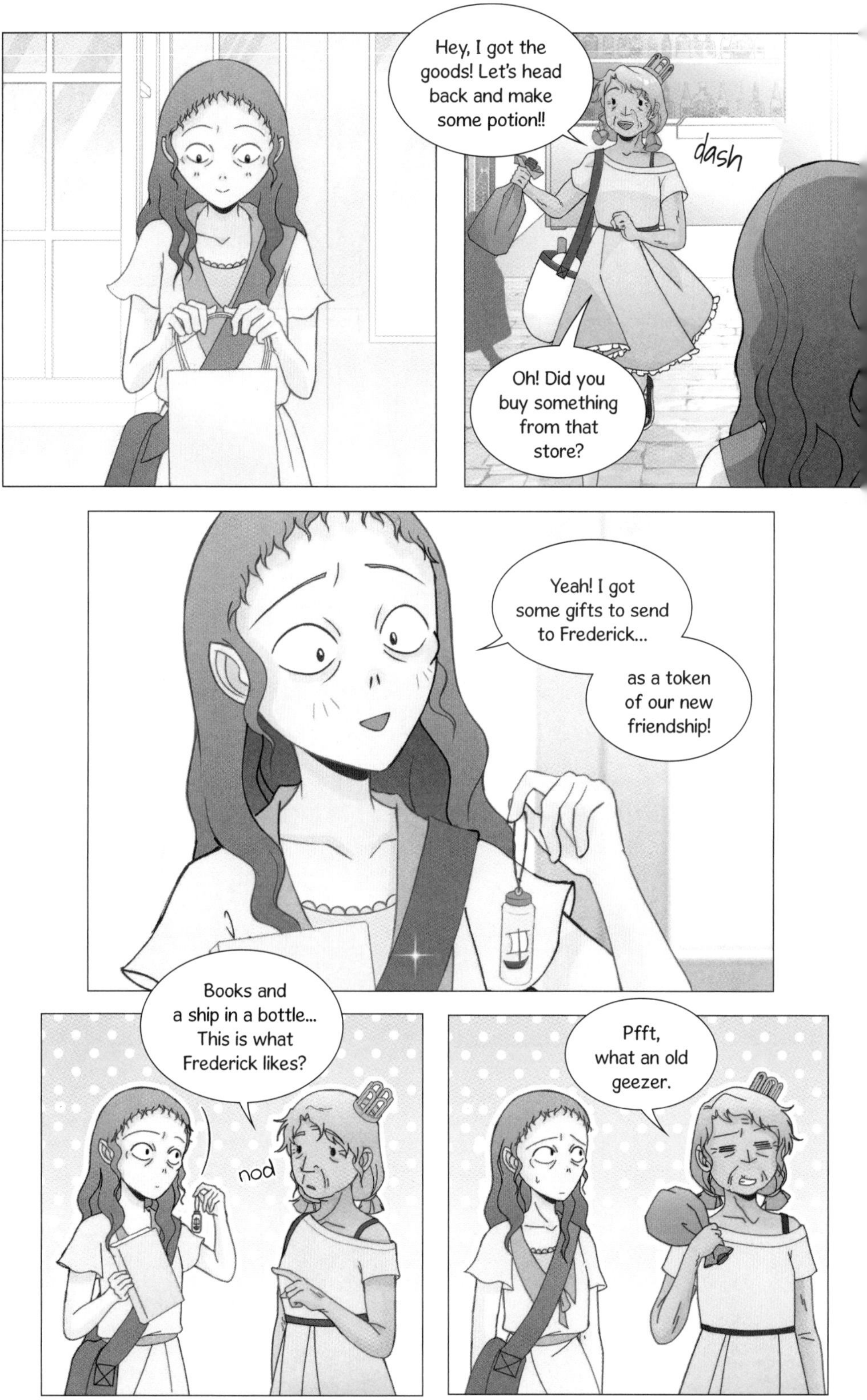
Hey, I got the goods! Let's head back and make some potion!!
dash
Oh! Did you buy something from that store?
Yeah! I got some gifts to send to Frederick...
as a token of our new friendship!
Books and a ship in a bottle... This is what Frederick likes?
nod
Pfft, what an old geezer.

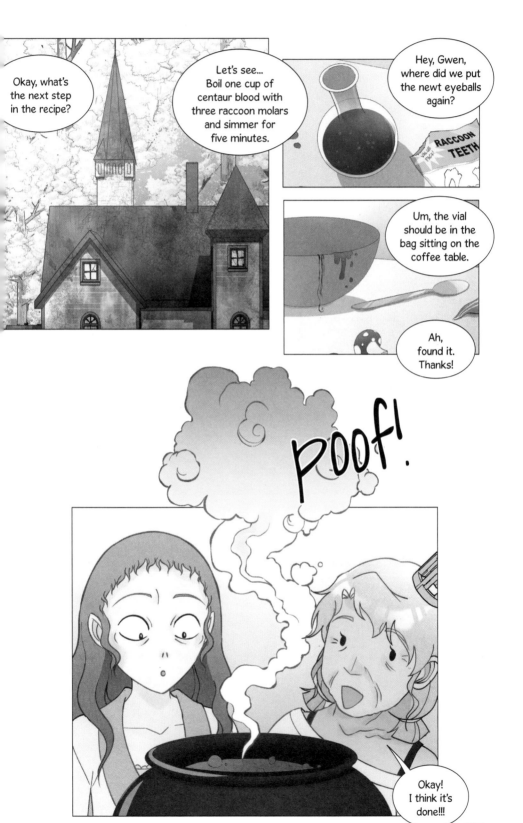

247

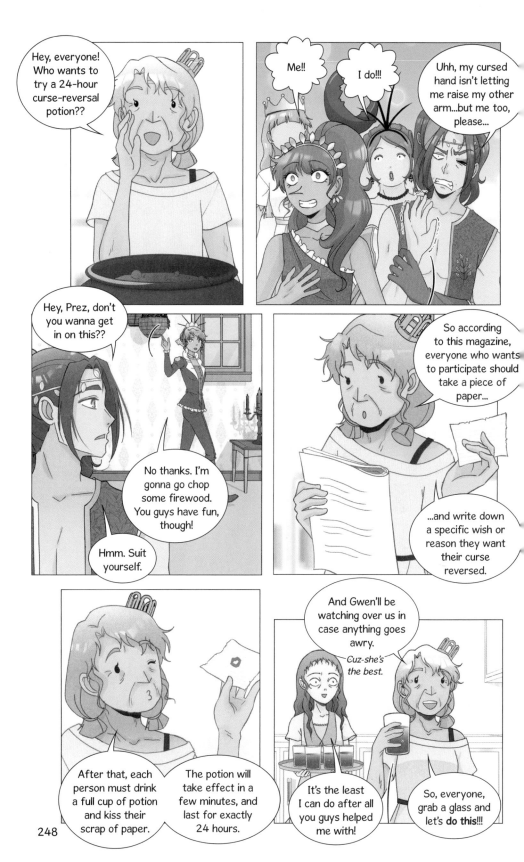

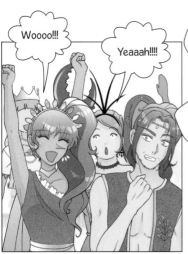

Woooo!!!

Yeaaah!!!!

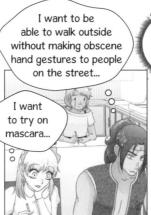

I want to be able to walk outside without making obscene hand gestures to people on the street...

I want to try on mascara...

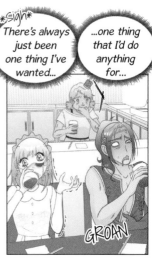

Sigh
There's always just been one thing I've wanted...

...one thing that I'd do anything for...

GROAN

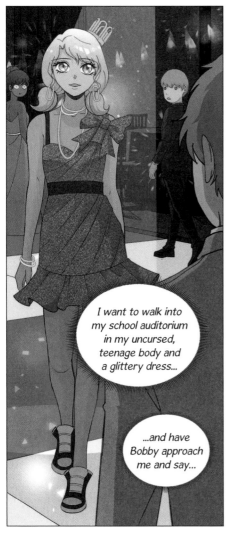

I want to walk into my school auditorium in my uncursed, teenage body and a glittery dress...

...and have Bobby approach me and say...

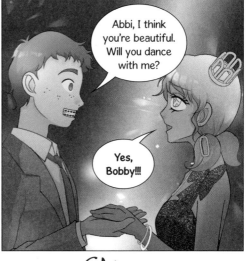

Abbi, I think you're beautiful. Will you dance with me?

Yes, Bobby!!!

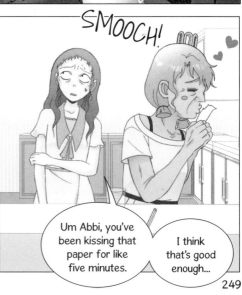

SMOOCH!

Um Abbi, you've been kissing that paper for like five minutes.

I think that's good enough...

249

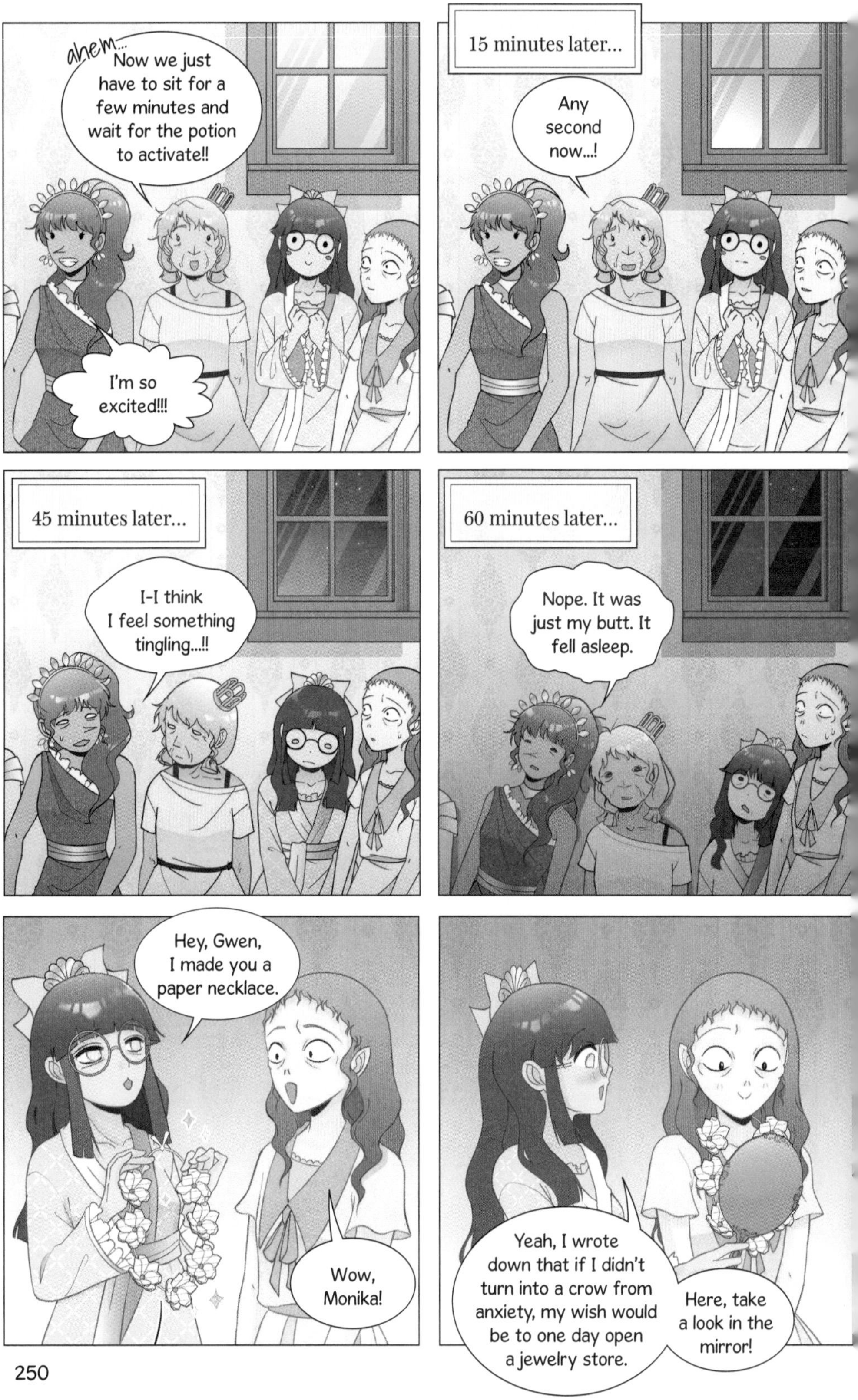
ahem...
Now we just have to sit for a few minutes and wait for the potion to activate!!
I'm so excited!!!
15 minutes later...
Any second now...!
45 minutes later...
I-I think I feel something tingling...!!
60 minutes later...
Nope. It was just my butt. It fell asleep.
Hey, Gwen, I made you a paper necklace.
Wow, Monika!
Yeah, I wrote down that if I didn't turn into a crow from anxiety, my wish would be to one day open a jewelry store.
Here, take a look in the mirror!

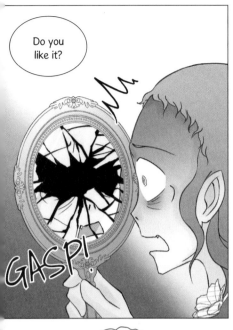

Do you like it?

GASP!

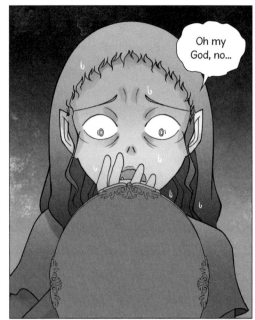

Oh my God, no...

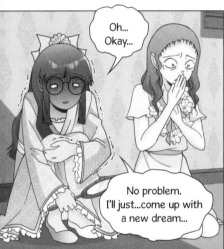

Oh... Okay...

No problem. I'll just...come up with a new dream...

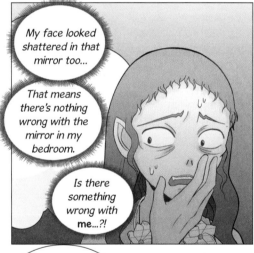

My face looked shattered in that mirror too...

That means there's nothing wrong with the mirror in my bedroom.

Is there something wrong with me....?!

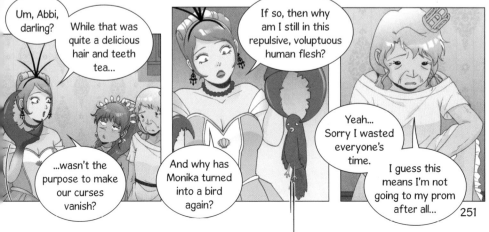

Um, Abbi, darling? While that was quite a delicious hair and teeth tea...

...wasn't the purpose to make our curses vanish?

If so, then why am I still in this repulsive, voluptuous human flesh?

And why has Monika turned into a bird again?

Yeah... Sorry I wasted everyone's time.

I guess this means I'm not going to my prom after all...

251

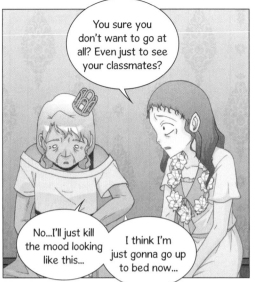

You sure you don't want to go at all? Even just to see your classmates?

No...I'll just kill the mood looking like this...

I think I'm just gonna go up to bed now...

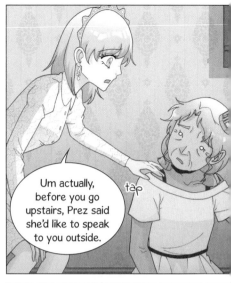

tap

Um actually, before you go upstairs, Prez said she'd like to speak to you outside.

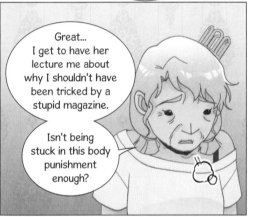

Great... I get to have her lecture me about why I shouldn't have been tricked by a stupid magazine.

Isn't being stuck in this body punishment enough?

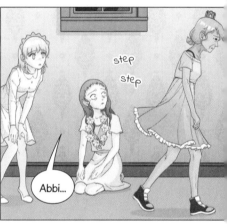

step
step

Abbi...

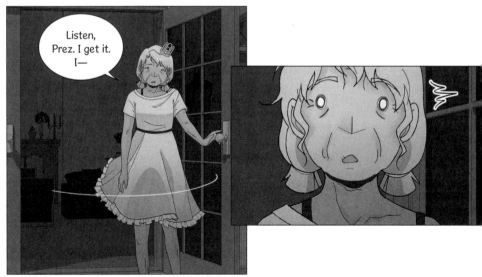

Listen, Prez. I get it. I—

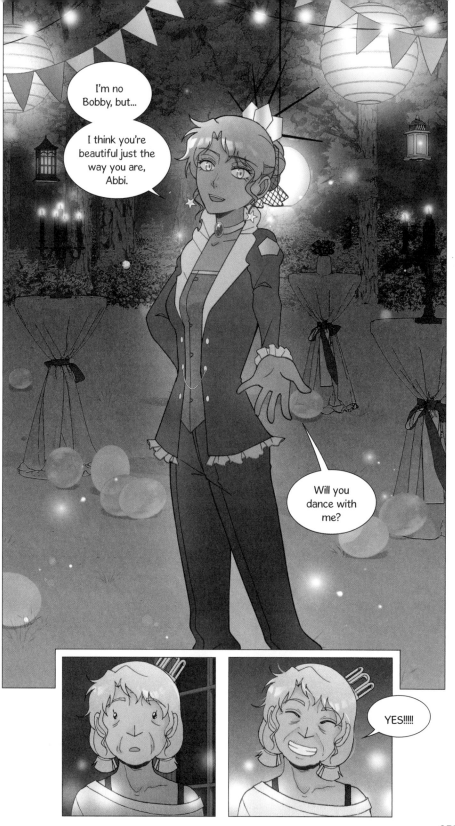

253

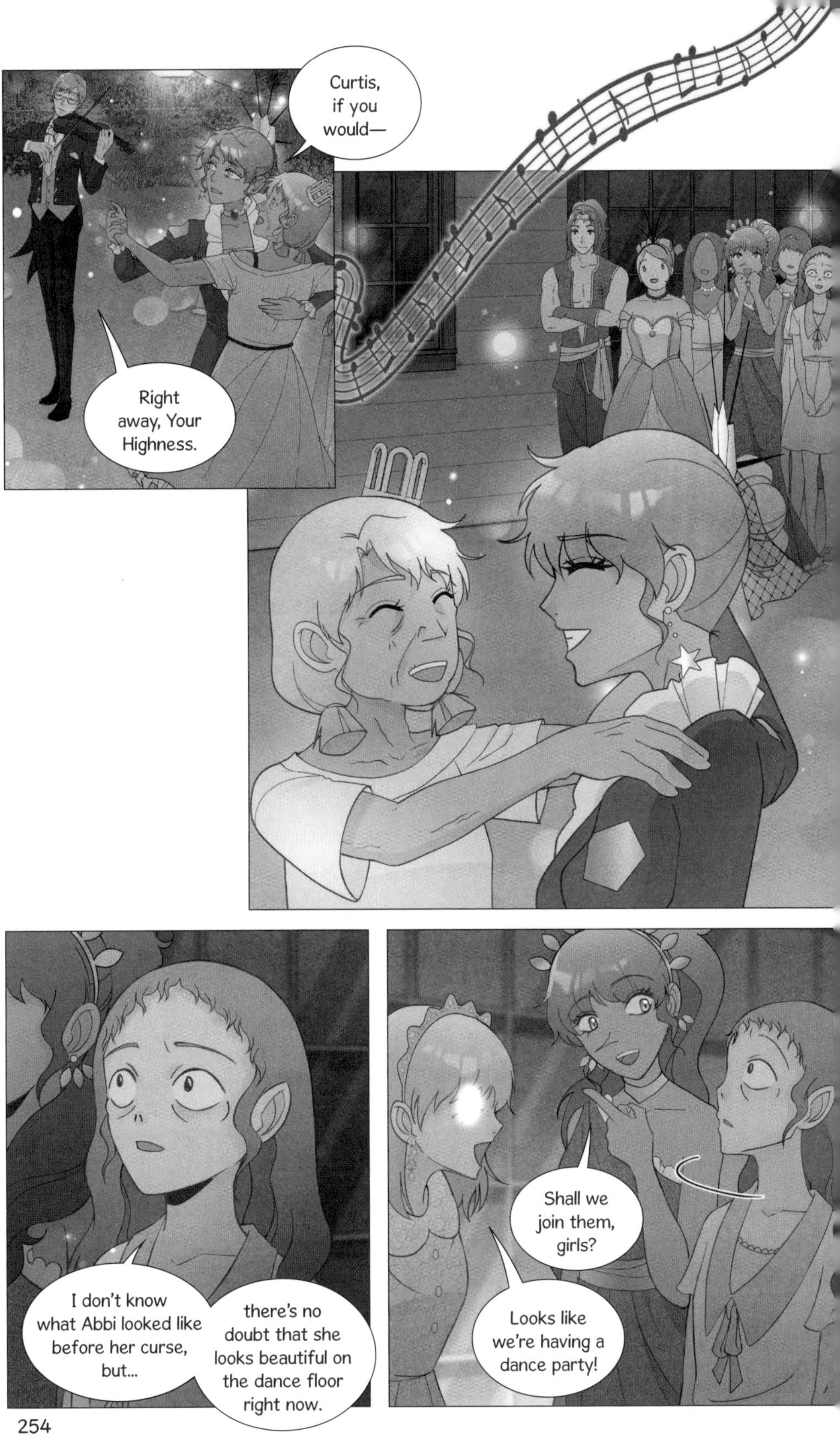
Curtis, if you would—
Right away, Your Highness.
I don't know what Abbi looked like before her curse, but...
there's no doubt that she looks beautiful on the dance floor right now.
Shall we join them, girls?
Looks like we're having a dance party!

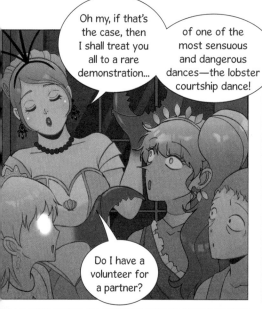

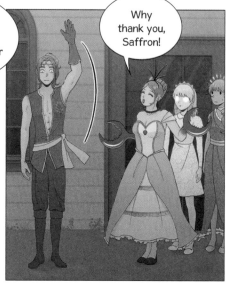

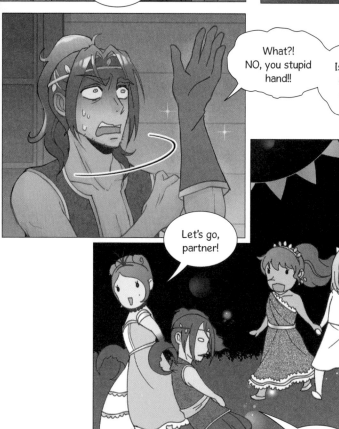

255

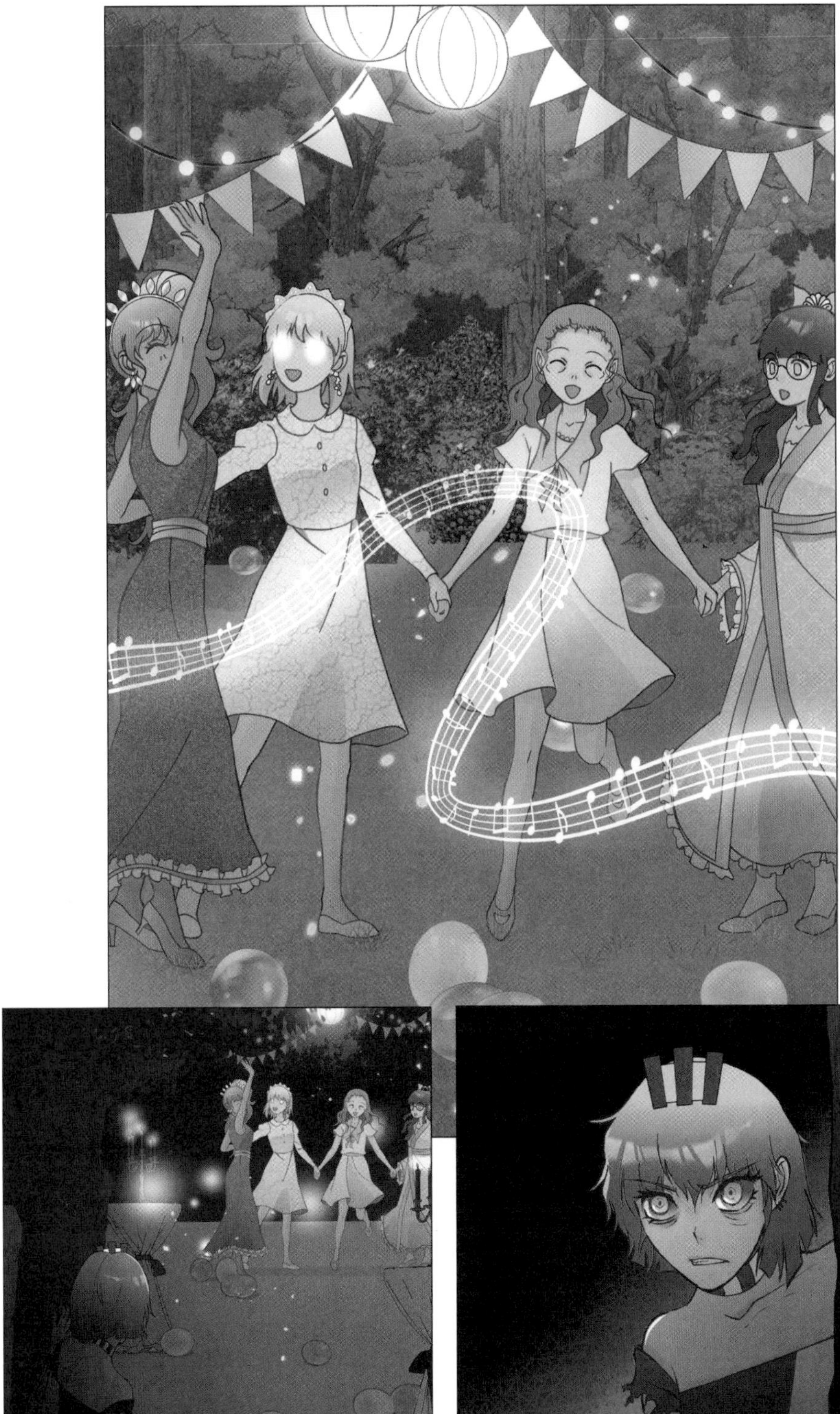

Chapter

11

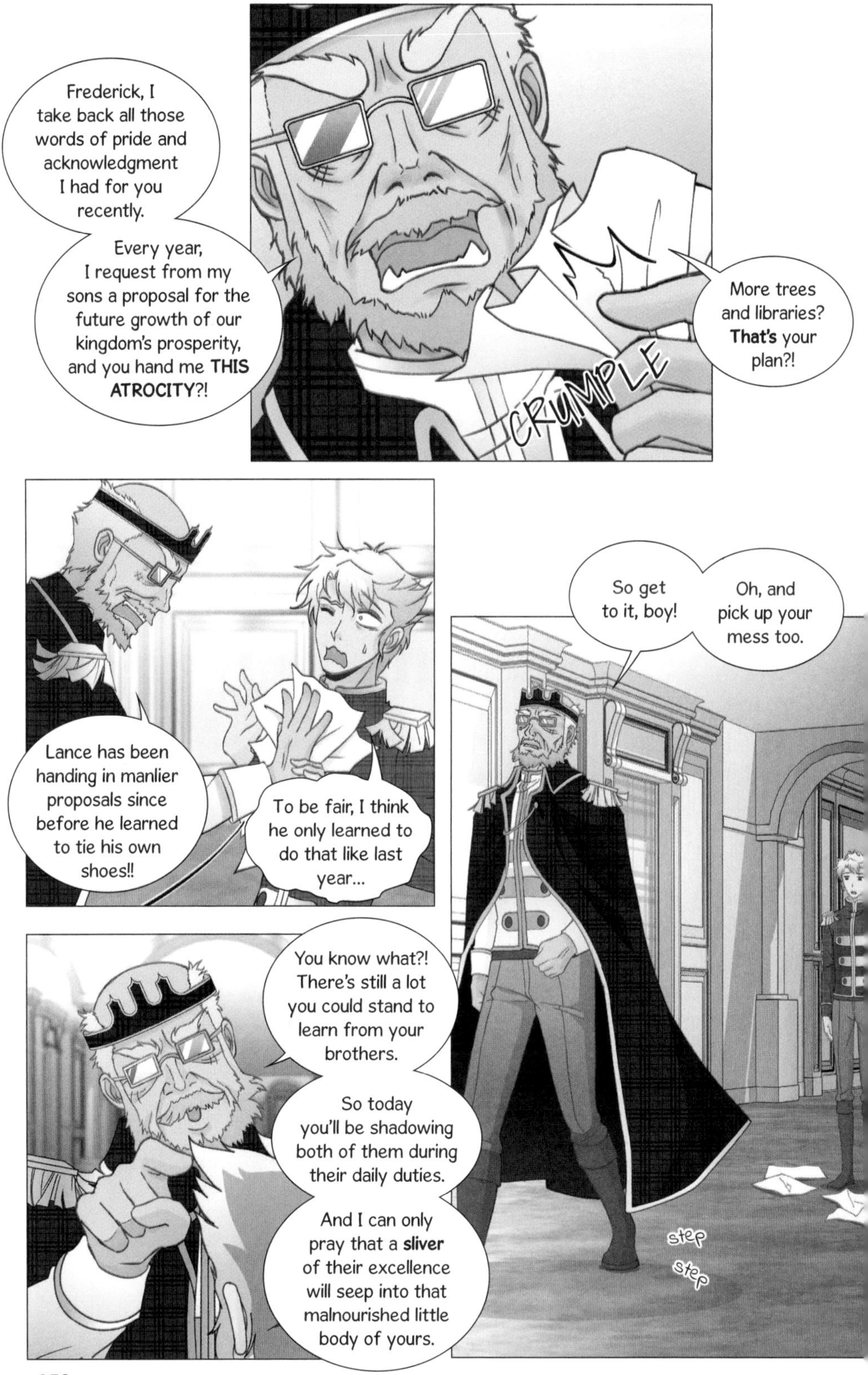
Frederick, I take back all those words of pride and acknowledgment I had for you recently.
Every year, I request from my sons a proposal for the future growth of our kingdom's prosperity, and you hand me **THIS ATROCITY**?!
More trees and libraries? **That's** your plan?!
CRUMPLE
Lance has been handing in manlier proposals since before he learned to tie his own shoes!!
To be fair, I think he only learned to do that like last year...
You know what?! There's still a lot you could stand to learn from your brothers.
So today you'll be shadowing both of them during their daily duties.
And I can only pray that a **sliver** of their excellence will seep into that malnourished little body of yours.
So get to it, boy!
Oh, and pick up your mess too.
step
step

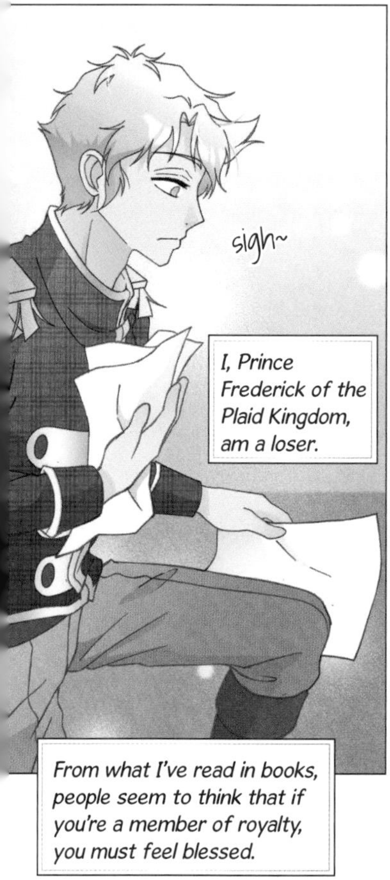
sigh~
I, Prince Frederick of the Plaid Kingdom, am a loser.
From what I've read in books, people seem to think that if you're a member of royalty, you must feel blessed.

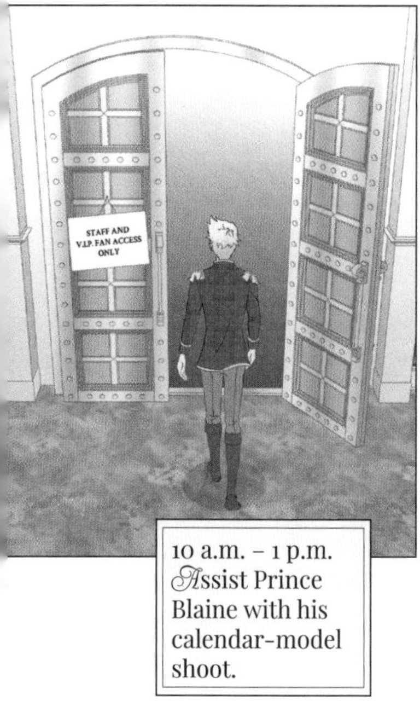
STAFF AND V.I.P. FAN ACCESS ONLY
10 a.m. – 1 p.m. Assist Prince Blaine with his calendar-model shoot.

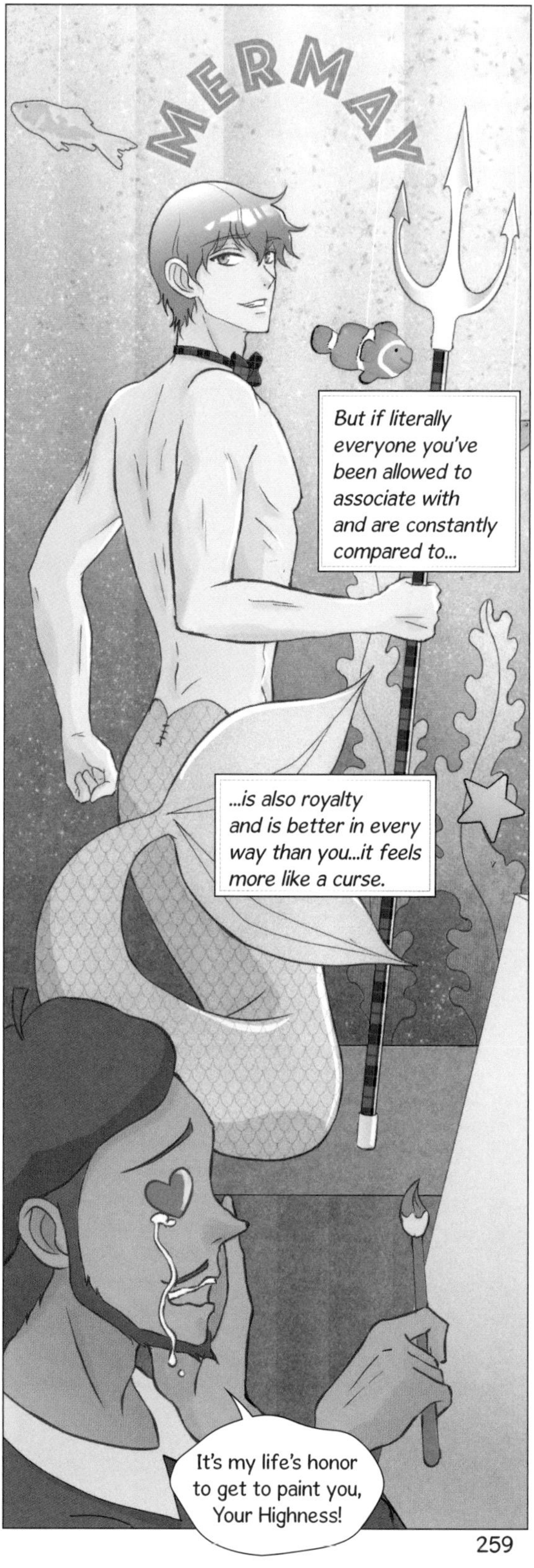
MERMAY
But if literally everyone you've been allowed to associate with and are constantly compared to...
...is also royalty and is better in every way than you...it feels more like a curse.
It's my life's honor to get to paint you, Your Highness!

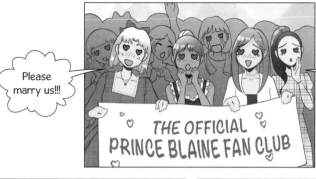

Please marry us!!!

You're pure perfection, Prince Blaine!!

THE OFFICIAL PRINCE BLAINE FAN CLUB

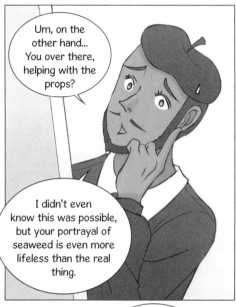

Um, on the other hand... You over there, helping with the props?

I didn't even know this was possible, but your portrayal of seaweed is even more lifeless than the real thing.

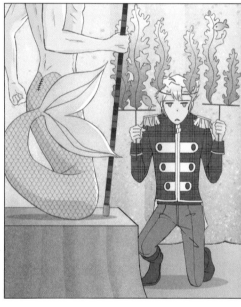

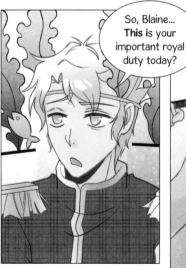

So, Blaine... **This** is your important royal duty today?

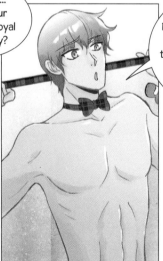

Oh, I'm sorry. Does your personal brand bring in two percent of the national GDP and raise awareness for numerous charitable foundations? Hmm?

...No...

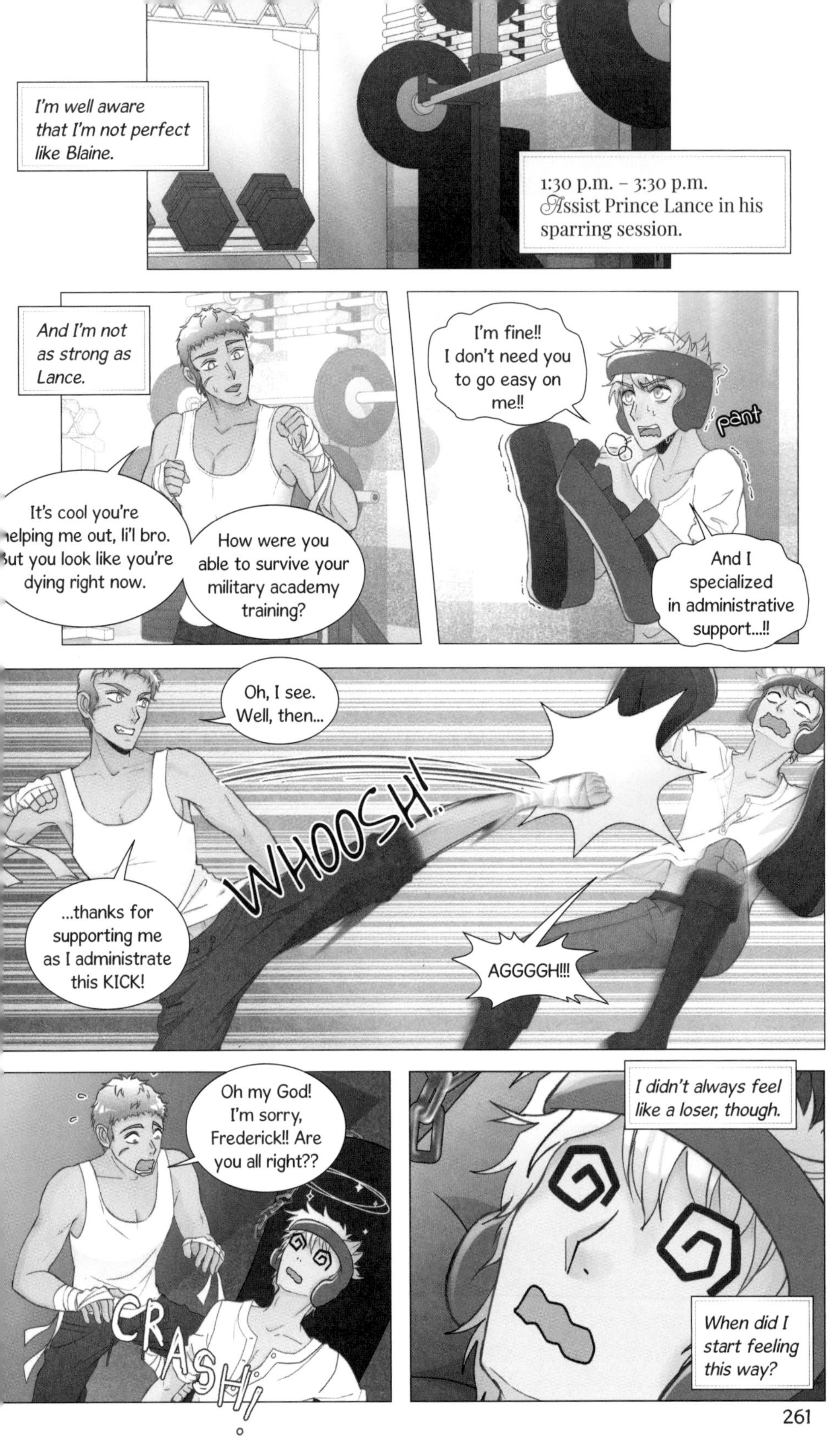

I'm well aware that I'm not perfect like Blaine.
1:30 p.m. – 3:30 p.m.
Assist Prince Lance in his sparring session.
And I'm not as strong as Lance.
It's cool you're elping me out, li'l bro. ut you look like you're dying right now.
How were you able to survive your military academy training?
I'm fine!! I don't need you to go easy on me!!
pant
And I specialized in administrative support...!!
Oh, I see. Well, then...
WHOOSH!
...thanks for supporting me as I administrate this KICK!
AGGGGH!!!
Oh my God! I'm sorry, Frederick!! Are you all right??
CRASH!
I didn't always feel like a loser, though.
When did I start feeling this way?

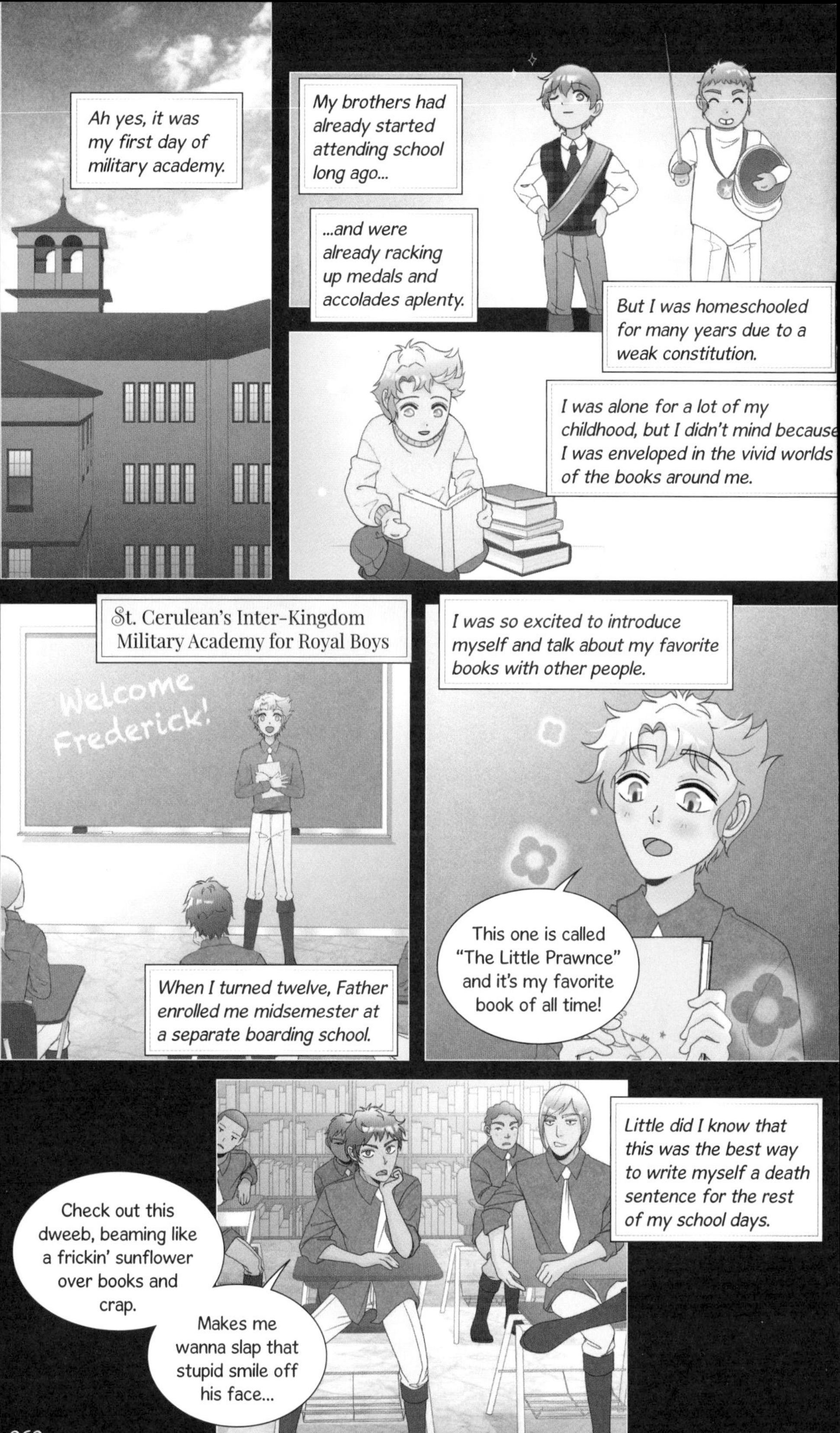

Ah yes, it was my first day of military academy.
My brothers had already started attending school long ago...
...and were already racking up medals and accolades aplenty.
But I was homeschooled for many years due to a weak constitution.
I was alone for a lot of my childhood, but I didn't mind because I was enveloped in the vivid worlds of the books around me.
St. Cerulean's Inter-Kingdom Military Academy for Royal Boys
Welcome Frederick!
When I turned twelve, Father enrolled me midsemester at a separate boarding school.
I was so excited to introduce myself and talk about my favorite books with other people.
This one is called "The Little Prawnce" and it's my favorite book of all time!
Little did I know that this was the best way to write myself a death sentence for the rest of my school days.
Check out this dweeb, beaming like a frickin' sunflower over books and crap.
Makes me wanna slap that stupid smile off his face...

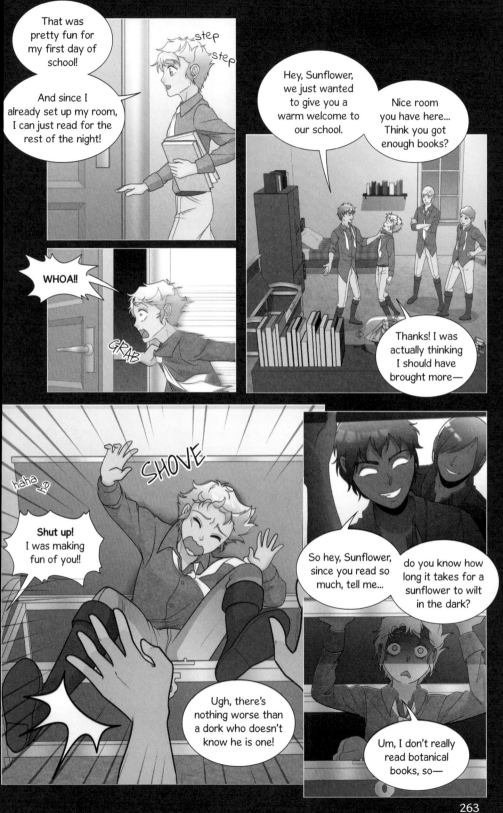

263

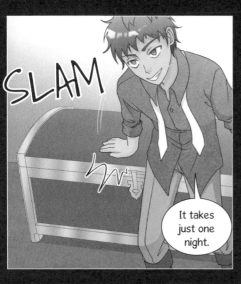

SLAM

It takes just one night.

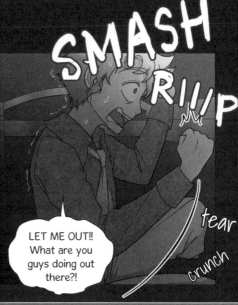

SMASH

RIIIP

tear

crunch

LET ME OUT!! What are you guys doing out there?!

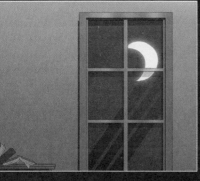

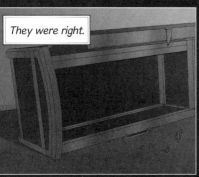

They were right.

One night was all it took...

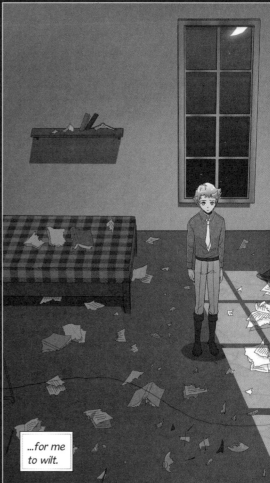

...for me to wilt.

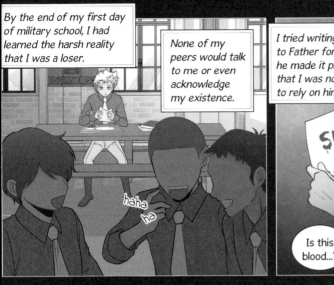

By the end of my first day of military school, I had learned the harsh reality that I was a loser.

None of my peers would talk to me or even acknowledge my existence.

haha ha

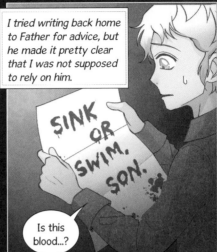

I tried writing back home to Father for advice, but he made it pretty clear that I was not supposed to rely on him.

SINK OR SWIM, SON.

Is this blood...?

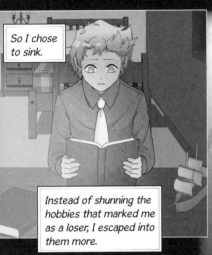

So I chose to sink.

Instead of shunning the hobbies that marked me as a loser, I escaped into them more.

I dreamed of sailing far away from school on one of my model ships...

...or pretended I was the protagonist of every book I could borrow from the library.

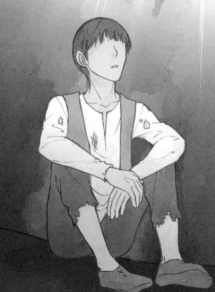

There was one tale I became particulary obsessed with about a man who lived at the bottom of a deep hole in the ground.

He could not climb out no matter how much he tried. And for that, he was the laughingstock of the village.

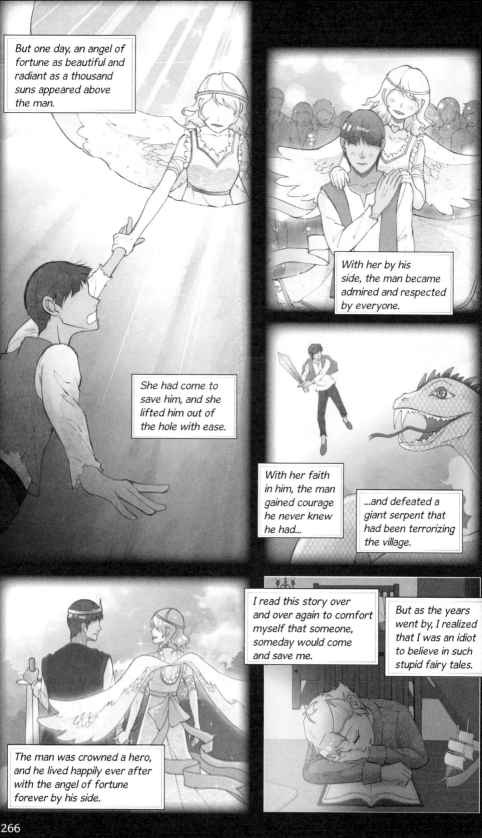

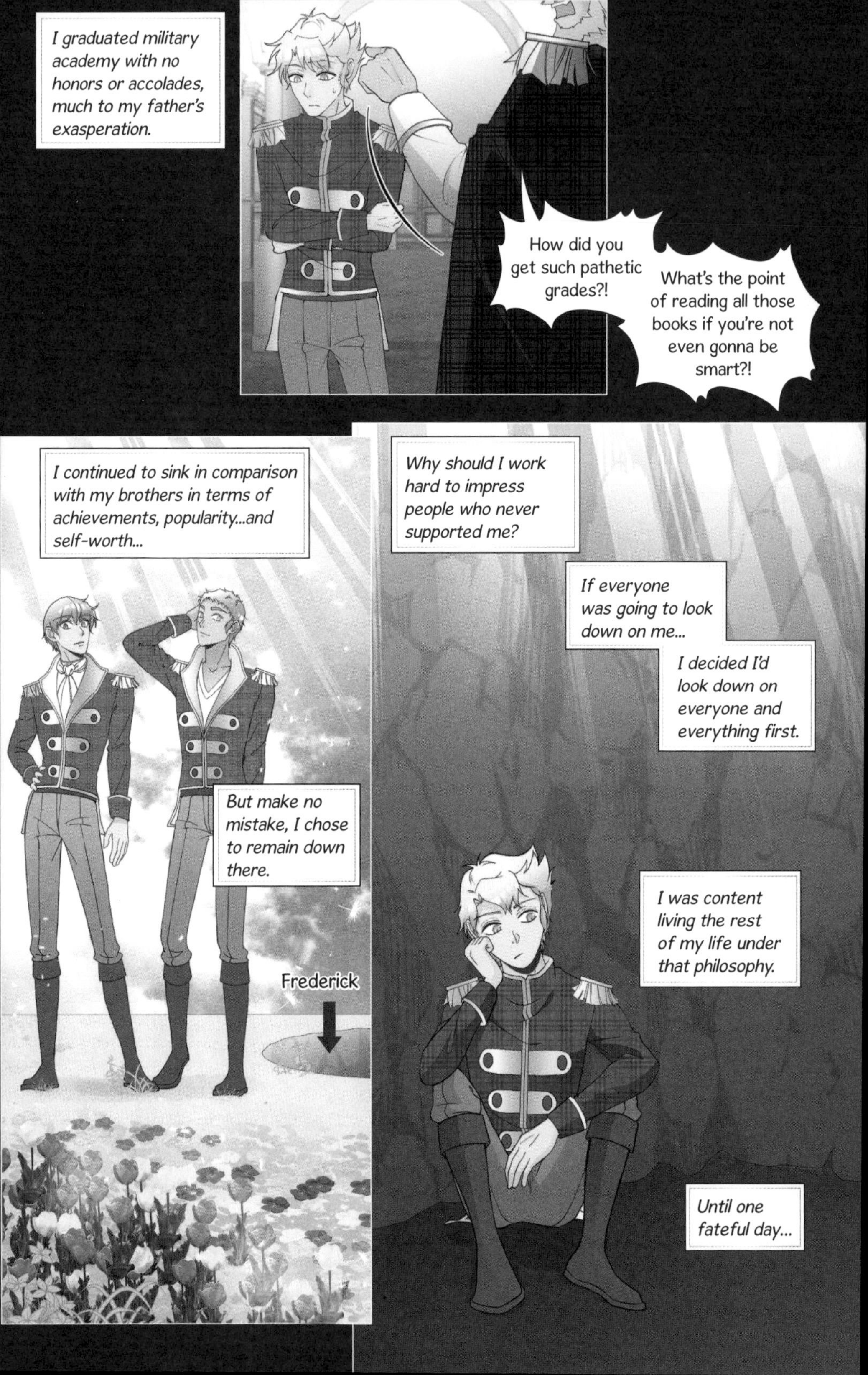
I graduated military academy with no honors or accolades, much to my father's exasperation.
How did you get such pathetic grades?!
What's the point of reading all those books if you're not even gonna be smart?!
I continued to sink in comparison with my brothers in terms of achievements, popularity...and self-worth...
But make no mistake, I chose to remain down there.
Frederick
Why should I work hard to impress people who never supported me?
If everyone was going to look down on me...
I decided I'd look down on everyone and everything first.
I was content living the rest of my life under that philosophy.
Until one fateful day...

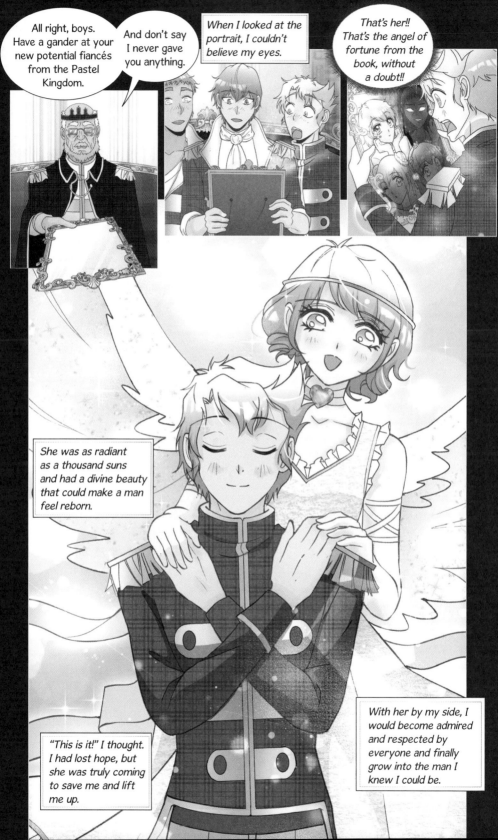

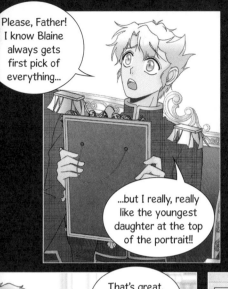

Please, Father! I know Blaine always gets first pick of everything...

...but I really, really like the youngest daughter at the top of the portrait!!

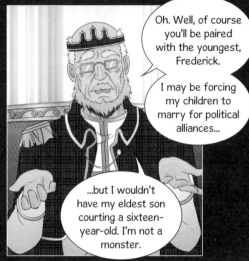

Oh. Well, of course you'll be paired with the youngest, Frederick.

I may be forcing my children to marry for political alliances...

...but I wouldn't have my eldest son courting a sixteen-year-old. I'm not a monster.

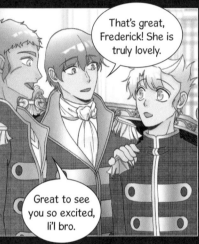

That's great, Frederick! She is truly lovely.

Great to see you so excited, li'l bro.

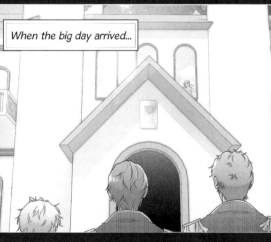

When the big day arrived...

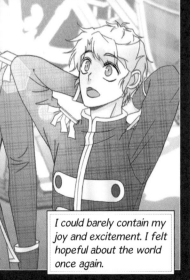

I could barely contain my joy and excitement. I felt hopeful about the world once again.

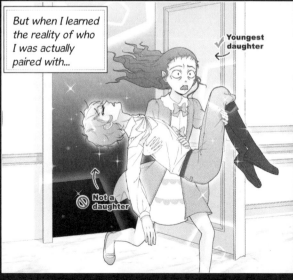

But when I learned the reality of who I was actually paired with...

Youngest daughter

Not a daughter

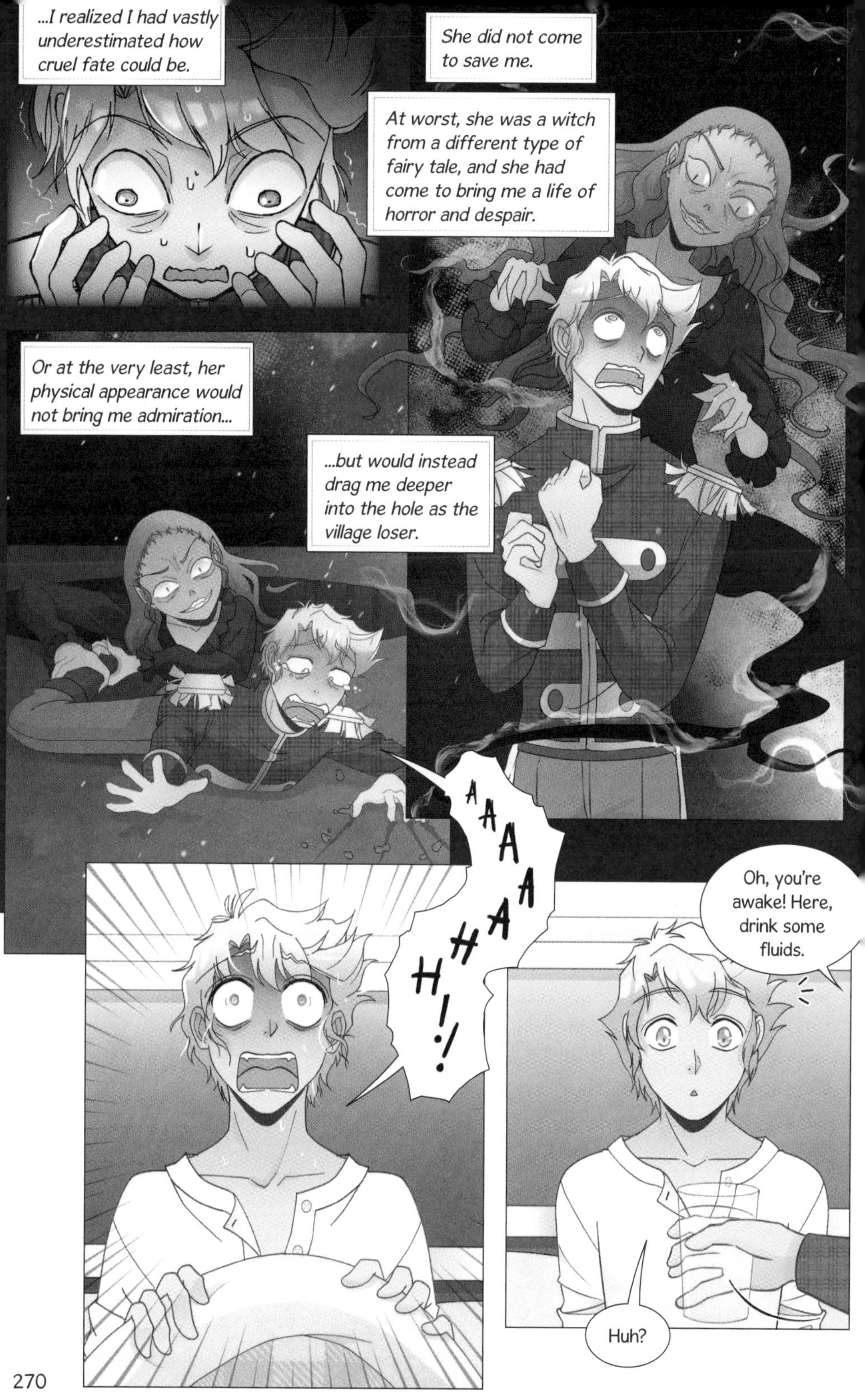

...I realized I had vastly underestimated how cruel fate could be.
She did not come to save me.
At worst, she was a witch from a different type of fairy tale, and she had come to bring me a life of horror and despair.
Or at the very least, her physical appearance would not bring me admiration...
...but would instead drag me deeper into the hole as the village loser.
AAAAAHH!!
Oh, you're awake! Here, drink some fluids.
Huh?

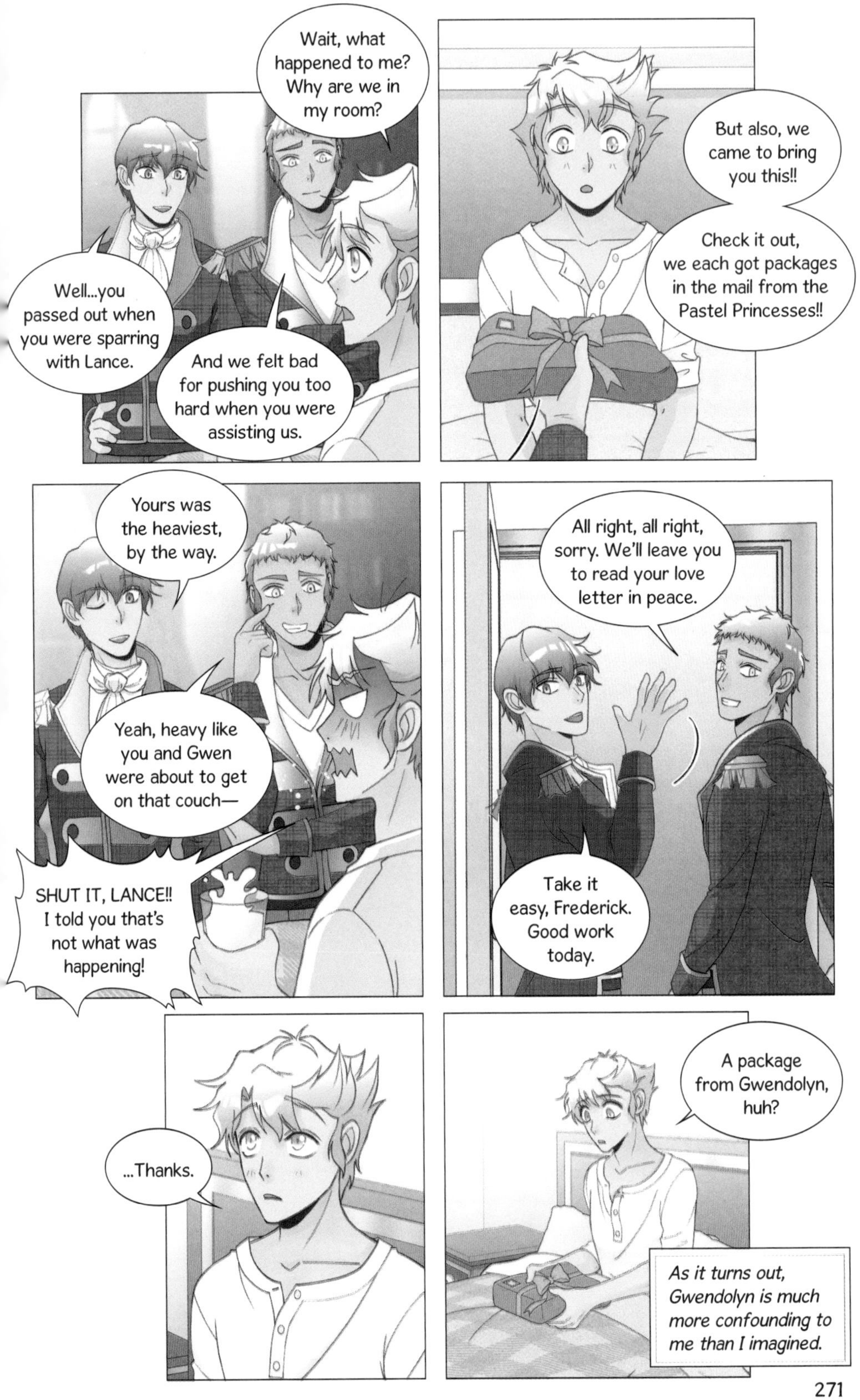
Wait, what happened to me? Why are we in my room?
Well...you passed out when you were sparring with Lance.
And we felt bad for pushing you too hard when you were assisting us.
But also, we came to bring you this!!
Check it out, we each got packages in the mail from the Pastel Princesses!!
Yours was the heaviest, by the way.
Yeah, heavy like you and Gwen were about to get on that couch—
SHUT IT, LANCE!! I told you that's not what was happening!
All right, all right, sorry. We'll leave you to read your love letter in peace.
Take it easy, Frederick. Good work today.
...Thanks.
A package from Gwendolyn, huh?
As it turns out, Gwendolyn is much more confounding to me than I imagined.

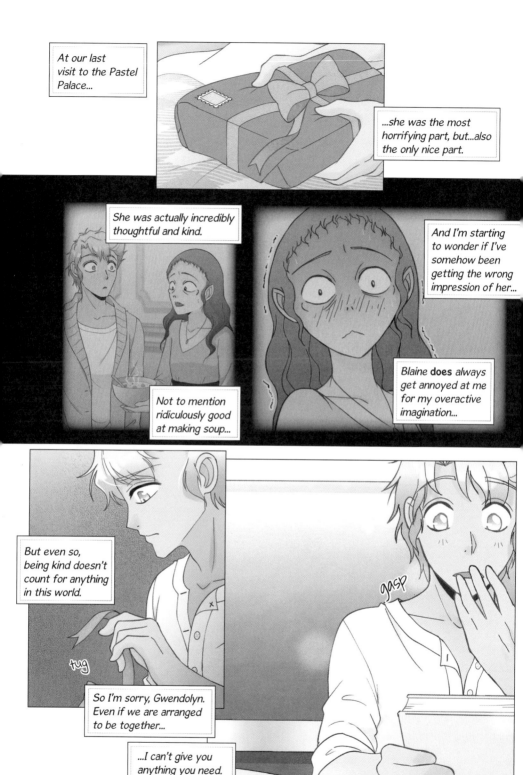

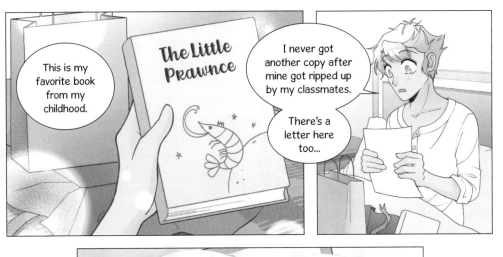

This is my favorite book from my childhood.

The Little Prawnce

I never got another copy after mine got ripped up by my classmates.

There's a letter here too...

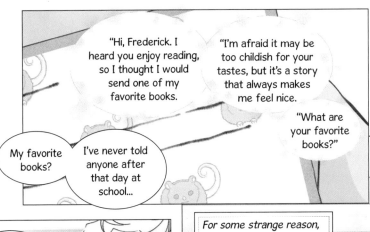

"Hi, Frederick. I heard you enjoy reading, so I thought I would send one of my favorite books.

"I'm afraid it may be too childish for your tastes, but it's a story that always makes me feel nice.

"What are your favorite books?"

My favorite books?

I've never told anyone after that day at school...

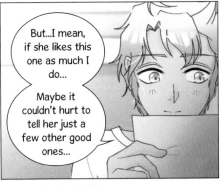

But...I mean, if she likes this one as much I do...

Maybe it couldn't hurt to tell her just a few other good ones...

For some strange reason, despite everything I said, Gwendolyn can sometimes make me feel...

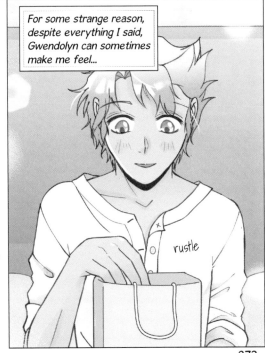

rustle

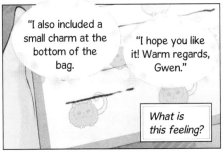

"I also included a small charm at the bottom of the bag.

"I hope you like it! Warm regards, Gwen."

What is this feeling?

273

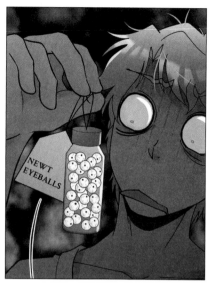

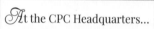

NEWT EYEBALLS

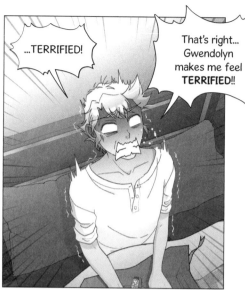

...TERRIFIED!

That's right... Gwendolyn makes me feel **TERRIFIED**!!

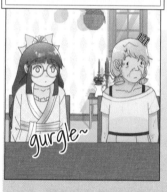

At the CPC Headquarters...

gurgle~

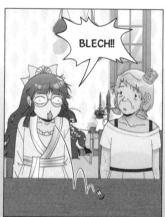

BLECH!!

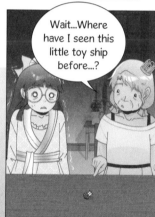

Wait...Where have I seen this little toy ship before...?

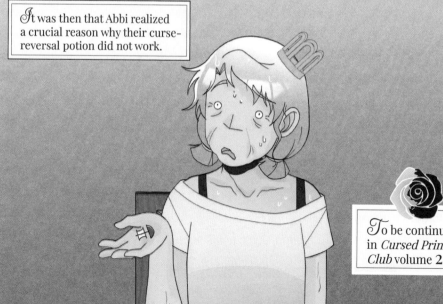

It was then that Abbi realized a crucial reason why their curse-reversal potion did not work.

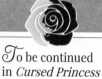

To be continued in Cursed Princess Club volume 2

Early Concept Art & Character Design Sheets

Cursed Princess Club

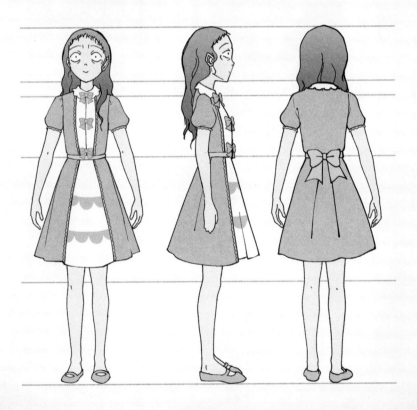

Gwendolyn

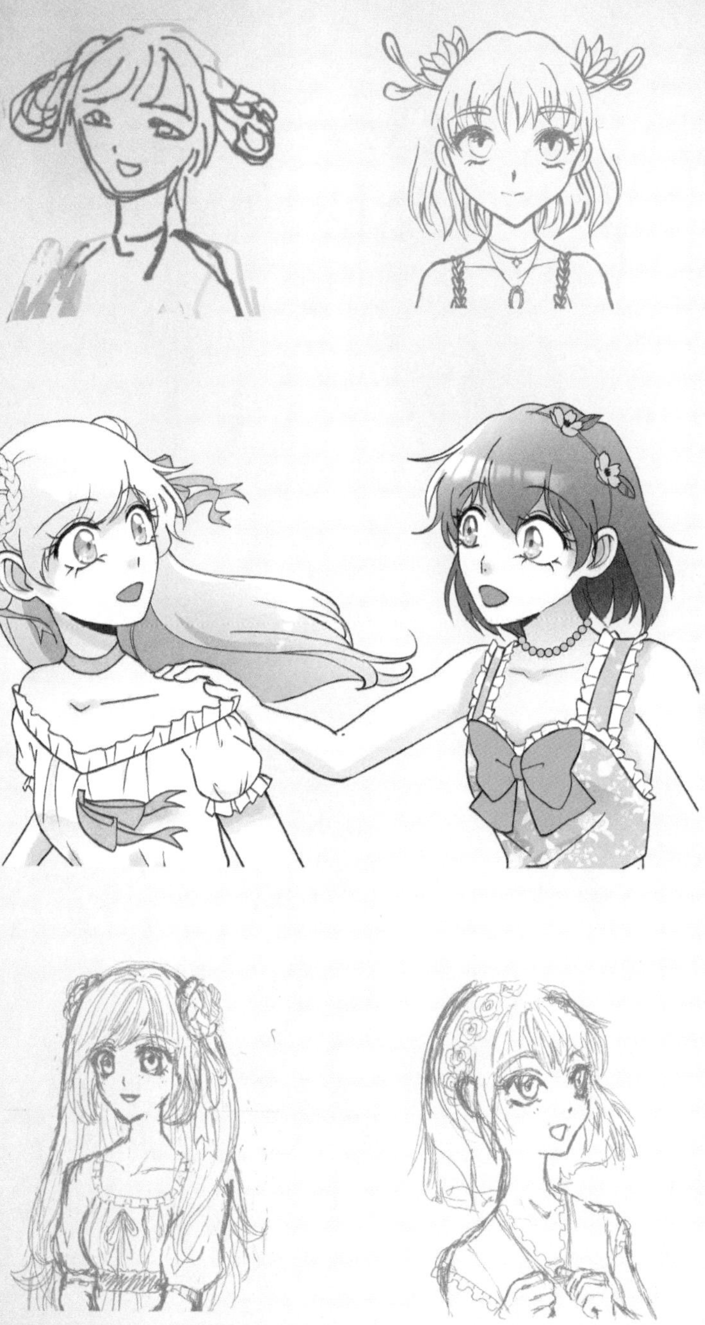

Maria & Lorena

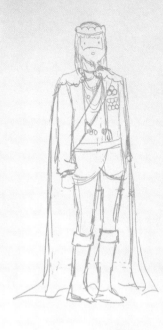

The Pastel King

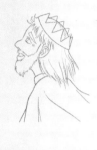

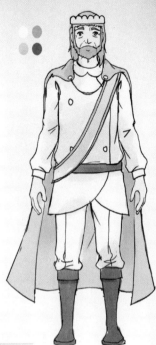

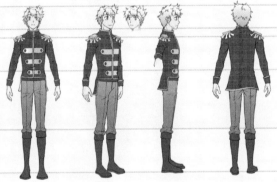

Frederick

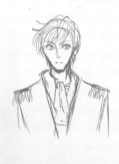

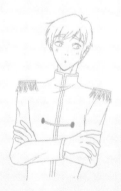

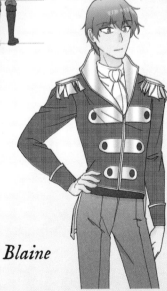

Blaine

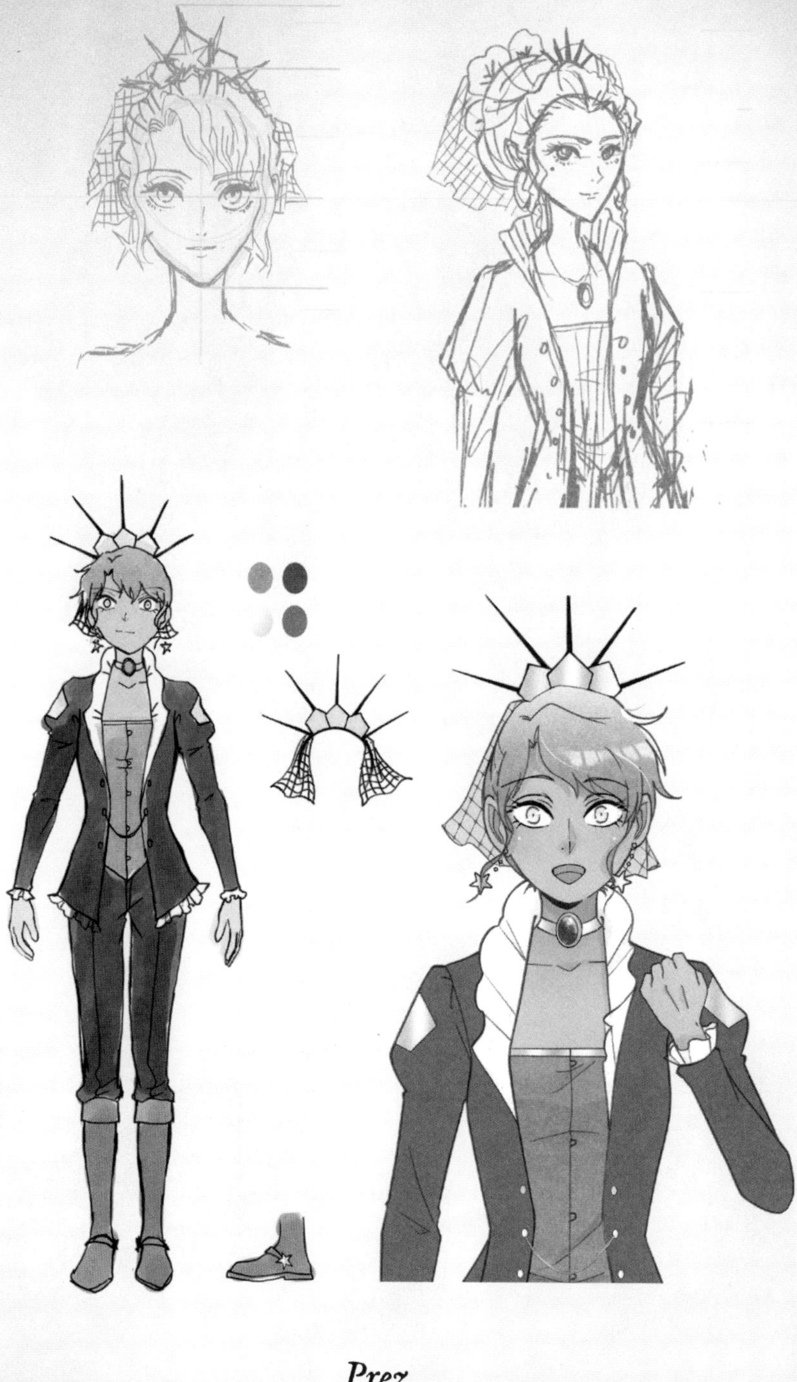

Prez

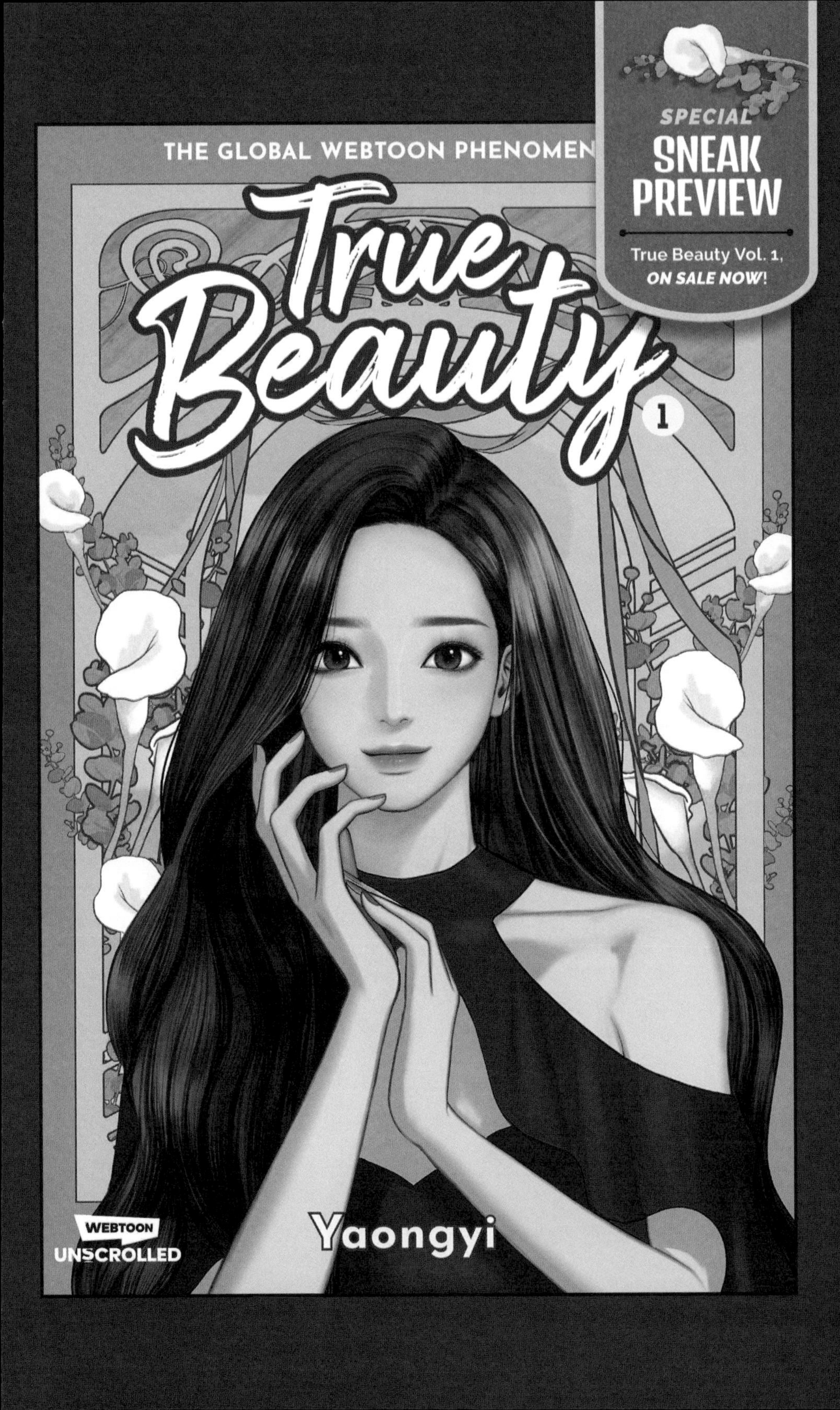
SPECIAL
SNEAK
PREVIEW
True Beauty Vol. 1,
ON SALE NOW!
THE GLOBAL WEBTOON PHENOMEN
True
Beauty
1
WEBTOON
UNSCROLLED
Yaongyi

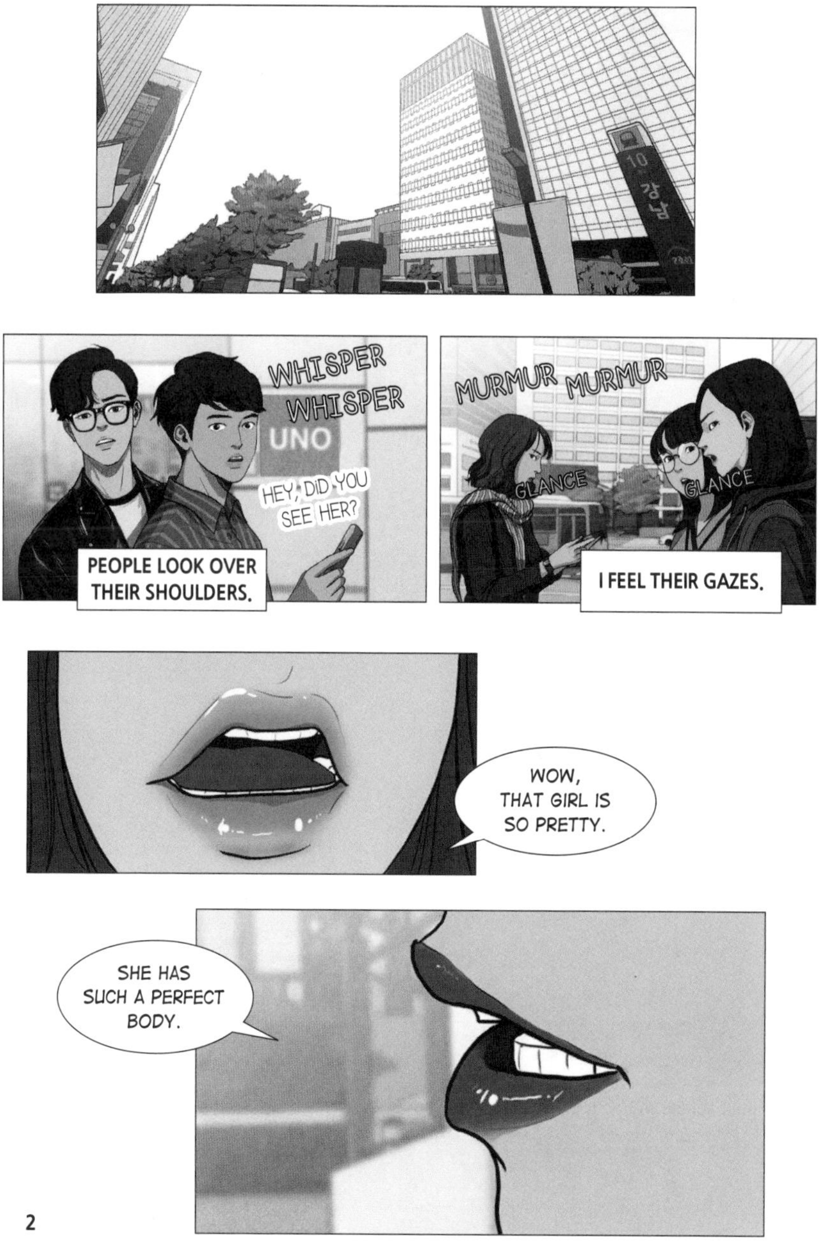

WHISPER
WHISPER
UNO
HEY, DID YOU SEE HER?
PEOPLE LOOK OVER THEIR SHOULDERS.
MURMUR MURMUR
GLANCE
GLANCE
I FEEL THEIR GAZES.
WOW, THAT GIRL IS SO PRETTY.
SHE HAS SUCH A PERFECT BODY.

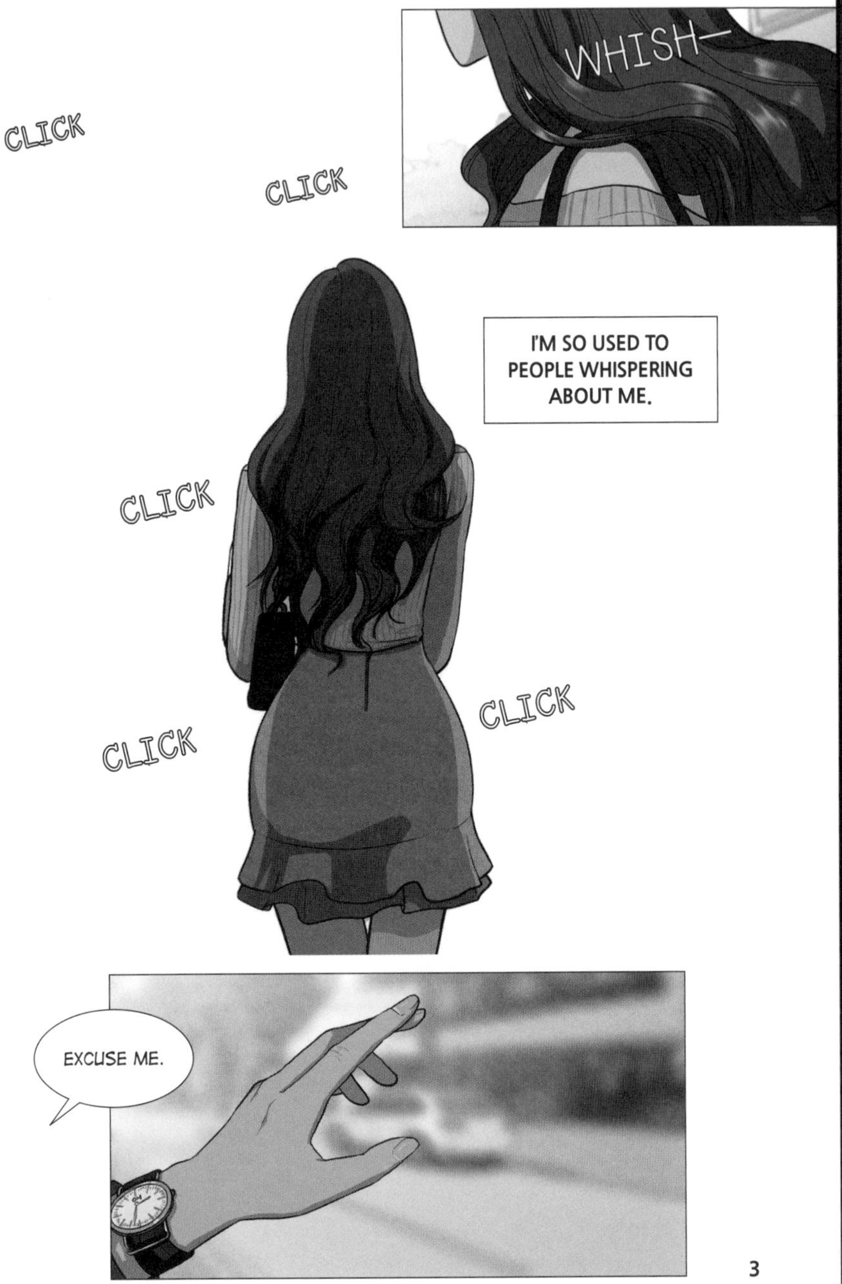
CLICK
CLICK
WHISH—
I'M SO USED TO PEOPLE WHISPERING ABOUT ME.
CLICK
CLICK
CLICK
EXCUSE ME.

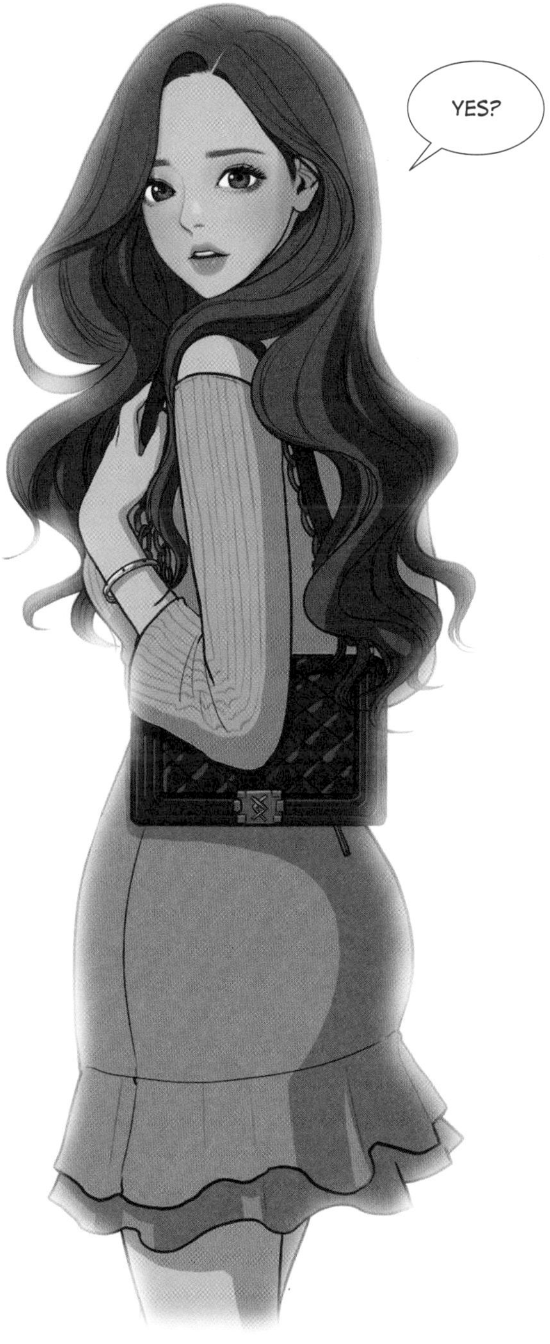
YES?

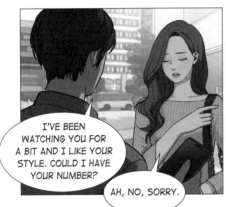

I'VE BEEN WATCHING YOU FOR A BIT AND I LIKE YOUR STYLE. COULD I HAVE YOUR NUMBER?

AH, NO, SORRY.

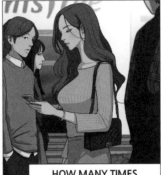

HOW MANY TIMES HAVE GUYS ASKED ME FOR MY NUMBER TODAY?

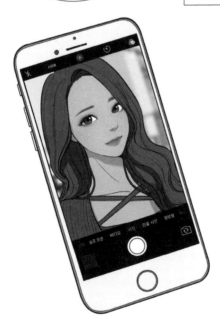

WHO AM I, YOU ASK?

A UNIVERSALLY RECOGNIZED

GODDESS!

5

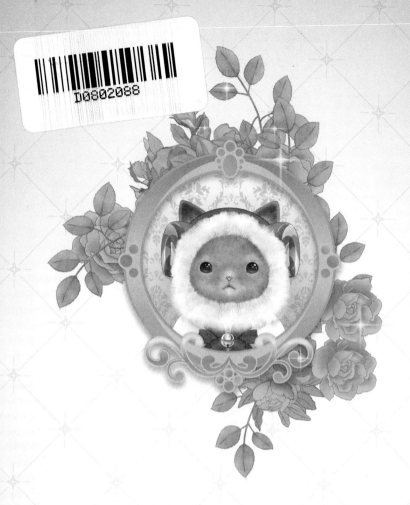

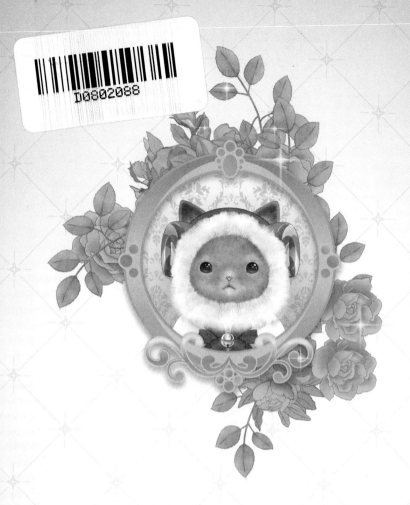

LambCat is a small, omnivorous,
and easily frightened creature who has burrowed deep
into the Pacific Northwest to draw comics and make music.
They can be lured out by Bill Evans records and
frosted animal crackers.

Read the original on www.WEBTOONS.com

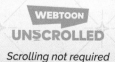

WEBTOON
UNSCROLLED

Scrolling not required